Step 2: Lust

A GAMER'S GU1DE 2 BEATING THE TUTORIAL

Step 2: Lust

Palt

Podium

To my friend and teacher Ida, who stuck with me despite The Killings

Published in 2024 by Podium Publishing
www.podiumentertainment.com

Step 2: Lust

FLOOR 8

THE MUDDY SLUICE

I

Swamp

My feet touch the pristine, cold, WHITE floor of the lobby.

Yeah, thanks. Appreciated.

The second I'm back in the lobby, I collapse to the floor. I place my head in my hands.

I don't know what to do. I don't know what to say. Is there anything to say or do?

<To repay your debt, your inventory has been sold for 9 points.>
<Current debt: 61,730 points.>

Oh, yeah, there's one thing I can say.

These gods are all kind of douches.

Alright, okay, uh, um . . . On to the next floor, I guess? I don't know. I feel kind of nauseous, even though any injury I got on floor seven has technically been recovered by now. It just doesn't feel like it. It still aches. But it's not like I can stop now, right?

I need to keep going. That's it. That's my only choice.

<Top—Status—Community>
<22:30:21 Day 150>
<The sixth attempt will begin in 1:29:39>
<The eighth floor will open in 23:59:54>

At least I was able to clear the floor right on time. As long as I clear a floor within twenty-four hours of the next attempt beginning, I won't have to go back to the lobby to redo the whole thing. And, sure, it's not like I lose much of anything by having to redo it, it's just annoying and tedious. Besides, the longer I stay in the lobby, the more willing I become to engage in the senseless act of auto-asphyxiation.

All in all, it's best for me to try to keep going.

I briefly consider sending Moleman a message, but I'm sure he's still busy, so I'll just leave it be.

The lobby waiting period goes just the same as it always does. Paint the room, mutilate myself, and after considering how one could best kill themself in a room where everything automatically regenerates within seconds, the floor finally opens.

<Floor 8 has opened. Do you want to enter?>
<Yes/No>

My hand shoots out like an arrow to press the Yes button and I almost cry with happiness when the floor shifts beneath my feet and the endless RED and WHITE is replaced by a foggy darkness.

This place is . . . ?

It's dark, but I can still see well enough to make out my own position. I'm standing at the shore of what I think is a river of mud. I can't see the other side of the river, and neither can I see whence it comes nor where it goes, and the entire area behind me is so foggy it looks like it came straight out of *Silent Hill*. It looks pretty spooky, but there's no real wind and it's completely silent otherwise, so at least I don't think I'll be accosted by any spooky ghosts. The only real area of interest is that right next to the shore, just beside me, is a single flickering streetlamp. It looks fire-lit and old, but I can't be sure.

I look back at the river. This has to be the thing I'm supposed to do, right? It should be . . .

<Tutorial stage, Hell Difficulty Eighth Floor: The Muddy Sluice.>
<[Clear Condition] Pass over the river of mud and reach the shore.>

Yeah, as I thought.

Still, this river is . . . I mean, it isn't going by very quickly or anything, but it's still made up entirely of mud. Thick, slimy mud. Hunching down, I stick my hand into it, and even though it moves slowly, the mud is so dense and strong that I almost get pulled along with it just by my hand alone. And then I feel something bite my hand.

I pull my hand out of the river to find a little sharp-toothed, eyeless fish trying to bite my finger off.

<Mudswimmer (Lv.4)>

And, miraculously, after a second or so, it actually succeeds, dropping back into the flowing mud together with my finger. Hm. Interesting. So, in other words, not only is it muddy, but it's also infested with weird piranhas? I guess that makes sense.

Standing up again, I look out at the river. It sure is broad. The fog lies so heavily over it that I can't even make out what's just a few meters ahead. Oh, apart from that shadow, of course.

Shadow?

I squint at the fog. Yeah, I wasn't hallucinating. That is absolutely a shadow. Pretty big one, too, moving slowly and smoothly toward me. If the shape hadn't been so weird, I would have assumed it was some muddy sea monster. But as the shadow passes closer, the silhouette becomes clearer and clearer, soon coming close enough for me to make out what it is.

It's a guy, standing in a little boat. I don't know how he's doing it, but he's paddling along, standing upright like a gondolier, without the stream of the muddy river seeming to have even the slightest impact. It's a strange sight, but I've seen weirder things in this tutorial.

As I watch, he lets his boat touch the shore, and even though most of the boat remains in the muddy river, it isn't moving even slightly. It's like it's nothing but a shadow. While I look at his boat, the man stretches out his hand and I look up, first at his open palm, and then at his face. Or, rather, where a face would be if he had one. I'm sure he'd have one if he didn't look like a fuzzy shadow.

<The Ferryman>

No level, huh? Is that supposed to suggest that he isn't meant to be killed?

"A piece of metal," the ferryman says, "for safe travels across the river."

I open my mouth and close it again. Deftly, I open up my inventory. Let's see here . . .

Leopard hide, wolf hide, boar hide, squirrel hide, bird hide, shade hide, gombie hide, bat hide, deer hide, elk hide, bear hide . . . Nope, no metal. What a bummer! I hope he accepts alternative forms of currency.

"How about if you take me across, I won't kill you and wear your skin like a pair of overalls?"

The ferryman looks down at me. I can't really tell his expression since he's lacking a face, but for some reason, I think he might be a little shocked. After almost a full minute of silence, he finally speaks again. "No money, no travels."

Ah, is that so. Shame. I shake my head. "No travels," I say. "*No life.*"

I leap at him before he has time to set back out into the river. I'm able to get a pretty good grip on him, hooking my legs around his midsection, but apparently I underestimated him, because after only a short quarrel, he finally pushes me off enough to smack me across the head with his oar, sending me hurling ass over teakettle into the muddy river below. Everything is cold and slimy and gross and—oh, there goes my hide again. Great.

Within just seconds of entering the mud, I can already feel numerous mudswimmers biting into every bit of my exposed flesh. To keep them from annoyingly blinding me, I begin to wheel my arms in an attempt to breach the surface.

<You have learned: Swim Lv.1>

After a few seconds of paddling through heavy mud, I finally get my head to escape the mud, where I take a deep breath and pull off a mudswimmer stuck to my ear, ripping off half my ear in the process.

For a second or so, I just look around, trying to catch a glimpse of the ferryman. No luck. He's gone, and I don't think I'll have too much luck trying to find him again. He didn't have a level, so I don't think I need to defeat him or anything, but it still feels empty. What a guy, huh? What kind of person would smack someone over the head with an oar, just like that, completely unprompted? Total lunatic.

Anyhow, now that I'm in the mud, it's not like I have any other choice but to start swimming.

Swimming in mud feels weird. Since it's thicker than water, it's thicker than me, so I don't sink as easily and rather bob at about chest level. But at the same time, it's also so thick that taking a single stroke through it leaves my arms tired and trembling. And that's not even mentioning the current. I'm lucky I only have to get to the other shore, or this would have been a practically impossible task. It's very close to it, but not quite there.

I begin to doggy-paddle my way toward . . . toward . . .

Huh. Which way was the shore again?

It's the same mud whichever way I look, and I can't see any shore, be it the one I came from or not. It's just the same mud and the same fog on both sides.

No way. Did I . . . ?

Did I already get lost?

And lost I was. I'll spare you the details, but since I faithfully checked the time for the entire duration, I can speak with absolute certainty when I say that I doggy-paddled around in that river of mud for no less than thirteen days straight.

Sometimes I would actually reach a shore, but every time, it would be the wrong one, and I'd get no message about the boss stage. I got so desperate that at one point when I got to the shore, I paced up and down, trying to ensure that it was really the one I started out at. But it had the same lantern, so it must have been the one.

The river never took me anywhere, and when I reached the wrong shore, I would always be back at the lantern. My only theory is that as I swam, the river was actively turning around, constantly, always. In my exhausted, blood-drained state, I imagined that the river actually ran perpetually in a circle around a little island—that island being the place where I entered the floor. But that couldn't be the case, because once I got up to the wrong shore—again and again and again and again and again—no matter how far I walked along the shore, never did I circle around to find the lantern. Only by going into the river of mud and emerging back up again did I encounter the lantern.

After this, I stopped going up on the shore anytime I found it, and just focused on my new favorite pastime: eating live fish.

Fish is good for you. If you eat lots of fish, you'll be able to swim as well as one. That's what my mother always told me, and that's what I'm sticking to. Maybe swimming for almost two weeks straight and doing nothing but eating fish wasn't too good for my brain, because once I ran out of fish, I was genuinely bummed out about it to the point that when I saw the lantern and the shore again, I decided just to go right on ahead. Nothing left to lose, and all that.

I went past the lantern and beyond the shore, into the fog, and after about half a day of walking . . .

<Tutorial stage, Hell Difficulty Eighth Floor: Boss Stage>
<[Clear Condition]Pass through the swamp to reach the lighthouse.>

I stare at the message in front of me. I lift my head upward. Far ahead, I spy the only light shining through the thick mist—far away, yet close enough where I can tell that it's got to be a lighthouse of some sort.

Seriously? That was it? That was all I needed to do? Did I seriously swim around in mud for like two weeks just . . . *because?* Seriously?

<THE GOD OF CRUELTY chuckles.>

If I ever find you, if I ever were to meet you face-to-face, I would make sure that when we part ways, you won't have a face anymore. And if I find out that you gods don't have faces as we mere mortals do, then I will learn divine magic strong enough to give you a face, and then rip *that* off. Does that sound good to you? How's Sunday at three? That work with you, Cruel?

No answer. Should've guessed. Cowards, the lot of them . . . !

Now, what's this about a swamp?

But before I can inspect the area around me more closely, a message pops up.

<You have received a message.>

The only one I can imagine who'd send this would be . . .

<SuperMoleman[F39]: Hey Kitty! Sorry I didn't say anything earlier; my party basically ran right on ahead into the next floors as well to prepare for the next Server Symposium. How have you been faring? I just now remembered that you need a piece of metal for the ferryman, but he'll settle for almost anything as long as it's metallic. Even your braces or a titanium implant will do. Aside from that, good job with the seventh floor! Glad you were able to beat it. Hope the eighth floor hasn't been too hard on you!>

I quickly type in a response.

<PrissyKittyPrincess[F8]: f7 was bad bt now im kk so is fine but wdy mean wit sympossum>
<SuperMoleman[F39]: You didn't get the memo? Then again, you seem very busy, so I'm not especially surprised. By the end of this attempt, there will be another Server Symposium. We still don't know what the purpose of the symposiums are, but HookedOnBach[F23] has hypothesized that it commemorates whenever something important happens or is unveiled in the server. Let's talk more At the symposium, I've got to go. Good luck!>
<PrissyKittyPrincess[F8]: kk thx u2>

Another symposium so soon? The last one was only . . . Uhh . . .

<Top—Status—Community>
<22:37:57 Day 164>
<The seventh attempt will begin in 16:01:22:03>

Seventy-five days ago! Or ninety days, if you calculate from when it will start. Hm. If I remember correctly, the last one was exactly ninety days after the tutorial opened. That's an interesting coincidence. Will I have to meet a bunch of people every three months? No idea. I almost hope not. The last time was kind of stressful. I certainly hope there won't be any insurrections this time . . .

Anyhow, back to the swamp.

I squint at the area in front of me. It's still so foggy I can barely see my own nose, but I think what I'm looking at is something of a woody area. There are trees, that's for sure, but they're squat and twisted. The area between the trees is basically just BLACK. And if I look back up, there's the lighthouse. Pretty far away, but not far enough for me to hesitate.

I move toward it.

After only a few steps, I feel my bare feet plunge into cold, slippery mud. Oh, God, more of this? Alright, fine, it's not like I've got any choice.

I move forward. It really is a swamp. The completely BLACK mud I move through is filled with what I hope are vines and the roots of whatever plants exist here. It's really disgusting, having your foot brush up against what feels like a head full of hair, but there isn't much else I can do but grit my teeth and continue.

The mud and sludge stand pretty high, but it never gets higher than my navel, so I'm able to trudge forward without having to commit myself to the tedious task of swimming through it. And things go somewhat fine until I accidentally bump into what I assume is a log or something, but when I look down at it, I find a pair of yellow eyes looking back up at me.

Cr—crocodile?!

<Shade (Lv.38)>

Oh, phew, it's just a clone of me. Before it can do anything, I shove it underneath the muddy surface, holding it down as it kicks and flails and scratches up my arms. After a few minutes it stops moving. I hold it down for an extra minute or so until I get a message.

<Shade (Lv.38) Defeated.>

So, if I am to understand this right . . . there are shades on this floor?

I look down at the wide-eyed shade floating face-up in the mud.

But they only look like me, so it's fine. Honestly, unlike the other shades, I don't even know if these shades are sapient at all. They don't say anything other than hissing and stuff, and if you so much as look at them, they attack like a raccoon on crack. A crackoon, if you will. Maybe there's something wrong with their programming? Who knows.

I continue. There are quite a few shades, more and more as I get closer to the lighthouse. Thankfully, they only attack if I physically touch them, so all I need to do is to place myself in the perfect position to disembowel them and break their neck at the same time while also tearing out their throat. That usually lets me take of them pretty easily.

Once the lighthouse comes nearer, it isn't even all that much trouble to take care of them.

Almost casually, I snake my hands around a nearby shade standing and staring at a tree. With only the simplest movements, I kill him.

<Shade (Lv.40) Defeated.>
<[Level Up]>
<You have reached Level 41.>
<Agility has increased by 4.
Strength has increased by 2.
Stamina has increased by 3.
Magic Power has increased by 1.
Dagger Tooth has increased by 1.
Swim has increased by 1.
Clutch has increased by 1.
Exhaustion Resistance has increased by 1.
Starvation Resistance has increased by 1.
Dehydration Resistance has increased by 1.
Parasite Resistance has increased by 1.>

Not bad, all things considered. With this level, I might actually be able to give Moleman a run for his money, hehehe!

But the lighthouse is very close now, so there's no need to linger anymore. I've already been wandering through this swamp for over two weeks in order to kill all of the shades, so it's about time to get moving. I can't smell any more warm blood, and the only sound in this swamp is from my own movement. The time is now.

As I move closer to the lighthouse, the muddy swamp retreats, and with each step, the level of mud falls slightly, slipping below my hips, down to my knees, down to my ankles and even further. Soon, I'm standing completely freed of mud, and the lighthouse is right above me. I take a quick peek at the time.

<Top—Status—Community>
<23:37:57 Day 179>
<The seventh attempt will begin in 1:00:22:03>
<The Server Symposium will begin in 22:03.>

Perfect.

I step close enough to touch it.

<To clear the eighth floor, please knock on the door.>

The door? What doo—

Oh, this one? The one to the lighthouse? Huh. That sounds kind of suspicious, but it's not like I can just refuse, so . . .

Knock knock knock.

No answer. I do a knock to the tune of "Shave and a Haircut." No response either. That's pretty wa—

The door flies open but by that point I'm already gone, right back in the lobby, with a series of messages floating in front of my vision.

<You have cleared the eighth floor.>

<You have received 1,000 points for clearing the floor. You have received an additional 1,000 points for being the first to clear the floor.>

<For clearing the stage completely, you will receive an additional reward.>

<To repay your debt, the additional reward has been traded for 5,000 points.>

<4 Gods have shown a positive response to you. You have obtained 4,000 points.>

<36 Gods have shown a negative response to you. 36,000 points have been deducted.>

<To repay your debt, the floor clear reward has been traded for 1,000 points.>

FLOOR 9

THE FLAMING TOWER

II

Harassment or Assault

They just keep on coming, huh? At least my gods are staying loyal, for once. One of these days, I'm going to have a hundred gods on my case about doing this or that or even about not doing this or that. Unreasonable, the lot of them.

<To repay your debt, your inventory has been sold for 2 points.>

Are my shade innards really *that* worthless? You know, if that ferryman hadn't had God-buffs and been level-less, I would totally have been able to sell his boat for a pretty penny. Not that you'd ever let me do anything to get better, of course.

<Current debt: 85,728 points.>

Okay, so, um, what you're trying to say is, uh . . . When I beat the next floor, I'll be in six-figure debt? Is that it?

I can't even muster a fitting amount of annoyance at the situation. If I were still on Earth, this is the moment when I would fake my death and pick up a new identity in Cuba. This simply isn't sustainable, and I'm not just talking about me! Think of all the poor, innocent little challengers who accidentally angered a few gods because they liked to drink their coffee BLACK, or with cream, or actually preferred *tea*. And just like that, they'd be a million points in debt and there would be nothing they could do. Why not have sympathy for *them*, huh?

No one's going to rebuke my perfectly sound argument, eh? Yeah, keep your silence, cowards, I know I'm ri—

<The God of Cruelty helpfully informs you that only Hell Challenger Lo Fennrick is currently indebted to the Gods.>

Okay, now that's just some bullshit.

No way that's true. There's just no way—

<The Server Symposium will begin in 0:00:00.>
<The Server Symposium has begun. You will be automatically summoned in 00:10.>

H—hang on, I'm not done here! This guy can't just go around saying whatever he wants whenever he—

The floor shifts beneath me and I stumble forward and bash my head into a table.

O—ow.

"H—hiiik?!" someone squeals.

I pull myself up from the floor. Alright, yeah, it's the same old Hell lobby room. In that case, the only voice that that could be, would have to be . . .

"K—Kitty? Is that you?" Virgil asks, her eyes trembling. Huh. I shouldn't look *all* that different from the last time I was here. Weird.

"Yeah," I say. "Of course, it's me. Who else would it be?"

She looks away. "Yeah, I guess, but it's just that . . ." She gestures at the whole of me. "It isn't very, um, obvious?"

What isn't very obvious? Just to follow her line of sight, I look down at myself. I'm covered from top to toe in a thick layer of muddy goo. Oh. Ah. Um. "This is, uh . . ." I shake my head, making a few pieces of mud fly everywhere. Virgil steps back. "It's not important." I take a step toward her, trying to make my voice as sympathetic as I can. "Listen, I saw how it went with the, uh, *lobbies*, and I just wanted to, um, say that, well, ah, it's . . ." I gulp. "It's not your fault, okay? You did your best, and I'm sure you'll do great next time around, so just—"

A hand reaches out in front of me. It isn't Virgil's.

I look up and meet the eyes of some normal-looking dude. "Hi," he says. "I'm Almos." He smiles.

I don't take his hand. Not answering him, I look over at Virgil. She gives a small smile. "I did it," she says quietly. "I got one of them to stay."

I look back at this . . . *Almos* character. He waggles his hand at me. After a moment's consideration, I take it, splattering his hand with mud and probably more blood than you'd expect. One shake up, one shake down. He's got a firm grip. But mine is firmer, thanks to the wonderful doping effects of leveling up. I clench his hand until I feel his bones creak, and only after he gives the smallest, tiniest "Ow" do I let him go.

"I'm Kitty," I say to him with maybe a little more assertiveness than the name would normally command.

Almos looks down at his muddied hand and after visibly wincing, he shakes it off before wiping the last bits off on his short pants. "Virgil told me you like to be referred to by your username, so . . . If you want, you can call me Magus."

I'm not sure if my frown is visible through the thick layer of mud on my face.

"I'm not calling you that."

His smile turns a little strained. "I understand that, haha. It is a pretty . . . *flashy* username, I suppose." As I cross my arms, his eyes gain a strange gleam. "Though I'm surprised to hear you speak Hungarian so fluently."

"I'm not speaking Hungarian."

"Is that so?"

"Yeah." After my firm words, a bout of silence follows. I don't want to have to randomly exposition to this strange man, but now the silence is quickly turning awkward, and Virgil looks very curious about him being able to understand me and me being able to understand him, so even though I don't want to, I heave a sigh and explain the effects of the all-tongue skill.

Almos's eyes gleam in that strange way again. I don't like that look. "A language skill . . . Interesting. And only *you* have this?"

"No idea. I'm pretty sure the gods gave it to me as a punishment, but who knows?"

"The gods . . . !"

Being standoffish with this man is strikingly ineffective. I don't know why he decided to stay in the lobby, or how Virgil convinced him, or why he picked the Hell Difficulty at all, but right now, I really couldn't care less. I don't like him. He's got an ambitious glint in his eye that I feel like I recognize from somewhere.

"Hey, K—Kitty, how come you've been able to get so far in the tutorial? What's your secret?" Almos asks.

He hesitated saying my name. I get it, but . . .

"Luck." That's all I have to say. The word makes his expression falter a little, but that doesn't make me change my answer.

After a second or so, he's able to gather his wits again. "Then what would you say—"

I put up my hand at him. "I don't have time to talk 'cause I'm gonna go have a rematch with Moleman and I'm gonna totally bust his butt and you're kind of in the way with your dumbo questions so I'm actually going to leave now and you can't stop me 'cause as you're familiar with you're just level zero and I'm leagues above that so yeah I'll be going now bye." And then, before he has time to reaffix his jaw in place, I leave the room, despite Virgil calling out to me.

Sniff sniff sniff sniff. Moleman . . . !

Getting down on all fours, I initiate my fastest running possible by using haste in every single part of my body while also using dagger nails to be able to run on walls for when the hallways are too crowded. For some reason, a lot of people scream when they see me bolting at them at Mach speeds. Even the well-armored beef heads make sounds like startled schoolgirls. Weird. Maybe I'm being followed by some spooky ghost? Who knows.

After running for maybe a minute or two tops, I finally get to the right place. At the end of the hallway, there's an open door that seems to enter into a massive hall filled with countless tables and even more people.

I leap at the open doorway and splatter into an invisible wall.

Slowly, I slide down from the wall before collapsing just beneath it. What in the heck is this—oh, it's the Easy Lobby. I should have noticed the sign. How dare he be in a place where I can't readily attack him? So inconsiderate. Once I get my hands on him, he'll wish he really lived up to his namesake so he could go bury himself in a hole, haha!

Not that I'll actually kill him or anything. No, I just need to have a wonderful little rematch to prove to him that I am the superior gamer. That's all. Hehe.

I stare into the Easy Lobby. I notice someone staring back at me. I have no idea who she is, but as she looks at where I sit crouched on the floor, she suddenly turns deathly pale—almost more so than me—and hurries off. Weird. Lots of weird stuff is happening at this symposium, and we aren't even ten minutes into it.

Since I've got nothing else to do, I start pacing back and forth in front of the doorway. He's got to come out of there someday, right? I think I can see people looking at me from within, but one harsh glare is enough to make them look away, so I'm not worried.

After a minute or so, I see that pale girl from before, except she's walking together with some well-armored girl who looks strangely authoritative. Not to me, though. Rules are for chumps, and rulers only have power over those that let them. The two of them are heading over here. Interesting. I keep watch on them from my peripheral vision all the way until they reach the doorway.

"You do know that harassment is a punishable offense under the Lawbook of the PRR?"

My jaw falls open and I freeze in my step. I look up at her. "Um," I say. "I didn't consent to . . ." Her eyes sharpen slightly. I turn toward her fully. "Okay, um actually I'm not harassing anyone and there's absolutely no proof that I would ever do something weird like that because as you can see, I'm just a totally normal sort of guy and besides the only reason I'm here is because I'm waiting for Moleman to come out so I can beat him up until he begs for his mommy"—I take a breath—"so it's not harassment."

She makes the sort of face you make when your toddler is trying to express that they're having prophetic visions of the heat death of the universe. "So, what you're trying to say is . . . You're not harassing anyone; you're just premeditating assault?"

I snap my fingers, making mud splatter. A piece of it hits her cheek. "*Exactly.*"

The woman wipes off her face before looking back at the pale girl and then returning her vision to me. "That's worse. You do know that premeditated assault is worse than harassment, right?"

"Uh," I say intellectually. "Um." Okay, I need to find some way to de-escalate this situation. Option one: kill her. She's standing just behind the barrier, out of reach. Shoot. Option two . . . "Officer, I have no idea what all of this is about; do you have anything to base these accusations on other than shoddy witness testimony and baseless accusations? You should know that witness accounts are the most gullible and easily tempered kinds of evidence, so all of this is actually completely meaningless."

Her eyebrows shoot up and her eyelids flare. "You—you *just* confessed to premeditated assault! How is that in any way baseless? If I reported this to Leader Bach, we could have you—"

"Ursula? Is everything alri—"

My eyes fall on Moleman. His eyes fall on me. For some reason, the gentle smile on his face suddenly slips off. After about half a second he's able to muster up another—if somewhat tense—smile, and he steps closer. Not close enough to leave the Easy Lobby, but close enough that he's part of the situation. He looks down at me. "Eh, erm . . . Kitty? Is that you?"

I take a few steps back. "Hey, haha, yeah, it's me, your buddy Kitty!" I hold out my hand. "Why don't you step out of the lobby here and greet me? A handshake, just for old times' sake, right? How's that sound, old buddy, old pal?"

Before Moleman can react to my words at all, Ursula puts her hand on his chest. "He just confessed to premeditating your assault. I wouldn't approach that . . . *thing* . . . if I were you."

Hey! How am I a thing? This is discrimination on the basis of animation!

Moleman looks away from Ursula and back to me. He takes a deep breath, like you do before walking into a minefield of a conversation. "Kitty, will you please explain just two things to me?" I tilt my head at him. "Actually, three. Um . . . First, why are you covered head to toe in mud?"

"Floor eight was muddy."

He nods, gives a short, almost self-deprecating chuckle, and then continues. "Second, why are you crouched down like—like . . . *Gollum*, or something?"

I look down. Huh. Yeah, I suppose this position could be considered kind of like that. Hm. "If I'm crouched down, they can't spot me."

Moleman looks like he has a lot he wants to say about that, but, in the end, he says nothing. "Alright. Third—"

"Hang on," I say, holding up my hand. He pauses. I continue, "You've asked me a whole bunch of questions now, so I think it's only fair if I get to ask you something in return."

He takes a deep, deep breath. "Sure," he says. "Ask away, friend."

I hesitate for a second. See, sure, he was level forty when he was on floor twenty-three or something, but now he's way beyond that. So there's a chance, just a tiny little chance, that . . . "What level are you?"

"I'm level eighty-three."

I can feel my jaw drop. I physically put it back in place. "I—I see. Um, okay. Yeah. Alright. Yup. Mm-hm."

Moleman takes a single step closer, moving out of the barrier. "Now, question three." He looks down at me. I feel like a child about to be reprimanded. I take a step back. "What's this about premeditated assault?"

"Uh—um, uh, ah, th—that's . . ." I gulp. "I was just . . . The, um, the rematch, and, it's . . ."

He heaves a sigh. Then he looks back at Ursula and the pale girl. "It's alright, he wasn't going to do anything. Just . . . just leave this to me, alright?"

She looks down at me. She's got that same look in her eye that you have when you look at a rowdy dog. Still, she seems to trust Moleman a fair bit, because after only a second or so, she replies, "Well, alright . . . Just, well, be careful, okay?"

He smiles back at her. "Don't worry." And so she leaves. The mud caked around my entire body feels awfully stuffy all of a sudden. Right as I start considering whether it's possible to fake your own death in the tutorial, Moleman squats down in front of me. He puts one hand on my shoulder. "Let's talk somewhere else, alright?"

"Uh," I say. "O—okay."

Before I can do anything else, he grabs me by both shoulders and pulls me to stand upright. It feels uncomfortable, but I can't find it in me to refuse him. He stares into my eyes intently. "When you're with people, try to act like one, okay?" I nod fiercely at him. "Great. That's rule number one."

Rule?

He grabs hold of my muddy hand in his left one and drags me through a bunch of weird, winding hallways and staircases, the number of people around us quickly turning to basically zero. Eventually, we get to what I think may be one of the tops of the castle, and he brings me into a little room overlooking the grassy hills outside. There are quite a lot of people out there. Some are training together, others are talking, yet more are just lying down in the grass, and some have apparently started playing football.

"Before we do anything else," Moleman says, and I only just have time to look at him before he points at me with his left ring finger and suddenly I'm lifted off the floor in a tiny hurricane and all of the mud and goop caking my body is violently ripped off me. As I swirl around like a lone sock in a massive dryer, he empties a few bottles of water into the whole thing, and while I'm still too shocked to do anything at all, I suddenly fall out of the ball and watch with fascination as he gestures the ball of swirling mud out of the window and then just lets it drop down into a gutter below.

Huh. Whoa. Wow. Is—is that the power of magic?

"Right, now that you're clean, we can—" He turns back to me, eyes widening as he notices that I am completely in the nude. "You—you're—why—" After a second or so of wild stammering, he pulls himself together enough to speak. "W—well, for, um, for starters, you can . . . Put something on. P—please."

Huh? Oh, yeah.

I pull one of my dozen leopard hides out of my inventory and wrap it around me like I usually do. Hm. It seems that I've gotten pretty used to wearing these things, huh? I turn back to him. "Is this better?"

Giving a sharp nod, Moleman wanders over and takes a seat at the small round table in the middle of the room. He gestures toward the only other chair, and I reluctantly sit down across from him. This feels like a parent-teacher conference. In that case, the best thing to do would be to start this on the right side of the street. I draw myself up as best as I can in my seat, even though it feels uncomfortable with the wood beneath my bony behind. "Um, thank you for cleaning off the mud, very n—"

"What level are you?"

My jaw snaps shut. Wearily, my eyes wander over the room. Oh, wow, I didn't notice that tapestry before. Isn't that neat?

"Look at me and tell me what level you are, Kitty."

I glance back at him. I look down at my hands. My palms have gone all sweaty again. "I'm, uh . . ." My voice falls to something just below a whisper. "Level forty-one . . ."

"Forty-one, huh? Not bad for floor eight," Moleman says casually, nodding as he does. When my eyes meet his, they harden. "But considering that I'm at floor forty-six, you've still got a long way to go before you can even *think* about having a fair rematch. Not to even mention trying to . . . What did Ursula call it? *Premeditating my assault?* Yeah. Not to say that it isn't possible, but . . ." He lays his hands flat on the table. "You might want to wait until you get to Purgatory before you try anything like that."

To say I feel like a schoolboy being scolded for getting into trouble again is a vast understatement. There's basically nothing I can do but sit here and stare down at my lap. That said, one word sticks out to me, and I muster the courage to raise my face to him again. "Get to where now?"

He blinks at me. "Oh! That's, um . . . It's one of the topics that'll be brought up at the Leadership Meeting in . . . Let me just look at the time." While he brings up his clock, I sneak a peek at it.

<Top—Status—Community>
<00:34:21 Day 180>
<The seventh attempt will begin in 23:20:39>
<The Server Symposium
will end in 23:20:39>

"Around fifteen minutes," Moleman finishes.
I feel my brows furrow. "Leadership Meeting?"

He jumps a little in his seat like he forgot I was here at all. "Oh, it's, uh . . . It's a meeting for the leadership. After the Delegate Commission got overthrown, *someone* had to step in and make sure people followed the new rules, and Bach decided that that should be, well, *us*. According to her, we've already shown the drive and passion needed to lead people, so . . . yeah. To simplify things, we just decided to make her the leader of our little band, too."

"Uh-huh," I say. "Alright."

He pauses for a second before continuing. "This meeting has been a long time coming, and all members of the leadership are required to be there. That includes me." He looks me up and down and gives a small sigh. "Since one of my formal duties is to keep track of you, I guess I have no choice but to ask you to, well, come along to the meeting."

I perk an eyebrow at him and point a hand at my chest. "*Me?*"

He nods, maybe a tad bit too gravely for the situation. "Yes, *you*. You won't need to say anything—in truth, it might be better if you kept quiet—and all you need to do is keep in my line of sight. I'd appreciate it if you didn't go and tattle to everyone about everything we talk about, but from what I can tell, you don't really spend too much time in the message boards anyway."

"Too busy grinding," I add with a sage bow of the head.

For almost a full minute, Moleman doesn't say anything else. Then he looks back down at the clock and just stands up, saying, "So, uh, yeah, we'd better, um . . . get going. There's no reason not to get there as early as possible." As I make to stand as well, he suddenly drills his eyes into me and I freeze midlift. "I'll say it again just so we're clear. *No* monkey business, okay? Unless you're asked something, you'd best keep your mouth shut. That's rule two here—try not to mess with the leaders."

He stands up fully, straightening out his back. Then he turns to look out of the window. For some reason, his face looks older than it should be for his age.

"Bach may not have succeeded in executing you last time, but that was because they didn't know that you were immune to poison. The next time, they'll go with the axe first." He turns back to look at me. The fact that he's technically still a teenager—much like myself—is not visible in the least. "The next time, I won't be able to stop them."

I look down at the table. "If they . . ." I close my mouth again. Lifting my face, I look straight into his eyes. "If they come to kill you, then I will protect you. I don't mind if they kill me instead, but you're not the kind of guy who should just get killed by some idiot bundle that doesn't know any other punishment than killing. That's just dumb." My hands clench into fists. "No matter what, I won't let you die again."

Dumbfounded, he stares at me for several seconds, until he finally bursts into laughter. "Hahaha, you sure do know how to ramp up the tension, huh?" He smiles warmly. "Thanks, though. I'll trust you on it, alright?"

"Just like how you'll trust that I won't do any monkey business while you're not looking?"

He hums. "That's a bit far, don't you think?"

"Alright, alright, that's true," I huff. And for a second or so, we just smile at each other.

He looks back down at the clock. "The time is starting to get a bit late. How about we get going?" I nod at him and step away from the table, but right as we're about to leave the room, he pauses and points at me. "Before that, though, is there anything you'd like to have brought up at the meeting? Anything you've learned in the difficulty we might like to know?"

"Uhhhh . . ." I tap my thumb to my lower lip. Oh, yeah, there was that *one* thing, wasn't there? I grin at him. "Today's my eighteenth birthday. Two more years and I'll be able to drink!"

"Hey, congrats!" Moleman says, and pats me on the back, but then his expression shifts into thoughtfulness. "But you know, I'm pretty sure you can still drink even now."

"Huh?" I say. "Why?"

Moleman shrugs and gestures at the room around us. "Dude, we're in a *fantasy world* here. Different rules and laws apply. From what I've heard, according to our new rulebook, there's no age you need to be to start drinking." He grins at me. I can feel something warm and fuzzy form in my chest.

"You're telling me that I can get BLACKout drunk?" I breathe.

He nods at me. The world fills up with birdsong.

"This is the best birthday of my life," I mumble. "This is the peak. From here on out, it's just downhill."

He slaps my back twice. "Hey, no need for those kinds of thoughts! Today . . . today, we will celebrate. But for now, we'd better get to the meeting!" I nod at him numbly and he pulls me along through the winding hallways again. I have no idea how he knows this castle so well. Maybe he has a skill like my great values sniffer? Anything is possible in a world as wonderful as this one.

After a few minutes of walking, we finally reach a larger room containing a few tapestries depicting unknown battles and flags, with the centerpiece of the room being a large round table fitted with a total of twelve chairs. Just for the sake of it, I check if there's any nameplate above the entrance to the room, but there's nothing like that.

The only other thing of interest would be that the main source of light in the room is a blocky dome of stained glass above the room, which looks pretty cool, to say the least. And now that I look closer at the table itself, there are little pieces of paper at every seat, each having a username written on them. Let's see if we can find Moleman's . . . Yup, there it is! Right next to Hooked-OnBach. Curious.

Obviously, there's no name tag for me since I haven't got any place at the table.

Moleman looks at the table for a second or two before turning to me. "I'll go get you a chair; just stay here and try not to cause any trouble, alright?"

"Yes, sir!" I say with a joking salute. He squints at me suspiciously and then leaves. Alright.

What's the most amount of monkey business I can cause in around a minute's time? Well, first, I could give those name tags a bit more of a, uh, non-insane-ifying color. WHITE . . . bad. Slowly, I creep toward the table.

"What are you doing in here, Princess?"

I jump a foot off the floor and twirl around midair like some sort of ballerina. In the entrance to the room stands a woman I know very well. "Bach . . . !"

She leans against the doorframe, crossing her arms. "If you're trying to mess with the seating arrangements out of foolish spite, then I can tell you with full certainty that no matter what order we sit in, we'll still talk about the same things. It would be a silly prank at best."

I scowl at her. There's no one else in the room. My personal record for disassembling a shade is only a single minute if I work at top speed. Since I'd be stressed by the situation in this case, I could do it even faster. If I use hurry across my entire body, then . . .

"I'm level sixty-six," she says. "Don't even try it."

Tch. I really don't like her. She's got that look to her. Mad with power. If she could order my execution once, she can do it again. Even though I don't exactly have any way of beating her, it doesn't mean I'm powerless or anything. Silently, I hunch down into a prepared crouch. If she tries something, I can drop into a FPB roll within the span of a single second. My body tenses. Where she stands, Bach doesn't even look remotely fazed.

Before I can do anything, someone shuffles down the hallway and I have the brief hope that it might be Moleman, but their appearance shatters those thoughts. This guy . . . I do not recognize him. He's pretty big, and he doesn't look Nordic.

"What's happening in here?" he asks as he steps inside. His eyes quickly train on me. "Isn't that . . . ?"

"The former Hell executive?" Bach fills in. "Yeah."

The guy thumbs his lower lip. "Didn't we execute the executives?"

Bach sighs in obvious frustration. "Not this one. So if you want to kill him, you'll have to face the consequences yourself."

He looks at me. I look at him. He's well-armored and big, but that doesn't mean anything. If he's got a throat, then I can claw it open. Simple as that.

His nose wrinkles. "Dunno about that one, Leader. It looks kind of . . . feral. Are you sure I won't catch some kind of disease touching it?"

In response, Bach shrugs dismissively. "How do you expect me to know?" She turns to me with a sly grin. "Why don't you try it out yourself? Maybe you'll get yourself a nice new tolerance from it." Her smile fades. "Either way, pesky stray cats like that shouldn't be wandering around in here. How about it, Princess? Why don't you show yourself out before Brutus here helps you?"

Brutus takes a step toward me. Alright, that's it.

I drop into a roll and dart across the floor, between Brutus's large legs and out into the hallway, where I promptly crash into Moleman, making him fall over and the chair in his hand go flying and then falling to the ground with a loud clatter just a step away. I'm atop Moleman. He seems confused. In the greatest haste I'm able to muster, I leap off his body. Should I keep running? Should I fight? Would Moleman be a proper hostage? What should I—

"K—Kitty?" Moleman asks from where he lies, still on the floor. He puts his hand to his right temple and glances up, just past me, his eyes falling right on Bach and Brutus. "Ah."

"Oh, Mole!" Bach says. "Excellent timing, I was just about to find you and ask why you haven't been keeping an eye on this guy."

"Well, first," Moleman says as he slowly pulls himself up, dusting off the front of his robe, "he *does* actually have a name." Just to help out somehow, I dust off Moleman's back, to which he whispers a small "Thanks." Moleman looks back at Bach. "Second, I *was* actually keeping track of him. For that purpose, I had invited him to join me at the meeting so that I could do just that. And since we only had twelve chairs, I went to get another one, asking him to remain in the room. And, if I may ask you a question in turn"—his eye gleams sharply—"how come I now meet him trying to escape that very room like it was filled with snakes?"

Bach doesn't say anything in response.

Man, I should have gotten this guy as the lawyer for my trial, then I would have gone free without any issues! Hm. Hang on . . .

After a fair amount of time, Bach finally finds her voice again. "I'm just as surprised as you are! As soon as Brutus here showed up, he just darted for it. I was questioning him regarding his presence, but he gave no real response, so . . ."

"So?" But even though Moleman's prompt is well-placed, she doesn't actually continue the sentence. The silence is just about to turn five degrees beyond awkward when the tension is broken by an approaching presence down the hall.

"Hey, Moleman, you're already here!" some guy that I think I vaguely recognize says as he comes close. But no matter how much I rack my brains, I can't come up with any name. Something with fish? The man stops a few meters away from the whole gang, his eyes jumping from Moleman to me, and then to Bach and Brutus before returning to Moleman. "Heh, did I walk in on something, or . . . ?"

"Not at all, Herring," Bach says with undue confidence. "We were just about to take our seats. You don't happen to have any word on when the rest will arrive?"

III

Birthday and Party

Herring—weird name—gives a small nod, but it's clear that he doesn't find the situation here too relaxed. "I talked to Yurt just the other minute. He went off to find the others, so they should be here any moment."

"Great!" Bach says with a clap of her hands. "No need for us to wait out here, though. How about we go inside the room and mingle a little? It's been a while since we met face to face, after all." The group agrees, and slowly we file back inside the room, though I wait just a few seconds for Moleman to grab the chair off the floor. Together with the rest, we enter. Sometimes I wish I were more oblivious of these things because the feeling of people looking at me with this air of suspicion is skin-crawling.

For a minute or so, Moleman and I discuss where I should sit. I think I should sit next to the entrance, but Moleman argues that since he considers me to be a proper part of the meeting since I'm the only one who can speak for the Hell Difficulty, I should sit at the table with the rest of them. And despite my best efforts, he gets his way through. Unfortunately, this puts me right between Moleman and Bach.

It's far from my first choice, but as you may be familiar with, as of right now, I basically don't have any human rights. So who cares.

After a few minutes, the rest of the leadership drops in one by one. Some I recognize, but most of them are complete strangers to me. To make things worse, they don't even try to introduce themselves, so I have no way of knowing so much as what their names are. There are too many of them in total for me to make a mental list of them, so for now, I'm not even going to bother to put their names and faces to mind. It probably won't be important in the future.

"Alright, let's take our seats, shall we?" Bach says to the group as a whole.

Until now, most of us had just been hanging around and mingling—with me following Moleman around like a lost sheep—but now we start moving properly. Everybody shuffles over to the table and after only a minute or so of people looking for their names and sitting down in their proper seats, we finally have the whole gang in one place. Bach makes a gesture at Moleman, and he silently points at the door, making a small gust of wind close it.

"Before we begin," Bach says, drawing herself up, "I will distribute the plan for today's Leadership Meeting. Please look through it carefully."

Nobody says anything in response, so she just goes right on ahead by pulling out a small pile of papers from her inventory and passing them to the right. The small pile moves through the people, and everyone takes one copy each, until it reaches Moleman on my left, who receives the final one. Leaving me empty-handed. N—not that I actually wanted a plan for the meeting or anything. Plans are for dumbos who can't get it right on their own.

Slyly, I peek at Moleman's copy. It's handwritten on a piece of textured paper with elegant, slightly swirly letters. It's a nice handwriting, but I don't want to say anything else because I've got a hunch that Bach may have written it herself, and I don't want to compliment her.

Most of it is just bureaucratic nonsense, though, so I give up trying to read it pretty fast.

"If you've all read through it properly, then I will henceforth declare the meeting opened." Pulling a small brass hammer from her inventory, she lightly bangs it against the table. "First, I nominate myself as chairman for the meeting. Are all in favor?"

A scattered chorus of "Aye" arises from the various members at the table. Not wanting to be left out, I parrot them and say, "Aye," too. But then Moleman elbows me in the ribs for some reason and Bach gives me a side-eye.

"To repeat what is already written in the program," she says sternly, "only those formally part of the Leadership of Rebel are allowed to have a vote at this meeting. Unauthorized persons present due to extenuating circumstances must remain quiet. Is that understood by all persons present?"

"Aye."

"A—" Moleman elbows me in the ribs again before I have time to instinctually say *Aye* like everyone else. It—it was just so tempting!

"To continue where we left off, since all are in favor of accepting HookedOn-Bach of the twenty-seventh floor as chairman, this motion is accepted." And then she bangs her little gavel and I have never before wanted to bonk a table with a brass hammer so badly. "On to our next point; HerringFerry of the fourteenth floor has nominated SuperMoleman of the forty-sixth floor as secretary. Are all in favor of accepting this motion?"

"Aye."

"A—" Moleman quickly silences me by stepping on my foot. I bite my tongue.

There's a bang of the gavel. "In that case, the meeting formally accepts Super-Moleman of the forty-sixth floor as secretary."

"Thank you," Moleman says politely as he pulls out a bit of stationery, mainly a few sheets of paper, a quill, and an inkwell. Even though I know that the shop doesn't exactly have access to much modern-day stuff, seeing him use such ancient things still feels weird. Almost archaic. I watch with fascination as he quickly jots down the events of the meeting being opened and the choice of chairman and secretary.

"To start," Bach says, "we will have each person describe how the last three months have gone for the floors they supervise, alongside what punishments have mainly been executed and in response to which crimes. Allow me to go first. As the supervisor of the Hard Difficulty, as well as floors twenty and above . . ."

I regret agreeing to this. I thought I would be getting some interesting information, but this is just the Delegate Commission chat all over again. Unlike that chat, however, now, I can't even clock out by just not reading it. There's nothing I can do *but* listen. To make the time go by faster, I begin silently ripping up my thighs just beneath the table. Wherever this is, it isn't like the lobbies, so I can hurt myself as much as I want without it healing straight away. Neat! "Now, I wish to leave the word to HerringFerry of the Hard Difficulty, supervisor of the first twenty floors."

"Thank you, Bach," Herring says. And then he begins to do a report, just as detailed as Bach's. I have no idea for how long he talks, but it feels like years.

Oh, I just reached my femurs! How neat. I'm going to try giving myself skeleton legs, hehe.

"In conclusion, since more people have understandably become far more desperate to finish the tutorial quickly, mistreatment among challengers and toward the inhabitants of Purgatory have unfortunately become more common than before."

Bach nods at him sagely. "Thank you. Continuing on . . ."

To make a horribly drawn-out situation a bit more manageable, I'll just summarize and say that nobody said anything of value and then they skipped over Moleman. But by the time we got here, I had already completed my goal of removing all the flesh on my legs. Great success! I feel slightly woozy, but it's already getting better.

<You have learned: Bleeding Protection Lv.5>

Hey, neat! Level up!

With the final report, Bach bangs her gavel again. "Let us continue. Since I'm sure that this news has undoubtedly hung heavy on everyone's minds lately, let us—" Her eyes widen slightly and her lips almost instantly dip into a frown. She glances at me in what seems to be disgust. Her mind seems to rush with thoughts and conflict and after a second or so she finally makes up her mind and says, "Did you never learn how to use a bathroom!? What the hell are you—"

She looks underneath the table. I don't know what she was expecting, but it was clearly not my skeleton legs, because just as soon as she looked beneath, she looks away, sitting back up straight to stare at a tapestry on the wall for a few seconds. Her eyes slowly open and close a few more times. After gathering herself, she looks back under the table. The rest of the leaders at the table—too confused to say anything—mirror her actions by looking under the table.

I feel Moleman's eyes burn into me. "Kitty?" he asks. "What did you do?"

I purse my lips. "I—it's not like I was hurting anybody; just the opposite actually, because in a sense, training my tolerances and resistances and stuff is very good for me, because it prevents me from dying in the future, so this is really less hurting and more saving, and saving someone is always a good thing, even if it hurts a little, so I haven't done anything morally reprehensible."

He stares at me for a few seconds more, and then, carefully, he places his face in his hands.

"A—a potion!" someone says hysterically.

"Moleman, you know a healing spell, right? Moleman, please, you need to—"

"Okay, guys, I'm buying an elixir right now . . ."

Bach slowly stands up again, and even though her eyes are foggy and dead-looking, she still finds it in herself to look me straight in the eyes. "Why did you do that to yourself?" she asks bluntly.

"Um," I say. "To train my tolerances?"

"You aren't in pain or going to die?"

"Uh . . ." I give a quick glance at Moleman. He's still got his head in his hands. "No?"

Bach claps her hands. "Great! Okay, meeting, you heard him. He's not going to die. Let's just ignore the pile of human flesh and blood under the table and try to continue the meeting, okay?"

"C—continue the meeting?! But he's—" A single look from Bach shuts them up.

"Perfect, glad we're all in agreement." Slowly, despite some of them not being able to pull their eyes away from me, the rest of the leadership takes their seats. Since this is apparently important to these people, I quietly activate my moving meditation to heal up. Slowly, flesh returns to my bones. Beside me, Bach folds her hands on top of the table. "Now, then. Where was I?"

*　*　*

"Since some here at the table may not be familiar with it, I will do my best to summarize the revelation that arrived with the new challengers this attempt," Bach says. Somehow, her words, although light, bring a weight to the room. It feels like everyone is holding their breath. "Namely, the fact that there has been an alien invasion of Earth. I hesitate to call it this, but there isn't exactly any better word for it. Normally, this kind of rumor wouldn't even faze us, but the fact of the matter is that a number of challengers have expressed similar accounts." She turns toward me, but she's actually looking at Moleman. "Mole, will you call for our witnesses?"

Moleman nods at her and types something into his PMs. I didn't mean to pry, but seeing an inbox that wasn't overflooded with hate mail felt somehow off.

Still, uh . . . Alien invasion? Wh—what?

What's that even supposed to mean?

After a minute or so at most, the supposed witnesses arrive. I'm unhappy to see a certain familiar face. To make matters worse, Almos is not only among the three or so witnesses but actually at the very front of them. As they close the door behind them, Almos steps to the forefront, greeting the collected group with a slight bow. "Greetings, esteemed leaders. I am MagusDownBelow of the Hell Difficulty."

"Thank you for coming to give your testimony, and to represent the rest of the witnesses in their stead. I understand that your presence was decided on a very brief note, and that you must find this whole situation very confusing, being from the first floor," Bach says mildly. How come she's never that polite with *me*? I call humbug!

Almos softly shakes his head. "Not at all, Leader." He glances at me. I don't like that unfamiliar look in his eye. Why is he smiling at me like that? "Upon arriving at this symposium, I had a very helpful guide." Yeah, Virgil's a nice gal, what else is new?

She nods at him. "In that case, please recount to us, as you told it to your fellow witnesses, the manner of your invitation."

His smile twitches, but nonetheless he speaks openly. "Of course. I was in my dorm room when it happened, trying to sleep, when all of a sudden, the whole building started to shake. And then I heard the explosion. I didn't know what was happening, so I looked out the window, and from there I saw just the strangest sight. The whole sky was full of lights, and I could hear fighter planes screech by, and every two seconds there would be a massive bang, enough to make my ears ring. I wouldn't have thought anything else of it if I hadn't seen the birds. I . . . I *think* it was birds, at least."

He takes a deep breath before resuming. "One of them crashed down close to my dorm. It was pitch BLACK and midnight, so I could barely see what it was, apart from that it was dead. It almost looked like a bird. I don't know. It was like if you'd tried to taxidermy a pigeon, but you'd filled it up too much. It looked bloated and cracked, and the cracks were all purple and glowy. I don't know if I'd personally call it an alien, but it didn't look like it came from anywhere on Earth." He pauses again, eyebrows knitting together for a second or two. "And—and while I looked at it, in the distance, I suddenly saw one of those fighter jets going down, being accosted by a swarm of the things. It was the strangest thing I'd ever seen." He cracks into a sudden smile. "Before, heh . . . before all *this*, of course," he says, gesturing at our perfectly normal gathering.

"And this didn't happen to you alone?" Bach asks, cutting through his personable humor.

He softly shakes his head. "I was actually talking to Porcupine here about the whole thing, and he had something similar. That's why I got roped into this whole, uh, witnessing thing, but, um . . ." He nods. "They both saw similar things. Porcupine was just taking a midnight walk when he came across some sort of person who looked like that pigeon did—bloated and cracked—and Ledge was watching the news when he saw an urgent report about a recent hoax of aliens being seen here and there." He scoffs. "I don't know if I'd personally call them aliens, but . . ."

Bach seems thoughtful. "Thank you for the testimony. Dismissed."

Almos seems surprised by how brief the whole thing was, but since he can't bring himself to say anything against her, he just gives another small bow and leaves. For some reason, he gave me a weird look before he left that I have no idea how to interpret.

Once the door is closed once more, the leadership turns back to Bach, who weaves her hands across the table. "Combined with the various other posts you've doubtless seen on the message boards regarding this, the fact that something strange is happening back on Earth is not under discussion. Instead, the problem is that we don't actually know *what* is happening. These aliens—if that is what they are—don't seem to be from Purgatory, nor do they seem to be fully synonymous with the aliens you would imagine upon hearing the word. We do not know what they are, and we do not fully know what the situation is on Earth following these attacks."

She continues. "As you are doubtless familiar with at this point, for every attempt that occurs here, only a single day passes on Earth. Until the next attempt, when the next challengers arrive, we cannot in complete certainty ensure that the information we gather is pertinent. It may be true, but if we go and make some sort of statement regarding this and the next challengers explain that it was only a worldwide robotics test and nothing more, our credibility as a governing body will sink. They are trusting us to make a suitable statement. It is better for us that what we say is correct, rather than it being soon.

"For the time being, we will neither confirm nor deny what the new challengers say. Is this acceptable according to the membership?"

The members of the leadership share glances for a few seconds.

"Aye."

"Aye."

"Aye."

And after everyone has verbally agreed, she bangs the gavel again. "Glad we could all agree. To speak informally, I'm not sure if we will be able to hold off on making a statement until the next Server Symposium. Hopefully, we will be able to say something earlier than that, but for now, we will hold our tongues—even when speaking privately."

The leaders don't seem too keen on that last part, but nonetheless, she continues, taking a quick glance at the meeting guide first. "Now, then. We are drawing close to our final point of discussion, which gives me the honor of congratulating SuperMoleman on being the first to beat the first part of the tutorial!"

On what? Huh?

I can't even really process all of that before the people around the table start clapping. I raise my hands to clap as well, but they're still covered in blood from when I made my legs into skeleton legs, so I quickly lick them off before clapping as well. Moleman seems both embarrassed by the applause and silently numb at whatever it is I'm doing wrong now.

Once the applause dies down, everyone's left looking at him expectantly, so even though he seems much more excited to write down what everyone else is saying, he smiles and speaks anyway. "Well, I, erm . . . I'm very honored, of course, but the achievement is equal between me and my party members. Not to even mention that none of this would have been possible without your gracious assistance, Leader Bach."

"Nonsense," Bach says firmly. "You were able to construct a working guide for the final floors of Inferno, and now you're allowed to reap the rewards. Without your excellent guidance, your party would surely have perished long ago."

"Haha, um, I really hope not . . ." Moleman mumbles.

Bach's eyes sharpen. "That said, we are *much* more interested in your report regarding Purgatory; no offense."

"None taken," Moleman replies coolly. For a second or so, he gathers himself up until he's sitting straight and serious. "As I explained in my posts, Purgatory—the second part of this tutorial—is completely unlike the first part. Instead of us simply acting in small, closed scenarios called *floors*, we are instead placed wholesale into this world that we have been acting parallel to. Since we were only able to act within Purgatory for a few days before the Server Symposium, there isn't much I can say regarding it. However, I can with full confidence say that it is mainly governed by a race of sentient humanoids known as *goblins*."

For some reason, he gives me a weird glance before looking back at Bach. "The world of Purgatory, compared to that of Earth, seems to be in the Middle Ages or so. I can't say exactly what time frame this is, but their technology is sorely lacking, and their main form of government is monarchy. They speak a language different than ours, and I have good reason to believe that they have never seen humans before."

Bach trains her eyes onto him like a hawk watching a mouse. "And you are still of the belief that goblins should be counted as fully sapient beings?"

Moleman nods resolutely. "There isn't a single doubt in my mind of that fact. That they look different from us and speak a different language has no bearing on their sapience."

Silently, Bach rubs her chin. "I see. In that case, I believe we should do an anonymous vote on the sapience of goblins and whether we should recognize them as such. It is a bit kindergarten-like, but if everyone would just close their eyes, and those that are in favor of considering goblins as sapient, please raise your hands . . ."

Since I'm not a part of the vote because I'm not a real human being, I'm able to see pretty clearly how seven of the twelve present raise their hands, Moleman being one of them. Bach counts them quickly, using her fingers to help, and then she says, "You may open your eyes again." They follow along. "Since seven to four, not counting myself, were in favor of regarding goblins as properly sapient beings, the meeting will hereby recognize goblins as such." She bonks her gavel. "Specific rules regarding the treatment of goblins and what circumstances allow for some to be broken will be discussed at a later date. For now, though, I move that—in general—the same rules that apply to our fellow challengers will likewise apply to goblins, not counting the case in which specific goblins must be defeated in accordance with the floor clear requirements. Is the meeting in agreement to accept this motion?"

"Aye."

Slam. "Motion accepted. Now, Moleman, when you explained this to me, you mentioned that you met a Korean?" Silence descends upon the table, suffocating us all.

A—a *Korean?*

Moleman just nods as if that isn't anything weird at all. "Yes. More specifically, a South Korean and his party of other Asians. Only the Korean spoke proper English; the others were near incomprehensible, but it was enough. We spoke to them, and we exchanged words. As we thought, our server isn't the only one. They were from the Asia Server, which had over three thousand current challengers, according to him." He passes me a quick look. "I asked what the state of their Hell Lobby was, and he said that they had never had anyone pass the first floor."

Unlike the rest of what he just said, that final part isn't especially surprising.

"How many other servers are there? Did he know?" Bach asks.

"From what he said, he had previously met a party of challengers from the Africa Server, who also don't have more than a thousand challengers. Personally, I think it would be rational to assume that there is an America Server, but I'm not sure whether there's an Oceania one or not. Either way, it seems that not many have reached Purgatory in total. Though, with the speed many challengers have gained now, before long, there may be several hundred challengers within Purgatory. At that point, we may need to make some sort of contact with the governments that exist there."

"But for now," he continues, "it is worth noting that the Asia Server seems to be governed by a representative democracy of sorts. Each country has a single nonappointed leader, and all leaders vote together on how to act and what rules should be obeyed. In that sense, it isn't much different from what we have."

"Very interesting," Bach says. "Since we don't have enough information to be able to make any decisions as of yet, I suggest that you simply continue to spend time in Purgatory. Write as detailed reports as you can, and we will continue this discussion at a later date. Now, on to our final few points . . ." I had hoped that something interesting would be saved for the end, but instead she just starts talking about the possibility of making a serverwide survey, and then a bunch of budgeting and stuff. I don't think anyone will fault me for zoning out completely.

And when I zone back in, my legs have regenerated again, and Bach is slamming her gavel onto the table.

"Does anyone have any final points of interest to bring before the meeting?" Bach asks.

Moleman gently raises his hand. I look at him. She gives him a nod, and he speaks those fateful, horrifying words: "Today is Kitty's birthday!"

Silence. Not even that—this is some sort of void of speech. Even if someone said something right now, the pure thickness of the nothingness that restrains us would have choked it to death and rendered it just as silent as everything else. My head slowly creaks to face Moleman. He's got a big, innocent smile on his face. Like he couldn't even consider the idea that maybe, just maybe, these people wouldn't be all that interested in celebrating my birthday in particular.

"Uh," Bach says, her narrowed eyes jumping between Moleman and me. "Congratulations?"

"Congratulations," someone says lamely across the table.

"Congrats," someone else says a second or so later. For almost half a minute, the word jumps like an obese toad between each mouth, tumbling off their tongues with increasing reluctance.

Ah. Hm. Hmm. I think, just maybe, that I had forgotten what it feels like to want to die. But now I can remember it clearly. Maybe even more strongly than before.

The circle completes when Moleman turns to me, face beaming, and says, "Congratulations!"

And then silence descends once more, but everyone's looking at me, expecting me to say something—maybe even give a speech—meaning that the responsibility for killing this murderous silence is on my shoulders alone. I look down at the table. "Th . . . thanks . . ." I mumble.

I am never again telling Moleman my birthday. Unfortunately, I doubt he's the type to forget a birthdate once heard. This is the worst thing I have ever experienced.

Without saying a word, acting mainly just on instinct, I pull my newly recovered knees to my chest and go into the fetal position. Seeing everyone's heads start to whirl around looking for me makes me feel a bit better. Hehe. They look silly.

"K—Kitty? Where'd you go?" Moleman says almost dejectedly, which makes my heart hurt a little, so I undo it and sit back down, normally. He turns back to me and scoffs a little at seeing me. "You sure do have some weird abilities, huh . . . ?"

Yeah. I guess I do.

With me found and the final point of the day concluded, they adjourn the meeting.

"But, as promised," Bach says just as I'm about to stand up, "lunch will now be served. On me."

My heart skips a beat. I can feel my pupils dilate. Is this . . . *Love* . . . ?

She brings forward a bunch of delicious food, and the other leaders also bring some stuff out, and soon the whole table is covered with yummy delicious exquisite *actual real human* food. It smells wonderful. Some of the food is even hot. *Steaming* hot. Not merely lukewarm because it's so freshly killed. Hot. Truly, actually *hot*. There's fresh bread, and butter, and sliced hams and smoked chicken to go on top, and a bowl of porridge, and sausage links, and jam, and pork brains in gravy, and a platter of fresh fruits, and a bowl of crisp salad, and a quarter of a wheel of cheese, and a bowl of oranges, and a plate of roast beef, and a small platter of biscuits, and a jug of fresh water, and a jug of juice, and a jug of milk, and a pot of tea that Moleman made using magic, and, and, and . . . !

Moleman puts his hand on my trembling shoulder. "Hey, dude, you're drooli—" His eyes widen slightly. "Are . . . are you *crying*?"

I hastily wipe at my eyes. "N—no. No, I'm just, it was just . . . the steam. The steam got—*hic*—into my eyes. That's all."

His mouth slowly closes. Then he turns to the table full of food. Taking a platter from his inventory, he begins shoveling it on. Two of each at the very least, making five different sandwiches with all combinations of meat, cheese, and jam, carefully balancing it all to fit as much food as humanly possible, the massive tower of meats and carbs and fruits and veggies leaning and wobbling with every new thing he adds. It's gotten to the point where if he didn't have his system and all his levels, he might not have been able to lift it at all. I stare at him, but more than that, I stare at the leaning tower of yummy.

Once it practically towers above the table and no one can help but stare, Moleman stands up, still holding his massive platter, grabs me by the wrist, and pulls me along as he makes for the door. Before he leaves fully, he glances back and smiles, saying, "Sorry, I forgot I made an appointment to eat lunch with someone else. I'm afraid I need to leave, but thank you all for today's meeting!"

They stare at him.

"Yes, thank you—" is about all I have time to hear from Bach before we're out of the room and in the hallway. I look back at the room we're leaving. What is even happening? Where are we going? If Moleman's having lunch with someone else, why is he pulling me along? This is all very confusing.

After less than a minute of walking, Moleman pulls me back into the room we went to first, with the table and the two chairs. He puts down the platter in the middle of the table and sits down, sighing deeply as he does. I'm still standing, just above him, my face affixed in a permanent expression of confusion. "What are you waiting for?" Moleman says lightly, with a simple smile on his face. He waves to the other chair. "Take a seat."

Carefully, I sit down. I look around the room a little. "So, um . . ." I say. "When will your lunch appointment guy show up? Should I leave before then, or . . . ?"

Moleman blinks at me. Twice. "You—" And then, surprisingly, he breaks out into laughter. A simple but loud laughter, pure and unhindered by anything at all. "Hahaha, hahaha, haha . . . Oh, Kitty, you really are quite something, aren't you?" He waves to the pile of food on the platter. "Go ahead. Dig in before it goes cold."

"Huh?" The sound erupts from my throat without any real thought. "What do you mean? Wasn't this for . . . ?"

"It's for *you*, birthday pig," he says, smiling broadly. His eyes shine with mirth. "Just eat. If I'd left you in that meeting to eat, you wouldn't have eaten a thing, right?" I make to protest, but he's quicker to speak. "You would have wanted to, sure, but then you would have realized that if you ate, you would have done it like a beast, and the leadership would have been angered by your lack of courtesy, or whatever. And that's rule two. So, since you wouldn't have been able to eat in any other way that wouldn't break rule two, you would have chosen not to eat at all. That's what would have happened. Am I right?"

"Well, uh, um," I say, crossing my arms. "M—maybe? How should I know? It hasn't happened yet!"

He smiles at me. "Your honesty is nice. I like it. Those other leaders are all full of hot air and none of them dare to stand up to Bach—but you don't care. About courtesy, or anything else. It's . . . refreshing."

I frown at him. This feels awfully weird. "Um . . . okay? That's kind of weird."

He chuckles again, and then he gestures at the platter of food. "So, now that we're away from them, you can eat to your heart's content. All this food is for you. Eat with your hands if you want to. I don't mind. I won't be angered by something so petty as you acting like you usually do."

I'm not entirely sure what he means by that, but . . . That jam sandwich there is looking mighty yummy. And the roast beef slices, too. And the fruit. And the biscuits. And the cheese. And the ham and the chicken. And the . . .

I glance up. He smiles at me and waves at the platter.

I can't stop myself anymore. I feel my body move as if possessed by a demon. Throwing everything I am to the wind, I attack, and my mind fills with *heaven*.

Fork and spoon and knife are optional and not necessary when I have sharp claws and fingers and a mouth. I shovel it in wholesale. Like some sort of trash compactor, I simply push the food inside, chew, shed a tear or two, and swallow. More and more and more and more. I eat and I eat and I eat and I eat and I can't recall a single moment in the past three months, or even the past six months, or maybe even the past eighteen years, when I have been this happy. I always thought crying tears of joy was a bogus concept, made up by people without the ability to sense their own emotions. But I get it now. I get it completely. I'm not sad, and yet my tears just keep streaming down, mingling into the food, making it slightly saltier, but still tastier than anything I've eaten in so long.

When the food starts running out, Moleman brings out more from his inventory. All kinds of food. Meats and potatoes and sauces and root vegetables and weird greens that must be from that fantasy world—Purgatory—and so many other heavenly delicacies, too.

I used to be a very picky eater. No onions, no carrots, no slimy boiled things, nothing too tough. But now it all just goes down. I'm not even really thinking about it at all. Everything just tastes so delicious and it's so easy to swallow that even if he had fed me his own hand, I would gladly have eaten it. Brussels sprouts and broccoli and asparagus are yummy. How could I ever have believed the opposite?

But all good things must come to an end, and even though I still want to eat, even though my stomach still aches, I can't physically eat any more. My stomach is bloated, and my heart is beating maybe a little too fast for comfort. But the table is wiped clear. Not a speck of sauce or a single crumb has been left behind. It is done.

I look up at Moleman, breathing slowly. Suddenly, a sly glint appears in his eye.

"Hang on, I need to buy something from the shop."

Dazed and stunned, I watch in silence as he opens the shop, and after just a few seconds . . .

A cake appears in the middle of the table. A *princess* cake.

"You do still have space for dessert, right?" he asks. I look up at him. I look back at the cake.

There's always space for dessert.

With trembling hands, I reach for the cake, but before I can gouge out a piece of it, he stops me. "Come on, man; this is your *birthday cake*. Let's be at least a little civilized with it, alright?" I don't know if I can still speak or if the food coma has made me mute, so I just nod at him dully. He smiles and brings out a small plate each, and a spoon for each of us. Then, finally, he takes out a simple dagger and a tiny candle. When he points at it with his left thumb, the candle lights up into flames, and he places it atop the cake. I look at the candle. Then I look up at him. He smiles at me. Then he pulls out a lute from his inventory. I'm not kidding. A *lute*.

The fact that he has a lute is quickly overshadowed by the fact that he can actually *play* it, and that fact is likewise overshadowed when he starts to sing "Happy Birthday" to me. My jaw slowly drops.

". . . Happy birthday, dear *Ki-tty*, happy birthday to you!" he finishes.

Ah. I'm crying again. That's weird.

He pushes the cake closer to me. "Come on, blow out the candle. Make a wish!"

I look down at the candle. In my heart, I make a little wish that I would never tell anyone. Silently, I blow out the candle, the words echoing softly through my heart.

I hope Moleman keeps being my friend forever.

He cuts two pieces out of the cake, one for me—topped with the obligatory marzipan rose—and another for himself. I take the spoon in hand and grab a piece of the slice, bringing it to my mouth. It's sweet. It's almost too sweet. It wasn't this sweet back when I ate it alone. Isn't that weird?

Even though it's a pretty big cake, we finish it together. Apparently he doesn't like marzipan, so he gives it to me, and I eat it happily even though it gives me heart palpitations. While I'm stuffing down the last of the marzipan, he suddenly stands up from the table and turns away, toward the wall. I can see him doing something suspicious, but I'm too focused on the yummy yummy yummy yummy to really care.

As I put the last piece of the cake into my mouth, a certain something slides across the table. I look down. There, a small, wrapped package lies.

"It's a present," Moleman says. "For your birthday."

My gaze jumps from him to the little package and back up to him. "Th—thanks," I choke out through the marzipan and the cake and everything else. I almost put my hands on the present, but then I realize how dirty they are, so I quickly lick them off and wipe the last on my legs. My hands are still dirty, but I can't restrain myself any longer. My clawed hands fall on the simple package, and I lift it off the table. It's about the size and weight of a book, sturdy, and wrapped in decorated paper, strung together with a little bow. I try to open it as carefully as my clawed fingers possibly can, first taking off the bow and then cutting off the paper.

It's a book. No . . . a *tome*. A *magic* tome.

My eyes widen at it. "Th—this is . . . ?"

"It's a basic introduction to magic and spellship," Moleman explains, standing just over my shoulder. "If you read it properly, you should be able to learn the mana sensing and the mana control skills at the novice level. You'll need other books for specific spells, but . . ." He smiles at me warmly. "I can always give you those at the next symposium, right?"

My mouth opens and closes a few times. My hands are trembling, and not just from the food and sugar. Gulp. "B—but if you give me this, then the next time I beat a floor, it will just . . ."

"In that case," Moleman states grandly, "it will also help decrease your debt. If you think about it like that, then it has a dual purpose, right?"

"But . . . but it's *your* book. Can't I just . . . ?"

I try to hold it out to him, but he just pushes it back to me. "Keep it. You might very well need magic in some of the upcoming floors, and even if you don't, it can't help to have a few more skills." I want to refuse it again, but then his eyes turn hard. "You aren't trying to deny it just because you don't like my gift, are you?"

"N—no! Of course not! I love it. It's the best gift I've ever gotten!" I blurt out.

He smiles down at me and pats me on the shoulder. "Glad to hear it! Since you love it so much, there shouldn't be any trouble keeping it, right?"

Damn it, he got me! He's too clever for me . . . !

I look back at the tome in my hands. It's thick. Bound in leather. It's even got one of those fabric bookmarks built into the spine of it. Unable to resist, I crack it open. That wonderful old-book smell hits me head-on and drags me so far back into my childhood—into sitting alone in the library at every recess, reading any and every old book I can get my hands on—that I don't even bother to check the contents. I know it will be educational. I can trust that Moleman wouldn't give me something useless. Before I know it, I've already put the book into my inventory. It's the only nonhide thing in there.

I've got one attempt to read it. Thirty days should be enough, right? Yeah. It better be, or I'll probably throw a tantrum or something.

"You can read it now," Moleman says, startling me out of my reverie. "I've got some reading to do on my own, so I don't mind if you want to check it out now."

I squint at him. Before I can agree or disagree, he's already pulled out a book of his own and taken his seat on the opposite side of the table again. He's basically giving me no choice, but . . . this book *does* look mighty readable. Not saying anything, I pull the book back out again. It's thick. It's heavy. It smells good. It's exactly how books should be.

I open it to the first page and start reading.

It is next to incomprehensible. Actually, scratch that, it *is* incomprehensible. Digit nexus? Arcarteries? Blood vessel awakening? Heart of sage? What does that even mean?

But since reading it is supposed to give me a skill, I keep going.

I'm not sure exactly how much time passes by, but even when the sun goes down and I'm a hundred pages in, I still haven't got a clue what any of this is. It's like I'm a kindergartner just about to learn the alphabet and someone dropped a thousand-page literary analysis of the origins of written language in my lap. And—and this is supposed to be *basic*?

I glance up at Moleman. He's reading a book titled *An Advanced Guide to the Practical Utilization of the Juurit-Porrs Theorem*. And he doesn't even seem slightly perturbed by it. Unwilling to give up, I continue reading, but after a few more minutes, Moleman puts down his hefty tome and looks me in the eye. "So," he says. "How about we get you smashed?"

"H—huh?" I say. "As in . . . bodily crushed?"

"No," he says. "I mean, it's about time you learned how to *party*."

I feel my heart flutter. "Is—is it time?"

He nods at me. "It is time."

I fly to my feet and he's already got two bottles in hand. "Hardest liquor you can buy in the shop," Moleman says. "Ninety-two percent alcohol content. There is one at ninety-eight, but it's way too expensive. This one, though?" He grins. "Just right."

He uncorks them. I have my first taste of the nectar of gods, and after that, I don't remember much.

At some point I think my poison protection rose, but that was probably just a mistake or something. Apparently, we two weren't the only ones partying. As the night grew darker over the castle, more and more challengers decided that what was needed right now was a good old party to liven our collective spirits. We didn't have any strobing lights, or thumping base, or smoke machines, but we *did* have magic, and a lot of people playing modern pop songs on medieval instruments. Moleman was one of them.

People were dancing and throwing their arms around each other and jumping around and mages were shooting bolts of flashy magic into the air and the alcohol flowed like water. Once people got a little more inebriated, they became a lot more generous with their points and their possessions, with people buying fine liquor left and right. Some people got so drunk they dropped, but there was always a mage nearby to give them a detoxification spell so they could drink more.

At one point, I think, I'm pretty sure I tried to impress someone by disemboweling myself, but they didn't react too positively to my trick. I'm not sure if the alcohol or my display made them puke their guts out. Could be either one.

And then, when the party was at its hardest and the trombones and the trumpets and the lutes and the drums were playing their hardest, everything ended.

<The Server Symposium will end in 00:00>
<The Server Symposium has ended.>
<Thank you for participating! You will now be returned to your lobbies.>

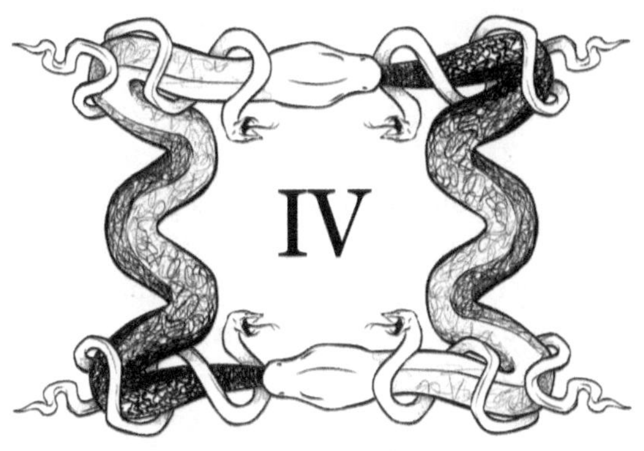

Me-atball

Ughh, my head . . .

Actually, that was a lie, my head feels pretty alright. My tolerances must be undoing the effects of the hangover I would otherwise be having. Neat!

And since I didn't have any money to use myself, I didn't spend a single point during the entire symposium. Ah, the perks of being poor.

I glance around at the RED lobby all around. Turning my attention to my inventory, I remove the tome that Moleman got me. I'd better keep reading. If I haven't finished this by the next attempt, I'm done for.

<Top—Status—Community>
<05:50:21 Day 181>
<The eighth attempt will begin in 29:18:09:39>
<The ninth floor will open in 18:09:39>

Right. Plenty of time.

Holding the tome gently, I hunker down with my back against one of the pillars. With the book in my lap, I try my best to make sense of the whole thing. I don't know what language this thing was originally written in, but it might as well still be written in it because I have no idea what it means. Sure, I didn't exactly finish high school or anything, but I should still be able to understand at least a chapter or two, right? This is just unnecessarily complicated.

Like—like chapter three, which is described as a *simple guide to sensing internal divinity*. Easy, right? It's described as simple, and it does seem to be step-by-step, but that's all it is. I follow the steps, and nothing happens. All it does is activate my meditation skills as I try to sense some sort of feeling deep inside. Maybe if the book actually described what the divinity is supposed to feel like,

I might have been able to properly tell if I had any at all. But as is, it's no better than a shot in the dark.

For hours on end, I try fruitlessly to sense the supposed magic inside me. This closed-eyes period is punctuated only by brief periods of frustration where I take out my irritation by either reading and rereading the same passages over and over again, or by just pacing around and breaking my own bones.

And after some time . . .

<Floor 9 has opened. Do you want to enter?>
<Yes/No>

But I haven't even finished reading chapter four! I'm barely halfway through, and I can't even fathom how I'm supposed to feel anything, so—

<If no answer is chosen, [No] will be chosen for you and the floor may be accessed on the next attempt.>

No, I can't . . . I can't stay here for a month. I can't. I absolutely can't stay here.

I clutch the tome tighter to me. Unwillingly, I stand up and put it into my inventory. Then I press *Yes*.

As the world whirls beneath my feet, I instinctually drop into a crouch, but unlike the last few floors, I'm not in any dark place, nor am I in nature or mud. This place is . . . ?

From what I can see, I'm standing inside a large, circular room. The farther-most walls are all covered with flowing satin and admittedly beautiful tapestries depicting what appear to mainly be snakes. The floor is completely covered by a number of different carpets and rugs, all of different weave and kind. Some are Persian, others simpler, but all have a feel of absolute luxury to them. The room itself is lit in part by candles placed along the walls in candlesticks and holders of crystal and silver and ivory. But the true centerpiece of the room, and what lights most of it, is a massive chandelier hanging from the domed ceiling. I can't tell entirely what materials it's made of, but it seems to be silver and pearlescent, with thousands of hanging pieces of finely polished crystals that diffuse the light of the candles inside in such a way where the whole room is illuminated.

I have never seen a more luxurious room.

The only problem is that almost everything is WHITE.

The soft carpets below my feet: WHITE.

The ceiling itself: WHITE.

The tapestries on the walls: WHITE.

The walls not covered: WHITE.

Everything, everything, everything: WHITE.

I can feel my left eye begin to twitch.

WHITE. WHITE. WHITE. WHITE. WHITE. WHITE. WHITE. WHITE.

Bad. Bad. Need to . . . need to remove the WHITE, have to . . .

<Tutorial stage, Hell Difficulty Ninth Floor: The Flaming Tower.>
<[Clear Condition] Endure until help arrives in [23:23:58:22].>

Help? For whom: *me?* N—now you're just being ridiculous! If anything, it's this room that needs help from *me!*

This room full of tapestries and carpets and rugs and paintings, all depicting . . .

Snakes?

As I stare at a certain piece of tapestry depicting a relatively large, thick snake, it seems to me that the WHITE creature is actually staring back at me, through its WHITE slitted eyes. Its WHITE forked tongue quickly slips out between its scaly WHITE lips, and I pause. Hang on. Paintings don't have tongues. The WHITE serpent blinks at me.

And snakes don't have eyelids! What is this?

With its bamboozling revealed, the snake hides no longer. Slipping out of the frames of the fabric, it drops down onto the WHITE floor, now thick and scaly. Like a proper snake. It slithers toward me on its belly.

Is this it? No, seriously, is *this* it?

I resist the urge to point and laugh at the pathetic little creature. Really, just a single snake? Hah, stuff that *help* down your throat, system! *I* can handle this just fine on my own. Casually, I stroll up to the snake. It raises its head from the ground, revealing that it isn't simply a mere snake but a cobra. The flaps on either side of its body beat threateningly.

"Hey, little buddy!" I say, hunching down toward it. "Aren't you a cute one, huh? Wouldn't you like to—"

"*Hiss!*"

And that's about all I have time to say before it sprays a concentrated stream of acid at my face, right into my eyes.

Argh! Heck, damn it, what the heck—!?

<You have learned: Acid Resistance Lv.2>
<You have learned: Corrosion Tolerance Lv.6>

Shoot, yeah, um, I can *feel* that; you didn't need to tell me. My vision has now successfully melted into BLACK darkness, which is typically preferable to WHITE, but right now, it means I can't really see that damn snake anymore. I *can*, however, feel it. As I lie squirming on the floor, trying my best to wipe the acid from my face while also using moving meditation, I can feel clearly how it crawls its way up my leg, coiling around it as it does. And then I can also feel it do the same thing to my arm. And then a thick, slick belly slips over my chest and I'm starting to think that maybe it isn't just *one* snake.

<You have learned: Corrosion Tolerance Lv.7>
<You have learned: Moving Meditation Lv.4>

My right eye finally heals enough for me to open it and I stare right into the dead, emotionless glare of a serpent as big as a horse.

<Snake (Lv.40)>

Uh, um. Moving my arms doesn't really do anything, but by using my intuitive problem-solving abilities, I'm able to figure out the reason behind this. I look down. The massive snake, five times my length and twice as thick at least, is wrapped around me twice over. Hmm. That's a bit worryi—

I don't even have time to finish my thought before the massive snakes gives an equally massive *squee—ze* that pushes the air out of my lungs. My ribs and pelvis both go *crack-crack* and my brain fizzles with BLACK and WHITE static. Then that massive WHITE maw opens before me to reveal an endless expanse of RED and everything turns BLACK.

My body fizzles and fuzzles and bubbles and churns. There's no air in my lungs anymore. There isn't any air at all. Wherever I look, a status message pops up.

<Snake (Lv.40)>

I can barely move at all. The heat is horrible and enough to melt me. Oh, wait, I really *am* melting! Haha, isn't that just silly?

I think this might be it. My brain isn't working too good anymore. It's like my skull's full of stuffy WHITE cotton and nothing else.

<You have learned: Acid Resistance Lv.3>
<You have learned: Acid Resistance Lv.4>
<You have learned: Acid Resistance Lv.5>

I don't want to die. I only just made another friend and I didn't ask him when his birthday was so when it's his turn I won't even be able to wish him happy birthday and sure it's not like I can actually buy him anything nice like a lovely cake or anything but I still want to give him something even if it's only words because even if it's only words they hold so much power and they can make you so happy despite what everyone says because sure they won't break your bones and dissolve you into goop but they can make you want such a fate they can make you want to die and it just isn't fair to assume that everyone has the mental strength to shrug off that sort of stuff because most people probably don't or else there wouldn't be policies regarding saying hurtful things so really the saying is superfluous at best and downright cruel at worst but I don't really want to die at all I don't want to die because I would miss him and I would miss Simel and I don't even know if goblins have birthdays so I need to ask him I need to live I need to survive I need to get out of here no matter what because if I don't then I'll be dead and I can't meet them again.

But the darkness is soothing and tempting and alluring and I have never felt sleepier. I just want to take a nap. I think, just maybe, that would be nice. A little snooze, and then I'll be off. But first, I should tell him.

My eyes are gone and my face has melted off but I can still see the screen in my head. I type up a message to Moleman.

<PrissyKittyPrincess[F9]: hy hee when ur brthdy srry i thnk im die now sry ssry i didn meen 2 im ssry plz l ssry i wuz mean 2 u srry sry plz>

Send. Now he'll know.

Now at least he knows. Which means that now, I can finally go to sleep . . .

<You have received a message.>
<SuperMoleman[F48]: Kitty, are you alright?! The ninth floor has snakes, right? Just try not to get too scared and face them with courage! It's okay. I've already forgiven you for being mean to me, so please try to survive. Don't die. You still have so much more you can do. And don't give up. We'll meet again soon, okay? Maybe we'll even meet in Purgatory one day! Please. Don't die.>

I stare at the message in front of me.

Don't die.

Survive.

Don't give up.

I clench my fingers. Most of my skin has melted off. That's alright. My claws are deeper than that. And I still have most of my sharp teeth. And that's all I need, because right in front of me, I have a perfectly eligible target.

I sink my sharp claws into the darkness in front of me and the harsh burning crushing around me gets even tighter, grinding some of my bones to dust, shifting my cranial plates, but it isn't enough. I bite. I tear. I chew. I gnaw. I claw. I rip. As the acidic sludge clinging to me is drenched with hot metallic blood, the acidic effects of it slowly weaken.

<You have learned: Acid Resistance Lv.6>
<You have learned: Corrosion Tolerance Lv.8>
<You have learned: Corrosion Tolerance Lv.9>
<You have learned: Dagger Tooth Lv.4>
<You have learned: Dagger Nails Lv.2>

Soon the flesh gives way to something far tougher, and I claw enough to see that this is the snake's scaly hide, letting in the tawniest amount of diffused light. I don't like harming the hide, but I have no choice, and with a thrust of my clawed hand, I finally break through. Dragging myself out of the snake, I suddenly feel that massive scaly body wrap itself around me once more. I hear its hissing breath approach to repeat its folly but I'm wise to its tricks now, and instead of letting myself get eaten, I stab my hands at where I can smell its open mouth to be, grabbing hold of it and pulling and clawing at it until I'm able to pull off its jaw. Warm blood spurts across my half-molten body and the body wrapped around me squeezes in an instinctual death grip, but I'm far from done.

<You have learned: Fracture Protection Lv.3>

As the snake tries to pull away its head, I instead grapple on harder, scratching and clawing until I'm able to get far inside enough to crush its neck in my grip.

<You have learned: Clutch Lv.10>
<You have learned: Crush Lv.1>
<Snake (Lv.40) Defeated.>
<[Level Up]>
<You have reached Level 42.>
<Agility has increased by 2.
Strength has increased by 3.
Stamina has increased by 3.
Magic Power has increased by 1.
Dagger Tooth has increased by 1.
Swim has increased by 1.
Crush has increased by 1.
Acid Resistance has increased by 1.

Corrosion Tolerance has increased by 1.
Corrosion Resistance has increased by 1.>

Haah, haah, haah . . . N—not bad for my first kill of the floor!

Right, I just, I can't really, um . . .

I cough and hack up something I can't really tell what it is. I still can't see anything, and my tongue is kind of half-dissolved, and I'm not entirely sure what happened to my bowels, but I'll be alright with just a bit of rest. That's right, I just need to meditate a little, and . . .

I feel something bite into my leg. It's not like I can tell by the pain, or even really by the way it feels. It's just that there's a sudden pressure and now something slick and cold is going into my leg. Hm. That might not be very good.

The floor gives way beneath me, and I can't feel my leg at all anymore and I drop to the ground with a wet squelch. Something wraps around my throat but I'm able to grab hold of it and pull it off before it does anything. I can't do anything else, so I grab what I think might be its head and push it into my mouth, crushing it between my jaws. It tastes bitter. I can feel my mouth start to go numb, which can only mean one thing.

<You have learned: Paralysis Resistance Lv.3>

Ah, there it is. Of course. Why am I not surprised?

But that's not the only serpent I can feel. All I have for skin now is jellified flesh and tendons, but I can still feel them coating me like a heavy, scaly blanket. Just how many are there? I try to pull myself up, but I'm completely covered, and I have unfortunately never been too good at push-ups. A couple of snakes is enough to completely immobilize me, huh? Well, how about . . . *this?*

I spin myself into a roll, the snake weight on top of me scattering off, and once I'm no longer restrained by their girth, I pull my knees to my chest. This should buy me at least a minute or two to regenerate properly. The floor sure is cold and hard for being carpet, though . . . Weird.

I close my eyes and meditate.

<A Canto appears to you.>

Hm? Oh, this again. Sure, hand it over.

<[He thrust away the thick air from his face, waving his left hand frequently before him; that seemed the only task that wearied him. I knew well he was Heaven's messenger, and I turned toward my master; and he made a sign that I be still and bow before him.]>

A thick one this time around, huh? It still doesn't make much of a difference, and being able to understand it also doesn't really change much. It doesn't change the fact that I just have to kill all of these snakes and I'll win, probably.

I just have to keep going.

After a few minutes, my eyes recover enough for me to be able to see again, but I keep them closed in order to continue meditating. Since I've got a feeling that my situation is somewhat precarious, I use moving meditation as well to speed things up a bit.

Nevertheless, after some time, I decide to peek anyway, just for a second, if only to orient myself.

I'm lying next to the rounded wall, below a tapestry of a goat fighting a snake. In the middle of the room, I can see the motionless horse-sized snake I killed, with its bowels torn open. Thanks to this, I can see with some relief that at least the inside of the snake is RED. The wonderful scarlet has dyed a fair bit of the carpet underneath the dead snake, which gives me a bright idea.

See, since I'm in the middle of a snake attack, I can't exactly waste blood and time by painting the whole room myself.

So why not use the snakes?

Wonderful! Inspired! Marvelous! Bravissimo!

Of course, before I put this ingenious plan into action, I need to recover a little. And that's where it gets a bit tricky. I'm not necessarily talking about the fact that I can now see with my very own eyes that my entire body has basically been jellified, with not a single part being any other color than a messy slobbery RED and the muddy WHITE of my bones and tendons. Hm. If I hold my legs tightly together while I recover, will they fuse into a single mermaid limb, or will they just regenerate normally? Very mysterious.

But my jellification isn't the problem here. The problem, as I've now noticed, is that I'm actually not lying on the floor at all.

I'm lying on a vast collection of entwined WHITE snakes, all bundled together into a cold, sleek carpet that almost looks woven. This is suboptimal for my desire to beat the floor and not die.

My only solace is that, at the very least, they haven't noticed me *yet*. A few of those lying directly beneath me seem less than comfortable, but the rest are fine. For now.

I just need to keep this position and hope that, somehow, my body doesn't heal itself into a single fused ball of skin and muscle and flesh. That would be almost as bad as getting walrusified. Ugh, the thought makes me shiver.

I close my eyes again, hoping that things won't go horribly wrong. Every now and then I try to shift my legs to make sure they don't merge, but if I shift them too much, I'll alert the snakes, so there's only so much I can do.

And after about an hour . . .

Uh, um, yeah. My body has kind of merged into one big meatball. I can't undo the fetal position blowover even if I try. I'm just . . . a meatball. Haha, does anyone have any spaghetti lying around? It's like I'm the meatball, and this whole room is a plate, and these snakes are the spaghetti, and my blood is the sauce! Haha!

I'm trying to distract myself from the existential horror of my transformation by making jokes, but if anything, it's having the opposite effect. I can't even really sob. My shoulders heaving just pulls on the skin connecting my knees to my chest. I wish I could somehow cut or bite this to make everything separate again but I can't reach. I just can't reach.

Before this moment, I never had nightmares that focused on the prospect of turning into a meatball. Now, though, if I ever have the misfortune of falling asleep again, I know what I'll see.

From the corner of my eye, I see a massive snake, a little larger than a horse, slithering out of a woven carpet on the floor. After flicking its tongue out for a few seconds, it approaches the horse-sized snake I killed earlier, and without any apparent hesitation, it just eats it, whole and unpeeled. H—hey, I was going to skin that! That's very rude. Ah, but, then again, I'm not sure if I'll ever be able to skin anything ever again.

Now I'm just making myself sad.

But the sight of the snake is giving me an idea. A horribly murky and crushing and burning and melting idea that I hate to even consider, but as it is, I genuinely can't think of any other option. Actually, there is one, but that would involve me numbly waiting for the next attempt, and then the next one, and then the next one, in perpetuity until the next Server Symposium at which I'll ask someone to cut me free. But that would also involve me fully dropping every single one of the three marbles I still have left, and I just . . . I can't. I just can't.

Between complete insanity and possible death, I know which one I'd choose.

Numbly, I roll toward the horse-sized snake.

Hello, mister snake. I have a weird request. Will you please eat me and then almost digest me but only almost? And *no* dying, please. Thank you.

Oh yeah, it can't see me. Or smell me. Or hear me. Or taste me. Ah, I want to cry again. I hate this.

Once the snake settles down, I roll, dejected, toward its head. I force myself into its mouth but then it starts gagging and hacking and before I know it, I'm lodged in its throat in such a way that, apparently, I'm choking it? It's trying to get me out of its throat but I'm just a bit too big so after squirming and writhing for a few seconds it finally gets me down. I feel horrible. My ribs are broken again. Maybe I should just stay down here and die? That would be preferable to being a meatball.

My skin is starting to melt again. My flesh soon follows. I'm trying to make my limbs move but my brain is starting to feel awfully sluggish and for some reason I really just want to go to sleep. Would that really be so bad? Sleeping is nice. You don't need to think about anything. It's just you and the darkness.

<You have learned: Oxygen Deficiency Resistance Lv.9>
<You have learned: Oxygen Deficiency Resistance Lv.10>
<You have learned: Oxygen Deficiency Protection Lv.1>

Except, on the other hand, what if I go to sleep and I dream of becoming a meatball?

My mind jolts awake. I absolutely can't have that. No way.

My whole body tenses, and my arms rip themselves from their place around my knees, and my legs finally straighten back out. With the frantic energy of a dying squirrel, I claw at the flesh in front of me, out, out, out, until I finally burst from within it like a certain sci-fi horror movie creature.

The snake tries to get at me, but I like to think that since this is my second rodeo, I know the game by now. Instead of letting it slither around me, I head back to the hole I already made, rip it open even more, and then just to finish it off, I rip it open all the way up to its throat. But by the point I get to its jaw, it has already bled out. Bummer.

<Snake (Lv.39) Defeated.>

Alright, but now I know not to just relax. I need to keep moving.

I take a deep breath. Almost the entire floor is covered in snakes, and although most of them are pretty small, I can't tell at a glance what effects they will actually have. A majority of them are probably just poisonous. But if I get bitten by one with a more exotic status effect that my tolerances can't handle, I'm done for.

But first things first, I'd like to wear something. My leopard hide got digested in the first snake, and since this might unfortunately not be my last time doing this, I don't want to waste yet another one. I'll need something new. Luckily, I think I've got the perfect candidate right in front of me.

Hunkering down, I get to work. Even though this is my first time skinning a snake, it still feels very natural, even if I am doing it blind. Not my first time skinning something I can't see, I guess.

The only trouble is that while I work, snakes will periodically show up to attack me, but I can fend off most of them by grabbing them and biting their heads off. Through this, I'm able to learn quite a few new tolerances, alongside leveling up a bunch of older ones. As time goes by, the snakes only get more and more numerous, but by the time I've finished skinning the snake, my vision has returned, making all of this a whole lot easier. The only problem with the hide now in my hands is that it is horribly, terribly WHITE. Bad.

But by sliding it around on the blood-soaked floor for a bit, I'm able to get it a nice, crisp RED. Neato. And then I just need to wrap it closely around my body. This way, I hope that should I get swallowed again, I'll be more . . . naturally protected.

Anyhow, my flesh and skin are starting to slowly regenerate. Oh, except my right leg, which is unfortunately rotted and necrotic. Whoops, I wonder how that could have happened?

I put my hands on my hips and look at a snake lying a pace or so away. Fi—do!

Canned laughter plays and there's a *whoomp-whoomp* trombone effect. You silly snake!

Grabbing it by the tip of its tail, I slam it back onto the floor a few times until it hasn't got a head anymore, and then I slurp down the whole thing like a thick noodle. Hmm. Not bad.

<You have learned: Necrosis Protection Lv.2>
<You have learned: Indigestion Resistance Lv.6>

Neato!

Most of my body still seems to be covered with a thick layer of pink jelly, and it aches to stand, but I should be fine. It'll take me a while to recover, but once I do, these snakes won't even stand a chance. Until then, though, I'll need to fight back.

A snake coils around my necrotic leg, but I rip it off first. It attempts to spray acid in my face, but I simply open my mouth and swallow it all instead, melting my already burnt throat into something that feels a lot like goo. I swallow the goo. The snake seems genuinely stunned by my actions, which is not an expression I thought snakes were capable of. While it's still confused, I shove its head into my mouth hole and chew its skull off.

One down, several thousand to go.

Well, nothing to do but get to it, right?

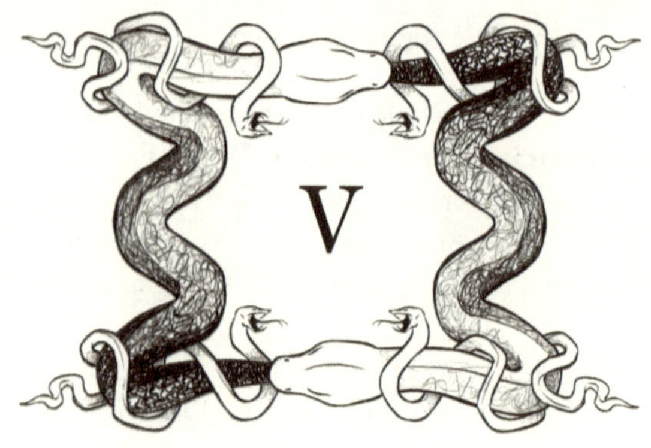

Yummy Gorgons

I start killin'. After an hour or so, my flesh has recovered enough to where I can go into fetal position blowover if I want to, but I choose not to. This way, the snakes will go for me. Some of them have really annoying effects, and it's starting to remind me of floor two and the ladies all over again, but none of the snakes cause vivid hallucinations strong enough to penetrate my hallucination protection, so I should be fine.

<Top—Status—Community>
<05:00:02 Day 182>
<The eighth attempt will begin in 28:18:59:58>
<[Help will arrive in 23:18:59:58]>

At least that's what I assumed just moments ago. That's changed a little now that I'm looking at a certain, uh, *lady* stepping out of a tapestry. Her skin is snow WHITE, and she isn't dressed in anything, but as she steps out of the tapestry, she's thankfully wrapping it around herself. Once she's emerged enough for me to get a grip on what in the world she's supposed to be, I find that she actually has long pointed ears like a goblin, and a bald head, too. But the most interesting part is undoubtedly the snakes she's got wrapped around her throat. Or maybe they're growing out of her neck? I genuinely have no clue here.

She meets my gaze and I feel a shiver creep down the hunch of my back.

"Foolish mortal, you dare invade this sacred sanctum of—" Her eyes fall on the hundreds of dead snakes littering the ground, and then the dog-sized serpent in my hand that I was using as a paintbrush on the wall until around four seconds ago. "Wh—wh—what—" Her eyes dart up to the ceiling, where I've thrown headless snake corpses onto the chandelier in an attempt to paint the ceiling, and at the splattered walls, and every other nice RED place. "What in the Gods have you . . ."

Only now do I notice the status message I get for her. And, more importantly, her *level.*

<Gorgon Megaera (Lv.15)>

Fifteen? That—that *has* to be a mistake, right? There's just no way that what is *clearly* a midboss would be *this* weak, right?

"N—nonetheless!" she says loudly, almost hysterically, pointing her finger at me. I hunch down, expecting a spell to come, but nothing happens, so it must just have been an ordinary accusation. Weird. "For the crime of intruding, I shall smite thee with my gaze of petrification!"

Oh, right, the snakes. Gorgon . . . that's, like, a Medusa, right?

Her eyes stare intently at me. She looks *really mad.* To avoid losing this battle of attrition, I make an equally mad face right back at her. It makes her flinch. Acting on the small opening, I fly at her, and she doesn't even have time to react before my claws slice through her throat and neck like a hot knife through butter, and without giving any other sort of fight, she just drops to the ground, completely anticlimactically.

Huh? Wait, was that it? That was *clearly* supposed to be some sort of midboss, so how come she just . . . died? Wasn't she supposed to block me, or petrify me limb by limb, or something else? This just felt wrong.

As I stare at her corpse, her death is quantified by the standard pop-up message.

<Gorgon Megaera (Lv.15) Defeated.>

I didn't even level up. Was that really it?

Well, uh, it's not like I have anything else to do, so I guess there's nothing better for me to do than to properly disassemble the body. I'm actually really curious about the snakes . . .

<You have learned: Disassemble Lv.7>

Just to ensure that there's nothing weird about these here snakes, I do a little taste test and compare their flavor to that of the regular snakes.

Hmmm. Chomp chomp nom nom.

<You have learned: Paralysis Resistance Lv.4>
<You have learned: Petrification Tolerance Lv.1>

In conclusion, the flavor and texture is almost exactly the same, but the ones from the gorgon have the added effect of making my joints feel crusty. So this is what arthritis feels like, huh? Very interesting. I have henceforth decided that I want to die young.

The remainder of the gorgon meat tastes very supple and gentle, with a delicate aftertaste. I was thinking of using the meat as snake bait, but it is way too delicious for that. High fat content, relaxed musculature . . . Oh, it's good alright.

<You have learned: Petrification Tolerance Lv.4>
<You have learned: Petrification Tolerance Lv.5>

And it grants me tolerance levels! How much better can it get?

As I sit chewing and chomping down on the meat, I feel a snake bite into my back. Almost casually, I reach back and bite its head off before slurping it down whole.

<Snake (Lv.17) Defeated.>

See? Even a regular snake has a higher level than she did! This is way too weird.

It takes me a few hours to finish eating it, which I only did because it really was *that* yummy, and once I'm done, I use the skeleton left behind as snake bait. The plan is simple. Since the snakes have terrible vision, they rely mainly on my scent and heat. So if I just pour a bunch of my blood onto this skeleton and then go into fetal position blowover, the snakes will all go into the skeleton. And then I can just pick them off one by one, eating them as I do. Very effective! I feel so full. This might be too much food.

Ah, I want to read my book. I *need* to read it, but if I bring it out now, it might get splashed by the snakes' acid and melt. Sure, it's going to get sold in about a month anyway, but at least that's part of Moleman's calculations. Me being a ditz and getting it destroyed certainly isn't.

All in all, though, the floor is simple.

Small and medium-sized snakes spawn every minute and every second. I cannot physically kill more than the amount that constantly pops in, but there is a cap to it, so it's not like the room is actually capable of being completely flooded with live snakes. Large snakes, like the ones that have jellified me, spawn once every hour. And, as I discovered with the third one, no, they do not necessarily need to be defeated from the inside. Sure, their flesh is weaker than their scales, but my claws and teeth are actually really strong. If I attack in a surprising manner and aim for one of its softer parts, there isn't any problem.

The main issue is that it's very easy for me to get crowded by the snakes. If I get hit by one particularly strong paralyzing bite, or necrotic bite, or acidic bite, or bacteria-infected bite, then the weakness that single bite grants me is enough to ensure that a second bite—usually of a different status condition than the first—will follow.

This can very easily lead into a downward spiral where every step I take earns me another bite and splash and I just get worse and worse and worse and worse until I want nothing better than to lie down and let it all end. But I don't because that would be weak, and I'm a gamer, which means I can't be weak. And so, with all of this, a full day somehow passes. I can't relax for a second or else I'll get bitten. I can't allow myself to die.

<Top—Status—Community>
<07:00:07 Day 183>
<The eighth attempt will begin in 27:16:59:53>
<[Help will arrive in 22:16:59:53]>

And on the seventh hour of the second day, another gorgon appears. Unlike the first one, this one appears by pulling herself out of a painting. Her neck snakes are wrapped up and around her head, covering most of her face apart from her right eye, which is very clearly crying.

<Gorgon Alecto (Lv.21)>

Another super low-leveled one, huh? I'm starting to think that these mid-bosses aren't actually scaled to the challenger but rather to the difficulty, or something like that. No idea. I glance at my stats just to be sure.

<Top—Status—Community>
<PrissyKittyPrincess
Human Level 42
Agility: 128
Strength: 80
Stamina: 150
Magic Power: 54>

Yeah, something's up.

She was already crying when she exited the painting, but as her one visible eye slowly moves across the room, it somehow, against all laws of anatomy, starts crying even harder.

"Y—you, um," she says through heaving sobs, "this—*hic*—um, you will, uh . . ." She brings up her hand and points at me, but, again, there's no magic behind it, so I don't get the point of it. "Y—you will face m—my wrath!"

Ah, yes, such a classic line. However, there's a very simple way to counter this.

The second she starts glaring at me like a wronged toddler, I leap across the floor and grab her neck with both hands, snaking my hands beneath her serpent hood, and then I just break it. It didn't even take all that much effort. It was just slim, and frail, and with only the slightest effort, it went *cra—ack!*

<Gorgon Alecto (Lv.21) Defeated.>

Another midboss, down for the count. What's even the point of these if I can beat them *this* easily? I feel kind of confused. Anyway, more delicious meat! I am so happy.

I hunker down beside the body and start removing the skin, but a snake approaches and tries to bite her foot. Hey, get out of here! She's mine! Grabbing it, I swallow it whole and without even killing it first. Ah, revenge. It tastes slippery and an awful lot like my stomach is being bitten from the inside.

Anyway, bottoms up!

I bite into the yummy yummy yummy yummy gorgon flesh and when that runs out I continue with the snakes. I really do think they're endless. This means that my best course of action right now is, simply put, to kill as many snakes as I possibly can. I mean, it's unlimited free exp! And, to boot, if I just also eat the dead snakes left over, I can also upgrade a lot of my tolerances and resistances. Neat!

The only downside is that I can't read while doing this. Even when I kill snakes at my maximum output, which usually nets me a lot of bites and a lost limb or two, I still can't kill more than the amount that spawns in every minute. Maybe if I could learn some AOE spell or skill I might have been able to instantly kill a bunch of snakes and do it that way, but there's nothing like that. I only have two arms and one mouth, and that just isn't enough.

But it will have to be enough, because until *help* arrives, there is nothing else I can do.

<Top—Status—Community>
<08:30:02 Day 203>
<The eighth attempt will begin in 6:15:29:58>
<[Help will arrive in 1:15:29:58]>

Two days left.

Dully, I turn my face to a weird bulge trying to press up against a literal mountain of snake corpses. It's been doing that for a while now, and I think it's the third gorgon. See, if you have more than one midboss but less than five, then you've got to have three. Since nothing else has appeared in these past ten days or so, I've been anticipating the third gorgon this whole time. I bet her flesh will be even more tender than the first two. Hehe.

That said, although the number of snakes that spawn in have a cap, this cap isn't affected by the number of snake corpses there are in the room. And since snake corpses don't despawn—much like real life—all the snakes I've been killing have started piling up. Like, literally. I couldn't bother to eat them all, so now the room has filled up with snake corpses to the point where I'm sitting at the same level as the chandelier. Snakes are still spawning in, but as soon as they do they get crushed to death by the weight of tens of thousands of dead snakes. It's a pretty weird situation, but until about half an hour ago, it gave me time to read.

Unfortunately, though, even though I've now made it through half the book, I still don't get it. Bummer. Maybe I'm just an idiot? Who knows?

Oh, a hand just popped out of the snake sea! Come on, miss gorgon, I know you can do it!

<Gorgon Tisiphone (Lv.40)>

"Paaah!" she gasps as she finally pulls herself out of the pile. The stuff below her midsection is still submerged in the serpentine ocean, but this is all I really need. Her face whips around. Oh, yeah, welcome to my crib. It's kind of small, but I recently had it redecorated, so now it's totally RED and cool. I don't really have much of anything up here, but I *do* have this cool snake, and this other cool snake, and another cool snake, and . . . "Did—did *you* do this?"

I perk my eyebrow at her.

"S—sorry, dumb question, uh . . ." She pulls her lips tight. It takes her a moment or so to pull herself together, but once she does, she's able to do that classical point-at-me-with-her-hand thing that these gorgons seem to love so much. And with as much grandeur as she can muster with only her upper body visible, she exclaims, "Challenger! For this crime against the God of Harvest, I will punish you with the most painful torment of petrification! *Prepare yourself!*"

I stare at her. She stares at me. I don't even feel slightly tingly, so . . .

She wiggles her finger a little. "Um, you aren't going to, like . . . take out a shield or something?" I shake my head at her. "No? I mean, it's fine if you want to use weapons, it just feels a little unfair if you're bare-handed and I'm . . ." Also bare-handed? She shakes her head, making the little snakes around her neck wobble. "No, forget it. I, uh . . . Where was I?" Petrifying me? "Oh, yeah. *Take this!*"

She drills her eyes into me and I leap to my feet, ready for anything.

We stare at each other for a solid ten seconds.

<You have learned: Petrification Resistance Lv.10>
<You have learned: Petrification Protection Lv.1>

Oh, nice! About time, if you ask me.

Her brows pinch together. "Huh? That's weird. You should at least feel a *little* creaky, um . . ." She smacks herself on the head like you do with an old piece of faulty machinery. "No, that wasn't quite right . . ."

I grin. Slowly, I walk around her until I'm standing just behind her. She's got a high level, so this probably won't kill her. Hehe. While she's still distracted trying to make her petrification gaze work, I claw up a gouge along her lower back and give her an instant slip of the disc.

"Eek—!" She squeals in pain. "Wh—what did you do to me? Why can't I feel my legs?"

I circle around until I'm in front of her again, and then I sit down. She looks up at me, eyes trembling. I pull out the magic tome Moleman gave me and hold it up to her. "Do you know how to read?"

She blinks. "Uh, um . . ." Her eyes travel over the line on the front. "Yes, uh, how so?"

Great. Step one complete, haha!

I open the book to chapter three. "In that case," I say, holding up the book to her, "you're going to help me study."

"Study wh—*what?*"

"How to make the magic happen. It's very simple. There's a step-by-step guide. See?" I point at the first page of chapter three. "Read this, and then try it out, and then you tell me how it went and what it felt like."

"You want me to learn magic?" she asks timidly. I nod at her. "But magic is . . . It's a God-given divine right. I'm just a gorgon—I can't . . ."

"You have a petrification skill, right?" She doesn't respond, but I can tell that I'm right on the mark. "Skills are given by the gods. If you can use a skill, you can probably also use magic."

"E—even then . . ."

I look at her. So it's like that, huh? Heaving a sigh, I make an exaggerated show of putting away the book. "We—ll, if you don't want to learn magic, I guess there's nothing I can do other than kill you and skin you and eat your flesh and use your minced brains to lure snakes. That sounds good to you too, right?"

Even though her skin is already WHITE, she still finds a way to blanch. "Um, uh . . . I—I want to learn magic. Yeah. P—please let me learn magic."

I grin. "Glad to hear it."

Timidly, she holds out her hands. "So, uh, the book . . . ?"

I slap her hands away. "You think I'm giving *you*—a filthy snake-goblin—my precious book?" Her eyes tattle on the obviously incorrect answer she's internally mustered to my rhetorical question. "The answer is: *obviously not*. So just settle in and I'll read it aloud, and you follow every single step and word I say, okay? We've only got like two days to do this, so try to follow along as best as you can."

"Uh, okay," she mumbles back.

Since she doesn't seem entirely focused, I decide to reiterate my point by piercing her with my eyes and saying, as clearly as I can, "If you even *consider* doing anything silly like trying to fight or whatever, I'll kill you. Got it?" She doesn't answer, so I helpfully repeat myself. "*Got. It?*"

"G—got it," she says, her voice trembling.

I smile. "Great! In that case, let's get into it, shall we?"

I start reading aloud. Since I've read the chapter several times over by this point, I know that it will take well over an hour to get through the entire thing. Probably even more than two hours since I'm reading it aloud, too. Regardless, she seems to be paying attention, and that's all I'm really asking for. A few paragraphs in, she closes her eyes, and a look of deep concentration befalls her face. Okay, good.

I continue speaking. After a while, a change seems to come over her. The concentration from before melts into a calmer sort of focus, with her facial expression softening considerably. She looks—dare I say—*relaxed*. I almost want to berate her for not working, but I can tell she's listening closely. Heck, even the snakes have closed their eyes, and they shouldn't even have eyelids to begin with!

As I reach the final step of the third chapter, I have seen her expression change several times, all leading up to this point where she's basically in a Zen-like state. I kind of want to stop talking to avoid the horrible truth of the situation, but my curiosity gets the better of me and I continue. As my lips speak the final lines of the guide, her body changes. From her previously WHITE chest, a swirling color starts to pulse out, spreading farther and farther with each beat of her heart, giving her pallid skin a standard, healthy, green hue. *Thump, thump, thump,* and the color spreads, across her torso, through her arms, into the snakes on her neck, and all the way up to her head and the tips of her long ears.

Slowly, her eyes open. They're a vivid orange. When she looks up at me, I can see them glimmer with enlightenment. Something bitter bubbles within the pit of my stomach.

"I—I can feel it!" she says excitedly. "Just as you said, deep in my chest, within the valves of my heart, I could feel the little rooms in there, and visualizing it as a house of four rooms as the guide said really *did* help! And to then also think of the presences within there as a family . . . It felt weird, but I get it. I can feel the father, in the upper right valve, and the mother in the upper left, and the son in the lower right, and the daughter in the lower left. Their names were weird, but if you read it to me again, I'm sure I could remember it! The son was, was . . . Aort? Was that it? I'm sorry I can't remember it, but . . ."

"What did it feel like?" I ask, slicing through her enthusiasm. I can feel my right hand curl into a fist.

She blinks at me before laughing a little. "What it felt like? Well, that's a bit hard to describe, but . . ."

My hand flies out and carves a chunk out of her exposed throat.

Her mouth opens and closes and then opens again and her eyes are wide as her hand lifts, trembling, to touch the blood-puking gash in her throat. She pulls her hand back and it's covered in RED. She looks back up at me again and she looks more confused than anything else as her mouth opens again, but no sound will come out, and all I can hear is her breath hissing out of her opened throat. The little snakes around her neck try to close the gash but they can't, and after a few more seconds, her eyes turn misty, and she slumps over.

<Gorgon Tisiphone (Lv.40) Defeated.>
<[Level Up]>
<You have reached Level 43.>
<Agility has increased by 3.
Strength has increased by 2.
Stamina has increased by 3.
Magic Power has increased by 1.
Dagger Nails has increased by 1.
Crush has increased by 1.
Corrosion Resistance has increased by 1.
Irritation Resistance has increased by 1.>

So, in other words, that experiment was a bust. Since I can't learn how the feeling of having magic power can be described, I can't exactly tell when I have it myself. Isn't that just a bummer?

Oh, that's weird. Now that she's dead, the gorgon's skin is turning WHITE again. I wonder if the whole having-magic thing will make the flesh taste any different?

<You have learned: Disassemble Lv.8>

Let's give this one a taste . . . Nomch. Hm. Hmm . . . Nope, it tastes the same. Maybe if I'd let the magic marinate in her for a while it might've tasted different?

That sounded kind of weird, but my intention is good. Still, whether it's magic-marinated or not, it's still far yummier than snake meat. Snacking on this nice bit of gorgon sashimi, I continue reading the book. And within time . . .

The entire mound of snakes beneath me, including the gorgon skeleton and the horse-sized snakes and the small cobras and the tiny snakes, all explode into colorful smoke, and I fall down approximately ten feet until I hit the floor hams first, the distinct feeling of my tailbone snapping in half making my body jolt up. Wh—wh—what the heck is—

<[Help has arrived.]>

I hear a door creak open and a stream of natural sunlight shines in, making a silver line around a person standing in the doorframe. My eyes train on the figure. Who the heck is this guy?

<Knight of WHITE Roses>

"Fret not!" the dude shouts, brandishing a sword. "Your ardent savior is he—" As he boldly steps inside, his eyes fall on the room. Every single inch of it is RED, which is something I'm very proud of. His entire body is covered in armor apart from his face, which means that I have an excellent view of his prominent eyebrows furrowing. "Huh. Have I come to the wrong place . . . ?"

But I'm not looking at his face. I'm looking at his armor. His horrible terrible awful dreadful lousy no-good abominable bad WHITE armor. My right eye twitches.

"N—nonetheless! Dear Miss Kitty Princess, I am here to rescue you, and to assist you in killing the horrible Gorgon Medu—" And he can say no more, because like a raging macaque, I've already thrown myself bodily across the floor, hooking my legs around his armored midsection. My claws wheel and scratch at his face, tearing it up within seconds, turning it into less of a face and more so fleshy strips of skin and meat.

<You have learned: Maul Lv.3>

A howl that might be considered a scream erupts from the torn-open cavity that used to be his throat and I take the opportunity to shove my entire arm into that same hole, down as far as it can go, until I hit flesh, which I tear open, and farther and farther, until my clawed hand finally grabs hold of something hot and pulsating and I tear it out, holding the still-beating heart in my hand like a trophy.

He takes one step forward, and then one back before wobbling left and right and then with a familiar sigh his lungs give their final breath and he falls over. Not that I go down with him, of course. I'm used to this situation, so with an acrobat's grace, I simply leap off, letting him fall as he pleases.

I look at the heart in my hand. Might as well, am I right? I take a chomp out of it like it's an apple. Hm. Not bad. It tastes like the heart of a shade, so I guess this guy really was some sort of shade or human instead of a pinkish, discolored goblin. Interesting. Chomping a little bit more, I finish off the heart. Hm. I'm not getting any pop-up message for his being defeated, but he should be dead considering that I literally just ate his heart. Maybe it has to do with the fact that he didn't have a level? It seems like people without a level or without a status message at all don't need to be killed to get a complete clear, but I mean . . . Why *wouldn't* you kill them?

Leaning down, I touch my hand onto his armor, smudging it with RED. This armor will be sure to sell for a whole bunch. And his heart was pretty tasty, too.

<THE GOD OF ADVENTURE SIGHS.>

<THE GOD OF CHIVALRY GROANS AND ALERTS THE GOD OF HARVEST OF THE SITUATION.>

<THE GOD OF HARVEST SILENTLY SURVEYS THE SITUATION.>

<THE GOD OF HARVEST WAVES HIS HAND.>

Huh? What the heck is happening now—

There's a sudden shift and my stomach turns just a bit lighter, as if something in it was abruptly removed. I look down at my feet. The body of the knight is gone. It just—it just *disappeared*! That makes no sense. What the heck did those damn gods do this time?! That was *my* lunch and/or dinner! You can't just steal a guy's meal for no reason. It isn't fair!

Damn these cruel gods . . . !

<Tutorial stage, Hell Difficulty Ninth Floor: Boss Stage>
<[Clear Condition] Defeat the Gorgon Medusa with the help of help of
—··· ppppppp—.11414>

<A CHANGE HAS BEEN MADE>

<[Clear Condition] Defeat the Gorgon Medusa.>

Uh-huh. Didn't like me killing the NPC, did you?

But the floor hasn't collapsed on itself or anything, so whatever. Let's see, the time is . . .

<Top—Status—Community>
<00:18:02 Day 205>
<The eighth attempt will begin in 4:23:42:58>

I have five days left until the next attempt.

I'm not entirely sure how the final gorgon will appear, but I've got a hunch that the door half-hidden behind a curtain over there just may have something to do with it. It certainly wasn't there a minute ago. Speaking of doors, that entrance the knight came in through just a few minutes earlier is completely gone now, almost as if it didn't even exist to begin with. Weird stuff.

Anyway, there's nothing better for me to do with these last few days than to try to finish the book Moleman gave me. I've got a feeling I won't learn anything, but I might as well try, right?

With that in mind, I hunker down on top of the softest rug I can find, with my back to a wall of soft velvet. No more snakes are appearing. I can't tell if this is a good or a bad thing, but it also doesn't matter that much. I just need to focus on reading. That's all.

And read I do. Making absolutely no headway whatsoever.

The chapters are just as incomprehensible as they were the first time around. I never did have dyslexia or anything, but it's almost starting to feel like I've developed it just by trying to read this thing. The words barely even look like words anymore. They're just little squiggles and dots. I refuse to believe that *aortic* is a real word. That's got to be made up. I won't have it.

Unfortunately, since there aren't any more snakes, and that irritating guy transformed all the snake bodies into colorful dust, there's nothing I can take out my frustration on other than my own body.

How lucky for me, then, that my prayer is heard. Right as I'm starting to consider the merits of auto-asphyxiation combined with cranial hemorrhage, the clock switches for the better.

<Top—Status—Community>
<00:08:02 Day 210>
<The eighth attempt will begin in 23:51:58>

The time has come. With only twenty-four hours of this attempt remaining, I have no other choice but to get going. Running my hand over the incomprehensible tome one final time, I put it into my inventory. Then I stand up and face the door.

I walk over to it in three large strides, put my hand to the doorknob, and tug at it. And then I realize it's a push door, so after dramatically pushing it open, I step inside.

A puff of perfume hits my face the second I enter. The intense light makes me squeeze my eyes shut, but on account of this not being a very strategic choice all things considered, I force myself to open them again, letting my gaze fall on the bizarre sight in front of me.

<Gorgon Medusa (Lv.47) [BOSS]>

She's lying on her stomach, on a regal-looking bed, with a carved pipe in hand. If it hadn't been for the way she looked, I might have mistaken her for some teenage girl, lying in bed and kicking her feet. But, as it is, the several meter-long snakes curling around her neck and upper back, alongside her shining RED eyes, make that a hard conclusion to draw. Silently, I hunch down a little in preparation for the fight.

"No need for violence, my love," Medusa says, a stream of perfume-scented smoke trailing out from between her lips. Oh, did I mention that she's huge? Yeah, she's easily bigger than the horse-sized snakes I fought earlier. She smiles at me. I feel a patch of goose bumps sprout across my back. "Would you like to see a magic trick?"— Um, actually, I'd rather no— "Look at your feet." And then she winks at me. I almost want to just, you know, *not*, but when the devil sends you an invitation, you can't refuse. I look down at my feet.

Ah. They've turned to stone, have they?

I look back up at her. She bursts into a fit of laughter. "*Bwahahahaha*, you should've seen your face! Oh, that is *priceless*. Could you just hold that face while I turn the rest of you into stone? I *need* to immortalize that one."

Okay, see, funny thing about petrification: It doesn't hurt. Like, at all. It's just that one second you can feel your legs, and the next, they just aren't there. The pain comes when you move them and rip the stumps from the petrified bits.

Namely, what I'm doing right now.

"Oh, come on; stay in place, won't you?"

No, I will not. I may not have anything left below my knees, but having knees is enough to go into a fetal position blowover-style roll, which is exactly what I do. She can't zap me with her gaze if I'm just not visible at all.

But I don't roll far before she enacts her countermeasures. The snakes that had previously simply remained coiled on top of her now spread out, each stretching out as far as its body can go, all of them laying themselves across the floor like a complex spider's web. I think I've said this before, but it's worth noting again that while I'm rolling, I'm basically blind because the whole world is just spinning around me too fast to really understand. To make sense of what's happening around me and where things are, I typically use scent, which is why I even realized that this was happening to begin with.

However, this all came just a second too late, as my escapades are abruptly stopped in their tracks as I run over one of these many snakes, and it, like a spring lock failing, instantly wraps tightly around me, choking the breath out of me and straightening me out into a boardlike shape.

"There you are," Medusa coos, her eyes training on me. Unluckily for me, this isn't the kind of situation where me not seeing her will cancel the effects of the skill. There's only one thing I can do.

I claw at the snake wrapped around me, successfully ripping off its head fully, making the body itself go limp. But by this point, I've already lost my upper left arm to the petrification.

That's alright, though. I'm still alive, and that's all that matters. While still falling, I pull myself into the fetal position as best as I can. As soon as I hit the floor, I book it for the underside of the bed. I'm able to make it there while tripping over only one snake. While she's still searching for me, I meditate a little, just to abate the bleeding and lessen the pain to an extent where I can think properly.

It's a simple situation, really. I just need to treat it as such.

I look down at the limbs I've still got.

Simple situations require simple sacrifices.

I bite my lip. This is going to hurt, but as long as it works, it won't matter in the end. Even though I only have one arm, it will have to be enough. I push my claws into my right thigh, sawing around my femur and then through it. All the while I use moving meditation to keep the wound from getting too serious.

"I know you're under there," Medusa says from just above. "There's no point in hiding."

I agree with her on that one, but there's one thing she's forgotten.

Hiding works best when coupled with diversion.

Pulling off a large segment of my leg, I waste no time to let it go cold before I throw it as hard as I can across the room. The snakes on the floor instantly bound for it, hissing in joy as they crowd around the piece of warm flesh. And right at that moment, before she can figure out that this isn't all that I am, I leap out from beneath the bed, climb the side of it with only one arm, and jump on top of her back.

"Huh—?" she exclaims beneath me, if only a second too late. Leaping toward her head, I place myself on top of her neck, and before she can properly react,

I press my clawed hand into her right eye, and then her left, blinding her. She tries to grab at me, and the snakes turn around to come for me, but I've already started digging into her throat, pulling out arteries and opening her throat. A few of the snakes bite into my torso and my one remaining limb but I can tell that it's already too late.

She tries to stand, but instead she just stumbles forward, over the side of the bed, and onto the floor below with a crunchy *squelch*!

<Gorgon Medusa (Lv.47) [BOSS] Defeated.>

<[Level Up]>

<You have reached Level 45.>

<Agility has increased by 6.

Strength has increased by 5.

Stamina has increased by 7.

Magic Power has increased by 2.

Dagger Tooth has increased by 1.

Crush has increased by 1.

Petrification Protection has increased by 1.

Exhaustion Resistance has increased by 1.

Exhaustion Protection has increased by 1.

Salamander Healing has increased by 1.

Moving Meditation has increased by 1.>

Haah, nice stuff!

As Medusa finally dies, the death grip that her snakes kept on me is finally let up, allowing me to breathe properly. To tally up the damage, I've lost three of my four limbs, and I'm pretty sure more of the bones in my body are broken than not. *Fracture protection* my ass.

<You have cleared the ninth floor.>

<You have received 1,000 points for clearing the floor.

You have received an additional 1,000 points for being the first to clear the floor.>

<For clearing the stage completely, you will receive an additional reward.>

<To repay your debt, the additional reward has been traded for 5,000 points.>

<2 Gods have shown a positive response to you. You have obtained 2,000 points.>

<43 Gods have shown a negative response to you. 43,000 points have been deducted.>

Ah, it's beautiful. Were my actions on this floor really *that* reprehensible, gods? Huh, gods? Care to explain why you aren't too hot on my playstyle? No? Right, got it.

<To repay your debt, the floor clear reward has been traded for 1,000 points.>

Let me guess. Now you'll abruptly send me back to the—

FLOOR 10

THE BURNING CITY

100,000 points

—lobby. You really are too predictable, system. You know that, right? And now you'll sell my inventory because I'm clearly not using any of it.

<To repay your debt, your inventory has been sold for 3,500 points.>

That's . . . a very exact number. Considering that I don't think I had anything sellable in my inventory apart from the book, that would mean that this was the price for the book, huh? I wonder how much it hampered my ever-growing debt?

<Current debt: 115,228 points.>

Ah. Yeah, uh, that actually makes sense. Still . . .

Six-figure debt. Here we are. I wish I could react more strongly, but I just feel numb. There's really no realistic way for me to pay this back, is there?

So, as you usually do with impossible problems, I'm just going to ignore it! Hakuna matata and all that. Let's check the time in the meanti—

<You have received a message.>

Hm? A message? From who?

<Status—Community—Top>
<Personal Messages>
<[NEW]SuperMoleman[F52]: Congrats on beating the floor!>
<[NEW]SuperMoleman[F52]: Checking in again. Please respond if you're able to.>

<[NEW]FarmerOfBlades[F32]: Have u die yet?>
<[NEW]SuperMoleman[F52]: Checking in again, did everything go alright with the floor?>
<[NEW]ExplosionBeyond[F29]: Wither In A Hole, You Inhuman Martinet>
<[NEW]SuperMoleman[F52]: Are you okay? Sorry to spam your inbox but I'm worried.>
<[NEW]SuperMoleman[F52]: Did everything go alright with the floor?>
<[NEW]PranksterGangster[F47]: I'm with your mother. She wants you to also suck me.>

For a minute or two, I just stare at my inbox.

I forgot to tell Moleman I survived. Erm. Uh . . . With trembling hands, I open the most recent PM.

<SuperMoleman[F52]: Congrats on beating the floor! Sorry that I sent so many messages, I could see that you were still alive since your profile hadn't gotten auto-deleted, but I still felt worried. There are worse fates than death, after all. But I'm happy to see that you were able to beat the floor! I didn't doubt it for a moment. How did it go? I talked with Bach about the floor, and she said a pair of gorgons would appear after five and thirty-one hours respectively. Did these go alright?>

Slowly, I draw in a deep, deep breath.

He isn't mad at me. He was just worried. That's all. I don't have to feel afraid or anything. Still, for some reason, I don't want to reply. If I just ignore him, I won't have to worry about his response. But—but that's cowardly! And I'm not a coward. Never.

My fingers tremble, but I still put them to the keyboard.

<PrissyKittyPrincess[F10]: um ya i beat da flor it wuz kind of hard n stuff an uhhhh da reson i messaged u is cuz a big snek 8 me witch wuz bad bt now im ok i bcame a meatball at 1 point but i jus had 2 get 8 by anotter snek and i wus ok srry 2 worry u i relly thoght i wuz gonna die>

I press send. Silently sweating, I wring my hands, trying not to let the thoughts get to me. He isn't mad at me. He said so. But what if he's mad at me anyway? Sometimes people say they aren't mad but they're actually super mad. People do that a lot, now that I think about it. They say they're happy but they're actually sad, or they say they're disappointed when they're actually angry, or they say they love you when they really hate you. I don't get it. Wouldn't everything be much simpler if we were just honest with each other? I just don't—

<You have received a message.>

I press the pop-up faster than my brain can even read it.

<SuperMoleman[F52]: Eaten by a snake . . . Glad you made it out alright! I just hope you didn't escape it the, uh, *natural* way, but I'm happy you were able to make it through regardless. On Easy, you only need to stay in the room for four hours, and according to Bach, the Hard Difficulty challengers had to stay there for forty-eight hours. I can't imagine having to stay there for an entire attempt, with all the snakes, their bodies piling up higher and higher . . . But you made it through, and that's what matters. You really do amaze me sometimes, you know that? Good luck with the tenth floor; it's a real doozy!>

I don't really know how to respond to that. I made him worry that much, and I didn't even send him a single message, and now he just wants to smooth it over like it never happened? That's just . . . *so much* like him. Why do I always expect him to blow up in my face? This is all so weird.

Anyhow, I can't just leave him on read, so I quickly type up a response and send it.

<PrissyKittyPrincess[F10]: thx u2 ur messag ment a lot withut it i prolly woulda died so thx ur a good friend>
<SuperMoleman[F52]: You're a good friend too, Kitty. See you soon!>

I stare at his message, stunned. He—he said it. He agreed. He . . . he said I was his *friend*.

My vision turns a little blurry but that's quickly undone by fiercely wiping at my eyes. I—I'm okay. I'm fine, I just . . . I mean, Simel is also my friend, but he never said it back, it was just kind of there, but Moleman, he just, he just went straight out and . . .

Sniffle. A friend. We're friends.

I have a *friend*.

<[NOW THAT YOU'RE FINISHED WITH YOUR PERSONAL AFFAIRS,]>
<A change has been made.>

<Would you like to enter Floor 10 early?>
<Yes/No>

H—huh? Wh . . . what? What's that supposed to mean?

I blink, and I rub at my eyes, but the message isn't going away. It's just hanging there, motionless. Asking for a simple response.

I can feel my nose wrinkle. This is . . . weird. Bad. Untrustworthy. The gods are up to something, again. I don't trust it. Not in the least. I've seen more trustworthy signs in gas station bathrooms.

<The God of Harvest sighs.>
<If [Yes] is chosen, 100,000 points will be erased from your debt.>

C—come again? A *hundred* thousand? With a big *H*?

Frankly speaking, this bribe just makes the whole deal even *more* suspicious, but on the other hand . . . A hundred thousand points. A HUNDRED THOUSAND. Do you know how many princess cakes I could buy with that?! Technically zero, but that doesn't matter! A hundred thousand . . . That'll bring my debt basically back to zero. And, sure, maybe they'll still hate me and make it go right back up to a hundred large again, but . . .

A hundred thousand. It's an offer I can't refuse.

Even though it's suspicious, even though I don't trust a single god, I still press the Yes button. Because of course I do. I don't exactly have any choice, now do I—

The world wobbles and shifts and somehow it feels wrong, even worse than the other times this has happened, because my stomach does a flip and I feel like I'm upside down but only my body is upside down and my brain is upright, but then it switches again, and my body, weak and wobbly, falls to the ground in a mess of limbs and confusion.

The first thing I notice, before I've even had time to get off the ground, is the overwhelming smell of smoke and fire. But it isn't just smoke. It isn't just that. It's something else, too.

Slowly, I pull myself to my feet. Before me stands a wall at a height of around eight meters or so. In the middle of the wall is a closed gate. I recognize this wall. I recognize this smell of smoke and fire. I recognize this gate.

The sight of it brings a tremble to my hands.

<Tutorial stage, Hell Difficulty Tenth Floor: The Burning City>
<[Clear Condition] Enter what used to be the Shore City of Acheron.>

Gulp.

Th—this place again, huh? Well, uh, the clear condition is easy enough, I guess.

But first, it might be a good idea to check out what else is around, right? I look over my shoulder. There are houses farther down the road, but I can't smell anything coming from them. No goblins, no food, no animals . . . nothing. And as I try to make out what lies farther away, all the way toward the horizon, I get a sudden and powerful sense that I shouldn't go there. It doesn't feel like my own emotion, or something that I should be feeling at all, but that doesn't mean it isn't there. So even though I want to try my hand at leaving this floor behind fully, I have no choice but to turn back to the wall and the gate and the smoke.

I really can't do anything for myself, can I?

I walk up to the gate and push it open. A gust of scalding hot air and blinding smoke hits my face and I want to leave, but I still push myself inside, closing the gate behind me.

<You have entered a Holy Area.>

Holy area? What is that supposed to—

<Tutorial stage, Hell Difficulty Tenth Floor: Boss Stage>
<[Clear Condition] Free the unhappy citizens of the burning city and kill the herald of the God of Kings.>

Two in one, huh? Now who's this *God of Kings* supposed to be?

<[Right your wrong. Undo the damage you have done. Quench the fire.]>

Hm. That's, uh, kind of interesting, if you ask me. See, pardon me for saying as such, but didn't the boss stage clear requirements basically beg me to kill the entire city? Sure, only the king *needed* to be defeated, but I got a bonus for defeating all enemies. Trying to say that this is *my* fault when I've done nothing but follow your orders is a little, well, I don't know . . . *cruel*?

But whatever, I guess. Gang up on poor Fennrick. Who's going to stop you? The police? No way.

Let's see, now. What is this place?

<You have learned: Heat Resistance Lv.3>
<You have learned: Heat Resistance Lv.4>

Yeah, it's scorching hot, that's one.

It is absolutely the city from floor three. Every single house is on fire, the roads are paved with soot, and the skies are darkened by BLACK clouds. Oh, and it's hot enough to melt my flesh off. Neat. I've been in sore need of a tan.

Slightly more worrying is the fact that I'm not exactly alone. I didn't notice it at first because it's sitting perfectly still, but on the side of the road is a BLACK-ened, crispy-looking little creature that seems to be fully made of soot. I'd assume it was a dead goblin if it weren't looking at me. Unlike its BLACKened, charred body, its eyes are still visible, and they are weirdly purple. And it's a very vivid shade, too. I think it's mauve, but it might be periwinkle. These things are hard to tell, and I kind of don't want to step any closer to it on account of the whole not-exactly-being-alive-or-dead part.

<Possessed Cinders>

No level? Does that mean I don't need to kill it? On the other hand, the clear requirement *did* say that I had to free the citizens, and I can't really smell anything other than soot, so . . . Yeah.

I walk up to it. Its gaze follows me. Um, hi. You don't happen to be suicidal, right?

It stares up at me. Experimentally, I stab my entire hand into its head. It doesn't even blink at me. Oh, uh, um . . . Okay, let me just . . .

You know that scene in dumb romance movies where the guy is taking off the girl's glasses and all of a sudden, she's a supermodel? That's kind of what I'm doing here, except I'm removing its eyeballs, and instead of making it turn into a supermodel, it just collapses into a pile of dead ash.

<Free the unhappy citizens: 1/8,792 Freed.>

Okay. That's one. Out of eight thousand seven hundred ninety-two.

I stare down at the bright purple eyeballs in my hands. They're weirdly squishy. I wonder how they taste? Sure, they look pretty radioactive, but that doesn't necessarily mean anything, right? Without hesitating any further, I pop one of them into my mouth, chew, and swallow.

<You have learned: Alpha Particle Tolerance Lv.1>
<You have learned: Beta Particle Tolerance Lv.1>
<You have learned: Gamma Ray Tolerance Lv.1>
<You have learned: Divinity Tolerance Lv.7>

It tastes like grape gummies, but without being sweet at all, and it's making my tongue kind of tingly. Looking at the tolerances I just got, I've got a feeling I might know why. I glance back down at the other eyeball in my hand. So it really is as radioactive as it looks, huh? On the one hand, radiation poisoning. On the other hand, grape gummy eyeball.

Bottoms up!

I pop the second eyeball in as well. Chewchewchewchew swallow. Yummy. I can't say the lack of sweetness is especially appealing, but I've eaten too many eyeballs at this point to really care.

<You have learned: Alpha Particle Tolerance Lv.2>
<You have learned: Alpha Particle Tolerance Lv.3>
<You have learned: Beta Particle Tolerance Lv.2>

Mmm. Yummy radiation.

I've got a theory. See, I didn't notice it before because I got distracted by the soot child, but now that I'm properly looking at it—unlike the rest of the city—the castle isn't on fire. Sniff sniff sniff sniff. If my hunch is correct, then that is where that so-called herald is.

But for once, the system actually understands me, because in order to beat this floor, I need to literally kill—erm, *free*—every single enemy available. I can't beat the boss without it. Or, I *can*, but I don't think I'll be sent back to the lobby by doing that. Hm. The next attempt should begin in less than twenty-four hours. I don't think there's any way for me to beat this entire floor and free all the citizens within that amount of time. Ugh. Should I just bite the bullet and accept that I'll have to waste an entire day here before the floor begins properly? What a bothe—

<[As an envoy of the Gods' will, you are exempt from the relaxation time for the remainder of the floor.]>

Oho? An exemption, is it? For little old me? Why, thank you! It sure feels nice to be heard now and again. But to see that hellish period in that hellish lobby described as *relaxation* feels somehow icky.

Either way, thanks to the gods finally caring about me for once, I have all the time in the world to properly do this floor. Yippee! And the first step to that is to ask Moleman what his tenth floor looked like, because I have a sneaking suspicion that it did not involve becoming an *"envoy of the gods' will,"* whatever that means.

I pull up my PMs.

<PrissyKittyPrincess[F10]: hey mole whts ur f10 liek>

Speedy as always, he sends me a quick response.

<SuperMoleman[F53]: It involved assisting a village of shades in defeating a flaming beast the size of an ox. Why? Is yours different?>
<PrissyKittyPrincess[F10]: ya bt dont worry ill b fine kk bye good lukk wit da floor>
<SuperMoleman[F53]: Thanks, you too!>

Alright, so this really is some weird custom thing. Hopefully, it wasn't just put together to punish me or something. These gods seem to have a weird obsession with making my life harder. Then again, so far with this floor, they've been surprisingly non-dickish about it. Dare I say, they've been almost *kind*. It's suspicious. People are only kind when they want something from you. Oh, excluding Moleman and Simel, though. They're just good people, which is an exception to the rule and therefore should not be counted.

Whatever this situation is, I can be fairly sure that the gods have some sort of stake in it. They actually *want* me to succeed, for once. Because of that, I'll need to move with caution.

I stick my nose in the air. Sniff sniff sniff sniff. Everything smells like soot and ash, but in many places, the scent intensifies. This must be those cinder people I'm supposed to free. The first one I met wasn't exactly aggressive, but that can always change. From now on, I'll move forward with slow caution. All the while gorging myself on yummy grape eyeballs, of course.

I make my way toward the nearest ones. It's a small cluster of I think three or so, which I'm able to confirm once I get close enough to see them.

All three are about the same size, and I can tell that they—much like the first one—used to be goblins. Mainly because they have those huge damn ears. Shouldn't they have gotten burned off with the fire? Weird. Anyway, they turn toward me as I approach and I briefly pause to check if they'll do anything, but nope. They just stare at me, and that's it. Since they aren't exactly doing anything, I wander closer, until I'm standing right in front of them. They look up at me. I pluck the eyeballs out of the nearest one's head and its body collapses into ash. The others simply stare at me as if their buddy didn't just die. Well, whatever. I pop both eyeballs into my mouth and chew them up as I simultaneously pluck the eyes from the next one. Once I've swallowed down the first eyeballs, I pop the next ones in my mouth and, using my newly freed hands, I un-eye the last one.

<Free the unhappy citizens: 4/8,792 Freed.>

Four down, eight thousand seven hundred eighty-eight to go. Simple enough.

<You have learned: Alpha Particle Tolerance Lv.4>
<You have learned: Beta Particle Tolerance Lv.3>
<You have learned: Gamma Ray Tolerance Lv.2>
<You have learned: Divinity Tolerance Lv.8>

Yeah, yeah, I know they're radioactive, who cares? I swallow the last eyes and pop in the next two. Maybe I was too cautious about this whole deal? This is easy stuff!

Leaving the piles of ash to dissipate into the fiery winds, I continue walking.

<You have learned: Heat Resistance Lv.5>

As I casually stroll down the half-familiar roads, I bump into cinder people here and there. None of them make any attempts whatsoever at fighting their fate. They just look at me, and then I take their eyeballs, and then they can't look at me anymore. It's all so simple and brainless that after only a few hours, I start doing it purely by routine. Step up to a cinder, grab its eyeballs, eat the eyeballs, step up to the next cinder, repeat. It's so easy it becomes dull.

<Free the unhappy citizens: 27/8,792 Freed.>
<Free the unhappy citizens: 166/8,792 Freed.>
<Free the unhappy citizens: 321/8,792 Freed.>
<Free the unhappy citizens: 690/8,792 Freed.>
<Free the unhappy citizens: 1,211/8,792 Freed.>
<You have learned: Alpha Particle Tolerance Lv.5>
<. . .>
<You have learned: Alpha Particle Tolerance Lv.10>
<You have learned: Alpha Particle Resistance Lv.1>
<You have learned: Beta Particle Tolerance Lv.4>
<. . .>
<You have learned: Beta Particle Tolerance Lv.10>
<You have learned: Beta Particle Resistance Lv.1>
<You have learned: Gamma Ray Tolerance Lv.3>
<. . .>
<You have learned: Gamma Ray Tolerance Lv.10>
<You have learned: Gamma Ray Resistance Lv.1>
<You have learned: Divinity Tolerance Lv.9>
<You have learned: Divinity Tolerance Lv.10>
<You have learned: Divinity Resistance Lv.1>

I spot a cinder.

I approach the cinder.
I grab the eyeballs.
I eat the eyeballs.
I spot a cinder.
I approach the cinder.
I grab the eyeballs.
I eat the eyeballs.
I spot a cinder.
I approa—

I stumble and fall. My head is filled with static. This is weird. When did I get these pop-ups?

<You have learned: Cancer Tolerance Lv.6>
<You have learned: Organ Failure Resistance Lv.5>
<You have learned: Brain Damage Protection Lv.2>
<You have learned: Unconsciousness Resistance Lv.7>
<You have learned: Irritation Resistance Lv.3>
<You have learned: Rash Tolerance Lv.4>

I feel weird. This is weird. Hm. I try to stand up, but when I push off the floor with my arms, I notice that they're covered in weird rashes and stuff. That isn't good. I'd better get rid of it. Raising my arm high, I slam it back into the ground a few times until I can feel my arm break, and then I gnaw it off. Weirdly enough, my blood looks a bit too dark. More than the usual. And where did my bone marrow go?

This is all so weird.

<Top—Status—Community>
<04:20:02 Day 227>
<The ninth attempt will begin in 13:19:39:58>

Day two hundred twenty-seven?

That can't be right. I only started yesterday. And yesterday was day two hundred and ten. It's only been one day. Not seventeen.

I heave myself up, but as I get on my knees, my mouth opens, and I puke again. A half-digested mush of WHITE slime falls out of my throat. I wipe my mouth and stand back up again fully. I fall again and my jaw falls off but then I stand back up again, and I stagger a little.

Down the road, I can see a shadow staring at me. The world is dark and fuzzy but I can see it. If my body weren't covered in weird crunchy bits and open wounds I can't recall getting, I would have. Have. I would. I don't remember where I was going. What am I doing? Who is that man?

I want to greet him but my jaw fell off and it's still on the ground. It's a weird thought, but I want to eat it. Wouldn't it be a waste otherwise? It would. Would. It.

He steps toward me. And I step back. And he steps toward me. And I step . . . step. My legs. Are they still there? Do I still have my legs?

I look down but instead of looking at my legs I look at my hands and in my hands I hold a pair of bright purple eyeballs that look up at me and I'm so startled that my whole body jerks and they fly out of my hand and I look up and he's standing right in front of me, eyeless, and the BLACK sockets of his eyes meet me, and his mouth is open, but he doesn't say anything, and he doesn't see, and before I can scream the wind takes the ash of his body and he goes away.

<Free the unhappy citizens: 3,488/8,792 Freed.>

I fall to my knees, my hands groping after the eyeballs I dropped, fervently searching, and once I have them in hand, even though they're covered with a layer of soot like pieces of purple fudge rolled in dark cocoa powder I still stick them into my mouth. They don't taste like anything other than soot. But since my jaw isn't here anymore, I can't chew them, so I just stuff them down into the hole of my throat.

<You have learned: Divinity Resistance Lv.3>

I feel weird. I feel weird. I feel weird. My body isn't supposed to feel like this. I can't remember the last weeks. It's just a blur of BLACK and purple.

I take a staggering step forward. The pressure of the step makes one of my eyeballs fall out again and by habit I grab it, pluck it from my eye socket, and stuff it down into my throat. Weird, this one didn't taste like grapes.

<You have learned: Cancer Tolerance Lv.10>
<You have learned: Cancer Resistance Lv.1>

I see a group down the road. They turn to me. Their judging eyes bore into me and I want to go dig a hole and bury my head in it. I—I didn't have any choice! It was you or me, so even if I had wanted to let you live, it's not like I could've! I never wanted to hurt anyone. You're all just, just . . . *casualties* of war! Every war's got to have a few sacrifices. It's how it works. So why are you upset that you were the unfortunate few? Shouldn't I have that right? I'm the one forced to do all of this! Shouldn't us soldiers deserve a little pity for having to do these acts?

Oh, sure, look at me with those unblinking eyes and mouthless faces, I know what you want to say. You don't need to say anything; I can hear you just fine.

I eat their eyeballs. They don't react.

<Free the unhappy citizens: 5,309/8,792 Freed.>

I hate goblins. I hate them. I hate their ears and their height and their bald heads and their stupid green skin. Killing them, a *crime*? Ha! If anything, I did the world a service by removing a few more of these annoying creatures. Eat eat eat eat eat eat eat.

Grape jelly. Grape jelly. Yum yum yum yum.

I haven't done anything wrong. And if I did, it wasn't that bad. And if it was, then it's not a big deal. And if it is, then it's not my fault. And if it is, then I didn't mean it. And if I did, then they deserved it.

Ashes ashes they all turn to ashes. I wish I could turn to ashes too. I don't like it when my body hurts. I can't get used to it. Every new injury hurts just as bad as the first one and my body reacts in the exact same way. I don't like getting hurt. Did I really deserve this fate? Wasn't I forgiven? He forgave me. So why am I here?

My hand grips an eyeball. I accidentally grip it too hard, making it pop. I lick the purple goop from in between my fingers. While licking, I accidentally bite off my own finger. Weird, it doesn't taste like grape. That's strange.

When did my jaw return? Strange. Strange. Weird. Odd. My eyeball, too. Huh.

<Top—Status—Community>
<00:00:01 Day 258>
<The tenth attempt will begin in 13:23:59:59>

I eat the final eyeball.

<Free the unhappy citizens: 8,792/8,792 Freed.>
<You have learned: Gamma Ray Resistance Lv.10>
<You have learned: Gamma Ray Protection Lv.1>
<You have learned: Alpha Particle Resistance Lv.10>
<You have learned: Alpha Particle Protection Lv.1>
<You have learned: Beta Particle Resistance Lv.10>
<You have learned: Beta Particle Protection Lv.1>
<You have learned: Divinity Resistance Lv.10>
<You have learned: Divinity Protection Lv.1>

I stare at the sight ahead of me. Slowly, I swallow the eyeballs.

The road in front of me is covered with a thick layer of flaky soot. I can't smell fire and smoke anymore. The city feels cold. The smell of cinders is no longer alive. And somehow, through it all, my brain feels clear.

<You have freed all unhappy citizens. Please return peace to the city by killing the herald of the God of Kings.>

Uh-huh. Uh-huh. Uh-huh . . .

My body feels . . . It's starting to feel better, but, um. What the heck was that?

I can still feel my brain fizzle a little, so even though the message is urging me to go and face whoever this herald guy is, I still sit down, cross my legs, and meditate a little.

<A Canto appears to you.>

Considering that I can't remember this showing up, I must seriously not have meditated a single time this past . . . month? Has it been a month? No, uh, I think it's been more than a month. But, anyway, um . . . Yeah, sure. Show me the canto.

<[And yet the Lady who is ruler here will not have her face kindled fifty times before you learn how heavy is that art.]>

Another nonsensical line. What is even the purpose of these? If they're supposed to be hints, then they aren't especially good ones. Hm. On the other hand, I usually just brute-force my way through whenever there's a weird, nonsensical puzzle to be done, so I might not be the best judge of these things.

But right as I'm starting to feel my body recover a little, another message pops up.

<The herald of the God of Kings has noticed your presence. Prepare yourself.>

VII

Hello, Herald

Seriously? You're not even going to let me heal up first? Really? Isn't that just a bit too—

A massive weight slams into me and I fly off the ground, bound through the air, and skid across the ground, scraping up my entire chest before finally coming to a stop a few paces from where I started out. Standing up, I blink open my eyes. There, on the other side of the road, right where I was until just a moment ago, stands a, uh . . . creature? Or something?

It looks like a dead goblin, with pallid green skin and a wrinkled, almost mummified look to it. Even weirder, other parts of it are weirdly bulbous, and others have cracked open, like someone tried to stuff a fortune cookie full of purple goop. This is the most evident with the head. Not only are the eyes a vivid purple, but the goop inside is even bursting out of them, flooding down the side. The mouth is also drooling purple stuff, but the drool and the stuff doesn't actually go anywhere, because instead of just falling off, it floats in beads around the face.

But the real showpiece is the stuff above the face. See, its head is exploded. It looks like a water balloon burst, but then it got frozen mid-pop, so it looks very strange. A large, blooming bubble of purple goop is swirling around, protruding from the open skull like a massive maggot. It looks strange, but since the purple goop on top has the same physics as a lava lamp, it's strangely hypnotic to look at. I just want to look at it, forever and ever and ever and . . .

"Are you the envoy sent by the pathetic God of Multitudes?" it asks, spitting goop as it does.

Um, me? Well . . . Yeah, I guess I am. That's what the system calls me, not that I actually get it personally.

It stares at me. Technically speaking, the body itself seems to be a she, considering the lack of mane and the fact that it's wearing a torn dress. But for some reason, I don't think whatever it is that's possessing it can be considered female, or even male for that matter. I mean, I'm pretty sure it's just goop, so . . .

"No answer? Do you perhaps not understand my language?"

No, I understand it. I just don't feel like talking right now.

It stares at me. Or maybe it's staring at something behind me. It's hard to tell since the eyes are just one solid color without any border between eye WHITE and iris and pupil. It crosses its arms. "You're a silent one, I see. But you don't seem especially enlightened by the situation. Do you know who I am?"

Um, yeah, the status box said—

"I am the herald of the great God of Kings, who in His gracious generosity has decided to accept these measly planets into His powerful bosom," it says grandly. Pfft. Bosom. Its right eye twitches. "Unfortunately, unbeknownst to you poor inhabitants, your Gods have decided to make things difficult for us all by resisting. Isn't that horrible? And now they're using you as unwitting pawns without even explaining the situation."

Um. Look, if you're doing a hostile takeover of my planet, then I'll probably try to fight back, unless—

"As the God of Kings pities you so much, He has through me asked most gently to make you an offer." It gives a pause for what I think might be dramatic effect. "Become His herald."

Herald? But aren't *you* his herald?

It places a hand on its chest. "I may be His current and most fortunate herald, but for His will, I do not mind relinquishing my life and my position. To be His herald is to feel His power at all times, and to exert it as though it was your own. It is a wonderful thing. I am happy. So, so, so, happy. And you can be, too. Unlike your God of Multitudes—or if you'd rather believe in your former God of Love—the God of Kings will be most kind with you, and He will tell you what He is to do in the future, and He will never abandon you."

You mean how he's currently totally abandoning you? Listen, I don't want to assume anything, but didn't you *just* say that if you stop being his herald, you'll literally die? Isn't this a textbook example of him letting you die?

"Ah, I can tell by your face—you do not believe in His kindness. But, you see, even in death, I shall fulfill His wants. If I should die in His name, how could that possibly be called abandonment?"

It's very easy, actually. I just called it such.

It gives a strained smile. "You doubt yet. It is unfortunate, but . . . The only reason you refuse is because you have yet to taste the sweet fruits of His strength.

Come—come closer, and I shall allow you a taste of His divinity." Saying so, it holds up one of its hands. A big glob of purple goop seeps out of a crack on its palm, beading in its hand.

I kind of want to keep my distance, but since I'm a purely close-quarters fighter, I don't really have much of a choice. If this will let me get close enough to beat it up, then so be it.

Cautiously, I step closer to it until I'm right in front of it. It's a fair bit shorter than me, but that just means that my face is right at the level of the pulsating mass of purple goop protruding from the top of its head. This makes it pretty hard to try to keep eye contact. I look down and find its hand reaching up toward me. There's a small bit of goop in it. The way it's holding it up to me feels a whole lot like a little girl offering a sugar cube to a horse. Like, is there no way for us to do this in a non-creepy way? No? Ugh, fine.

Hunching my back farther down, I let my head fall into its hand, and I lap the goop off its palm. Slurp slurp slurp. When did I stop being a proper human?

But the thought leads nowhere as my body freezes in place, my tongue still extended, my eyes wide. Th—this is . . .

MywholebrainexplodesintolightandmusicandsoundandmagicanddancingandIcanseethestarsandthemoonandthesunsandtheplanetsandthenebulasandeverythingthereisandeverythingthereeverwasispresentedtomeintechnicoloranditsliketheworldhasgoneastepbeyondsimplebeingthreedeeandIcannowseeitforwhatittrulyisanditisbeautifulitisgorgeousandIcanfeelpowerandenergyandmightandrightflowingthroughmyveinslikebloodbloodbloodbloodandmybodytremblesbecauseIHAVETHEPOWERtodoanythinganythinganythingandeverythingallatonceIamomnipotentIamaGodIamTHEGodIameverythingthereeverwasandeverythingthereeverwillbebecauseIamthebeginningandIamtheendandtherehasneverbeenanythingbeforemenorwilltherebeanythingaftermeforIamGODIamTHEGODIamIamIamIamIamIamIamIamIam . . . uh . . .

<You have learned: Divinity Protection Lv.2>

What was I doing again?

I look down at the little goblin apostle thing. It looks up at me. Even though it hasn't had much control over its facial expressions so far, now it is somehow able to narrow its eyes and furrow its brows, all at the same time. "How were you able to withstand that? That should have put you under my power!"

Withstand what? That yummy goop?

I stare at the bulbous blob of purple goop in front of me. I can feel a trail of drool inch down my mouth. Y'know, I'm not sure what this herald guy is trying to say about controlling me or whatever, but that goop I just ate tasted a whole lot like grape jelly, and right now, I can see a big lump of grape jelly, right in front of my eyes, wiggling back and forth like an experienced belly dancer . . .

With a mind clean of ill thought, I reach out and grab hold of the jelly. My hands sink through but that's alright. Leaning my head forward, I thrust my entire face into the blob of purple and begin sucking it down.

"H—hey! By the God of Kings, what are you—"

Gulp gulp gulp gulp gulp gulp gulp gulp gulp gulp gulp gulp gulp gulp gulp gulp gulp gulp gulp gulp gulp gulp gulp gulp gulp gulp gulp gulp gulp gulp gulp gulp gulp gulp gulp gulp gulp gulp gulp gulp gulp gulp.

My brain fires up again. I can see the lights. Ahahaha . . . hahahahah . . . hahahahahahah. Hahahahahahahahahahahahahah! *Beauuuuuuutifuuuuuuuu uuuuuuuuuuuuuu—~~l!*

The herald pushes me away, but by this point, I've sucked up most of the jelly it had on its head. As it tries to take distance from me, it sways from side to side. "You damn mortal . . . ! How dare you consume my divinity?! You should be within my *power*! This is ridiculous . . ." It points its right index finger at me. "*Fall before your king!*"

<Kneel.>

I stare at it. It stares at me. I've got a big goofy grin on my face from the grape goop. Man, I feel good. People who tell you not to do drugs are all a bunch of dweebs. This is the life!

Or, it was, because now I can feel the happy happy yummy fade out of my system, leaving me feeling cold and slimy and horrible inside. Luckily, I happen to know just how to get a refill. My eyes fall to the herald standing just a pace or so in front of me, wiggling its finger at me. Or, more accurately, at the small bit of purple goop still protruding from its head. Mmmm . . . Yummy grape . . .

"Kneel! *Kneel!* Why won't you kneel? How can you consume my divinity and then refuse my orders?"

I don't know and I don't care because I'm hungry for that jelly. Grinning like a lunatic, I sneak closer. But right as I'm almost close enough to make a grab for it . . .

"Agh, be off, mortal!" it exclaims, rudely pointing its middle finger at my stomach.

<Remove.>

Hm. I suddenly feel a lot lighter. By looking down, I'm able to discern the reason for this, which is that a hole has been blasted in my midsection.

Beneath my ribs and above my pelvis is a gaping hole with the only remaining thing being my pristinely WHITE spine. Huh. That's weird. Where'd my abdomen go?

I try to take a step forward, but without any abdominal muscles, my upper body just folds and falls forward limply, my legs unwillingly following along, leaving me to fall to the soot-covered ground without any stop whatsoever. As my mind is whirling, my arms desperately stretch out for something—anything—that allows me to grab a hold of the herald's legs, though my grip is too weak to pull it off its feet or anything like that.

The herald looks down at me. "That's a better position for mortals like you. Strange, though, that my divinity had no effect . . . Are you perhaps the apostle of the God of—hey, cut that out!"

Hm? Cut what out? You mean to tell me that you don't think I should be sucking the goop out of your legs like a vampire feeding on a human? I'm sorry to say, but this is *way* too delicious for me to possibly stop. Ah, it's so good . . . Weirdly enough, I can also feel my abdomen again. I'm not sure how, but the second I got more of this deliciousness into me, the area that just got blasted off returned.

And since I can now do things, such as stand up, I begin clawing my way up the herald, clawing up gashes in its soft goblin flesh as I do, sucking out all the purple and also eating the flesh as I do, because, like . . . *Why not?*

"You—you—how *dare* you?!" the herald cries. "My royal divinity is not for you to—to *eat*! Accept my righteous punishment, mortal!" It points at me, and another blast of what I assume to be pure magic shoots out, this time hitting my chest head-on, cleansing it of exactly everything, save for my bones. But I'm still eating its flesh and sucking the goop, so before I can even feel my heart stop beating, it has recovered again. "Why won't you die?!"

Because, obviously, I've got better things to do than dying. Like eating this grape jelly, for example.

The herald blasts me again and again and again, ripping out big chunks of my flesh, removing entire limbs at a time, at one moment even aiming straight for my skull, but the rays couldn't penetrate my bone, leaving my brain intact, which was all I needed. Yummy yummy yummy yummy.

By this point, the herald is basically just a skeleton with a purple, gooey head, and I'm doing just fine.

"Curse it all . . . !" the herald says. "Fine! If you should not only reject my want for peace, but so too spit in my face, then I will simply leave. *Escape!*"

<Escape.>
<Error! Escape Spell blocked.>

"H—huh? Wait, no, that's . . . that can't be. There must be something wrong, why can't I—"

I bite into its neck. Chomp chomp chomp. Hmmm. Maybe it's because this is holy ground or something? We're also inside a floor stage, which means that we're surrounded by an invisible barrier. As the boss monster, you can't exactly leave, can you? But my perfectly sound reasoning falls on deaf ears as the herald tries over and over with increasing desperation to leave the area.

<Flee.>
<Error! Flee Spell blocked.>
<Return.>
<Error! Return Spell blocked.>
<Leave.>
<Error! Leave Spell blocked.>
<Withdraw.>
<Error! Withdraw Spell blocked.>
<Retreat.>
<Error! Retreat Spell blocked.>

"Damn it, damn it, damn it . . . !" the herald says. Since it hasn't got a neck anymore, and the rest of its body is just a skeleton I gnawed the skin and meat off, all that's left of it is a purple goopy head that I'm currently holding with both hands and eating like a whole head of lettuce. It's actually kind of soothing, just peeling off layers of skin and tissue, biting off an ear or two . . . I almost wish I had a movie to watch this with. Maybe a bowl of salty snacks to balance out the grape flavor? Yeah, that'd be nice.

The streams of purple goo going down its bursting eyeballs seems to intensify as its face twists in despair. "This isn't fair, it isn't right!" it croaks somehow, despite not having a throat anymore. "I am a herald of the God of Kings! This is wrong, my fate was to be something far more grandiose! Please, God of Kings, don't let me die like this, please . . . !"

I can sense a shift. There's no status message, nor is there a presence, and nothing is technically altered with the head in my hands, but suddenly, like a switch being pulled, the goop in my hands stops swirling and bending against the laws of physics and the light in its eyes fades in an instant. Gravity grabs hold of the goop but instead of pulling it to the floor, it instead starts collecting, gathering onto itself, pulling itself together around the herald's decapitated head, tighter and tighter, crunching up the head itself as it goes, using it as fuel in its transformation. Tighter and tighter and tighter and tighter, until, finally, what I hold in my hand isn't a head at all, but instead a small, purple crystal.

I stare down at it. It gleams softly in the light. It looks valuable. Hm.

I wonder if it also tastes like grape?

I pop it in my mouth. When I try to chew it, the thing that goes *cr—ack* is instead my teeth, so I have no choice but to just swallow it down as it is. Hm. There *was* a certain kind of grape flavor, but it was much more muted. Almost quiet. Hmm. I like it!

<SHARD OF DIVINITY CONSUMED.>

Oh! Am I going to get a skill from it? Man, the gods sure are being nice to me on this floor, giving me skills and stuff. Oh, boy, I can't wait to hear what this does!

. . .

I said, I can't wait to hear what skill I get!

Okay, fine, I'm not getting anything. Boo-hoo, poor little me doesn't get anything for killing the literal herald of a *God*! Gee, that's so fair. Next time the gods ask me for a favor, I will *totally* listen and not at all decide to just, you know. Not.

Psh. What was even the point of this floor if I didn't get anything ni—

<THE GODDESS OF WANT ADMIRES YOUR STRENGTH OF DESIRE AND WILLINGNESS TO FULFILL IT AT ANY COST.>
<THE GODDESS OF WANT HEREBY INVITES HELL CHALLENGER LO FENNRICK TO FULFILL HER APOSTLESHIP TRIALS IN ORDER TO BECOME THE APOSTLE OF WANT.>
<WILL YOU ACCEPT?>
<YES/NO>

Huh? Wait, what the heck is this? Um, let me read that again . . . Admires my strength . . . fulfill her trials . . .

This is . . . ?

<THE GOD OF COWARDICE IS SUDDENLY STARTLED AWAKE FROM HIS NAP.>
<THE GOD OF COWARDICE PANICS.>
<THE GOD OF COWARDICE ADMIRES YOUR [FILL IN CHALLENGER TRAITS HERE]>
<THE GOD OF COWARDICE HEREBY INVITES HELL CHALLENGER LO FENNRICK TO FULFILL HIS APOSTLESHIP TRIALS IN ORDER TO BECOME THE APOSTLE OF COWARDICE.>
<WILL YOU ACCEPT?>
<YES/NO>

Okay, that one was absolutely done on a whim. You didn't even fill in what traits about me you liked!

<THE GOD OF COWARDICE RACKS HIS DIVINE BRAIN EQUIVALENT.>
<THE GOD OF COWARDICE ADMIRES YOUR CONFRONTATIONAL ABILITIES.>

Hey, my ability to call you out has nothing to do with these! Compliment me properly, damn it!

<THE GODDESS OF WANT AGREES WITH HELL CHALLENGER LO FENNRICK THAT THE GOD OF COWARDICE'S APOSTLESHIP INVITATION SEEMED A BIT UNINSPIRED, JUST LIKE ALWAYS.>
<THE GOD OF COWARDICE TRIES TO HIDE BUT FAILS.>
<THE GOD OF COWARDICE RELUCTANTLY ARGUES THAT JUST BECAUSE SOMETHING CAME AT THE LAST MINUTE DOESN'T MAKE IT ANY LESS THOUGHTFUL THAN WHAT CAME FIRST.>
<THE GODDESS OF WANT LAUGHS AND MAKES A CRASS INNUENDO.>
<THE GOD OF COWARDICE FEELS ASHAMED.>
<THE GOD OF COWARDICE EXPLAINS THAT THIS IS WHY THEY BROKE UP TO BEGIN WITH, AND THAT IF SHE WOULD JUST TREAT HIM WITH A LITTLE RESPECT, THEY WOULDN'T BE LIVING WITH NON-BETROTHED.>
<THE GODDESS OF WANT IS APPALLED THAT THE GOD OF COWARDICE WOULD SUGGEST THAT THIS WAS HER FAULT ALONE.>
<THE GODDESS OF WANT MAKES THE POINT THAT IF HE HAD ONLY TAKEN THE INITIATIVE NOW AND AGAIN, SHE WOULDN'T HAVE HAD TO NAG HIM ALL THE TIME.>

Am I, uh, in the middle of something . . . ?

What's the Deal?

<THE GODDESS OF WANT EXCLAIMS THAT IF HE HATES HER SO MUCH, WHY DID HE LET HER KEEP HIS ANGEL?>
<THE GOD OF COWARDICE WINCES AND TRIES TO EXPLAIN THAT THE BETROTHAL IS PERMANENT, AND THE EXCHANGE OF ANGELS IS LIKEWISE.>
<THE GODDESS OF WANT REFUSES TO ACCEPT ANY EXCUSES.>

Okay, uh, this is all great, I'm glad you both have, uh, *reconnected*, but I'd like to finish this floor before the next attempt starts, if that's okay with you both?

<THE GODDESS OF WANT WARNS HELL CHALLENGER LO FENNRICK NOT TO MEDDLE IN THE AFFAIRS OF GODS.>
<THE GOD OF COWARDICE SILENTLY REMEMBERS WHY THEY BROKE UP IN THE FIRST PLACE.>

Jeepers. This really is some sort of lover's spat, isn't it?

<THE GODDESS OF WANT KINDLY INFORMS YOU THAT THEY ARE NOT LOVERS.>
<THE GOD OF COWARDICE KINDLY INFORMS YOU THAT THEY ARE NOT LOVERS.>

Right. Sure.
Um, so, aside from that . . .
I have no idea what to do. I don't know what being an apostle means or how it's different from being a herald. I don't know what'll happen if I refuse. I don't know if I can accept both or if I have to choose between either the cat or the dog, so . . . I just don't have enough information to make a proper choice. Honestly, though, I kind of just want to . . . not. Sure, these two gods have almost always

been at least somewhat on my side, and they have given me a pair of skills that have saved my life more times than I can count, but at the same time . . . Why would I ever trust a god?

Not a single god I've met so far has been trustworthy. To them, I am almost certainly nothing but a toy, running around in the tutorial for their divine amusement.

But I can't be sure that refusing them is the proper choice, either.

The only clear positive in this situation is that I'm not getting any prompt to answer them within a specified amount of time, and the messages themselves aren't going away either. So it would probably be fair to assume that, for once, they'll give me all the time I need to make up my mind for it. Hypothetically, this means that I could probably put off answering for as long as I want, but they'll probably declare shenanigans eventually and take my lack of answer as a *no*.

Hrrm. If I were a cartoon character, this would be the point at which steam started shooting out of my ears. I just don't know enough.

<[SINCE THE GODDESS OF WANT AND GOD OF COWARDICE HAVE FINISHED,]>

<You have cleared the tenth floor.>
<You have received 1,000 points for clearing the floor. You have received an additional 1,000 points for being the first to clear the floor.>
<For clearing the stage completely, you will receive an additional reward.>
<To repay your debt, the additional reward has been traded for 5,000 points.>
<12 Gods have shown a positive response to you. You have obtained 12,000 points.>
<24 Gods have shown a negative response to you. 24,000 points have been deducted.>
<To repay your debt, the floor clear reward has been traded for 1,000 points.>

T—twelve gods liked what I did!? Hey, not too shabby! Sure, twice that many disliked it for whatever reason, but twelve is . . . It's a good start. With this, it shouldn't take me any time whatsoever to build up an empire of points, heheh . . . !

<[AS PER THE PROMISE,]>

<You have received 100,000 points.>

Ohohohoh, now we're talking! Oh, it's beautiful. I have never seen so many zeroes outside games before. I now understand why people willingly enter the rat race.

<To repay your debt, your inventory has been sold for 0 points.>

Makes sense, considering that I haven't put anything in my inventory since the last floor. Still, somehow, I feel mysteriously insulted.

<Current debt: 19,228 points.>

My debt isn't quite back at zero, but with this, I have a chance. If I can just get the gods on my side, lick their boots a little, then getting back in the green shouldn't be completely impossible.

<Congratulations! You have beaten the tenth floor of the Tutorial on Hell Difficulty. You are hereby invited to meet the Hell Difficulty Administrator to make a request.>

Hm? Request? Oh, yeah, I think I saw someone mention that every tenth floor, you got to meet the difficulty admin and make a wish. So this is that, then? I wonder what kind of creature the admin will be. If it's a goblin, I don't think I'll be able to restrain myself.

Huh. The pop-up isn't really changing. Do I need to . . . ?

I accept?

<Please stand by.>

A—alright. I'm standing by. Should I put on a better hide . . . ?

After about a minute or so, a new message pops up.

<Thank you for your patience. The Hell Difficulty Administrator will see you now.>

Suddenly I'm standing in a massive dark space. I can't see how big it is, but even though it seems to be completely BLACK, I can still see perfectly. Which might be because of—

Before I even have time to describe the massive pajamas-clad moon-man sitting in the middle of the room, he grabs hold of me and presses me close to his chest and gives me a hug.

He removes me from his chest, smiling down at me as if that weren't the most painful thing I have ever experienced. My body is still trembling. What was that. What was that. Who is this. Where am I.

"Kitty!" the massive being bellows. When I say he's massive, I mean that he's literally the size of a skyscraper. The yellow-and-blue pajamas with a teddy bear

print and the fact that his face is like a big crescent moon with a face on it makes the whole being-huge thing feel ten times weirder. He doesn't look like he should be anything at all, but he is. Lifting me up, he holds me closer to his humongous face. Now I notice that he's actually got a little bell dangling down from the top of his moon-face. It jingles with each movement he makes. **"Welcome, my friend! I have been waiting on you for so long, and now that you are finally here, I couldn't be happier."**

His hands are literally squeezing the air out of me, but I recognize the feeling of him talking all too well. "A—are you, like, an, um . . . *god*?"

His smile remains, unmoving, chiseled onto his face like a permanent groove. **"All in its time, my good friend."** He holds me to his chest, bringing me into a hug and it—

He removes me again. My breathing is shallow. If I had felt this kind of pain before the tutorial, I would have died. I would have had a heart attack, and then a seizure, and then another heart attack, and then I would have died. That's just what would have happened. "P—please, don't . . ." I stammer, my throat ragged. "Don't do that again. I beg of you."

He looks down at me. **"Is that your wish?"**

My wish? Oh, yeah, I need to . . . I need to make a wish. A wish . . .

I look at his chest. My brain briefly blanks out at the thought of him hugging me again, but I can't afford to ask him not to. It's just a hug. It doesn't kill me. It makes me want to die, but it doesn't kill me. That's what matters. It won't kill me. I need to make a better wish.

"What can I wish for?"

"Hmmmm . . ." he hums, rubbing at his weirdly pointed chin with one hand. **"Just about anything!"**

"Anything?"

"Almost anything."

Almost anything . . . "Like a million points? Or an insta-kill skill? Or a magic spellbook with every spell in it? Or a piece of super-strong armor? Or a potion that heals any injury with one sip? Or a magical staff? Or a powerful pet dragon?"

"Is that what you want to wish for?"

My jaw snaps shut.

I can't be stupid about this. I can be stupid about a lot of things, but right now, I can't afford to make a dumb choice. A pet dragon can be killed. A piece of armor or a magical staff can be broken, a potion will eventually run out, I can't necessarily learn every spell in a spellbook, I can't know what the effects of the skill will actually be, and a million points will get used up. But there's one thing I know that I need, that I *really* need, that can't be bought in the store and won't be found with the other challengers and is pertinent to my future.

<You have been invited to join the Apostleship Trials.>

<Will you accept?>

<Yes/No>

I look up, drilling my eyes straight into his.

"I wish for information."

"Information, is it?" His smile broadens. **"Is that your wish?"**

"Yeah, I literally just—yes. Yes, that is my wish."

He snaps his fingers. **"In that case, I shall grant this wish to the best of my abilities."** Gently, he places me on the floor, and before I can really understand what's going on, the space around us shifts once more. Suddenly I'm standing behind a lectern, and he's in a weird tuxedo, holding a couple of cue cards like a game show host. I'm being half blinded by a number of harsh spotlights, but I can still see that in front of us are several rows of empty seats. No, not quite empty . . . If my eyes haven't degraded into mush, I'm pretty sure that the seats are all occupied by singular fireflies. One in each seat.

Behind the both of us is a big screen, currently showing a logo that says *What's the Deal?*

"Welcome, welcome!" he says to the firefly audience, stretching out his arms as he does. **"On today's episode of *What's The Deal*, our dearest contestant—Hell Challenger PrissyKittyPrincess—will compete in finding out the answers to life's biggest questions! As usual, all questions and answers will be provided by our dear contestant, so give a hand for Kitty!"**

The tiniest round of applause erupts from the fireflies. What the heck is going on . . . ?

"As usual, I am your host! I doubt anyone here is unfamiliar with the rules, but I will still explain it as simply as I can. Rule number one: Only ten questions may be answered! And that was all we have in terms of rules. Now, let's begin with the first question, shall we?"

Only ten? But I haven't asked anythi—

The graphics on the screen shift around, transforming into the question *Who the heck is this guy?* I stare at the question. The question stares back at me.

"Nice question!" he says, turning to me. **"Well, shall we hear it?"**

Four answers pop up on the screen.

A. The God of Sleep.
B. The God of Pain.
C. The God of Comfort.
D. Not a God at all.

I blink at them. Uh. Hang on, I'm supposed to answer? Hey, that's unfair! How am I getting my wish if *I'm* the one answering the questions?!

But the *host* isn't saying anything, and the audience is holding its insect breath, so . . . It's up to me. Answer D is an obvious fake-out. If you're going to say what something is, you don't do it by explaining what it isn't. That's just weird. Sleep, pain, or comfort. Sleep would be my first guess, because of the moon-and-pajamas theme. But he *does* look pretty comfy, all things considered. On the other hand . . . Him being the god of pain would explain why him hugging me felt so . . . Yeah.

I look down at the lectern in front of me. There are four buttons, labeled *A*, *B*, *C*, and *D*. Even though I feel unsure, I press *B*.

A horn toots and a spray of confetti arches over the scene as the screen flashes green.

"Nice deduction!" he says. **"I am, indeed, the God of Pain! Very impressive. For that, you get one point!"**

Something *ding*s in the lectern. Leaning over it, I'm able to look at the front of it, which bears the *What's the Deal?* logo, alongside my username, and a screen that now shows a big *1*. What is that even . . .

"Oh, we've got another question! Let's see it on the big screen, folks," Pain says, and I turn to the screen just in time to watch it change one more time, in this case showing the question *What is that number even for?* After a second or so, four answers pop up.

A. Just for fun.
B. Each point grants another wish.
C. Each point grants one point.
D. At the end the points are tallied and if they are less than 5, Hell Challenger PrissyKittyPrincess dies.

Uh. I hesitate to ask since I don't want it to turn into yet another question, but what the heck is that last answer supposed to mean? Th—that can't be the right one, can it? Slowly, I glance over at the god of pain. He looks like a tricky fellow, but he doesn't seem to really hate me, and I can't see why this would lead to my death at all. No, I think there's a much simpler answer here.

I press the A button.

The screen lights up in green.

"That's correct! It's just for fun, so there's no need for you to worry about getting any answers wrong. Let's move on to the next one, shall we? This one's a doozy!" The screen shifts again. I try to clear my head and think only about the questions I really, really need answered. I've already wasted two of my ten questions on useless stuff, so I really need this one to be good.

A question pops up on the screen. *How come everyone's always so mean to me?*

I feel my jaw drop.

"Let's take a look at the options!" The four answer options pop up. If they can be called four, that is.

A. Because you're mean to them.
B. Because you're mean to them.
C. Because you're mean to them.
D. Because you're mean to them.

I gulp down a lump. Did the spotlight always feel this hot? The audience is completely silent. Pain is likewise silent, just staring at me. Waiting for me to choose an answer.

I look down at the buttons on the lectern. I didn't . . . I didn't think that. I didn't think anything like that.

My hand hovers over the buttons. This isn't true. I didn't . . . Th—this is a scam! I just—I'm not . . . Scowling, I push down on a button at random. The screen behind me lights up in green.

"Ouch, that's got to hurt! Good on you for being able to empathize with others and to see their perspective, Kitty. It sure isn't easy to admit that you've got no one else to blame but yourself, but you did it. Well done!"

I wonder if a god of pain can feel pain himself? I should test it out once I get the chance.

"No need to dillydally. Let's see what question four holds in store for us!"

W—wait, I don't need that question answered! I don't care whether he can feel pain or not, I really don't!

The screen flashes with the next question and I freeze in place. *What is the purpose of the tutorial?*

I can feel my eyebrows squash together. Okay, that one I *really* didn't think. Is this guy just messing with me? I bet he can't even read my thoughts! But I don't feel like talking today, so . . .

The answers pop up.

A. To torment humans just for the sake of it.
B. To train humans who would otherwise have died into becoming receptacles for divinity.
C. To steal away humans from the God of Love.
D. To birth a new God.

This is . . . ?

I look over at the god of pain, but he won't show me any expression other than that permanent *everything's-alright* smile. Is it seriously up to me to figure this out? Well, I doubt it's A. I also don't think it's C, because if they were going to steal a bunch of people, then why would they let us die? There is clearly some other purpose to this whole tutorial thing. Since I already know that the first part of B is factual, that would suggest that B really is the situation. I don't know what it means to be *receptacles for divinity*, and it sounds kind of ominous, but that doesn't make it less true. I guess.

I press the B button and sigh in relief as the screen lights up in green.

"Four in a row—what a prodigy! As you've deduced, the tutorial is a way for Earth and Purgatory to work together in beating back the forces of the God

of Kings! It's a very simple alliance. It all began when the God of Kings gave us an ultimatum, to join Him or die. As a polydeus, joining Him would have meant that all of us, save for one, would have to be killed in order to become more manageable in His eyes. To save ourselves, we reached out to the God of Earth—your God—the God of Love. Living up to His divine name, He agreed to assist us in creating this tutorial—designed by the God of Harvest. We were allowed to bring in humans such as yourself on three conditions: One, joining the tutorial would be completely voluntary; two, we would only invite those who would otherwise have died within twenty-four hours; and three, after they had completed the tutorial, they had to return to Earth."

He—he's actually giving me an explanation? No way. Am I having brain hallucinations?

I really need to put this to mind. This is important stuff! Uh . . . What did he say just now? Something about the god of Earth being the *god of love*? Oh, lord, please let that be a joke or something. Shouldn't our god be, like, a God of Power, or a God of Death, or a God of Awesomeness? Love. *Ugh.* I do not have the vocabulary to properly express how dumb that is. I mean, *Earth*? Really?

"The Tutorial itself," Pain continues, **"is designed in order to strengthen you so that you may be used in this war against the God of Kings. By defeating enemies and clearing floors, you earn levels and skills, both of which are granted directly by Us Gods. Equipped with this divinity, you will be able to resist the power of the God of Kings. Neat, huh?"**

Uh . . . Okay, wait just a minute. Sure, I *chose* to join the tutorial, but I never agreed to be part of this fight against this *god of kings* fella. I only killed his herald because I had to in order to beat the floor. Once I'm back on Earth, I'm going to go back to gaming, and that's final!

"Let's continue on to the fifth question!"

H—hey, wait a second, I'm not done digesting that last one yet! What the heck does that all even mean?!

A question pops up on the screen. *What is an angel?*

What is an—I, uh, I honestly haven't thought about that. Sure, Want and Cowardice mentioned angels in their lover's spat, but angels are . . . Isn't it only obvious that a god would have angels?

The answers quickly take space on the screen.

A. They are the servants of Gods.
B. They act in the name of their God by using their Divinity in a more focused manner.
C. They are exchanged in the ritual betrothal ceremony between Gods and Goddesses.
D. All of the above.

Uh. Uhh. Okay, this feels like another one where the answer is kind of obvious. I know that C is the correct answer because that's what Cowardice said. On the other hand, just because this is what the angels are used for doesn't necessarily mean that this is what they *are*. C isn't the right answer, but it also isn't incorrect. A and B both feel plausible, and they are both direct descriptions of what the angels are in and of themselves, which would suggest that several answers are correct.

In that case, there's only really one answer.

I press the D button.

"Ding ding ding ding! That's another correct answer, folks! Our dearest challenger sure is on a roll, isn't he?" Waving to the audience, Pain turns to me. **"If you're wondering, these wonderful moving stars—these firefly angels— are the gift I was given by the Goddess of Pleasure upon Our happy day. In return, I gifted Her my little sheep. Like this, I can use Her powers, and She can use Mine. Isn't that lovely?"**

Actually, I kind of don't care about your marriage status. Why should it matter to me if you gave some lady a bunch of sheep for a wedding gift? If you ask me, that's just plain weird, not to mention inconvenient. Do you know how much grass and hay sheep need to eat daily to stay alive? This is more of a WHITE elephant than a proper wedding gift.

"Angels are differently strong individually depending on how many angels one God has. Since I and Pleasure both have so many angels, each individual contains a relatively small fraction of Our Divinity, but the amount of Divinity is the same between Gods. An angel is an angel, no matter what God it serves."

Uh-huh. Right. Honestly, I don't care a lot about angels. If you ask me, they seem more like glorified wedding rings than actual individuals.

Before I even have time to finish my train of thought, and without waiting for the host of the show himself to say anything, the next question pops up on the screen.

Why is the God of Pain such a dork?

I read the question. Then I read it again. It still says the same thing. Slowly, I turn to look at Pain.

Much like I am, he's staring at the question. The cue cards he's holding fall out of his hand, startling him out of it. **"Oh! That was, erm, haha, uh . . ."** Falling down on his knees, he begins gathering up all the cue cards again. I catch a peek at one of them. It says, *Salmon Tuna Indigo Bream*. Standing back up again, Pain nervously chuckles. **"That's, um, you know, I mean, I'm not trying to say anything here, but calling me a dork is a bit, heh, uh . . ."** He shrugs dejectedly. **"I just thought that making it like one of your Earth game shows might make it a bit more fun, so, I just, erm . . . N—not that it matters or anything,**

haha! I'm the God of Pain, so, uh, obviously, a hurtful word or two from my favorite little challenger won't do anything! Haha. Erm . . ."

Usually, the thought of apologizing never even crosses my mind, because I rarely feel like I've done anything wrong. But right here, right now, in a situation where I don't think I've technically done anything wrong, the urge becomes too much. I look down at the lectern and the buttons. "Um," I say. "I don't . . . I don't think you're a, uh, *dork*. It was just, I was only . . ." I gulp. "I'm sorry. The game show is . . . It isn't . . . It's fun, I guess."

He perks up. His eyes, gleaming with appreciation, stare into me. **"So you don't think I'm silly? You want to keep doing the show . . . ?"**

I take a deep breath. In, out. In, out . . . "Yeah," I bite out after a long pause. "Sure, I want to keep doing the show."

He lights up and the possible answers flash on the screen.

A. Glad.
B. To.
C. Hear.
D. It!

Robotically, I look back up at Pain. He's still smiling. Silently, while still keeping eye contact, I press *B*.

The screen fills with green and confetti but I don't remove my eyes from him. **"Let's see what the seventh question has in store for us!"**

I refuse to turn away from him, but the next question that pops up is too much for my curiosity to withstand, and I glance away to check it out.

How is Simel doing?

I look back at Pain. He doesn't seem to find the question odd in the slightest. Before I can make up my mind on whether to verbally explain to him in the strongest words I can muster why this question is way too personal to put in front of this audience of insects, the answers pop up.

A. He's doing good.
B. Recently picked up a new hobby playing the flute.
C. Never been worse, suffers daily nightmares, has unwillingly taken a leadership position.
D. Recently married.

Hah, this one's so easy I don't even have to think it over in the least!

I press the A button.

A harsh *BZZZZZZZ* explodes across the scene and the screen lights up in a bright, deadly RED. Wh—what did I—

"Uh-oh, wrong answer! That's a shame. Better luck next time!"

N—no, wait, which answer was right? Was it B? I can see him playing the flute, but I think it's more unlikely that he'd get married, he didn't exactly seem like the romantic type, but you never know with people, no matter how closely you know them they can always change their minds, so . . .

"Here comes question eight, good luck!" Pain says as he points to the screen with a flourish.

The question blinks into existence. *Where the heck do these questions come from?*

Hm. So you're telling me that I only have two opportunities left to get the one question I really need to have answered pop up? Is that it? How useful. I hate this world.

The answers show up less than a second later.

A. The God of Pain makes them up on the fly.
B. They mirror questions asked the other Difficulty Administrators by previous challengers.
C. They are decided by the fireflies doing a vote.
D. They are ripped wholesale from your mind, memories, and thoughts.

Hm. Okay, uh . . . Getting this right means that I'll know better how to manipulate the questions that pop up in the future. If I get it wrong, it won't get answered at all. Right. My whole life is one big scam and I'm the sucker at every turn.

It wouldn't be weird to assume that Pain has seen everything I've done for the past floors, but I also don't think he'd purposefully use my own verbal mannerisms. That's just plagiarism, and I am not shy to sue.

I don't think other challengers have asked about how a single goblin in Purgatory is doing, especially not Simel personally.

The fireflies, despite being angels, are still insects and therefore can't know me personally.

I press the D button. The screen flashes with green and I sigh in relief. This means that I have a way of getting the question I want. I only have two left. I need to make them good ones.

"Nice one! Indeed, the questions get dragged straight out of your lovely mortal brain. To say that I can read your thoughts, as you put it, would be disingenuous, but not entirely false. I simply understand your intention, and by comprehending your brain's simple structure, I'm able to add your mannerisms to be able to read approximately what you're thinking!"

That's way too convoluted to be true.

"It isn't!"

I blink. W—wait. So, you've, um . . . You could understand me this whole time? All of it?

"Pretty much!"

Uh. Okay, um, that's, ah . . . I think I'm going to ignore that? Y—yeah. Let's. I mean, if this was true for *every* god, it would mean that no matter where I am or what I'm doing, they are constantly peeking into my head. Sure, I had a feeling that might have been the case, but to have it spelled out like that, face-to-face, is completely different.

"I can imagine that," Pain says with a sage nod. I almost want to tear his face off, but he could easily counter it, what with the mind reading and all. **"Though, since you've been such a good sport, I might as well mention that the more divinity you hold, the harder it will be for Us to understand your brain. But I don't mean Our divinity. Even if you were at level five hundred, since your divinity comes from Us, We would still understand you. But that shard of the God of Kings's divinity that you consumed earlier is a whole different story. It wasn't much, but it's already making your brain slightly more indecipherable. Not much, but if you continue to do us favors in killing the God of Kings's heralds . . . Who knows?"**

His smile turns enigmatic, but all I hear is that the more purple goo I eat, the more privacy my brain will have. It's like a VPN, but for your lobes. Interesting!

"And now, on to our penultimate question!"

H—huh? Wait, shoot, um, I need to send out my brain waves as hard as I can! Apostle, apostle, apostle, apostle . . . !

The question appears on the screen with a fun, colorful graphic. *What is an apostle?*

I gulp. Okay, sure, this isn't a bad question, but I don't need to know what it is to be able to be it. While I'm still reeling over the fact that I only have one chance left, the answers quickly appear.

A. A mortal whose form has been flooded with a God's divinity to the point where they lose their individuality to become a perfect servant of the God.

B. A God briefly taking the form of a mortal to act physically.

C. A mortal granted a fraction of a God's power in return for their contractual servitude.

D. A mortal who acts in the name of a God to further Their desires.

Okay, this one's a bit complicated. Hrm. I doubt it's B since nothing I got from Want or Cowardice suggested that they would be the ones doing anything. I don't think it's D either. Tons of mortals do stuff in the names of various gods, but that doesn't really make them apostles, specifically. It's either A or C, then.

I think it's C, because I've got a hunch that A just happens to perfectly describe a different sort of divinely sponsored being.

Namely, that herald. If that purple goop was divinity, then it was beyond flooded with it. It also had no individuality to speak of, and frequently spoke as though it considered itself to be the God of Kings. It matches up. And if A describes what a herald is, then there's only one real option left.

My finger flicks the C button.

Green floods the stage and the fireflies give a teeny tiny round of applause.

"That's exactly it! Gee, you sure do know your stuff, huh? It's almost like you didn't need to wish for information at all, haha!" Pain jokes. At least, I *think* it's a joke. I don't know for sure, but I really hope it is. If he's telling the truth, then I'm using my next wish to ask him to take an acid bath and dry himself off with sandpaper. **"Well, boys and girls, angels and mortals, we've finally reached the last and final question for the night! The tension is palpable. Will our most favorite challenger answer the most important question in life, or will his hopes and dreams be squashed right before his mortal eyes? Let's have a look!"**

A—already? Hang on, I haven't cleared my brain yet! I need to meditate before you—

The final question flashes onto the screen.

Whose apostle should I become?

"Now that's a spicy question!" Pain exclaims, his face one big grin. **"Before we let our dearest challenger see the options and give his answer, I feel that it is most opportune for Me to mention that in this space, no Gods other than Myself and the Goddess of Pleasure are able to see what is happening. You are free to make whatever arguments you please without fear of the possible repercussions. Now, on to the answers!"**

Before my eyes, four choices pop up, staring me down like brands of fire.

A. The Goddess of Want.
B. The God of Cowardice.
C. Both.
D. Neither.

It's exactly the question I was hoping to be brought up, but now that I think about it, this actually doesn't help me in the least. I don't know the answer to this. That's why I wanted it to pop up. But if I don't answer it correctly, I won't receive any answer at all. I have a twenty-five percent chance of getting it correct. That's it.

This game is rigged. I have no choice but to knowingly go with a choice that may be wrong for the sake of seeing what might be true.

But this does reveal something important. Namely, it is possible to choose both, and to reject both. I don't know what this does, though. The description of what an apostle was didn't directly state that a mortal could only be the apostle of *one* god, but it also didn't say anything about being able to follow several ones. Then again, from what I've seen and what Pain has said, all of the gods of Purgatory are technically just one god. I have no idea how that's supposed to work, but that might mean that since the divinity given by two gods is the same, it might be doable. However, if receiving the divinity of two gods is too much, then I may just literally burst and become a herald.

This is way too complicated, and I don't get anything, but . . . I mean, if the purpose of the tutorial is to make us receptacles of divinity, then isn't there a chance that—unlike goblins—I could become an apostle of two gods? On that note, if it *weren't* possible, then they wouldn't both have suggested it, right? I mean, they're *gods*. Shouldn't they be smart?

I glance over at Pain where he stands staring at me with that big, goofy grin.

Okay, I've changed my mind. *Smart* would be the last word I'd use to describe any divine entity. If they were smart, they wouldn't be against me.

In that sense, the argument is less a matter of whether I can or can't choose *both*, but more if I *should*. I don't know if you've noticed this, heh, but, um . . . These two gods in particular kind of hate each other? If I accept both, I might just get slapped in the face with them deciding to fight over me like two kids with a doll, each giving me more divinity than my body can hold, with the eventual outcome being that I get ripped apart in the process. Sure, you *could* call that a nightmare scenario, but the fact of the matter is that any interaction I have with these *literal gods* is always mere words away from my death.

This god of pain guy is no different. Sure, we're amicable right now, but if he wanted to, he could literally make me feel so much pain that I wouldn't even have time to bite my own tongue before the sensation short-circuited my brain. The only reason I'm not actively panicking is because if he wanted to kill me, I'd already be dead. Also, he looks like the mascot for a knockoff Nytol. How can I possibly take that seriously?

To return to the subject at hand, what I really need to know right now is whether I should accept this at all. Getting divinity from a god would be cool if the gods themselves weren't such doofuses. Additionally, the idea of being in their servitude makes me physically violent.

With all of this combined, there's only one button I can possibly press.

I slap my hand down on the D button.

Neither.

* * *

The scene flashes with RED and a loud angry *BZZZZZZ* slashes through the air and I feel my heart drop. I look over at Pain.

"Ooh, bummer! So close. Well, eight out of ten points is still quite high, so for your admirable efforts, you get the wonderful prize of—"

I slam both hands on the lectern faster than my brain can process what's happening. "W—wait!" I shout. "Why shouldn't I pick either? What will happen to me? Will they hurt me? Will Want try to kill me for it? Will I get hurt further down the road? Will they revoke my sovereign skills? Will they remove skills they gave me that I didn't know about? And if I have to pick one or both of them, which should I do? Want or Cowardice? What happens if the god of cruelty tries to jump into this mess? I wished for information, so give it to me!"

He pauses briefly, turns to me, and smiles. Then he turns back to the audience. **"As I said, for being such a champ, Kitty will receive the wonderful prize of getting another hug from your most beloved God of Pain!"**

My eyes widen and I want to say something, but no words will come out and I can do nothing but stare as he slowly approaches me, one step at a time, his hard leather shoes going *clack-clack-clack* against the stage, his arms stretched out and his chest bared in a gesture of friendliness and compassion. I back away from the lectern. "No, no, I don't want a hug, please, oh, God, please, I—I won't ask any questions anymore, so please, just . . . I'll do the tutorial as many times as you want, anything at all, just so long as you don't—"

He brings me into his arms.

Through the WHITE silent shrieking PAIN I hear only His voice.

[To those that know me, I am large.]
[To those that Love me, I Love them.]
[I am Pain, and I will walk with you, now and forever.]

The pain abruptly ends and I jerk out of it, sweating and shaking and trembling and with a dry mouth and staring eyes, the same way you feel when you startle out of a horrible terrible nightmare that never seemed to have an end.

Except the nightmare looks so silly when you look back on it that you can't understand why you felt so scared about it at all.

The God of Pain hugged me. Why do I feel my heart beat quicker and my breath turn into panting hyperventilation when all that happened was that I got hugged by a stupid moon-man? I don't get it. I just don't get it.

<THE GOD OF COWARDICE HEREBY INVITES HELL CHALLENGER LO FENNRICK TO FULFILL HIS APOSTLESHIP TRIALS IN ORDER TO BECOME THE APOSTLE OF COWARDICE.>
<WILL YOU ACCEPT?>
<YES/NO>

<THE GODDESS OF WANT HEREBY INVITES HELL CHALLENGER LO FENNRICK TO FULFILL HER APOSTLESHIP TRIALS IN ORDER TO BECOME THE APOSTLE OF WANT.>
<WILL YOU ACCEPT?>
<YES/NO>

I stare at the two messages in front of me. By giving a quick glance around, I can tell that I'm in the lobby of the next floor. Wonderful. The WHITE wallpaper really does give it that insanity-inducing glow that's so chic nowadays.

But I can't afford to put this off any longer.

I can't refuse them both. I don't know if I should choose one, and in that case, which one would be the proper choice. Even if I assume that picking one will relinquish the support of the other, I still can't decide. Both of the sovereign skills they've given me have been equal in how useful they are, and losing just one of them would hamper my progress and survival chances immeasurably. Likewise, whatever they give me should I become their apostle will no doubt be just as useful.

Even though Want has given me an additional skill and let me keep my pelts, I can't say that I would be too excited to be her apostle. Considering that her main facet of being is *greed*, there's no doubt in my mind that being her servant would be less of a two-sided partnership and more of an indentured servitude. I'd basically just be a little butler, or some kind of tamed brownie. There isn't a single doubt in my mind that she would mainly just use me to get stuff. Do I really want to be the underling of a sugar mama? The second she finds a new sweetie to take care of, I'm as good as a pair of outgrown pants.

But that doesn't mean that Cowardice is the right choice, either. I don't think he'd make a slave out of me, but I also don't think he'd be too keen on protecting me if things went wrong.

If I were his apostle, should shit hit the fan, instead of getting an umbrella to shield us, he'd just toss me aside and run for cover himself. Or, even worse, use *me* as cover. After all, I *am* nothing but a mortal.

Neither of them is a good choice. Not in and of themselves, at least.

But if you combine them, you get a completely different story. If one of them has me, then I'm disposable. However, if they're fighting over me—over my attention and gratitude—then I have a chance. There is only one real option here.

Twice the gods, double the rewards.

I place my index fingers to both Yes buttons and press them simultaneously.

<YOU HAVE ACCEPTED THE APOSTLESHIP TRIALS OF THE GODDESS OF WANT.>

<YOU HAVE ACCEPTED THE APOSTLESHIP TRIALS OF THE GOD OF COWARDICE.>

<WANT APOSTLESHIP TRIALS PROGRESS: 0/365>
<COWARDICE APOSTLESHIP TRIALS PROGRESS: 0/23>

Huh? Wait, that's it? I thought the apostleship trials would be, like, a floor or something where I had to defeat enemies or fight my way through mazes and puzzles or whatever. What the heck is this supposed to be? I can't press it, so I have no idea what these trials are even supposed to be. Do I need to defeat certain types of enemies? Should I collect X amount of gold? What about treasure? Maybe I need to beat the floors themselves? I have no idea! How do you expect me to clear your dumb trials if I can't even know what they're for?! I demand an explanation!

But, as usual, no such response arri—

<THE GOD OF COWARDICE CLEARS HIS THROAT EQUIVALENT AND PREPARES TO GIVE A LENGTHY EXPLANATION.>
<THE GODDESS OF WANT BARGES IN AND CHASTISES THE GOD OF COWARDICE FOR HIS IGNORANCE.>
<THE GOD OF COWARDICE ATTEMPTS TO DEFEND HIMSELF.>
<THE GODDESS OF WANT GETS INTO A SPAT WITH THE GOD OF COWARDICE.>
<THE GOD OF COWARDICE GETS INTO A SPAT WITH THE GODDESS OF WANT.>

Okay. So, in other words, I seriously should just never try to get these two in the same room, huh? What a lovely couple.

<THE GODDESS OF WANT KINDLY INFORMS YOU THAT THEY ARE NOT A COUPLE.>
<THE GOD OF COWARDICE KINDLY INFORMS YOU THAT THEY ARE NOT A COUPLE.>

Yeah, yeah, I get it, so buzz out of my screens already. It's starting to get annoying.

FLOOR 11

THE BROKEN ROCKS

IX

Washed-Up Gentleman

Alright then. New floor, new horrors.

That whole boss fight took exactly twenty-four hours? Huh. I feel like some time-warping effects of some sorts might have surrounded this all, but . . . Well, whatever. It isn't *that* important. What *is* important is that this lobby is still totally WHITE, and you all know what that means.

From doing this schtick so many times, I've actually started getting a hang of how to best do it. It's all about controlling the rate at which you heal, and to use the natural pumping of my blood to accurately use it almost as a hose. It takes some skill, but by this point, I've got skill in excess. Within less than an hour, the lobby is all nice and painted.

Only twenty-three hours left to go. I wonder what I should use all of these hours for? Training my tolerances would be my first option, but it also doesn't hurt to train my movement skills. Hmmm . . .

No. No, now that I think about it, there's just one thing I have to do that's a touch more important.

I open up my PMs and type one up for Moleman.

It takes me a few minutes just to write everything He told me. Apparently, I was already starting to forget a lot of things, because now that I'm actually thinking about it, a few of the things I recall feel very new. Whether or not Moleman knows any of this is up to fate, because I sure don't know. He might have asked about this way back and even made a post about it. I don't really check that kind of stuff, so I wouldn't know.

After I've finished dictating this behemoth of a message, I give it a quick once-over just to make sure I didn't accidentally lie. Since I didn't, I quickly send it off.

And now, we wait. And wait. And wait . . .

How long has it been since I sent it?

<Top—Status—Community>
<01:15:01 Day 259>
<The tenth attempt will begin in 12:22:44:59>
<The eleventh floor will open in 22:44:59>

No way, only five minutes have gone by? That makes no sense!

Well, in that case, I guess I'd better just try to make the time pass quicker by training a bit. I wonder, if I knew magic, could I have used it on myself to gain higher divinity resistance? Or would it just not have had any effect on me? Hmm. I almost want to learn magic just to figure out how this works, but I think my brain just isn't suited for it. Kind of a shame that one of my stat points always falls into the *magic power* category each level up . . . I wonder if I can wish that away? Eh. For now, I'll just do my best to continue. I'll take it when I get there.

I continue training. And then . . .

<You have received a message.>

My hand flies out to poke it but only then do I remember that I experimentally bit off my arm to gain higher bisection resistance. Damn it! I try to poke it with my stump, but by that point, it's too late.

<Floor 11 has opened. Do you want to enter?>
<Yes/No>

Really? *Now?* Come on, I literally don't have any arms!

Oh, hey, my arms grew back. Hey, why couldn't you do this a second earlier so I could poke the message?! I demand a refund!

<If no answer is chosen, [No] will be chosen for you and the floor may be accessed next attempt.>

D—damn it . . . ! Fine, I'll just check his message once I'm on the floor! How's that?

As usual, the world holds no answer for me. Scowling, I press the Yes button and pretend to be surprised when the floor shifts beneath my feet and I'm suddenly standing on a rocky alcove overlooking a stormy sea. Wow, how original, a sea. As if those don't exist on Earth. What's next, are you going to show me rocks? Oh, I see rocks leading out into the ocean! Real original, god of harvest. Or should I call you farmer boy? Yeah, I think that sounds better. Damn hippie.

<Tutorial stage, Hell Difficulty Eleventh Floor: The Broken Rocks>
<[Clear Condition] Pass over the sharp rocks to reach the small island.>

Oh, wow, I need to go over the rocks that lead out to sea. How novel. Let me guess, there'll be tons of sharks, and maybe a sea monster or two. Will there be mermaids? Oh, oh, maybe a siren or two will lure me into the seas!

Rolling my eyes, I open up my messages, but before I can even check his message, a song calls out to me from the seas. A beautiful aria. I don't like music, never really have, but this can't be called music. It's beautiful in the same way that the baritone notes of the sea are beautiful, in the humming of a whale, in the song of a seabird. It is music only in the sense that it is a sound that is beautiful to the ears. If this is music, then so is the wind, and the rain, and the rustle of leaves.

I head out onto the rocky path. Moleman's message can wait.

The rocks beneath my bare feet are sharp and I leave behind a trail of blood, but that's alright. The wind pushes me and beats me around, but I have wind resistance, so I can avoid falling into the humming, trilling waters. The music is all around me. The ocean itself is singing. The farther out I go, the more beautiful it is. I'm not walking anymore, I'm simply skipping from rock to rock, caught up in a dance. My heart beats to the rhythm of the waves and I feel my brain slosh around in my head, spinning and circling and up and down and down and up.

Eyes look at me from just below the waves, with giggles and laughter following closely after. My dearest audience watches me!

The hands of maidens reach out from the sea, clapping and clapping and I bow to them. I can't see the shore anymore. I turn around and bow to the audience behind me. See, see! With a song as beautiful as yours, how can my strutting dance compare in the slightest? Oh, sing louder, fair nymphs! Let your song reach my very innermost being and cleanse me through it!

Their hands reach up and I take one to kiss it, bowing as I do, but just beneath the waves, beyond the fair hand, I see not a woman but a beast. Its hide is a deep blue, with a knotted, bumpy surface out of which a dozen human eyes peek. Atop its sharklike skull, a single lipped mouth opens and closes, singing— singing, so beautifully.

The maiden's hand I hold grasps mine and tugs at me, inviting me into the water. Well, I wasn't planning on staying, but if you're so insistent . . .

I join them below the surface for supper.

They swarm me and tear me apart with questions and inquiries.

"Where did you study?"

"Have you ever had a betrothed?"

"How is your family?"

"Is your father proud of you?"

"What do you do in your spare time?"

"Do you find your work fulfilling?"

"What's your best memory from your childhood?"

L—ladies, ladies, these questions are a bit . . .

Hm? Where'd my arm go? Hey, I need that to open my messages! And now my leg, too? Where are you going with that, Mary? Lilyanne, I happen to treasure my left hand quite a lot; it's very important for pressing the WASD buttons, so please—Belle, please, not my other leg! Now I haven't got anything left!

Petunia? You want my—? Well, I suppose . . . I guess it's alright if you want my internal organs . . . But you'd better give them back afterward, or I'll be very upset!

Hmm . . . the water is starting to look . . . awfully . . . dark . . .

—Ah! Wh—where am I?

I'm lying on something hard and rocky. Hm . . . Oh, I know! It's rocks, isn't it? I try to get up, but then I remember that all the ladies borrowed my limbs. Bummer. I wonder what they need them for? Anyway, by turning my neck, I'm able to tell that I am, indeed, lying on top of a rocky alcove. I knew it! Sadly, this means that I'm all the way back at the start of the floor. Damn it.

But my limbs have started to slowly heal, so within time, I should be able to get them back. I hope . . .

Hm? Oh, hello there, weird seagull. You look kind of, uh, REDdish? What's that all about?

Flap flap flap flap. Oh, another one! Is this your friend? Flap flap flap flap flap flap. Boy, uh, there, um . . . Sure are a lot of you, huh? You look just about ready to have a feast! But, erm, how come you're looking at me like that? N—now, wait just a moment, I'd actually rather you didn't come any closer. You see, I'm kind of in the middle of meditating here. It's very important to me, and it takes utmost concentration. I'm talking nobody-within-one-meter sort of concentration. And even though I do think your plumage is wonderful, I'd rather be able to keep . . .

See, this is what I mean! Standing two inches away from my face makes me feel very uncomfortable, and it isn't respectful in the least. I would like for you to—

H—hey! Stop pecking my eye! That just isn't—oh, and now you just took the whole thing. *Very* unprofessional. And the missus, too? Oh, come on, keep your kids away from my bowels, that's just—I barely had any intestines left, and now your whole family is eating it. That's just rude! Isn't it common courtesy not to take the last of something until you're sure nobody else wants it? Or am I not a part of this group?

Hey, don't turn away from me! You—damn—bird!

Craning my neck, I bite a hold of the bird's supple throat, biting through the feathers, ignoring the way it's started squawking and flapping its wings like crazy, and with just one strong bite, I completely behead it.

<Breezebird (Lv.27) Defeated.>

I toss the corpse at the rest of its family, who flap their wings and take a few steps back. But it wasn't enough, because now they're just approaching again, not caring that the head of the house is now both headless *and* houseless.

I may have neither limbs nor organs, but that doesn't make me helpless, damn it!

Another bird approaches to peck at my face and I snap my teeth at it. It takes a step back, recalibrates, and then approaches from the top of my head rather than the side. It pecks at my eyes and I can't really stop it. But I know how these birdbrains think. I open my mouth slightly and begin to wiggle my tongue like it's a worm. I don't have eyes to see it anymore, but I can smell and hear it. I take slow, calculating breaths through my nose. And once it foolishly pecks at my open mouth . . .

I bite!

My teeth clamp down on top of its head and I clench my jaw with all my strength, crushing the skull and making its soft brains splatter the inside of my mouth.

<Breezebird (Lv.25) Defeated.>

Another one down. A dozen or so left. That's doable, I think.

A lot of them are still pecking at my bowels and stumps, but some are approaching my head and face. The *worm* in my mouth is just too tempting to ignore, I guess. Slowly, one by one, I whittle down their numbers, until the final one perishes from my mouth.

<Breezebird (Lv.29) Defeated.>
<Breezebird (Lv.26) Defeated.>
<Breezebird (Lv.27) Defeated.>
<[Level Up]>
<You have reached Level 46.>
<Agility has increased by 2.
Strength has increased by 3.
Stamina has increased by 3.
Magic Power has increased by 1.
Dagger Tooth has increased by 1.
Swim has increased by 1.
Crush has increased by 1.
Blindness Resistance has increased by 1.
Evisceration Resistance has increased by 1.>

Alright. I'm lying pretty exposed here, so I should probably . . .

A beautiful song reaches me, even through my burst eardrums.

Yeah, I need to heal up so I can return to the party. Leaving the ladies all on their own is very unbecoming.

Using my head and my jaw, I drag myself toward a small hole in the rocks. There, I'm able to take some sort of shelter. There's a lot of crabs taking tiny crab-nibbles off me, but since I can just crush them by bashing my skull onto the rocks, it's fine.

<You have learned: Concussion Tolerance Lv.10>
<You have learned: Concussion Resistance Lv.1>

Yup, totally fine.

I close my eyes and meditate.

<A Canto appears to you.>
<[Along the upper rim of a high bank formed by a ring of massive broken boulders, we came above a crowd more cruelly pent.]>

Alright. Sure.

Once my arms recover, I use them to eat the crabs. I don't get any messages for doing so, which means I don't need to eat all of them, but I still do. Yummy! Very crunchy, and with a soft, surprisingly sweet inside. After some time, I recover enough to emerge and return to the party.

Staggering across the rocks, I try to regain my groove, but for some reason, the groove just isn't there. Weird. When I look down into the depths, I find that all the ladies have food in their mouths, so they can't sing. Not talking with their mouths full is far from disrespectful, but the fact that they're eating the limbs and organs they borrowed from me is very uncouth. I was expecting those to be returned, thank you very much.

One of the ladies notices me and quickly swallows a few of my fingers. She sticks her arms out of the sea, inviting me for a dance, but I've got a better idea. I'm kind of tired of always coming to visit you, so how about we take this dance—*I take her hand*—at *my* place?

Pulling her out of the water, I expose her for what she truly is. A bulbous, bony creature, with four maidenly arms emerging from the top of it, its thick, scabby tail beating furiously in the air. And now, out of the water, her singing sounds less like something a pretty lady could create and more like a hoarse blubbering from a beastly throat. Ew, gross. As she flails through the air briefly, I simply stick out my arm at her, straight, stabbing her through the chest. But as it slides in, her beastly, sharp-toothed lower mouth also bites into my shoulder, which is very unseemly for someone unwed. However, as close to her as I am now, I can finally see what she is.

<Lady Lure (Lv.43)>

Uh-huh. *Lady?* You sure about that?

Well, alright. For her crimes of being unladylike, I sentence her to death. Are all in favor? Great!

Pushing my clawed hand into the side of her head, I make a drilling motion until I get far inside to grab her neck. Fish or not, a broken neck is a broken neck. I clutch my hand hard enough to feel the bone break.

<Lady Lure (Lv.43) Defeated.>

The second she goes limp, the song sung by the other ladies turns chastising. Hey, why are you taking her side? She wasn't being respectful in the least! All I wanted to do was to invite her over to my place. Is that really so bad? Oh, damn it, these songs are just . . . !

Biting off the fingertips of both of my index fingers, I stuff them into my ears, effectively sealing out their annoying song.

Hm. That's weird. Where did the ladies go?

<You have learned: Delusion Resistance Lv.5>

Hmm. Something weird is going on.

I look down into the watery depths. A lure looks up at me.

<Lady Lure (Lv.40)>

Ah. So that's how it is.

I let my eyes go up the path of stones. Yup, still can't see where I'm supposed to be headed.

That means I've got plenty of time to do away with these lures.

I won't bore you with the details, but there's a pretty simple way to catch the lures. See, they aren't as smart as they seem. Not in the least, as a matter of fact. At first, I just did what I did with the first one by pulling them up on the rocks. This was a pretty good idea. Facing one of these things underwater is a very, very bad idea. The agility buff they have down there is ridiculous, so it's best not to even try it unless I want to wash up on the shore again without any organs or limbs. From what I can tell, they don't like eating bones, so they usually don't go for the skull, or even the neck. This is technically good for me, but it's also very annoying since it means I have to redo the whole damn thing all over again if I get caught.

After a while, though, the lures caught on to the fact that I'm not actually going to join them for a dance, so they stopped inviting me, which totally didn't hurt in the least and I took it without crying even once.

So how do I catch them, then? Well, that's very simple. I just use my own bowels as a lure. My small intestine works well as a rope, and my spleen—which I don't use anyway—is apparently yummy enough for them to bite. I use one of their own teeth as a hook, so then I just reel them back in. Easy stuff.

By the time I finally reach that damn island, there aren't any more lady lures to try to do away with me. Aside from a number of breezebirds that tried to peck me to death, there weren't any other enemies with levels, so once I took care of the breezebirds, I was finally free to try to beat the stage for real.

I step onto the small, rocky island. It can only be considered an island because it's the end of the rocky path. In terms of what it actually is, it's basically just made up of rocks, big and small, with the island itself being one big rocky outgrowth.

<Tutorial stage, Hell Difficulty Eleventh Floor: Boss Stage>
<[Clear Condition] Answer the three riddles of the tomb to put its inhabit-ant to rest.>

Tomb? What tomb?

What, is that big square rock supposed to be a tomb? Pretty weird shape, but alright.

As I approach the only structure that isn't just a sharp rock on the island, I find that it does actually have a door. Interesting. Pushing it open, I step inside.

It's dark, but I can still see, because there's a small dome-shaped window atop it, letting in a bit of light. With this light, I can see what I assume to be the tomb in question. It's really just a coffin, though, standing upright at the end of the room.

I step closer, which lets me see that there are actually a few inscriptions on the tomb itself. I can't understand what they mean, though, so I'm not sure how I'm supposed to—

<Riddle 1: [I am clad in the finest of furs, yet have killed no beast. What am I?]>

What? Uh . . . Shoot. Okay, yeah, I admit it, I've never been very good at riddles. Um . . . Wears furs, without killing anyone. Could it be a standard woman? Just a woman. A lot of women wear pelts without killing it themselves. Like, they just bought it in a shop. Totally normal.

Yeah, that's my answer. A woman.

<You have answered: A woman.>
<Incorrect!>
<The answer was: A cat.>

I . . .

You . . .

That's—

I call bullshit! What the hell, that's not even—! How the heck can you say that cats don't kill things?! Sure, it's not like they wear the furs of the things they kill, but how can that answer possibly be correct while mine isn't?! This just—

Thump. Inside the tomb, something rattles. A crack spreads across the front of the tomb. Uh. Okay, that's . . . worrying.

<Riddle 2: [I sing, and yet I have no breath. What am I?]>

Okay, okay. Let's think this through. I want to say the lady lures because they literally sang without breathing, but that's too easy. It's not going to be that. I have no idea what it'll be though, so . . . Singing, with no breath. So it's inanimate. That means . . .

Right, um, I think I know it. The answer is . . . the wind!

<You have answered: The wind.>
<Incorrect!>
<The answer was: An instrument.>

Damn it, this is bullshit! An instrument? Which instrument?! Instruments don't sing! They toot and whine and that's it! How can you sing without breath? The wind sings! It whistles and it howls and that's exactly what the wind does! And you can't say wind has a breath because you have to be alive to be able to breathe. And you kind of have to have a throat and breath to be able to sing, but apparently instruments sing, too. Absolute bullsh—

The tomb thumps again and the crack spreads farther, an ominous RED light streaming out from inside it. Sh—shoot. Okay, um . . .

<Riddle 3: [In all the world, there is only one of me. I am never seen, but always known. I hold no rallies, yet I have countless followers. What am I?]>

I'm calling my lifeline.
I open up my PMs.

<PrissyKittyPrincess[F11]: hey mole umm In all the world, there is only one of me. I am never seen, but always known. I hold no rallies, yet I have countless followers. What am I?>

Leaning back, I await a response. But within only a few seconds . . .

<Please choose your answer or it will be considered incorrect. You have 29 seconds left to answer.>

My jaw drops open. I—you—that's . . . !
I stare at my PMs. Come on, Moleman . . . ! You're always so fast with this stuff, so just be a bit quicker this time, come on, please—!

<Please choose your answer or it will be considered incorrect. You have 11 seconds left to answer.>

My mind whirls. Shoot. Shoot. Shoot. Shoot.

<Please choose your answer or it will be considered incorrect. You have 4 seconds left to answer.>

D—damn it! Okay, okay, it's the wind! I don't care anymore, so let's just say it's the wind again! That's my answer: the wind!

<You have answered: The wind.>

<Incorrect!>
<The answer was: The north wind.>

I fall to my knees.

That's it. I can't handle this anymore. Let the tutorial kill me, I don't care. I accept it. Just, please . . . let me die with dignity.

The tomb before me thumps and beats and the fiery crack begins to web across the entire tomb. A message pops up in front of my eyes.

<SuperMoleman[59]: Oh, that's a tricky one! Let me see here . . . It could be a lot of things. This is for the tomb, right? Hmm . . . How about "the north wind"? or maybe something simpler, like "direction"? It could also be a concept, like "faith," but that might be too far out. Hope this helps! Good luck! It's alright to fail one or two of the riddles, so don't worry if you get it wrong as long as you get the other ones right!>

Uh-huh. Thanks, Moleman. Appreciated.

<Riddle 1: incorrect. Riddle 2: incorrect. Riddle 3: incorrect.>
<The wrath of the Flaming Risen has been awakened.>

Ah, here we go.

The tomb bursts open with sharp bits of rock flying everywhere, one stabbing deep into my chest and breaking a rib or two, which is totally uncool. I don't know exactly what I expected the inhabitant itself to look like, but a burning skeleton wasn't exactly it. Not that I'm complaining, it looks awesome, I'm just a bit surprised, is all.

<Flaming Risen (Lv.53) [BOSS]>

Hm. Okay, I want to quickly consider the pros and cons here. First, being killed by a burning skeleton for failing to answer his riddles three is both cool and lame. I mean, burning skeleton? Awesome. Being remembered for failing three trick questions? Not quite as cool.

Oh, and I never did check out what Moleman's earlier message said. Hmm. Okay, fine, I'll fight.

I stand up, but only a second too late as the skeleton stabs his hand into my chest. My skin bursts into flames and my flesh starts to cook and I can feel it groping after my heart. Very rude. I grab onto its skeleton arm and break it off, but the skeleton hand inside my chest keeps going. Hm. That's worrisome. Also, holding the skeleton's hand is making my hands cook and char, which in turn makes my fingers curl up and close around the skeleton's arm, so I can't even let go. Not good.

In a fight like this, I can't exactly afford to lose both of my arms, so I keep my grip on it. I have no idea if this skeleton can be beaten through normal means, but that doesn't actually matter too much. I have more than just normal means to work with, after all.

Still gripping it, I activate touch of reverse tolerance.

<[TOUCH OF REVERSED FRACTURE TOLERANCE (LV.7)]>
<[TOUCH OF REVERSED DIVINITY TOLERANCE (LV.7)]>
<[TOUCH OF REVERSED DROWNING TOLERANCE (LV.7)]>
<[TOUCH OF REVERSED COLD TOLERANCE (LV.7)]>
<[TOUCH OF REVERSED BLUNT TOLERANCE (LV.7)]>
<[TOUCH OF REVERSED OXYGEN DEFICIENCY TOLERANCE (LV.7)]>
<[TOUCH OF REVERSED FEVER TOLERANCE (LV.7)]>
<[TOUCH OF REVERSED HYPOTHERMIA TOLERANCE (LV.7)]>
<[TOUCH OF REVERSED BALANCE NAUSEA TOLERANCE (LV.7)]>
<[TOUCH OF REVERSED ACID TOLERANCE (LV.7)]>

<YOU HAVE LEARNED:
TOUCH OF REVERSED TOLERANCE LV.8>

The skeleton's flames flicker and it starts to crack here and there. But I'm far from done.

<[TOUCH OF REVERSED FRACTURE TOLERANCE (LV.8)]>
<[TOUCH OF REVERSED DIVINITY TOLERANCE (LV.8)]>
<[TOUCH OF REVERSED DROWNING TOLERANCE (LV.8)]>
<[TOUCH OF REVERSED COLD TOLERANCE (LV.8)]>
<[TOUCH OF REVERSED BLUNT TOLERANCE (LV.8)]>
<[TOUCH OF REVERSED OXYGEN DEFICIENCY TOLERANCE (LV.8)]>
<[TOUCH OF REVERSED FEVER TOLERANCE (LV.8)]>
<[TOUCH OF REVERSED HYPOTHERMIA TOLERANCE (LV.8)]>
<[TOUCH OF REVERSED BALANCE NAUSEA TOLERANCE (LV.8)]>
<[TOUCH OF REVERSED ACID TOLERANCE (LV.8)]>

That was apparently enough, as the bones I hold my hands turn brittle enough for me to crush it fully. The flames don't even cover the entire skeleton anymore but rather only its head alone. So that's where it's coming from, huh?

Since my hands are curled anyway, I just clench them fully. Time to punch some skeleton.

And I'm just about to do so when I feel something hot and burning clutch around my still-beating heart. Oh, yeah, that hand is still in there, isn't it?

My mind speeds up to subsonic levels and I throw my punch, right at its cracked and weakened skull.

With a loud crack, right as I feel its hand tighten around my heart, I punch my hand straight through its skull.

<Flaming Risen (Lv.53) [BOSS] Defeated.>
<[Level Up]>
<You have reached Level 49.>
<Agility has increased by 2.
Strength has increased by 2.
Stamina has increased by 4.
Magic Power has increased by 1.
Dagger Nails has increased by 1.
Hit has increased by 1.
Burn Resistance has increased by 1.
Heat Resistance has increased by 1.>

The grip around my heart weakens. The skeleton turns to dust before my eyes and so does the hand still in my chest.

<You have cleared the eleventh floor.>
<You have received 1,000 points for clearing the floor. You have received an additional 1,000 points for being the first to clear the floor.>
<For clearing the stage completely, you will receive an additional reward.>
<To repay your debt, the additional reward has been traded for 5,000 points.>
<6 Gods have shown a positive response to you. You have obtained 6,000 points.>
<42 Gods have shown a negative response to you. 42,000 points have been deducted.>
<To repay your debt, the floor clear reward has been traded for 1,000 points.>

Hey, wait a sec! I thought you guys liked me now? What did I do this time?! This is—

FLOOR 12

THE RIVER OF BOILING BLOOD

Mi—/Hydra

—ridiculous! Oh, I'm back here. Yeah, of course I am. Always back here, always . . . !

<To repay your debt, your inventory has been sold for 121 points.>

Oh, yeah, I did grab a fair bit of lady lure parts. You know . . . just for the sake of it.

<Current debt: 47,107 points.>

Really? One floor, and I'm back here again? I hate this place. Even if I *did* get out of debt and escape skid row, the second I inevitably beat a floor—or better yet: *die*—I get sent straight back to the pits. I *want* to buy food and clothing and weapons and magic books and ropes and tools and whatever else is in there, but I just can't. And even if I could, it would eventually get sold off anyway. This place sucks. Should I just go die?

Nah. Then the gods would win. Can't allow that. I need to prove them wrong. This difficulty *is* beatable, and that's final.

<Top—Status—Community>
<00:04:38 Day 271>
<The eleventh attempt will begin in 29:23:55:42>
<The twelfth floor will open in 23:49:30>

Huh? The tenth attempt has already begun? Did I really spend almost two weeks on floor eleven . . . ? I want to say it's weird, but I also can't remember a lot of what happened on that floor, so . . . Yeah. Time is weird.

Anyway, you know how this goes by now. I'll just strut around and paint this here room, and you'll . . . hang around? Is that okay with you? Yeah, alright.

If you ask me, this talking-to-you deal is at least half a step up from keeping a diary. I am not a wimp. I detest that description of me.

Hm. I wonder . . .

As I go about making the room pretty, I check the apostleship thing.

<WANT APOSTLESHIP TRIALS PROGRESS: 2/365>
<COWARDICE APOSTLESHIP TRIALS PROGRESS: 1/23>

Hey, they went up! Interesting. I have no idea how or why, though, so I'll hold off on making any theories until later. That said, the room is nice and RED, so now it's only a matter of waiting until the timer ticks down. And, as it always is, it eventually does.

<Floor 12 has opened. Do you want to enter?>
<Yes/No>

Duh, of course I do.

Casually, I press *Yes*.

The second I enter the floor, I feel a sweltering heat assault me. It's worse than a sauna. As soon as my body starts to understandably sweat, it instantly evaporates, leaving me even more exposed than before. The culprit is obvious enough for me to not instantly assume that I've been teleported inside a volcano. Namely, I'm standing right in front of a river of boiling, bubbling, churning RED blood. I know it's blood. I can smell it. There's no smell like blood.

<Tutorial stage, Hell Difficulty Twelfth Floor: The River of Boiling Blood>
<[Clear Condition] Wade across the river to reach the other side.>

Boiling blood is a very accurate description of what I'm looking at, but it feels like the description is hampered by the fact that it isn't *just* boiling blood. To be specific, it is far from empty. I can't count them exactly, but the river is crowded by shades of RED, all covered in dried and caked blood. Each and every single one of them is either fighting the others, snarling and spitting like beasts, clawing and spilling more blood to feed the river, or they're apathetically floating in it, either by staring up at the BLACK, formless sky with unblinking eyes, or with their faces deep in the blood. I have no idea if the latter ones are dead or not. All of them have the same level as I do, though.

I have to go through . . . *this*? Seriously? And, since I want to completely clear the floor, I'll also have to defeat *all* of them? Really?

Well, okay. It's not like I have any choice, right?

So even though the mere heat is making me dizzy, I step toward the river. It's broad but not especially strong. Silently, I enter it. They don't exactly turn on me as one, but the ones closest to me aren't shy about dragging me into their own squabble. And I—being equally bold—join them.

It's pretty easy to kill myself. After all, I know my own weaknesses. My heat and drowning resistances aren't very high, and I can't survive for long without a heart. My spine is still important to my bodily functions, and so is my brain. Breaking my neck works wonders. Evisceration—not so much.

<Shade (Lv.49) Defeated.>
<Shade (Lv.49) Defeated.>
<Shade (Lv.50) Defeated.>
<Shade (Lv.50) Defeated.>
<Shade (Lv.50) Defeated.>

I fight on. It's pretty simple once you get into it. Sometimes I get myself mixed up with the shades because we smell the same and look the same and sound the same and feel the same but that's alright. We don't taste the same. It's hard to find a moment of stillness to skin a few of them, but it works out in the end.

I fight on.

<Shade (Lv.50) Defeated.>
<Shade (Lv.51) Defeated.>
<Shade (Lv.51) Defeated.>

I fight on.

I fight on.

I fight on and on and on and on and on and on and on and on and on and on and on and on and on.

<Shade (Lv.51) Defeated.>
<Shade (Lv.51) Defeated.>
<Shade (Lv.51) Defeated.>
<Shade (Lv.51) Defeated.>
<Shade (Lv.52) Defeated.>
<Shade (Lv.52) Defeated.>
<Shade (Lv.52) Defeated.>
<Shade (Lv.52) Defeated.>
<Shade (Lv.53) Defeated.>
<Shade (Lv.53) Defeated.>

Everything is RED and RED and RED and RED.

Everything looks like RED and smells like RED and sounds like RED and feels like RED and tastes like RED.

If I get too hot I dunk myself in the boiling blood, and the brief coolness of the blood evaporating keeps me going.

After some time, I realize that I forgot to kill the me's floating in the blood without fighting.

But I just kill those too. They're easier. They don't fight.

I kill I kill I kill I kill I kill I kill I kill I.

<Shade (Lv.53) Defeated.>
<Shade (Lv.53) Defeated.>
<Shade (Lv.53) Defeated.>
<Shade (Lv.53) Defeated.>
<Shade (Lv.53) Defeated.>
<Shade (Lv.54) Defeated.>
<Shade (Lv.54) Defeated.>

And then I get to the other side.

As I step out of the blood, my whole body is RED and crunchy and some bits of me are half-cooked but that's okay. Because right now, I've got bigger problems.

<Tutorial stage, Hell Difficulty Twelfth Floor: Boss Stage>
<[Clear Condition] Escape the minotaur.>

Which I would do if there *were* a minotaur. But there isn't. I'm just here, and there isn't anything else. So, like . . . What now?

<Error! [BOSS] missing. Recalibrating . . .>
<[Clear Condition] Escape the hydra.>

Hydra? Hey, wait just a minute, a hydra and a minotaur are *very* different— Oh. There's a hydra here, now.

<Hydra (Lv.59) [BOSS]>

Ah. Yeah, uh . . . I see how it is.

Turning around, I run back into the river. It's littered with corpses, but the five-headed hydra doesn't seem to mind as it leaps in right alongside me.

But it's not like I'm actually trying to escape. No, it just so happens that the river is a lot better for me to fight in. As I expected, the hydra doesn't seem too hot on the heat, but that won't kill it. However, I happen to know something that probably will.

As soon as we're both in the river, I dive down and start swimming. From above, the large hydra can't possibly see me, smell me, or even feel me. I'm basically invisible. But I can remember where it is. Swimming around it, I get close enough to latch onto one of its back legs, where I instantly go for the hamstrings and the heel, chewing through so fast that it doesn't even have time to react before its leg goes down for the count. And then, as one of its heads begins to blindly snap at me through the blood, I jump off and swim for the next leg, where I repeat the process. Now it's on its knees, most of its belly exposed to the blood. I *could go* for it straightaway, but that's too easy.

Instead, I go for its arms. One of its heads succeeds in grabbing hold of one of my legs, but I'm willing to sacrifice it. Like a lizard severing its tail, I simultaneously break and slash along my thigh until the whole thing pops off. I'm bleeding like crazy, but it's not like I'll die, so, eh.

Then I go back into the blood and remove the support of its arms, forcing the whole body of the hydra to fall into the blood, each and every one of its five heads screeching in pain. Apparently, though, it's a bit more pragmatic than I originally thought, because it decides to sacrifice four of its heads to keep a bit of its body above the blood. But that just gives me four heads to bite off.

As I now find out, the hydra is not the sort that is capable of growing out its heads. If it were, I'd probably be screwed, so I'm glad that that is the case.

With its only supports gone, the body of the hydra falls into the blood.

And now, I finally stand up and out of the blood. I'm not sure which tolerance to thank, but as I've discovered, I can currently hold my breath for well over twenty minutes. Neat, huh? Anyway, the final head of the hydra is growling up at me, but I kind of don't care.

Hm. This hide . . . It's way too nice to give away to the system. Yeah, I need to be able to keep this. Walking around the hydra, I grab hold of its tail and drag it up onto land, where I start skinning it and dissecting it bit by bit. The meat will get sold anyway, so I make sure to munch it. The whole river-of-boiling-blood thing means that some parts are actually cooked, which is extremely yummy. Warm food! Delightful.

After an hour or so, I finally have the whole skin in my inventory, at which point I give the hydra its final beheading.

<Hydra (Lv.59) [BOSS] Defeated.>
<[Level Up]>
<You have reached Level 55.>
<Agility has increased by 2.
Strength has increased by 4.

Stamina has increased by 2.
Magic Power has increased by 1.
Disassemble has increased by 1.
Burn Resistance has increased by 1.
Heat Resistance has increased by 1.
Oxygen Deficiency Protection has increased by 1.
Drowning Resistance has increased by 1.>
<You have cleared the twelfth floor.>
<You have received 1,000 points for clearing the floor. You have received an additional 1,000 points for being the first to clear the floor.>
<For clearing the stage completely, you will receive an additional reward.>
<To repay your debt, the additional reward has been traded for 5,000 points.>
<5 Gods have shown a positive response to you. You have obtained 5,000 points.>
<45 Gods have shown a negative response to you. 45,000 points have been deducted.>
<To repay your debt, the floor clear reward has been traded for 1,000 points.>

Even fewer this time, huh? I don't know why I would expect anything else. Still, it's nice to get a level up. I guess this is when the floor—

FLOOR 13

THE WEEPING WOODS

XI

Enemy

—closes. Yeah, thanks, very appreciated. And now, we'll get the message about my inventory. Go on, don't be shy. How much did my own flesh go for? It's okay, I'm brave. I can hear it. I picked up a lot of my own skulls and hands, I'll have you know.

<To repay your debt, your inventory has been sold for 1 point.>

I purse my lips. Yup. Yeah. That's . . . I'm not upset. Why should I be upset that all my shade stuff only sold for one point? That would be silly, haha! Y—yeah, really silly . . . Sniffle . . .

<Current debt: 79,106 points.>

Okay, so, one more floor and I'll be right back where I started? Doing that favor for the gods meant nothing? Wow. This really is such a wonderful world, isn't it? You know, maybe—just maybe—I'd be able to act in your graces if I actually knew what it was you didn't like me doing? How can you fault me for completing the stage requirements that *you* made?

Ugh, I hate these gods . . .

Hm. Hang on a second—I just now remembered that I forgot to check Moleman's message! That's weird, I was so interested in reading it, too . . . Well, better late than never, I guess.

Let's see here . . .

<SuperMoleman[F63]: Wow, interesting stuff! I'm surprised you would ask for information, but I'm beyond glad to hear that you did. This is far

more detailed than what the Easy Difficulty admin told me, especially regarding the purpose of the tutorial. All of this about apostles and the God of Kings is completely new to me, so I'll be sure to ask the Easy admin about it once I complete the second task of Lust. Oh, and since you might not be familiar with how the Purgatory stage works, erm . . . It's not what it sounds like, okay? A shame you were only allowed to ask five questions, but the ones you asked were very good, if you ask me. I mean, angels? I didn't even know Gods had them, so . . . Very interesting. Thank you for telling me! If it's okay with you, I would love to write an official post with this information. The other servers will also no doubt be overjoyed to hear about it.>

I feel cold sweat break out across my back. Okay, so, um . . . This was the kind of message asking for a reply, huh? Well, gee, that's, um . . .

Now I just feel bad. I can't believe I forgot to read this before going into floor twelve. What the heck was going through my mind? Sometimes, I barely recognize myself. Now that I think about it, I'm still covered in dried, caked blood, but . . . That can wait.

I pull up a PM and start typing.

<PrissyKittyPrincess[F13]: hey mole sry i forgt 2 respond bt um ya sure spred it or wtvr is cool>

I hope that's enough. If it isn't, I'll just have to apologize in person the next time we meet.

<You have received a message>

I click the pop-up faster than greased lightning.

<SuperMoleman[F63]: No worries, thanks for the permission! I'm certain you've had your hands full with the last two stages. I'll be sure to credit you for the information! Good luck with the next floor. It's a bit tricky, but I don't think it should be much trouble!>

Right, great, wonderful. That isn't foreboding at all.

<PrissyKittyPrincess[F13]: thx u2>

Alright. Mission: successful. Hearing Moleman describe it as a bit tricky worries me since I'm not very good with tricks, but I should be able to brute-force my way through somehow. At this point, that's my only real option. Before that, though, I need to clean myself. How am I supposed to face monsters and animals while covered head-to-toe in RED? I look ridiculous!

Also, just for the sake of it, I take a quick look at my stats.

<Top—Status—Community>
<PrissyKittyPrincess
Human Level 55
Agility: 159
Strength: 99
Stamina: 181
Magic Power: 63>

Lookin' good. Now, about the RED . . .

After carefully licking off all the blood, I remember that this room is bad, so I take an hour or so to paint it properly. You all know the routine by now. Since the next floor apparently has an unknown number of tricks in store, I train up my drowning resistance by expertly poking holes in the inside of my throat to flood it with blood. And then, just for the sake of it, I train my concussion resistance by repeatedly bashing my head into one of the many pillars.

<Floor 13 has opened. Do you want to enter?>
<Yes/No>

Once the message finally pops up, I at first assume it's a hallucination brought on by the whole bashing-my-head-into-a-pillar thing. Thankfully, I recognize it just in time to press Yes before it automatically chooses for me.

It isn't just my head that whirls as I stumble forward; the world around me shifting from RED to a dark grayish within moments. A strong wind almost brings me back onto my feet, but it isn't strong enough to counteract my wind resistance, so I still end up falling and face-planting on the ground. Eughh. Yeah, that's a good start. I can feel the pebbles and dirt between my teeth . . .

Grumbling to no one in particular, I push myself to my feet. This place is . . . ?

<Tutorial stage, Hell Difficulty Thirteenth Floor: The Weeping Woods>
<[Clear Condition] Make it through the weeping woods to reach the tower of ash.>

It almost looks like the forest of the fourth floor, but I can't say for sure, because—for one—I can actually see this floor. It's a big leafless forest. All that's above us is a dreary gray sky, but it isn't especially dark, so I don't think it's night-time. Will this floor have the passing of time? I have no idea.

That said, the forest itself is honestly completely overshadowed by a tiny little detail that is actively making my skin crawl.

All that I can hear, even louder than the whine of the wind, is loud weeping and sniffling and sobbing and wailing. That's all. It's ever-present, and it sounds like it's being made by several hundred people, all at once, everywhere around me. Some close by, others far away, all in their own tempo and tone. Some are wailing so loudly they can be heard from several kilometers away; others are simply sniffling and weeping, almost in complete silence.

But I can't see anyone. I can't smell anyone. Not a single human or goblin is present for miles around. However, even in the absence of actual humans or goblins, I can still smell blood.

It's not coming from me, but I smell it as though it were only meters away. Everywhere around. The whole forest is filled with the scent of blood. But most closely, I can smell it coming from that tree over there. It isn't very big. Its swirling bark is rugged and scarred as though it's been clawed at by beasts and its branches are crooked and jut out in random directions without any clear sense of purpose. I step close to it. It doesn't smell like a tree at all.

In the trunk of the tree, I can see a gaping hole, just beneath two hollow openings. Through that hole, a low, mellow moan can be heard, painfully rasping out of the wood. What is—

A clawed foot like that of a massive bird snakes around the trunk of the tree, gouging deep gashes through the bark. From those gashes, RED blood seeps in the place of sap.

I stare in stunned silence as a goblinlike creature, with the wings and under-body of a massive bird but the torso and head of a female goblin, cranes around the side of the tree.

<Harpy (Lv.41)>

I'm less surprised by the appearance of the harpy than I am by the fact that the loud sobbing and wailing is coming not from the tree, but from her. Never-ending tears stream down her face, briefly washing away some of the blood that stains her mouth and the front of her chest. A single whiff of her scent makes me acutely aware that apart from the blood-filled trees, the entire forest is filled with nothing but harpies.

Her flaming eyes look me up and down. "Meat? Meat?" she squawks, her voice hoarse from the crying and screaming. I take a step back. She reluctantly detaches herself from the tree and goes onto the ground. But she doesn't walk like a bird does. Even though her legs are double-jointed like those of a bird, she has the entire lower part planted firmly on the ground, as though she were walking on normal feet.

Fanged jaw trembling, she reaches out her bloodied feathers toward me, like a beggar asking for spare change. "Meat? Please, let me have your flesh, only an arm will do! Please, I beg of you. Whatever creature you are, from whatever clan you herald, let me have some of your flesh so that I needn't feed off Petyr anymore!"

In firm confusion, I can do nothing more than continue taking steps back, away from her. But she's as persistent as a beggar, and for some reason, she won't attack me. She's just stepping closer. Why ask when you can take? As soon as she attacks, I'll fight back. Not when she's just approaching me, though. She isn't doing anything. Why won't she attack?

"Please. Please," she whimpers, and she was probably about to say something else, but an overhead flock of massive, screeching birds stops her in her tracks. Oh, no, wait, it's not birds—it's harpies. Big difference. "No, no," she whispers in terror, and before I can gather myself to ask her what the big deal is, she backs up to the tree she was previously feeding off, placing her back against it and her wings spread wide. Her eyes bore into me. "Hide!" she whisper-shouts. "Hide before they get here!"

Hide? From what? Those guys up there? I look up. The harpies are circling high above us, their bright yellow eyes staring down as one. I barely even have time to wonder what they're trying to accomplish when they suddenly swoop down in one large cluster, descending on me and the other harpy. I look back down at her, and her eyes are so urgent that without really thinking about it, I crouch down into the fetal position and roll over to one of the nearby trees. Now that I look closer, this one also has what could maybe be described as a face, but when I cut one of its roots, it won't bleed. I think it's dead.

With a mighty flapping, the swarm of harpies descends on us, most of them landing in the nearby trees, perching in the dead, leafless branches. However, one of them, just slightly larger than the others, lands right in the middle of the small clearing, in front of the first harpy and her tree.

"Lilette," the large harpy greets her with a heavy voice. "We've come for him. I asked you before and I will ask you again—give him over, or we will take you both to the same grave."

"Never!" the harpy—apparently named Lilette—cries. "You'll suck him dry and kill him within days. I cannot give my love to you bloodsuckers!"

"Tut tut," the large harpy coos. "Nobody loves a hypocrite. If you give him to us, we will let you join our ambush. Wouldn't that be nice? It'll happen sooner or later anyway. Within time, he'll be nothing but dead bark and dry roots. When that happens, should you not be one of us, we will simply make food out of you, instead. Unlike some, we don't differentiate between the blood and the flesh."

"I still won't let you have him," Lilette says firmly, her face set in powerful resolve. "I don't care if I'll eventually die. When that happens, I will die with him."

The large harpy gives an exaggerated sigh and the harpies in the treetops lean closer, mouths drooling, feathers furling. "In that case," the large harpy says, "why not do it now rather than later?"

The harpies all around draw closer. Lilette, in contrast, takes a step back, pressing herself even closer to the painfully groaning tree.

Alright, I guess this is about a good time to step in.

In complete silence, I roll up behind the large harpy.

<Harpy (Lv.58)>

Fun fact, most creatures have a very big weak spot situated on their back, and it's called *their back*. If you attack someone there, they can easily be critted and stunned depending on where you hit them. So, of course, this is what I aimed for.

Popping up behind the harpy, I stab both hands into her lower back. She squawks in pain and surprise, which is an interesting sound considering that she spoke perfectly mere seconds ago, but whatever. Grabbing her spine in one hand, I use the other to push her to the ground. This is a very good position for me to harm her maximally.

Once she is well on the ground, I crush her spine in my hand, and using the other, I tear up her throat. Very effective.

"Release her!" someone screeches, and I'm only barely able to swirl around in time to watch one of the many other harpies come barreling into me, her claws digging deep into my bowels. The both of us go flying all roly-poly, but I'm able to get a good grip on her throat even as we're rolling around. Tearing it up is no big deal, but the price of it is that while I'm squabbling with this featherbrain, the large harpy has started trying to take to flight, her paralyzed legs hanging limply.

<Harpy (Lv.48) Defeated.>

Oh, no you don't!

Running toward her I leap into the air with enough momentum and speed to be able to hook my clawed fingers into her soft belly, tearing a huge gash through which her organs spill out indiscriminately. It's actually kind of gross, but with her disemboweled as she is, she won't get far even by flying.

I let go of her and fall down right on top of another harpy that was apparently in pursuit. With strange hunger, she instantly starts biting into my bowels, eating and eating like she hasn't been fed for years or something. Still, her ravenous appetite is only a weakness in this moment, as it gives me ample opportunity to break both her wings and send us both flailing down to the ground. Since I'm on top of her, I can feel very closely how her ribs snap like glow sticks the second we hit the ground, her breath and half of my liver getting choked out of her in equal measure.

Almost casually, I rip out her throat.

<Harpy (Lv.50) Defeated.>

Alright, let's see how many we have le—

Before I'm even able to finish the thought, about five harpies descend on me as one, ripping and tearing at my flesh with talons of steel. But their legs are weak and thin and with only one well-placed clutch of the hand, I'm able to completely handicap them. By rolling into the fetal position, I briefly disorient them before leaping at the back of one of them, stabbing my hand through the back of her head and into her skull in one strike.

<You have learned: Stab Lv.1>

That sounds like the kind of skill that only a weapon would be able to use, but if I can get it for this, then I don't see the problem.

"E-e-escape! Escape! It'll kill us all!" one of the random harpies screeches, taking to the air rather than attacking me. Bad move for her, though, because while in the air, it's very easy for me to grab one of her legs to pull her back on the ground. And maybe also to bash her head into said ground, too.

Nonetheless, despite my efforts, a few of the harpies are able to escape with their lives intact. Though, of course, not all of them. Counting the corpses, I think I was able to defeat about a dozen and a half of them. Not bad, but I wish I'd been able to kill all of them. Well, I've got an entire attempt to do this floor, so it's no biggie.

I turn toward Lilette and the tree.

She visibly blanches as I look at her. "Wh—what are you?" she asks, her voice trembling. "Do you understand me? Did—did you save me on purpose . . . ?"

Hmmm . . . Now, what to do with this one? Since I must be wary of tricks, I'll need to figure out this floor properly. So far, I have no idea what's happening, so I kind of need someone to tell me. For some reason, she seems to treasure that weird tree, so if I just take it hostage, she'll probably tell me whatever I need to know.

Before that, though, her wings are an eyesore. I can't have her flying off on me, can I?

I casually approach her. She inches herself closer to the tree, her bright yellow eyes trembling in completely unfounded fear.

"P—please," she says. "Don't hurt him. I'll do whatever you ask of me, so, please . . . Spare him."

I grab her left wing and bend it in two ways at once, eliciting a nice, loud *crack*! I had expected Lilette to cry out in pain or something, but instead she's just biting her lip hard enough to draw blood. Interesting. I break the other one, too, and the only response she gives is a hissing, nasal breath. Now she can't escape.

Hunching my back a little more, I bring my face to the level of her trembling eyes. "If you even think about escaping," I tell her firmly, "I will remove all the bark off this dumb tree and make you eat it and then I'll pluck every feather from your bosom to make a new bark for this here tree so it'll survive the winter without you because you'll die of unrelated causes still directly linked to the mutilation in store for you. Got it?" Her head jerks up and down and I take that as a yes. "Good! Okay, so, I have a few questions I'd like to ask, and after that, I'll probably kill you. Is that alright?"

She blinks at me. New, fresh tears stream down her face. "P—please, spare him—"

"Okay, see, that's question one," I say, holding up my index finger. "Why are you calling this dumb inanimate arboreal nitwit a *he*? What's up with that? Are you dumb or did you just not pay attention in tree class?"

She squeezes her eyes shut before slowly opening them again. Since she doesn't seem especially willing to answer, I point my clawed index finger at the patch of bark right next to her head, and in one swift movement, I stab my finger into the wood down to the second knuckle.

<You have learned: Stab Lv.2>

Eww, it's all warm inside! Gross. I pull out my finger and find it broken and slightly mangled, but that's an easy fix. Sticking it into my mouth, I bite it off fully and swallow it down. The whole thing took less than five seconds, and by the end of it, when I turn my attention back to Lilette, she makes a sound I wouldn't be surprised to hear coming from a startled rabbit.

"H—he's—Petyr, he's—um . . ." Her eyes frantically move from the blood-spurting hole beside her head to my bleeding hand to the bloodstained ground and then back up to my face. Ah, she's crying again. It's starting to annoy me for some reason. But before I can tell her not to, she swallows down a lump and says, "Two years ago, I and Petyr had recently been betrothed to each other. As part of our vows, we made an offering and a prayer to the God of Attachment, but . . . but the witch of ash must have heard us."

Suddenly, her face perks up and she looks at me with such fierceness that I almost do a double take. "She's a jealous witch! She heard our love, and she despised us for it, as she has despised every unhappy inhabitant of these horrid woods. So she transformed us. With a cruel spell, she turned Petyr into a twisted tree capable of feeling only pain, and me into a horrible harpy, who can feed on nothing but flesh and blood!"

Transformed? "What were you before?"

"Before . . . ?" Her brows furrow at me. "Why, of course, we were normal goblins. Though, at the time, we could not be thankful for this, and like all others, we foolishly cursed the God of Goblins! Ah, now, as I love, I understand why He should choose to love the Goddess of Dragons, even though our kind are mortal enemies!"

"Okay, so, to recap . . . You used to be goblins, and then an evil witch transformed you into harpies and trees."

She scoffs self-derogatorily. "When you put it like that, it almost sounds like a wolf tale. Then again, in a sense, that's what it used to be. There's a story about these woods. An army heading to the nearby kingdom of Ret-inn stopped to rest, not knowing that a witch had made her tower here, and when she heard them lamenting over how they missed their lovers from back home, she decided to curse them for . . . I can't remember if it was that she was jealous or that she despised their lack of patriotism, but now that I'm here, I believe it was mere, petty jealousy." Her eyes turn muddy with memories. Then she looks up to me. "But what are you? Why have you foolishly entered these woods?"

I purse my lips at her. "So you don't have any idea about the fact that you're in a floor?"

Her face twists in confusion. "A . . . floor?" She looks down at the ground. "No, I'm not . . . Why would I be in . . . ?"

Hm. Pointing to the ground, I say, "This is the thirteenth floor in the tutorial. I'm here to beat the floor by going over to that tower you talked about and then probably killing the witch."

Her face lights up in hope and her lower lip begins to tremble. "R—really? Is that true? Have you truly come to save us all, to undo this horrible curse of bitter jealousy? Please, let me help you! Without my wings, I may not be able to fly, but I will do anything to see that horrible witch killed! I could ask for nothing m—"

Casually, I reach out my hand and grip her throat, squeezing it just enough to silence her. She gacks and gags for a few seconds, but just one stern look is enough to quiet her down. "Listen, that's a very sweet thing to offer and all, but I'm trying to completely clear the floor, right? You're not familiar with gamer terms so I guess that doesn't mean all that much to you, but it basically means that I've got to defeat all the enemies that come my way."

"E—enemies?" she chokes out.

"Yeah, *enemies*. So, basically, anything that's got a level is an enemy and needs to die, hopefully by my hand."

She seems like she wants to say something, and since I'm such a lovely, merciful guy, I release my choke hold on her just slightly to let her speak. "Wh—what do you mean by level . . . ?"

I blink at her. Huh. I . . . hadn't thought about that. "You can't . . . ?" I point to the space above my head, where she should realistically see my level and race. "Can you not see levels? Don't you have a system?"

"I—I don't understand what—" Since I don't need to hear any more on that, I squeeze her throat shut again. Hm, interesting. So only the challengers have a system and can see levels? Interesting. And, to make things even more interesting, not every enemy I meet knows that they're even in the tutorial to begin with. The shades know, and so did the gorgons, but I doubt the goblins on the third floor knew that.

So, what decides it?

I look back at Lilette to find her face turning a strange shade of blue and her eyes bugging out weirdly. Oh, right, I'm choking her. I let up on my grip a little and she draws in a large, rasping breath, her eyes returning to their normal state. "Haah, haah, haah . . ." she pants. After a second or so, her eyes widen just slightly, and with mechanical movements, she turns to look at me. "D—do I have a level . . . ?"

"Yup," I reply simply. "Level forty-one."

From being deep green due to the strangulation, her face almost instantly turns pale. It's an interesting turn, and just for the sake of it, I try strangling her for a minute or so to make her face dark green again, but then when I undo it, she doesn't turn pale again. Shame.

With my grip released, she speaks again, her voice hoarse and raspy. "D—does . . . Does Petyr . . . have a level . . . ?"

"Uhh," I say. Arching my neck, I look at the tree.

Weird, I don't even get a pop-up for it. That would almost suggest that it isn't even alive anymore, but I can't know that for sure, so, eh. "Nope, no level."

The words bring surprising relief to her as she gives a long sigh, but it was apparently too much on her sore throat, as she begins coughing and gasping. After a few seconds, she's able to pull herself together enough to speak, her eyes filling up with tears again. "Oh, thank the Gods, thank Them all . . . In that case—"

"Ah, but I'll still probably kill them, 'cause this whole area is pretty big, so if I can't kill all the harpies by the end of this attempt, I'll probably have to set a fire and try to take them out like that, which wouldn't be very good since I don't get as much exp from secondhand kills, but I still got to do it 'cause otherwise I won't completely clear it." I look down at her. "You understand, right?"

I don't think I've ever seen a face show even a single fraction of the despair that I now see on Lilette's face. It's a marvel, really, but I don't have time to fully absorb it before she snarls like a beast, her eyes flashing and her clawed feet shooting up to gouge a massive slash along the side of my face. However, on account of her wings being crippled, this desperate attack only sends her flying to the ground, her ferocious talons losing power halfway through my face and therefore unable to cause any lasting damage. Since she's already presented her legs to me, it takes barely any effort for me to just grab them out of the air, leaving her upper body to dangle mere inches above the ground.

"R—release me, you damned beas—"

Since she's asking so nicely for it, I break both of her legs before letting her down. Hissing in pain, she squirms on the ground. I stomp my foot onto her exposed chest if only to keep her from uselessly writhing any more than she already is. A rib or two cracks beneath my foot and she jerks in pain. "You done with your temper tantrum?" I ask, looking down at her.

Her eyes bore into me, burning with tears. "You're a monster," she snarls. "You're worse than a dragon. A dragon at least kills quickly. Their teeth bite down and then you're gone, but you . . . !" She grinds her teeth. "I don't care if you were sent by the Gods Themselves. Whatever it is that you are, you are worse than the witch. She acts on emotion. Emotion, I understand. But you . . . !" Her face twists in disgust. "You're below that. You're a monster! A *demon*."

Derecho. That was the goblin word for *demon*, wasn't it?

I look down at her. At her bald head and her green skin and her yellow eyes. "I—I'm not a demon," I say faintly. "I'm just following the floor clear requirements. It's not like I have a choice, so . . ."

She glares up at me with eyes of yellow fire.

So stop looking at me like that. Like I'm just doing this for fun. Like I *want* to hurt you. Like I don't care. Like the city didn't *need* to burn. Like I had a choice in any of this. Like I really am a demon.

Like I'm not your friend.

My chest feels tight and hollow and I look down at the enemy below me and I feel my foot start to press down, farther and farther, grinding my heel into the enemy's flesh, pushing and pushing and pushing and pushing and I can feel bones break and shatter and crack and snap and yet the enemy won't make a sound and won't stop glaring at me so I keep pressing down and down and down until the hard gives way to the soft and the crunch becomes soft and soft and my foot sinks into the enemy flesh and into the skin and I feel organs being pushed aside but not that one not the one that beats softly, slowly, carefully, as though it knows, as though it *wants* me to defeat it, to gain a level, to gain exp and maybe a new skill and to get one step closer to clear completion, and I feel this organ, the heart, the heart of it all, being squeezed just beneath my toes, and I look into the eyes of the enemy, but the enemy isn't looking at me with the fury of a thousand lovers anymore; it's looking at the roots of the tree right next to me, its broken, trembling wing reaching out to touch the scarred bark, and for some reason, it almost looks as though the tree is reaching out to the enemy, too, so I push down again, one final push, one final press, and the heart bursts beneath my foot and the enemy stops moving.

<Harpy (Lv.41) Defeated.>

Haah, haah, haah . . .

I didn't . . . get a level up . . . Not even for a skill.

I step off the body. Looking up, I find the tree looking at me, through hollow holes. It isn't moaning and groaning anymore. Maybe it's happy that its tormentor is dead. As I stare into its hollows, some sort of liquid rolls out of them, slipping in between the grooves and coils of the scarred bark. Like clear sap. What, are you crying or something? Why? For this—this . . . *monster*? Look at it! It's got nothing but sharp claws and sharp teeth! What's there to mourn over?

Or maybe that's just something trees do.

But for some reason, looking at this tree stupidly crying while still being all silent is getting me riled up. There's no reason for it to look at me like that when I'm only doing what must be done. What's wrong with making a few sacrifices for the greater good? Nothing! That's exactly it.

I step up to the tree. Planting a hand on it, I mentally recoil at the feeling of its warm bark. It's appalling.

I'll tell you what—if *I* were transformed into a tree, and a harpy kept screaming into my ear, and wailing and whining, and *also* cutting me up to drink my blood, and some friendly chap came around and took care of that annoying miser, you know what I'd be happy for that lovely fellow to do next?

Smiling to myself, I stab my hand into the trunk, jimmying it between the bark itself and the wood. And then I just peel off a bit. Blood is flowing in pints and gallons, but that's all part of the procedure. Once I've got a nice bit of bark peeled, I tear it off the trunk and give it a bite. It's lukewarm and tastes mostly like wood, though the added bit of blood gives it a very strange taste and texture. It isn't exactly bad, but I'm not very interested in eating any more of it.

With my tuppence taken, I begin chewing and scratching at the exposed wood. I had expected this to take way longer, but the fact that the wood was softened by so much blood made it quite a bit easier. After only a few minutes, I finally bite through enough to be able to say *Timber!*

I jump out of the way and the tree falls down with a loud *thwack* and a slightly quieter *splat.*

It's not like I *had* to kill this guy, but if I were a living tree, I'd want the same thing. After a few minutes, the tree stops bleeding, and I can turn my attention to the floor itself.

Okay, so . . . Sniffsniffsniff . . . Yeah, we have about a few hundred harpies. Around half of them are spread out and alone, very close to a blood-filled tree. Just below a third of all the trees here have blood in them. The other half of the harpies are crowded together in a number of smaller or bigger groups, the smallest at only two or three and the largest at around forty.

It's a lot, but I think it's doable.

I haven't checked the time in a while, but . . .

<Top—Status—Community>
<07:04:38 Day 301>
<The twelfth attempt will begin in 29:16:55:42>

Yeah, I've got a whole attempt to do this. Perfect.

Step one . . .

I look around my position. There's about a dozen dead harpies and one felled tree. Right.

I've got a few chickens to skin.

As I dismantle the harpies, I find with interest that there isn't actually that much structural difference between the goblin and bird parts. It just passes almost seamlessly into a leaner kind of muscle. Equally interesting, the harpies are all incredibly light. It makes sense since they're supposed to be able to fly, but it still surprised me to find that their bones are hollow. Logistically speaking, I don't think the size of the wingspan is enough for these to exist in a non-magical setting, but considering that they were made from magic, their flight is excused. I guess.

I hope I don't get salmonella from this. I mean, sure, it's magical chicken-women, but it's still chicken, right? Maybe I shouldn't eat it, you know . . . raw?

Well, only one way to find out!

With the world's biggest chicken thigh in hand, I dig in. Chomp chomp chomp chew chew chew. Hm. Erm . . . It's surprisingly slimy, and not in a good way. The flavor is fine, kind of bland, but it's all very lean. Chickens generally have a very high fat percentage, but that's mainly because of breeding. These are, in comparison, wild chickies. I almost want to set up a fire to try cooking them, but I literally don't know how to make a fire. Rub sticks together? I doubt that actually works.

Hmm . . . As I dig into a chewy chicken breast, a sudden thought strikes me. Is this . . . unethical? No, specifically, is this against the rules of the server? It's not like I care about breaking them or anything, but I don't want to accidentally blurt out something to Moleman that'll get me executed or whatever.

Let's see here . . .

Opening the community boards, I search until I find Moleman's profile. Luckily for me, by scrolling down only a little, I find that he made a post regarding the status of goblins within the tutorial and how we should meet them.

Alright, here we go . . .

Okay, so, to summarize, there's a fair bit about which floors have you meeting goblins and how you can interact with them in a positive and friendly manner. There's some basic goblinese you can learn, such as how to say your own name, and that, for example, *Kier tu un'lau?* means *Are you okay?* which would have been great to know a couple of months ago.

Anyway, on the note of how to recognize a goblin, Moleman lists the following traits aside from the obvious pop-up: One, they are usually pretty short; two, they are typically either green, RED, yellow, or blue in color; and three, they have long ears and either are completely hairless or have a mane around their necks. Hm.

I turn away from the screen and look down at the half-disassembled harpy at my feet. Hairless, check . . . long ears, check . . . green, check . . .

Leaning down, I pick her up and hold her in front of me. With her legs completely stretched out, she's almost as tall as I am.

Well, there you have it, folks! Not a goblin: confirmed. Wonderful. In that case, there's no reason to worry.

The only problem I have with the harpies is their skin. The goblin part is fine, and I have no problem skinning a chicken, but the part where the two skins cross into each other is where the trouble starts. That part specifically is unusually thin, so it often tears, and I also can't remove the feathers and skin from the wings without tearing it. It's all very frustrating, but in the end, after a dozen tries, I finally have a single complete harpy skin.

I almost want to try wearing it as a disguise, but I'm pretty sure it'll just get torn apart. Shame. If only for the sake of the floor theme, I put it on. It might be a bit late to say, but I haven't worn anything since the tenth floor. My hides kept getting washed away on the eleventh, and they burned to a crisp on floor twelve, so here we are.

Ah, clothes, wonderful clothe—

Erm. This is kind of . . . uncomfortable? Hrm. Well, uh, I'm sure I'll get used to it. Besides, it works as scent and visual camouflage, so I do sort of need it. I was just surprised by the feeling of the feathers. Not . . . not nice. Do not like. I've always been sensitive to the clothes I wear, but this is a new one.

Pulling on the harpy hide fully, I put the last of the other harpies into my inventory. I hope I'll have time to eat them. It's not that I mind them getting sold, it's just that it's more worthwhile for me to eat them and raise my indigestion tolerances.

With my preparations complete, I take a look across the forest. In the far distance, I catch sight of a dark, twisting tower, supported by a massive tree entwined around the tower itself, so large it casts a shadow across the land. That's my goal, then.

Looking to the forest, instead, I take a deep breath through my nose.

Now, where to start?

XII

Funniest Shit I Ever Saw

First, let's strategize. There are two distinct groups of harpies, the solos and the flockers. Sure, I *could* probably just go for whatever's the closest and hope to get them all eventually, but that won't work in the long run. The harpies will in time, as a collective, realize not to be close to me.

It would have been good if I could somehow lure them to myself, but that runs the risk of getting flocked by too many harpies to be able to defeat without getting killed first. No, if I want to do this, I need to avoid large group battles as much as possible. Fighting a lot of enemies is currently my biggest weakness. If I can just surprise them on their own or in smaller groups, I can take care of them pretty well.

But that still leaves me with the same question.

To return to the basis of the question, the flocks move about quite a bit, while the solos are on their own. Even if I kill an entire nearby flock, it's unlikely that a solo will leave. Meanwhile, the flocks have no attachment to the trees—I think— so they will just leave and go whenever and wherever they want to. They'll be harder to kill, even if I get them in smaller chunks.

In that case, since my time is limited, my best bet is simply to go for the flocks and take the solos as I find them. There's also a chance that even if the forest starts burning, the solos won't try to escape, so, yeah.

The flocks it is.

I look out over the forest. I don't like how exposed everything is. No matter where I am, I'm visible. There are no leaves, and it's kind of bugging me. Then again, this *does* give me a chance to train my fetal rolling.

Getting down on the ground, I get going.

I wish I could say that during the approximately twenty-seven days that followed that I somehow learned a few tricks and cheats that made the whole harpy-catching thing easier, but that would, frankly speaking, be a lie. I didn't learn shit.

Listen, I'd love to say that the harpies were easy pickings, but that was absolutely not the case. I thought I could do like I did with the shades on floor seven and easily split up these flocks, but that was disproven within days. Unlike the solos, the flocks were as tight-knit as a rat king. Every night and every day were spent so close together they looked like one big pile of feathers. And, for the record, yes, there was a difference between day and night. During the night, the sky was dark gray. During the day, it was light gray. Wonderful.

The only time they were even slightly distracted from preening and gossiping among each other was when they were trying to either kill or extort one of the solos, or while fighting with another flock.

As far as I can understand, every harpy in this forest has two choices ahead of them. Either they drink the blood sap from one of the warm trees, or they eat the flesh of other harpies. That's all the choice they have. The choice they make seems to depend mainly on whether they have a tree available.

The harpies that lose their tree, or who killed it themselves, or the extremely few who chose to abandon it, join one of the many flocks. Some flocks scavenge old, dead bodies and half-eaten trees. Others extort harpies for their trees, and some just attack the second they find them.

The obvious result of all of this is that many of the flocks find themselves fighting each other over discovered trees and solos. It was actually pretty interesting to follow, and in the aftermath of the larger and more equilateral battles, there's a lot of half-dead harpies to pick off as easy prey.

Because of the whole gang war situation, a lot of the harpies have no one else to rely on but their comrades. This means that it's actually very rare to see harpies turn on each other, even during starvation. They are incredibly close to each other, only comparable to soldiers in time of war. Because of this, it is incredibly unusual for harpies to go off on their own, or even in smaller groups.

The second I realized that this whole forest was filled with a bunch of warring harpy gangs, my first thought was obviously that I should try to create an all-out, massive gang war between the largest groups available.

This didn't happen.

I tried, that I can promise you, but I just couldn't make it happen.

First, I took out all the smaller groups of less than ten members, just to simplify things. Somewhere in the back of my mind, I had hoped that this would have kind of pushed the larger groups closer to conflict. If they couldn't quarrel with smaller groups, they would just quarrel with bigger ones, right? Simple. Also absolutely not what happened.

As I took out more and more harpies, the conflicts drastically decreased.

In hindsight, the reason was obvious, but it still confused me. Fewer harpies meant fewer clashes over food and territory, which in turn meant fewer fights in general. Food became more abundant as the competition decreased. Groups could eat more, more harpies could be fed better, more solos were able to avoid harassment . . .

The whole situation felt like introducing a wolf to a previously herbivore-eaten wasteland. Suddenly, everything just works better, even though it feels like it should have worsened things.

Did I do something wrong? I have no idea.

It's not like I left the harpy bodies lying around for anyone to eat, either. I disassembled them and put them into my inventory as usual, and still, for some mysterious reason, the larger harpy groups prospered.

My personal theory is that since they weren't exactly procreating, if left alone, they wouldn't reproduce at a rate that generated conflict on its own. If everyone was fed, then that was all that mattered. Useless conflict would only kill more. And, sure, that's nice for them, but I'd like them to die, so I'm quite unhappy.

The only time when I can pick them off one by one is at night, when most of them are asleep, or during the daytime when they're distracted. In those situations, I'll just randomly grab someone, use touch of reverse tolerance to almost instantly kill them, and then drag them off before anyone can react. As far as I can see, this did have a slight psychological effect on the other harpies, but it's not even close to what I was able to achieve on the seventh floor. Very upsetting.

Worse yet, even if one of them *did* spot me in the daytime, their usual reaction is always to either beg for a piece of my flesh or just attack on the spot. No fear whatsoever. In desperation, I once tried wearing a harpy disguise, but that literally changed nothing.

After about two weeks, I had eradicated every group with less than a dozen members, leaving me with only a few select larger groups left to go, but these would be the crux of it all.

I wish I could say that I formulated some sort of clever strategy to do this, but I really didn't. I just attacked at night, tried to take out as many as I could before everyone woke up, and then I rolled away and repeated the whole thing the next night until they were all dead. This strategy sucked. Every morning they'd have more bodies and therefore more food, which they ate mournfully after offering several prayers. This meant that the next time I attacked, they would be far healthier than the last time. Sure, many would have had a few tiring, sleepless nights, but that didn't make as grave a difference as the lack of starvation did.

Still, in the end, after doing this sort of stuff to several different groups every single night, I was able to whittle down their numbers enough for a full-on raid to be possible. One by one, I took down the groups. Funny thing was, at some point, the remaining groups actually formed into a single big group. Maybe it's just human instinct to do so, but—

Wait, sorry, *goblin* instinct. My mistake.

Anyway, since they were so kind as to form into a single group, I was able to take them on all at once. As they weren't soldiers or anything, they never pulled any strategies more complicated than having guards sit up at night and making some sort of buddy system, not that it helped.

By the final week, all flocks of harpies had been taken out. That left me with just the solos to take care of, which took a fair bit more time than I had expected. This was mainly because I had to actually go from harpy to harpy. My main mode of getting there quickly turned to my four-legged running, which was very effective.

One by one, I took them out with the greatest efficiency possible, without sleep and without food or anything else most people would usually need. I didn't even stop to disassemble the bodies but rather left them where they were. For some reason, this always made the tree they were clutching like a life raft drip clear sap from its hollows. Weird.

But even after all that, right now, with two days left of the attempt, there are still a pretty significant number of solos hanging around. So, what's my plan? As I said before, I have no idea how to set up a fire. But now, finally, I have a solution.

Finally, after almost a month of grinding, I've gained the much-awaited *touch of reversed resistance*.

<[TOUCH OF REVERSED RESISTANCE (LV.1)]
ANY [RESISTANCE] SKILL CAN BE USED IN THE REVERSE TO CAUSE THE EFFECT THAT IT PROTECTS FROM, TO THE STRENGTH OF THE SKILL. THE RESISTANCE LEVEL THAT MAY BE REVERSED DEPENDS ON THE SKILL LEVEL. THE TOUCH MAY ONLY BE USED ONCE PER RESISTANCE LEVEL. CURRENT POWER: LEVEL 1.>

Neat, huh? Also, as I had hoped, I still have touch of reverse tolerance! This means that I am now unstoppable. Well, not exactly, but it certainly feels like it.

Why is this important? You mean aside from the fact that I can now make people delusional and unconscious at the same time, while also giving them an ulcer the size of a small nation? Oh, only because now I can actually make a fire.

See, all I need to do is grab this handy-dandy harpy . . .

"P—please," she pleads for some reason, "I don't care if you kill me, just spare Riet—"

Put a few fingers to her forehead . . .

"I don't want to die, I don't want to die, I don't want to—"

<[TOUCH OF REVERSED DEHYDRATION RESISTANCE (LV.1)]>
<[TOUCH OF REVERSED HEAT RESISTANCE (LV.1)]>
<[TOUCH OF REVERSED BURN RESISTANCE (LV.1)]>

The dehydration makes them better kindling, the heat forms a teeny tiny little spark, and the burn ignites that little spark into an actual fire. And all of a sudden, I'm holding a beautiful, lovely fire. Isn't that just wonderful? The feathers are wonderfully burnable, and once she's properly alight, I toss her at one of the nearby dead trees, which easily catches the flames.

And in only three steps, you've got yourself an adorable little forest fire.

After repeating this with a few more harpies in a few more places, we've got the whole forest up in flames. It's a pretty sight, but the smell of smoke and burning blood and feathers is kind of gross. That said, I do think I prefer the slightly nostalgic sound of widespread screaming to the previous moans and wails. This really does confirm that whole thing about preferring the familiar over the unknown, huh?

<Harpy (Lv.41) Defeated.>
<Harpy (Lv.43) Defeated.>
<Harpy (Lv.39) Defeated.>
<. . .>

Anyhow, since the forest is burning pretty well and the defeat messages are rolling in like dough, I might as well head on inside the tower. I'm actually standing right at the base of it right now. I haven't gotten any message about the boss stage, though, so I think it only activates once I enter through the conspicuously visible—and open—front door.

Final note before I do that, though . . .

I think this big-ass tree twirling around the tower is one of those living trees. Why do I think so? For one, it's got those big hollowed-out holes, of which two are currently flooded with clear sap. Second, it's warm. I wonder if it provides any sort of internal isolation and warmth to the tower itself? If that's the case, then the witch is either very lucky or a genius. Either way, I'm starting to get a little excited to meet her.

Well, no need to procrastinate anymore. Let's head inside!

<Tutorial stage, Hell Difficulty Thirteenth Floor: Boss Stage>
<[Clear Condition] Defeat the wicked Witch of Ash and rescue the princ—
Princ—
/ppppppp./>

<A CHANGE HAS BEEN MADE.>

<[Clear Condition] Defeat the wicked Witch of Ash.>

Hm? Hey, wait, what's all that about? A princ . . . Prince? Princess? Hang on a second, are you trying to say that you don't think I'm capable of rescuing a prince or princess from a wicked witch?! I may not look like knight material, but . . . Actually, there's no *but* to that. Still!

Why, I'll show you that I can rescue a prince or princess just as easily as any other challenger or royally sponsored tin can!

Hmpf, what an insult.

Okay, so, what are we dealing with in here?

Stairs. Yeah, uh, I don't know exactly what I expected, but the tower is stairs. It's just one big spiral staircase, and that's it. It doesn't even have any windows! Any real estate agent would switch professions if they saw this place. Ugh. This is going to be dull. Be happy you don't have to watch me doing this whole thing.

Going down on all fours, I ascend the stairs like a dog.

Approximately three thousand five hundred two steps later, I arrive at the top. What meets me is so stunning I physically stop in place, glued to the floor.

There's a door, a completely ordinary door, and just below it is a mat that says *Welcome* on it in big, curvy letters. A little sign hangs on the door that says *No solicitors or armies, please* in similar cute, swirly letters with a little heart at the end. Stepping forward, I unconsciously wipe my feet on the mat before opening the door.

"Nyeheheh! Soon you will fall to my despicable curse, Princess Swee-Swee!" a comically standard witch—complete with purple, broad brimmed hat and door handle nose—says with a cackle as she points all ten of her fingers at a frail maiden goblin sitting chained on the floor. Orange bolts of undoubtedly magical lightning zap out from all ten fingers.

<Witch of Ash (Lv.62)>

"No, please, anything but that!" said frail maiden goblin moans, closing her eyes in pain. "I will do anything, so please don't turn me into one of your horrid beasts!"

<Goblin (Lv.9)>

"Nyeheheheh, oh, but you have no choice! Now, accept your fate or I'll—"

The witch meets my eyes. I meet hers.

Um, did I walk in on something . . . ?

"Uh," the witch says. "Do you mind? I'm kind of in the middle of turning this princess into a chimera, and you're sort of ruining the atmosphere." She gestures at the confused-looking princess.

"Oh, um," I stammer. "S—sorry. Should I come back in like five minutes or something?"

The witch rubs her wart-covered chin. "Hmmm . . ." She shrugs. "Yeah, that should just about do it."

"W—wait!" the princess stammers, her face whipping between the witch and me. "Don't listen to this foul ungoblic woman! Free me, please, and I'll give you my hand in marriage. The whole kingdom of Ret-inn will be yours to rule!"

I frown down at her. "Sorry, but, um . . ." I glance away. "I'm not really ready for that sort of commitment, you know? I'm sort of saving myself for, well, *the right one.*"

The witch shakes her head and crosses her arms. "Princess Swee-Swee, didn't anyone teach you manners? Proposing out of nowhere is *very* rude."

"Wh—what?" the princess says, brows furrowing. "I have nothing else to offer! How else should I—"

"To be honest," I say, interrupting her, "I've got to agree with the witch on this one. You can't just assume that guys will be into you just 'cause you're a person of power. It's pretty unfair, actually. And what if I was already married? Proposing to a guy out of nowhere can be really problematic to his social life if it gets out."

The princess's head jerks from side to side. "N . . . No, I was just . . ."

The witch shakes her head again. "Just because you're a pretty young girl doesn't mean you can get away with that sort of stuff." She looks over at me. "Now, my magic is starting to wear off, so if you'll just step out for a second, I'll be ready in a moment, alright?"

"Oh, yeah, sure," I say, stepping back out the door. But before I go, I peek my head back in briefly. "That chimera better have a cool-ass hide."

The witch grins at me. "You better believe it."

I step back out the door and gently close it behind me.

Wow, what a swell gal. She really gets me!

Hm. It feels like I've forgotten something . . . On the other hand, if I forgot it, then it must not be important, right? Right . . .

I hear a piercing, feminine scream, and as I mull over my thoughts, the scream slowly transforms into beastly growling.

Oh, wait, I was supposed to save the princess! Shoot—

I throw the door back open again. "Sorry to burst in, but I just remembered that part of the boss stage clear requirement was to save the princess, so can you just, like, not turn her into a—"

Inside the room, a big chimera with the head of a lion, the body of a bear, the legs of a tiger, and the tail of a shark stares at me. Oh, and it also has a pair of mismatched wings. I stare at it. My mouth falls open.

The witch's eyes widen at the sight of me. "You're telling me that *now*? It's not like I can un-chimera her! Just bursting in here is very inconsiderate of you."

I hold up a hand, stilling her talking. "No, I've changed my mind. To hell with the stage requirements, that chimera is *way too cool* to undo."

The witch blinks once before puffing up her chest in pride, putting her hands on her hips. "'Ain't that exactly it! It's like I've always said—a strong theme with just a few little breaks to that rule is how you make a great chimera! Just sticking together random bits of whatever animals you can find is super boring. You need some panache, some moxie, some damn chutzpah to make things happen!"

I hold up my hands. "I know we're supposed to fight or whatever, but I couldn't have said it better myself. Randomly cobbled-together bosses are a waste of an awesome concept, but this is . . . !" I clutch my hand into a fist. "Never before have I seen such beauty, such fierceness, such boldness! You, witch, are a true artist."

She nods in response, cheeks a deep green. "Indeed, indeed, you are quite correct. None of those pompous wizards at the university could understand this, but you—you!" Her eyes gleam. "You have a great eye. I am surprised the Gods would send a man of such culture to punish me for my supposed sins."

I shrug. "Those dumbos can't tell a diamond from a pebble."

She grins at me. "You truly are a worthy challenger. Come, face the chimera. If you beat it, I'll battle you one on one."

I frown at her. "It's fine if you want to go all at once, so . . ."

"No way, I have no idea what abilities this thing has. I'm not stepping close to it."

"Huh," I say. "Fair."

The witch takes a few steps back, closer to the back of the room. Oh, by the way, the whole room is full of potions and weird ingredients and a big BLACK cauldron and everything else a witch should have. It's a pretty fun sight because no matter where you look, you'll always see something new. But, for now, I need to focus on the chimera.

<Chimera Lv.59>

Well away from the two of us, the witch points at the chimera. "Uh, go get 'em, princess!"

And go get me it does. Leaping across the room, it flaps its wings, but they aren't especially big, so it doesn't actually start flying or anything. The whole wing thing is still pretty intimidating, though, so I'd better get out of the way. Since jumping to the sides or back is too predictable, I leap toward it, just beneath its displayed claws, rolling myself into a ball as I do.

"Princess, he's going under you!" the witch cries, and I don't really have time to wonder whether the chimera can understand actual words before a massive shark tail smashes into my face, fin-first. My nose goes *crunch* and the rest of me goes flying across the floor, but since I'm still rolled up into a ball, I resist the urge to turn into a pancake in order to uphold my invisibility. "Invisibility? No, more than that, hmmm . . . *Spot!*"

<**Spot.**>

I stay rolled up. Did she . . . ?

No, going by the utter confusion on her green face, she can't tell where I am in the least. Good. But even as I lie hidden, trying to figure out some sort of strategy here, the witch carefully scans the room. In the end, her eyes fall on me. Or, rather . . .

"There, princess! That pile of knocked-over tomes on the best ways to cook leaplizards and other four-footed amphibians! That's where he went!" she cries, pointing right at where I'm lying.

I expect the chimera to jump at me again, but instead it opens its mouth wide, a weird, hissing noise gathering in the back of its throat.

The witch turns to it, brows furrowed. "Princess, what are you waiting for? Go get—"

"HURHRGGHRHHHHHRHHHRHH"

I only barely get over my bewilderment in time to throw myself out of the way of a spray of BLACK barf shooting like a water cannon out of the chimera's mouth. My left foot gets caught in it, and it doesn't even hurt, but when I look down, I find that this is because it completely melted off, not including my bones. I've got a skeleton foot, and that's it.

<**You have learned: Acid Resistance Lv.8**>

Now that I also look back at where I was mere seconds ago, it's completely covered in BLACK goop, and everything has sort of lost its shape. Yeah, that's corrosive as all heck.

"No! My tomes on how to best cook leaplizards and other four-footed amphibians! They're *ruined*! Damn you, princess, is this your revenge for my turning your handsome prince rescuer into an outdoor heating system?" the witch shrieks, pulling down the flaps of her hat. The chimera, being incapable of speech, merely growls in response. The witch, exhibiting amazing linguistic prowess, growls back at it. For a second or so, I almost imagine that they're communicating through growls and snarls alone, but I easily snap out of it once I remember that I have a skill that would translate such an exchange. Since it doesn't, I can come to the rational conclusion that this is a matter of two beings on the same level speaking without words or thought. Very interesting to watch, but I kind of want to kill them both.

The problem right now is my foot. See, it's bleeding profusely, which isn't too dangerous or anything, but it means that even if I go into the fetal position and start rolling, I'll leave a trail of easily followed blood. Bummer.

So no tricks. Well, a few tricks.

I stand up, revealing myself.

"Ah, there you are!" the witch says, speaking properly for once. However, she's not the only one to notice me, and once the chimera lays eyes on me, things get complicated. The witch's eyes widen, and surprisingly, she shouts to it, "Don't you dare—"

But it dares, and it does. Since I have amazing powers of cognition, I'm able to predict it and deftly jump out of the way as it vomits BLACK goop at me again. The goop spreads out across the floor, absorbing half a chair and eating up part of a surprisingly comfy rug.

"Argh, my Liftan carpet! That thing cost me someone's arm and leg!"

As I jump around like a monkey, the chimera and its spray of goop follows closely, melting books and jewels and furniture and tools alike, all the while the witch cries out in emotional devastation. Finally, after almost a full minute of gymnastics, the chimera barfs at her big cauldron, which actually melts completely. It seemed pretty robust at a glance, but maybe it wasn't as high-quality as I thought.

"My GoodGoop(tm) Potion Brewer 6000 Deluxe with built-in divinity channels and detachable handles! Oh, that's the final pinch, princess! You're going *down*!" the witch says, raising her hands at the chimera and firing off a number of multicolored bolts of lightning. They strike the side of the chimera, making it writhe in pain. However, with one massive stroke of its shark tail, it smashes the witch off her feet and sends her flying right at me.

I catch her only barely, putting her down beside me. Her hat went flying, though, which means that I can now see her head. Her hairy head. No, I'm serious! She's got, I think, cornrows? It's some sort of braid, and it doesn't look half-bad. I'm surprised because this is the first goblin I've ever seen with a head of hair.

"Damn it—!" the witch cries, covering her head with one hand as she goes down on her knees and starts fumbling for her hat. The chimera makes to attack her, swiping with its paws for once, but I'm able to take the hit instead, attaching myself to its massive foreleg. I'm not sure why I did this, actually. It's too furry to properly scratch at; so without much else to do, I just start biting as hard as I can into its wrist. I can feel one bone break, but that's all the damage I can get in before it lifts its paw high up and then smashes me into the floor, crushing the air out of my lungs and forcing my mouth to open, releasing my grip on it.

My ears are ringing and my head aches and all I can really do is stare up as the chimera opens its mouth, BLACK goop forming in the back of its throat. Ah, that's going to blast away my skull, isn't it? Well, I had a good run, I gue—

<Blast.>

A bolt of RED lightning zaps into the side of me and I go rolling, tumbling ass over teakettle for several moments before appropriately smashing into one of the walls. Oww.

My instincts suddenly flare up and I leap to my feet, stumbling because one of them is literally just bones, but it's still enough to get out of the way of the charging chimera. Standing, I'm able to see the witch on the other side of the room. So it's a free-for-all, huh?

Though, then again . . .

I look back at where the chimera had me pinned just now. Where my head was, there's a big pile of smoking BLACK goop. Glancing back up at the witch, I find her staring at the chimera with an expression of pure rage, her fingers twitching and crackling with multicolored lightning. It *could* have been a coincidence that her blasting me just happened to literally save my life. She didn't have to know in advance that blasting me with magic has recently become pretty ineffective, and even more so that smashing into a wall wouldn't kill me, either.

She glances at me. I meet her gaze. Understanding shines between us. Ah, I see how it is.

We share a nod as one.

Time to tag-team the chimera.

The chimera seems abruptly capable of reading thoughts as it leaps toward the witch, cleverly going for the long-range fighter first. However, fetal position blowover doesn't confuse those looking for me alone. Leaping toward the witch, I briefly roll myself into a ball in midair, distracting the attacking chimera enough to avoid having it take out the witch. In the small opening this presents, I'm able to get on top of it, clutching onto its back by grabbing a hold of its mane. Hm. Now that I think of it, if this is supposed to be a female chimera, how come it has a male lion's head? That makes no—

<Zap.>

A bolt of lightning arcs toward us at the literal speed of light, flashing my vision with WHITE and striking the chimera—I think—headfirst. The chimera roars loudly, rearing up onto its hind legs while massively flapping its wings. It's like I'm on top of a bucking bull, and since I'd rather not get thrown off, my best bet is to just abandon ship. But, first . . .

<[TOUCH OF REVERSED EXHAUSTION RESISTANCE (LV.1)]>
<[TOUCH OF REVERSED IMMOBILIZATION RESISTANCE (LV.1)]>
<[TOUCH OF REVERSED STROKE RESISTANCE (LV.1)]>

And that's about all the TRRs I have time to get in before the thrashing gets too intense to stay and I leap off, tumbling to the ground in a less-than-gracious fashion. It's not exactly a superhero landing, but I didn't die or break any bones, so it's fine.

Even then, I am more than happy to find that the chimera is visibly worse off thanks to the TRRs. Not by any extreme amount, but it moves with less ferocious energy than before, if that makes any sense.

Like this, I think it's more than doable.

A bit more than doable, as a matter of fact. With our forces combined, the chimera was doomed from the start.

At first, she stupidly wanted to just zap it with lightning and stuff, but I was able to eventually dissuade her. After all, I can't exactly have her lightning go and stain—or even worse, *burn*—my lovely new hide, can I? More surprising, however, was that she apparently did not have any buffing spells. I'm serious. I tried to get her to buff me or something, but she just didn't get it. Not even when I explained the very basics of functional PvP did she understand the simple fact that having attacking spells alone is a shitty strategy.

I mean, with nothing but attacking spells, you basically have the same strategic might as a seven-year-old playing Pokémon. It's dumb, but at least her stunning spell was able to briefly immobilize it, allowing me to get a few hits in. It wasn't entirely easy to only go for its stomach, but once I got it nice and open, the rest was a cake walk.

<Chimera (Lv.59) Defeated.>
<[Level Up]>
<You have reached Level 57.>
<Agility has increased by 4.
Strength has increased by 6.
Stamina has increased by 6.
Magic Power has increased by 2.

**Disassemble has increased by 1.
Burn Resistance has increased by 1.
Acid Resistance has increased by 1.
Corrosion Resistance has increased by 1.
Maul has increased by 1.>**

The creature gives one last sighing breath before finally falling over, dead as dust. About time, too.

The witch paces up behind me, hands hooked around her waist. "Alright, the menace is dead, alongside half my laboratory." I glance up at her. She makes a thoughtful face. "This is the moment when we fight each other, right? I'm in pretty good shape, still got some divinity running through my archeries despite the Gods apparently hating me. So, what say you?"

I look back down at the chimera before returning my eyes to her. Lifting my hands, I form them into a capital-*T* shape. "Time out," I say, jerking a thumb at the chimera. "I need to skin this monster thingy 'cause if I don't put it in my inventory then it'll just disappear once I beat this stage by killing you, and I don't want that to happen 'cause it's a really cool skin and I just spent a lot of time for it, so can we just, like, take the fight in five minutes or something?"

She blinks at me and purses her lips. Then she shrugs. "Well, I don't see why not. Oh, but only on the agreement that I get to charge up all my spells in the meantime."

"Fair's fair," I reply, and turn to the chimera, already stabbing my claws into its soft bosom. With my fingers half-sunk into its pancreas, a thought hits me and I look at her over my shoulder. "Hey," I say. "How come you're so cool with me being here to kill you and stuff? Most people don't like it when I come to kill them."

With the tips of her fingers pressed together and her eyes closed in some sort of meditative trance, she briefly peeks one open to look me up and down. "You're assuming that I won't be able to kill you first." In response, I simply shrug at her, because obviously I'll be able to kill her. "Unsurprising. Nevertheless, the simple fact is that I have been waiting for you. Maybe not *you* specifically, but those detestable Gods sent me a sign. A very obvious one, actually." I can tell she's about to launch into a long tale, because her voice shifts into that standard storybook one, slightly wistful and all that. "I got a parchment sent to me. It was only . . . Yes, it was only a few hours after I had kidnapped the princess and taken her imbecile savior-to-be as well. I can't believe the Split Horizon Empire would be so foolish as to send their second-eldest prince all willy-nilly with nothing but a sprint drake and an heirloom sword. Can you believe what they let their kids get away with nowadays?

"Apparently, though," she continues, "that was the last straw. Who would have thought it? Here I go, kidnapping and transforming random passersby and army men for three hundred and a half years, but the second I bring in some little spoiled golden-rattle brat and her yet-to-be honeybunch, that was apparently one step too far."

"Those gods . . ." I mutter, shaking my head back and forth. "Buncha pricks, that's what they are."

She gives me an odd look. "Really, I had expected someone more . . . devout. Though, all in all, this is far from worse. In fact, I believe I prefer this. Had they sent one of those lanky rose knights, I might actually have done myself in instead."

Humming, I remove the chimera's lungs and stick them into my inventory. After this is done, I should definitely compare the flavor of these things to regular goblin lungs. You know, because . . . science?

As I dissect the chimera, trying to little avail to figure out how to handle the wings, the witch creeps up from behind. "Not to be pushy," she says in a pushy fashion, "but you don't actually have to remove the inner stuff from the wings. You can just leave them as they are and it'll work fine." Freezing in place, I find myself only just barely capable of turning my neck to look at her. She gives me a cheeky grin. "Trust me, it works very well."

I turn back to the chimera and follow her advice. As I continue disassembling it, she gives me a few comments here and there about how to do it better.

Out of pure curiosity, after a short time of silence, I ask her, "Hey, how come you're turning all these couples into harpies and trees? Haven't you got anything better to do?"

She gives me a blank look. "Well, obviously, because it's hilarious."

My jaw falls open a little. "You think it's funny?"

"You don't?" she asks incredulously. Standing up, she goes to one of the windows overlooking the now burning and smoking forests. You can't really hear any screams anymore. "I just find it so funny to watch them scramble for a solution, I mean, all they do all the time is moan and groan about how unfair everything is, and then they still go and eat their own lovers! Isn't that just the funniest thing you've ever seen?" She barks a laugh. "Really, this whole burning-the-forest thing is . . . When I first saw it, I thought it was quite unfortunate, but I think I've changed my mind. This is just the punch line to the joke I was already setting up!"

Scratching my chin, I stand up and join her at the window. Looking out, I can see, hidden within the trees the curled-up corpses of harpies, clutching onto the trunks of burnt trees, or in the arms of charred half-bird corpses.

"Huh," I say, thoughtfully. "Now that I think about it, you're totally right. That *is* really funny! I wasn't really thinking about it before, but chicks loving trees? That is actually golden. Hah!" Boy, do I feel foolish for not catching on to the joke here earlier. Man, what a master of comedy!

"It is, isn't it?" the witch says with this huge grin, her cheeks dipping into dimples. "Watching them run around like soggy rats is almost as funny as the moment when they realize their beloved flame got turned into a tree of all things!"

"Haha, yeah, that *would* be pretty hilarious," I say merrily. "Wish I could've seen it, but I guess I'll have to settle with imagining it."

"A real shame, that," the witch says with a sigh. She looks over at me, glancing at the chimera skin in my hands. "Anyway, you're done with that now, aren't you?"

I look down at the skin I'm holding. "Oh, yeah," I say as I turn back to her. "I guess I am, huh?"

She grins. "Well, then. How about a classic little fight to the death?"

I smile back at her. "Sounds good to me."

Honestly, the fight itself was kind of disappointing, but it was still fun if only because we got some nice banter going. She'd insult me, I'd insult her back, all the while we traded blows and spells and whatnot. She'd blast off one of my legs, I'd tear off her hand, she made a hole through my stomach, I ripped out her eye . . . Fun stuff.

In the end, though, I was able to win, if only by a small margin. The weakness of magicians here is that they can only blast you if they can point directly at you, which is obviously impossible if they don't know where I am. The weakness here, in turn, is that she was a bit too clever for fetal position blowover to work consistently, meaning that instead of just cheesing the whole fight, I had to switch up my strategies constantly. It kept me on my toes—not that I had any left—and was, in all, a very enjoyable fight. I haven't had many of those, but this really felt like it. If I could, I wouldn't mind doing it over again.

In the end, thanks to a cheap shot I got in by abusing her weakness in not being able to see above her, I was able to get the final upper hand on her.

And here we are. She's lying on the floor, and I'm just above her, holding two lungs in my hands, one big, the other small.

The witch draws in a raspy breath. "So how is it?" she asks, which is impressive, considering that she only has one lung.

"Tastes about the same," I say, mouth full of lung. "Apart from the size, it really is just regular old goblin, though the harpies also taste the same, so it's not like I expected anything different."

"D—does, haah, your kind taste any different? Whatever it is you are?"

"Me?" I ask. "Hmm, well . . . Humans and goblins taste pretty similar, but I do think there's a clear difference. It's slight, but in my opinion, humans taste slightly tangier, though that might just be because my own lungs have gotten a bit roughed up as of late."

"Human . . ." she whispers, her voice all raspy. "So that's what you are. *Hu-man.*"

"Yeah, human. *Homo sapiens.* Or, if you ask me, *dumbus idioticus.* But my name is actually Fennrick."

She gives a hoarse laugh that sends a few spasms through her mutilated body. "Dumb . . . aren't we all?" She smiles. "You didn't, haah, ask, but . . . I'm . . . Jalussa . . ."

I look down at her. "I kind of don't care and I'm just going to keep mentally referring to you as *witch*, but um, okay, sure. Also that's a kind of really dumb name, were your parents drunk at your time of birth?"

She chuckles. "It's not like . . . haaah . . . your name is . . . any . . . better . . ." She smiles and looks up at me through her one remaining eye. "Earlier, you saw . . . my mane. The foul one, on my head."

I take a bite of her lung, chew, and swallow. "Yeah," I say. "So what?"

"Your kind . . ." she breathes. "These . . . *humans* . . . do they all . . . have manes . . . on their heads?"

I purse my lips thoughtfully. "Okay, um, that depends on kind of a lot of things like some people shave their heads for various dumb reasons and others get cancer and lose it because their wills are too weak to keep a grasp of it and also we don't call it manes 'cause unlike animals we're civilized or so they say but like purely physically most people do have hair on their heads yeah, a bunch of them even have hair on their faces and chins, which usually looks dumb."

"And are they all . . . like you?"

"Um," I say intelligently. "Sort of?"

Her smile broadens. "I see. In that case . . . wherever you come from . . . must be quite . . . the Godless . . . place . . ." She looks off into some unspecified corner of the room. "I'd like . . . to go there . . . someday . . ."

And I'm just about to tell her some snappy and clever comeback when her eye goes dull and a message pops up in front of my eyes.

<Witch of Ash (Lv.62) Defeated.>
<[Level Up]>
<You have reached Level 59.>
<Agility has increased by 5.
Strength has increased by 6.
Stamina has increased by 5.
Magic Power has increased by 2.
Petrification Protection has increased by 1.
Enhanced Smell has increased by 1.

**Parasite Resistance has increased by 1.
Fever Resistance has increased by 1.
Enhanced Taste has increased by 1.>**

Oh, there she goes. Before I can really react in any other way, the lungs I hold in my hands suddenly shift, with the big chimera lung turning small and petite out of nowhere. That's . . . weird. Oh, and the living tree branches outside the window are also gone. Hm. Something strange is going on here.

But I don't have any time to ponder it before the floor clear message predictably pops up.

**<You have cleared the thirteenth floor.>
<You have received 1,000 points for clearing the floor. You have received an
additional 1,000 points for being the first to clear the floor.>
<For clearing the stage completely, you will receive an additional reward.>
<To repay your debt, the additional reward has been traded for 5,000
points.>
<8 Gods have shown a positive response to you. You have obtained 8,000
points.>
<46 Gods have shown a negative response to you. 46,000 points have been
deducted.>
<To repay your debt, the floor clear reward has been traded for 1,000
points.>**

There it is. Ah, beloved debt. It's a shame I wasn't able to eat more than one of her lungs, half of her heart, her entire spleen, and a spool of her arteries before I cleared the floor. Real shame, that one. Still, the chimera skin was a nice gain, as well as all the other harpy skins I picked up. So, all in all, I'm pretty happy with this fl—

FLOOR 14

THE SAND WASTE

XIII

Sandy

—oor. You know what? I'm starting to get annoyed at always having my internal monologue interrupted by a sudden scene shift. Can't whoever coordinates this teleportation thing be a bit more respectful? As their obedient, humble servant, I should at least be afforded an inch of dignity in th—

<To repay your debt, your inventory has been sold for 12 points.>

Hey! You did that one on purpose, you damn—

<Current debt: 109,094 points.>

Oh. Oh, okay. I see how it is here. You're *mocking* me! How dare you? Here I am, serving your every need, fulfilling your stupid clear requirements, and you go and do this!

I am, quite frankly, appalled. There is no justification for this blatant disregard of my—

<You have received a message.>

Ah. Aha. Right. Okay.
Whoever sent that message will die by my hand.
I pull it up.

<SuperMoleman[F66]: Hey Kitty, congrats on beating floor 13! I always knew you could do it. I'm not surprised that the gods have taken notice of

you, friend. That aside, since you're always so busy, I thought I might as well tell you personally that, apparently, there's another Server Symposium in the works. I didn't get this information personally, but I hear that it will actually take place on day 365, meaning that it will be on new years eve! Isn't that so fun? I don't mean to spoil, but I've been in contact with a few other members of the leadership, and we're going to hold a huge party to celebrate! I haven't taken it by Bach yet, she's gotten kind of weird lately, though I'm certain she'll love it, too. There'll be music, food, drinks, etc. But I'm sure you only had to hear "food" to be invested, haha. I hope I'll see you there, and good luck with the next floor!>

I stare at the message, and then I stare at an imaginary camera to pull off a deadpan expression. Um. Okay, just to be clear, that was a joke.

As I glance back at the message, my vision automatically zooms in on the word *food*. Damn. Moleman knows me too well. On the other hand . . .

The word *drinks* shines like a spotlight on an empty stage. Yeah. Alcohol . . . is good. People who tell you that drinking brings out the worst in you are dumb hippies, because if anything, it does the opposite. A New Year's party . . . My last New Year's Eve was pretty crap, so this will be a nice, refreshing take. If I drink enough, maybe this one will even erase my memories of all previous New Year's Eves, effectively giving me a clean slate? There's only one way to find out!

Though, of course, that will have to wait. I've got a room to paint and a floor to beat.

<Top—Status—Community>
<03:03:10 Day 331>
<The thirteenth attempt will begin in 29:20:57:50>
<The fourteenth floor will open in 23:57:50>

Day three hundred thirty-one, eh? In that case, I've got just a little over one attempt left until the Server Symposium. I'd better get to it.

Do I even need to say anything else? You know the gist by now. Paint room, mutilate self, zone out, wonder about life and death and the universe, decide to pick up yoga, eat raw skin, break a few bones trying to do yoga, decide to drop yoga, check if pillars are edible, panic because my saliva removed the paint, go into a state of mania, bash open my brains on the floor, taste my own cerebellum . . . You know, the standard.

<Floor 14 has opened.
Do you want to enter?>
<Yes/No>

As is also standard, this question only has one answer. I press the Yes button.

The world around me shifts and the first thing I feel is my feet plunging into something soft and burning, like feathers with the same temperature as the surface of the sun. Approximately, at least. At the same time, a sweltering heat takes hold of my body, making every inch of exposed skin I have start to blossom into RED rashes. Ah, the sun. I kind of missed seeing it, to be honest. Though, technically, this isn't actually *the* sun, but rather the sun of some fantasy world, meaning that it is a yet-to-be-named star. I could name it whatever I want. Hmm . . . Alright, for simplicity's sake, let's just call it *The Sun 2: Electric Boogaloo*, or *the sun* for short.

I stare up at the sun. I hate the color of it, but I still give it a cheeky wink.

Now, what are we dealing with?

Well, first, I am not standing in fiery feathers as I had assumed but am rather ankle-deep in what appears to be soot. As a matter of fact, soot is just about everything I can see. It's like I'm in the middle of a huge desert, but instead of sand, it's just soot. In the distance, I can see various clifflike structures, sticking out of the soot-covered ground. Hm.

Just to check for certain, I crouch down and dig around a little bit in the soot. It gets my arms completely BLACK, but it's fine. Oh, not to mention the fact that the soot is hot enough where, if it weren't soot, it would probably burst into flames again. Just touching it is enough to give me burns of the umpteenth degree, but I don't need working arms to be able to dig a little.

Ah, just as I expected. A foot or so below the soot is nothing less than the common sand. It's grayish and sooty, but if I dig for a few minutes, in the process peeling off all the skin of my arms, I'm able to expose a deeper layer of sand, which is just the standard yellow. Interesting.

Straightening back out, I look across the desert again. It's all BLACK. In the distance, I can see a huge, circular mound, only partially BLACK. I wonder what that's all about?

<Tutorial stage, Hell Difficulty Fourteenth Floor: The Sand Waste>
<[Clear Condition] Reach the round mountain.>

Uh-huh. Okay, so that's my goal, then? Oh, let me guess, there's some guy living inside the weird mountain that I have to kill? Is that it?

Before all of this, I used to hate escort missions and fetch quests more than anything else. But now, I'm starting to get really irate with all of these go-over-there missions. I wonder if there's anything stopping me from just going wherever I want to? Oh, yeah, the attempt thing. If I were the conspiratorial type, I might say that this was specifically put in place to keep challengers from exploring the whole of purgatory before they actually reached that part of the tutorial. But only a nerd would try to figure stuff out.

So, instead, I'm just going to blindly do what I'm asked to, because what else would I do?

Round mountain. If that's where I'm supposed to go, then that is where I will go.

First up, though, I need to get stylish. See, I don't know if I said it before, but it's hot. It's really, really, really, *really* hot. The sun burns, the sand burns, the soot burns . . . It's like I'm standing inside an oven set to max. Or like I'm a banana and someone is trying out that supposed trick where you can make bananas go ripe for banana bread by putting them in the oven. Either that, or I'm an uncooked banana bread, sitting in an oven that's a bit too hot, so my top will get dry and burnt while my insides will still be too goopy. Whichever parable you prefer, the situation is still the same. Me hot, me no likey.

<You have learned: Heat Resistance Lv.8>
<You have learned: Burn Resistance Lv.5>
<You have learned: Dehydration Resistance Lv.10>
<You have learned: Dehydration Protection Lv.1>

See what I'm talking about? I usually choose to mentally sift out most of these since they're starting to get irritating with how often they pop up, but yeah, this is how bad it is. I'm normally pretty cool with situations that let me increase my resistances, but this sweltering heat is just too much. So for once, I'm going to wear clothes properly. Specifically, I'm going to make use of my lovely chimera hide, assuming that the mane doesn't instantly burst into flames.

Humming to myself, I remove the chimera hide from my inventory, only to discover something truly horrific.

Wh—what happened to my chimera hide? This is just a stupid goblin hide! When the heck did this happen!?

Okay, now that I look more closely, I think this might actually be that goblin princess from before. To be fair, though, the regal status of the skin doesn't make it any better. I almost want to throw it away because of how sucky this situation is, but that's just a waste.

Damn it. Fine, I guess I'll just keep wearing this harpy hide or a wh—

Wait a minute. M—my harpy hides! They've all turned into goblin hides, too! Argh, this is horrible! What did I do to deserve this fate? No chimera skin, no harpy hides . . . It's enough to make a grown man cry.

After some time of totally tearless mourning, I put the goblin skins back into my inventory and pull out my snakeskin, since it's good for wrapping myself in completely. Alright. Even though it hurts, I must now continue. I'm sure this place will have plenty of fun hides to collect.

I'm sure . . .

And so began my journey across the sandy dunes.

I learned a lot of things and tasted a lot of things, including but not limited to soot, sand, rock, dog-sized scorpions, small but crunchy flightless birds and the lizards that hunt them, fifteen different kinds of hallucinogenic cacti, soot, a bus-sized woolly lizard that actually posed a pretty big threat before I figured out that they couldn't turn any faster than an arthritis-struck grandma, a couple of drakes, and also a bit more soot. Very few of these things were actually tasty, specifically one, but I'll leave it up to you to infer that. I'll give you one hint, though: It's not the soot.

Alright, alright, fine, I'll tell you which ones I found tasty. It was . . . drumroll, please . . .

The birds! Yeah, uh, those birds were pretty tasty. If you stomp around in a specific way, they'll peek out assuming you're a bug or tiny lizard, and then you can just dig them out of the soot and sand. The thick coat of feathers is annoying to remove, though, so I usually don't bother and just pop them as they are. If you do it right, you can use them as bait to catch a complimentary lizard, too. Neat, huh?

There is actually a surprising amount of life, most of it hiding just beneath the thick layer of soot. The vast majority of them are insects, but a significant number of plants and cacti hide down there as well.

The desert was, as a whole, a pretty interesting place to just explore as it was. There were plenty of small caves here and there, usually hosting some creature or another. Even though it's kind of a loser move, I actually rested in these a few times, just to cool down my head. I mean, what more can you want? Food, a place to rest . . . it was good.

It was less good at night, though.

See, unlike the day, nighttime was as cold as a mother's glare, so the caves no longer presented any real solace. Not that this was any problem, of course, it was just kind of annoying. Then again, it *did* allow me to train both my cold and heat resistance, so it wasn't exactly a bad thing, really. I just continued on as before. The night held other creatures than the day did, which meant more hides for me. Weirdly big and hairy tarantulas, a thick snake sifting through the soot with a snorkel-like tongue to breathe and smell through, a feather-light creature that ran on top of the soot, a flock of tall, three-footed creatures that resembled cacti . . . That sort of stuff. I did the sensible thing by killing, skinning, and eating everything I came across, all the while mentally noting down their effects and such.

I've started being able to tell when something does something to me, even if I have a resistance suppressing the effects. It's very subtle, but once you recognize it, it's impossible not to taste it.

A lot of things in this place are very poisonous, but not always what you expect. That tarantula I mentioned? No poison. Neither did the snake have any—no, as a matter of fact, that guy was a constrictor. That tiny, fluffy creature that was so light it could run easily on top of the soot, though? Poisonous enough to raise my protection to level six, which was nice, if a bit frightening. It left me queasy for days. Obviously, though, I still ate it the next time I saw it.

But the fauna was only marginally less hazardous than the environment itself. It should come as no surprise that by the end of my first day of trekking, I decided to do the unthinkable and start wearing shoes, because my feet had gone all skeleton-y twice already. The shoes were hardly anything to look at, just a pair of snake hides wrapped all the way up to my thigh, but they did their job by keeping me on my feet, literally speaking.

Oh, right, remember those caves I mentioned earlier? Yeah, they had more use than as an outlet for my hubris. During certain times, they were actually lifesaving.

Once every couple of days or so, the otherwise blue skies would abruptly darken, which would leave me with about ten minutes to find shelter before flaming BLACK snowflakes of ash would start falling from the heavens. Speaking from experience, I can tell you that this is far from enjoyable. The soot will start by just branding itself into your skin, burning away tiny patches of flesh. But the light sootfall will soon turn into something more resembling a blizzard than anything suitable for a pleasant Christmas view. Within an hour, the soot will be falling with such speed and consistency that it will easily burn its way through almost anything. Skin, muscle, fat, and bones stand no chance. The soot burns onto you in great thick irremovable sheets, as inseparable from you as your own skin. You can pull and claw at the heavy bits of soot as much as you want, but in time, it will only end up with your entire limbs getting pulled off.

This is the point where I was able to drag my half-dead body into the shade of a rock, but if not for that, I would almost definitely have died the first time it happened. But I didn't, so everything's fine!

The experience did, however, teach me something very important: don't die. Only losers die.

Aside from this and various other natural disasters, the desert did present me with one final oddity. Here and there, all angled toward that big round mountain I'm heading toward, you can find these smooth, soot-caked rocks. Or, at least, that's what I thought they were before I tore off the soot and cracked them open.

They're goblins. Fleshy, bloody, still-alive goblins, prostrating with their foreheads to the ground. If I hadn't torn their still-beating hearts from their chests, I would have assumed them to be dead. Or just inanimate. Heck, they don't even react when you kill them! What's the point in killing something that doesn't care about its death? Very dull.

Also, to answer your unsaid question: Yes, they taste like normal goblins. The flesh closest to the skin is a little broiled, though, but that's the only difference.

It's just goblins. This makes no sense.

Out of pure spite, I killed each and every one of these that I came across, even though they didn't have any levels.

Day and night, I trekked. And after only a little under a month, I finally reached the mountain. Or, at least, what I had assumed to be a mountain.

<Tutorial stage, Hell Difficulty Fourteenth Floor: Boss Stage>
<[Clear Condition] Put the giant out of his misery.>

Yeah, uh, that's a guy. He's got ears as long as those of a goat, and his skin color is ashen and gray and his proportions are really weird, but it is absolutely some sort of guy. Maybe a huge goblin, but a dude nonetheless. Much like the smaller guys, he's prostrated, forehead pressed tightly against the sand. He's not exactly breathing, but I can hear his heartbeat. It's actually so loud that if I stand too close, I can feel my entire body vibrate with every beat of it.

He really is the size of a mountain. At least a small one. A more apt description might be that he's the size of a skyscraper, but now he's all crouched down, so although he's still big, it's hard to tell exactly how big he is.

<Giant [BOSS]>

I can't even see his level, which is the *really* weird thing here. I mean, everything is weird, but that's just a step above.

So, uh . . . how do I kill this guy? He's huge!

Alright, alright, um . . . He's only really covered in soot on top, so I can get to his skin pretty easily. There's a gap between his elbow and knee that acts as a sort of opening, so I just kind of pass through there and put my hands to his flesh. It's surprisingly cold. Anyway . . .

<[TOUCH OF REVERSED POISON RESISTANCE (LV.1)]>
<[TOUCH OF REVERSED ORGAN FAILURE RESISTANCE (LV.1)]>
<[TOUCH OF REVERSED BRAIN DAMAGE RESISTANCE (LV.1)]>
<[TOUCH OF REVERSED INTERNAL DAMAGE RESISTANCE (LV.1)]>
<[TOUCH OF REVERSED BLEEDING RESISTANCE (LV.1)]>
<YOU HAVE LEARNED:
TOUCH OF REVERSED RESISTANCE LV.2>

Oh, hey, neat! Just what I wanted.

With this in hand, I give the same resistances a go at the next level, alongside a few other yummy treats. When I step back, I fully expect the giant to be basically dead, but . . . No. Nothing. He's breathing fine, his heartbeat didn't even twitch, his breath is still scattering sand everywhere . . . He's alive.

That's a problem.

FLOOR 15

THE BLACK DESERT

XIV

Long Time No See, Friend!

Welcome to the crib.

Huh? You don't know what crib I'm talking about? Why, obviously, *this* crib!

See, a while back, I realized something important. Sometimes—on a few rare occasions—violence isn't the answer. Such a moment is now. Kind of. It all began a few weeks ago—yes, yes, I know, just stay with me—when I was tasked with killing this huge-ass giant dude. I tried my whole arsenal. Poison, burning, strokes, immobilization . . . Everything you can think of, I forced onto him. But this guy, heh, *this guy*—!

He just wouldn't die!

Not just that, no matter what I did, he never even winced. Nothing at all. So I've decided to adapt a bit more . . . unconventional tactics. Which brings us back to this wonderful crib.

See, you enter here, through a gap I made between the ribs. It leads through one of his lungs, and then into the real showcase, namely, a roomy, extravagant living room mixed seamlessly with the kitchen, dining room, parlor, retreating room, lounge, and pantry. Natural light illuminates the place, entering through a flap in the roof that can easily be closed in the event of a sootfall. The bed, carved out of the lung, allows you to relax and lean back, being rocked by the natural breathing of the area.

But the real gem here has to be the fully organic walls, all of which are made out of pure grass-fed, cruelty-free non-GMO meat and flesh. It's like the Hansel and Gretel gingerbread house, except it's made out of flesh and organs! Isn't that just wonderful?

So, yeah. All things considered, I'm doing pretty well.

And this is the point at which you start to hyperventilate and ask me in hysterics about how I could just be hanging out when I was only days from the attempt ending when I got to the giant. Carving out a crib this sweet must have taken weeks!

Well, not quite, but you're also not wrong.

I *am* on the thirteenth attempt, day three-hundred sixty-three. I also didn't need to redo this floor. Why? I'm not entirely sure myself, but right as I was despairing because the attempt was about to end, I got a message. A message about a "*change being made.*" I have no idea what caused it, but all of a sudden, I got a message from the gods or whatever that I wouldn't be returned to the lobby until I had beaten floor fifteen.

Oh, also, apparently, I'm now on floor fifteen, I think? I have no idea. I'm still in the same place, doing the same thing, but on my community profile, it says I'm on the fifteenth floor. Yeah, I'm just as confused as you are. However, this *does* mean that I can take my time killing this guy with no worries.

This is especially good because he's fantastic to train TRT and TRR on. Apart from leaving the cavity in his chest that I gouged out to hunt random nearby creatures, that's really all I've been doing. Thanks to my efforts, I've actually been able to get my touch of reversed resistance to level five now, but since I only have so many resistances at level five, I've hit a natural roadblock. I also don't want to use all of the touches I have since I might need them for more specific situations down the road.

So, in conclusion: I've got a sweet crib, all the free time in the world, and an awesome New Year's Eve party in two days. What's the problem?

The problem is that I'm not really alone anymore. Okay, that's a bit disingenuous—it's not like I've suddenly got guests coming over for tea. But it's also not entirely incorrect.

I can smell them. Goblins. Not too far away, though not exactly nearby, either. They're sweaty, hot, and crowded tightly together. A couple hundred. Going by the smell of what they're wearing, there isn't a single doubt in my mind that they're soldiers. I first smelled them a few hours ago, and I wasn't worried then, and neither am I now. It's just goblins. By their level alone, they won't be able to get much farther through this hellish desert. And that's exactly what's happening. Now, finally, I can smell something new about them. Fear. Stress. Blood. Tears. It's all there, in all its exquisite glory.

I was going to just let them die—going by the smell, they're clearly engaged by a woolly drake, one of the more annoyingly ferocious creatures in the desert— but curiosity got the better of me. I mean, they're soldiers, right? That means they ought to be carrying at least a few rations with them. Rations mean food. Food is yummy.

It wouldn't hurt to swoop in, finish them all off, and then loot whatever's left, right? It's an excellent plan. Literally nothing can go wrong.

But I'm starting to smell a lot of death, so I'll need to move quickly.

Exiting the crib, I get down on all fours and start running like an animal. Since I've got a goal now, the smell of death and blood and sweat becomes even stronger, guiding me like a clairvoyance trail from Skyrim. Quadruped running isn't technically a skill, but it sometimes feels like it if only because of how fast I can get. Which is why it doesn't surprise me too much when I show up at the site within mere minutes. Alright, here we are.

Most of the army is still alive, but only barely so. It's a rather disorganized bundle, all in all. From what I can see, the army itself doesn't even have a single unified color. Some of them are dressed in RED, and others in blue. It's very confusing, and I really don't get it. Anyway, at this distance, it's clear as day that my hunch was correct. A woolly drake the size of a bus is tearing through the army, trampling some underfoot, eating others whole, and tearing yet more apart. It's a pretty cool sight now that I'm looking at it, sort of like a Godzilla fight gone wrong, but if I want to save any exp for myself, I kind of need to take out the drake as soon as possible.

Not to mention that a few of the goblins have already noticed my presence and are actively staring at me like I'm the coming of the Antichrist. Has nobody taught these goblins that it's rude to stare?

Well, anyway. I guess I'd better get to it.

Leaning down, I pick a half-dead soldier off the ground. He makes a weird wheezing noise like how I'd imagine a busted accordion might sound, but it doesn't really matter. The woolly drake doesn't react to sound, or even sight, but rather movement. Which means that I can grab its attention pretty easily by just throwing this guy at its face, which I do. The drake hisses and snaps its jaws in the air, turning its attention to me. Wonderful.

Without any hesitation whatsoever, it throws itself at me, stomping some guy beneath its massive feet and crushing his head into a flat pancake, which looked pretty funny. Unfortunately, since I have no time to laugh at silly slapstick, I restrain myself.

The woolly drake is very effective at running through the soot, which is unusual but easily countered. All I need to do is crouch down and get beneath it. See, unlike most lizards, it has really long, almost lanky legs specifically made for trudging through soot. This puts its abdomen and stomach high above the soot as a way of protecting it. Right at the perfect eviscerating height. So once it's close enough, I deftly dodge a slap of its paw, duck down beneath it, and stab my hand into the soft part just below its ribs. It cries out in pain and begins thrashing, but I've already affixed myself to its bosom by grabbing hold of its ribs, so I'm not going anywhere.

As a matter of fact, this just lets me do more damage, mainly in the form of digging around until I've grabbed one of its three hearts. One good squeeze and the heart goes *pop!* Another squeeze and the others follow suit.

The woolly drake cries out, thrashing like a maniac, trampling even more soldiers underfoot before finally buckling over, falling on its back into the soot. This means that I am currently standing atop the downed drake, covered head-to-toe in its blood. I must look hideous. Cleaning this off is going to be such a bother . . .

<Woolly Drake (Lv.54) Defeated.>

Perched atop the dead drake, I look out onto the rest of the collected group. A little above a hundred and fifty injured or exhausted goblins look up at me.

Well, I might as well get to it straightaway.

Leaping off the drake, I roll myself into a ball in midair. But I avoid crashing onto the soot-covered ground, partially because it'll make me easier to discover, and also because it takes an annoyingly long amount of time to heal from the full-body third-degree burns. Instead, I jump right on top of a goblin soldier, stabbing my hand into his throat at the same time as I twist his neck, which lets me tear his head off in one smooth movement. The head itself is only useful as shock material, so I simply toss it at the closest goblin.

And thus begins my little massacre. It was far easier than I had expected, but that was only because I had foolishly assumed that they would have an average level higher than eleven. I even saw a few that still had the title *gobling*, so, you know. Make of that what you will. Obviously, though, this wasn't enough to make me stupidly spare them or whatever. I just kept going from one to the other, tearing out throats and ripping out spines with speedy efficiency.

One by one, dozen by dozen, I took them out. Easy peasy lemon squeezy.

As I went along, I eventually realized that even though the sooty sands were now littered with motionless bodies, I could still smell the scent of living goblins. Weird.

It seems, in my frenzy, that I had missed the most obviously interesting thing on the battlefield. Namely, off to the side, right in the shade of a cliff, a pair of tents had been erected. Only one of them smelled like goblin, though, so I guess that's my next goal, huh?

Casually, I stroll up to it. When I pull open the flaps of the tent, a pair of soldiers stab their spears into my chest, impaling both of my lungs. Very rude. In return, I plunge my hands into their chests and tear out their hearts. They fall down, dead.

<Goblin (Lv.13) Defeated.>
<Goblin (Lv.12) Defeated.>

That leaves me with the tent's inhabitant, which is . . .

<Goblin (Lv.8)>

. . . just some guy. Well, sure, he's dressed extravagantly, but he's still just a guy. Though, then again, that *is* a very snazzy crown.

"P—please," he stammers pathetically. "Don't hurt me. You may have taken the life of my love, but—"

<Goblin (Lv.8) Defeated.>

But nothing, because now I've also taken the life of him. Oops. My hand just slipped; I swear that's all! Ah, his blood is sticky; that's kind of gross . . . I can't smell any other goblins around, so I guess I can take my time now. I wonder how much his crown will sell for? It looks important. I don't think I have the patience right now to skin every single one of these goblins, but this one seems important, so I might—

I hear a rustle behind me.

<Chain.>

I whirl around, my eyes falling instantly on the being standing behind me. Simel? Is that—

<Chain broken.>

No, it's just some commander-looking goblin in a hood, pointing at me. Whew, that *really* scared me! Not being able to smell some goblins is really start- ing to mess with me. I wonder what this guy is trying to accomplish, though? I almost wish I could see his face just so I could savor it once I kill him.

His finger, still pointing at me, trembles.

I cross the distance between us in a single stride, grabbing ahold of his throat as casually as one might pluck a soda bottle from a countertop. Since every gob- lin I've met so far is only barely at the height of my chest, it's no difficulty at all to lift him into the air with one hand. Sometimes I remember how this wasn't something I could do just a year back. Heck, if I'd just tried, I probably would've broken my arm, haha!

The goblin commander in my grip starts to struggle, his legs kicking, hands grasping at my arm in some pathetic attempt to escape. Just choking him a little harder is enough to stop this, though, and after a second or two, his hands fall limply to his side. Great success! Though not seeing the light fade from his eyes feels a bit unsatisfying. I *do* have a spare hand, so I might as well take a peek under the hood, here . . .

. . .

Simel?!

My hand instantly retreats and Simel—my friend, my good, *good* friend—clatters down to the floor like a dropped rag doll, arms and legs in a big, disorganized heap. What? What? What is happening? Why is he—? I fall to my knees, scraping him up into my arms. His head is all floppy. That's bad. That's bad. Alive people shouldn't have floppy heads. Grabbing hold of his head, I try to hold it in place. His neck isn't broken, is it? No, it's not broken, it doesn't smell broken, he smells okay, and his breathing is . . .

I press the side of my head against his chest. I can't hear anything. Damn it. Damn it. That's bad.

Why didn't he say something? If he'd just said something like, I don't know, *Hello there, my good friend Fennrick!* this wouldn't have happened! Damn it, you . . . Well, I can't fault him, m—maybe he just didn't recognize me. I mean, goblins all look pretty similar to me as a human; they all look kind of the same, so maybe Simel also has that same thing, that most humans look the same to him, and I'm also covered in a *lot* of blood, so it's not like he did it with any ill intent. I must have just surprised him, that's all, and then I started doing, um, *that* before he had time to say something like, I don't know, *Hello there, my good friend Lo!* which would easily have defused the situation, but now he's like this, and, and, and—!

A raspy breath claws its way through his throat. Deep inside his chest, I can hear something give a weak thump.

H—he's alive! Oh, thank God. I was just—I was so certain that he'd . . .

Not that it's, um . . . *important* what almost happened. It didn't happen, so now it's fine. He's okay. He's alright. Oh, God, Simel . . .

I press him close to me. For a while—I'm not sure how long, I wasn't keeping track—I just hold him close to my chest. Tightly. It probably wasn't needed in pure survival terms, but it made me feel better, and besides, when you've almost . . . been in a *bad* situation, isn't it good to wake up in the arms of a friend? That's what I think. Why, if I were almost in a bad situation, and everything went BLACK, and I were then to wake up, I would quite like to wake up in the arms of a—

Simel twitches. My thoughts come to a standstill, and I stare down at him with bated breath. Slowly, gently, his eyes flutter open.

His eyes meet mine. I smile down at him.

"Hi," I say.

His eyes roll back in his skull and he goes unconscious again.

H—hey, Simel, snap out of it! Stay with me here!

Damn it, maybe he still doesn't recognize me? My face is totally covered in blood and soot, so maybe that isn't so strange . . . I'd best clean up. But not here, and not with Simel in this state. Goblins don't usually like to look at corpses of their own species, so that might also be what spooked him. Holding him to my chest, I stand up, carrying him in a slightly ironic princess carry. I'll need to use my arms, though, so with some tinkering, I'm able to put him on my back in a piggyback ride. Now then.

My eye catches the glint shining off the crown on top of the random guy's head. Mmmm. That's just too good to pass up.

Before I leave the tent, I inconspicuously grab the crown and pop it into my inventory.

Exiting, I remember the fact that I hate this place. I hope Simel will be okay, even in the harsh heat. Just to keep him cool, I bend down and grab the luke-warm heart from a nearby body before squeezing it on top of his head. He won't like it, but it'll keep him cool for the moment being. When I was running at my top speed I got here in just a few minutes, but with Simel on my back . . .

I feel a rumble in the air and freeze in place. That better not be—

Looking up, I find that it is, in fact, *it*. Dark storm clouds are gathering high above, swirling and foaming like a whirlpool in the sky. Within only a few min-utes, the sootfall will begin.

I look up at my back, where Simel's head hangs low. I don't know what level he is, but it won't be enough to withstand the ashes.

This is quite the pickle.

Removing one of the snakeskins from my inventory, I tie it around both Simel and myself, affixing him to my back. This way, I should be able to do at least some quadruped running. Getting down on all fours, I start sprinting with all I have. I get around five steps in before the straps loosen to the point where Simel almost gets thrown clear off. Grumbling, I reluctantly tighten the skin before taking an upright position. This is my only choice, but I still need to be quick about it.

The desert turns darker and darker with each step I take toward the round mountain. Soon it's as dark as night, and I can smell the soot forming in the skies.

"GRRROUUUUUUUUU"

<Woolly Drake (Lv.58)>

Ah. Hello there, old friend.

Heh, can this day get any better?

Standing still is no use at this point. It's already noticed me. These things are also pretty dumb, because they don't hide in caves when the sky goes dark like basically every other creature. It just doesn't care, which means that right now, I don't have much of a choice but to fight. I'm not fast enough to run by it. I can't even put Simel down or he'll get burned by the soot.

I tighten the hide keeping myself and Simel close. This is all I can do.

The woolly drake bucks onto its hind legs, raising its heavy claws high. "*GRRROOUUUUUUUUUUUU*," it roars, and just as it attacks me, so too do I attack it.

Predicting the actions of its simple, reptilian brain, I easily dodge out of the way of a powerful strike from its right front paw, just in time to also leap over a swipe of the tail that it probably thought was very clever. With its tail stretched out, it gives me enough time to jump onto its back. Unfortunately, with Simel on my back, I can't afford to use my normal strategy.

The woolly drake howls and arches back onto its hind legs, stretching its long neck around to snap at me. This is exactly what I wanted. Grabbing two fistfuls of its hair, I sling down to the front of its neck, where I stab my hand into the exposed skin of its underside. I'm able to carve out a pretty deep wound, but it swipes at me just as I'm about to hit any vital arteries, and since a hit from this angle would mean Simel getting hurt, I have no choice but to jump off his neck, simultaneously angling my body so that the strike that would otherwise have hit Simel instead simply gouges out the flesh of my chest, snapping a few of my ribs like matchsticks.

Simel makes some movement on my back, and I almost get too distracted to dodge the jaws thrusting at me. I try to leap away, but apparently it only barely bit a hold of my left thigh.

With my feet off the ground, I'm unable to fight back as the drake snaps its neck, tossing me high into the air. I soar for just a second or two, right above the wide-open jaws of the beast. But instead of stupidly panicking or trying to escape, I embrace this flashing RED weak point that it has so kindly presented to me. When I then fall down, I helpfully thrust my clawed hand into the back of its throat, piercing a hole as I do. The drake, startled, clamps its jaws shut, but it isn't enough to fully amputate my arm, and with my arm still in its throat, there's no way I wouldn't take the chance to tear out its tongue.

Finally, with this, the woolly drake realizes that it's fighting a losing battle, opting to simply spit me out. Not that I'll allow it to get rid of me so easily, of course. Hooking my legs around its throat, I stab my hand into the same hole I made just a minute earlier, and this time, I won't let myself get thrown off. I dig and I dig and I dig and I dig and after what feels like much longer than the few seconds it really took, I finally find that beating hose of blood, which I easily pull out, biting it in half as I do. Blood sprays me from tip to toe and I leap off the throat and land a few paces away.

The woolly drake staggers once, twice, until it finally collapses fully, throwing up a cloud of ash as it does.

<Woolly Drake (Lv.59) Defeated.>
<[Level Up]>
<You have reached Level 65.>
<Agility has increased by 2.
Strength has increased by 2.
Stamina has increased by 3.
Magic Power has increased by 1.
Burn Resistance has increased by 1.
Cold Resistance has increased by 1.
Stab has increased by 1.>

As you can see, I've started getting fewer and fewer skill level-ups per level, for some reason. But that isn't important right now.

A BLACK sootflake just fell on my forehead.

Damn it, damn it, damn it, damn it . . .

I need to act fast. Just running won't help right now. I need shelter, but I know for a fact there are no caves until I get to the round mountain. I need to find some sort of solution, some way of doing this, some kind of . . .

My eyes fall on the woolly drake's corpse. Doing a tauntaun is out of the question since the sootfall will cake us in completely, but that doesn't mean it can't serve as some other form of cover.

I approach the head of it. I need to act fast, faster than ever before. With near-frantic movements, I cut off the head and neck before splitting the neck into two thick slabs and tearing off the lower jaw of the head. And then just a bit here, and with some time and creativity, we have ourselves a coat! I can't wear it with Simel on my back, so while desperately shielding him from the falling flakes of burning ash, I angle him again to place him against my chest, with the heavy head and neck of the drake atop us, shielding us enough so that I can move at least a little bit.

And it works. At least for a few minutes, until the sootfall turns into a true sootstorm.

I don't have any choice but to take out almost every hide I have and wrap them around Simel. I have no idea where I am, I can't see anything anymore, but I can follow the scent. It smells like home. Everything is BLACK. I hope Simel is okay. The soot has burned off a lot of my body now. I had to wrap the stuff I took from the drake around Simel because otherwise the soot would get to him, but it's left a bit of me exposed, and it's burning and it hurts but I need to get there. Fast. I think the wind or the soot or something stripped off something on my back because I can feel the soot eating and gnawing into my flesh and my ribs and my lungs. My skeleton creaks in ways it shouldn't.

But the smell is getting stronger. Home. Home. It's close. Soon. Soon. Soo—

My foot breaks off and I go down into the soot, but I can't fall, I can't fall with Simel beneath me, so I twist. I twist myself as I fall, and the soot goes into my back, burning, tearing, biting, like millions of tiny spiders, nibbling bites out of me, but Simel is still okay, and that's all that matters. It hurts. It hurts a lot. But I'm still able to pull myself back up, to get onto the one foot I have left. That's all I need. And I hop and I hobble because home is close now.

The big round mountain presents a brief moment of solace as the soot lets up and the winds aren't quite so harsh anymore.

I put my hand to the cold flesh of the crib and pull open the door and I go inside. Passing through the slowly breathing lungs, I move into the room, the room where I can live and exist.

Carefully, I place Simel onto my bed and unwrap the hides and the flesh and everything else that he's surrounded in. I press the side of my head against his chest, and even though my ears got scorched off, I can hear that he is still alive, that his heart still beats, and that his chest still rises, gently, so gently. And that's all I need to hear.

Since he's alive, I don't have to fear anymore. I turn my back to him, stumble away, and fall face first onto the floor, my remaining leg breaking off like a dropped gingerbread man and both of my arms following suit.

I'm not sure if what I enter at this moment is some kind of sleep, or if I just meditate so deeply, I might as well be in a coma, but everything goes dark and calm and I don't worry so much anymore.

It was probably just a dream of some sort—that's all I can imagine it being—but during my time in limbo lite, I thought I could hear someone stand up and walk over to me, carefully, quietly, like they were on their tiptoes and didn't want to wake me. Then they just stood over me. I almost thought that they had gone away again, but then I felt a nice warmth and my body didn't hurt so much anymore.

<Cure.>

And then they walked away again, as softly as a cat would, and I slept—if sleeping is what I did—much better.

When I woke up, or snapped out of my meditative trance, my limbs were all back, and so was my hair. It's a funny thing, but for some reason, the regeneration things all see my hair as a living part of me, so even when it gets cut off or burned off or melted off or otherwise destroyed, it always grows back alongside everything else. Weird, huh?

Carefully, still a bit unsure of my limbs, I get back onto my feet. Since the place is illuminated through the thin bit of skin I carved up on top, I can ascertain that the storm has thankfully passed, and the sun is now out and about. In here, you can't really feel its burning heat, though. Another one of the perks of this roomy, centralized penthouse available in three different exotic colors! Another one of the features is the combined living room, bedroom, kitchen, and—

My eyes fall on Simel. He's sitting up, as still as a stone statue, and looking at me.

I look down. I'm butt naked. Th—that, uh, that's . . .

I pull a skin from my inventory at random—a leopard hide by the feel of it—and wrap it around myself faster than I probably ever have before. Man, do I feel embarrassed. Here I am, with a guest over for tea and biscuits, and I just go and flash him! Very rude of me. I ought to be executed for that!

Now, this seems like the perfect moment to say something.

He's looking at me. I'm looking at him . . .

Wow, uh, erm . . . This got awkward *really* fast, didn't it? Oh, wait, I know why he isn't saying anything! It must be because I'm still covered in soot and blood. Boy, that's a real mistake on my part.

I leap into action, making Simel jerk back in fear, but instead of running at him like he seems to expect for some odd reason, I sprint at one of my many walls, burying my face into the moist flesh. After rolling around in it a bit, I pull out a goblin hide and wipe off the soot and blood before sticking it back into my inventory. There we go. I can't see myself or anything, but with this, I ought to look more, well, *normal*.

I turn back to Simel. He's gone a shade paler, which is impressive every time I see it. I wonder if he can do it on command?

Casually leaning myself against the fleshy wall, I try to make an expression that would to most people come across as friendly and polite. I'm not sure whether it worked, though, because for some reason, Simel just looks even more uncomfortable.

"So, um," I say after a long while of skin-crawling silence. "What's up?"

He stares at me. I can feel myself start to sweat again. Wow, with how much I'm sweating, I bet I could dry myself up again to get *even cleaner*. I think. I gulp. Suddenly, I really wish I had a mirror. Maybe I'm still too covered in blood and everything? Simel sure is looking at me as though I were covered in fifteen pints of blood, but that could be because of something completely unrelated to the physical presence of said blood.

I try to clear the air by chuckling. "Heh, um . . . Been a while, huh?" His expression doesn't change even a twitch. Not sure if that is a good sign or not. "Haha, yeah, uh, maybe you can't recognize me because of the, erm . . . But . . ."

I swallow. "It's me, Simel!" Smiling, I do a little pose. The movement does nothing but make him twitch again, which does not bode well. I laugh awkwardly. "Not—not that *I'm* Simel, just—*you're* Simel, so, I just . . . It's me. Fennrick!"

His teeth grind together so hard I can actually hear it from across the room. That's . . . not good. Isn't this the moment when he's supposed to fly to his feet and go *Oh, my good friend Fennrick, it's you!* and then run into my arms?

Then again, that might be a bit too clichéd, and Simel has always been a bit more . . . *original* in his expressions. I guess.

A cold, slimy feeling drags its way up my spine. "You—you do remember me, right? It, heh . . . It hasn't been *that* long, has it? We met in that forest, and you got my feet cut off, and then I was in a cage, and you took me out to see the stars, and then we got to the city of Acheron, and . . ." I chuckle self-deprecatingly. "And after that—hoo, boy! But it's not important, right? We both did some weird and wacky things, and then the floor closed, so . . ."

I look at him, expecting him to pipe in with some reply, or maybe a short anecdote from his side, or a funny story, but . . . nothing. He just stares at me. I'm starting to wonder if he's blinked even once since I woke up.

A little realization hits me. "Oh! You must be wondering how I can speak your language! Well, that's, um . . . Funny story, but after . . . after I . . . you know, last time we met? Yeah, uh, the gods didn't really like it, so they gave me this language skill as a, you know . . . *punishment* or whatever. It—it really isn't all that important, though. What matters is that you understand me, and I can understand you, so . . ." I try to muster a smile. "If you talk, I'll be able to understand you."

He stares at me. I stare at him.

Doubt seeps in. Maybe he really doesn't recognize me? "Um, hang on a second . . ." I pull out one of my many goblin skins at random and try to wipe at my face again, but as soon as I put it to my face, I feel something grab at it. Startled, I remove the goblin skin from my eyes. There, below me, stands Simel, one hand clutching the arm of my goblin skin. His face twisted in pale desperation. "Simel?"

At my word—at my gaze—his entire body jerks back and he lets go of the skin, practically leaping away from me and back to where he was mere seconds ago. But instead of sitting down calmly and nicely, he stands half crouched down, hands trembling and his eyes likewise—as though expecting me to attack or something. But, for once, he doesn't look only at me with his staring, blinkless eyes; rather, his eyes periodically twitch down to look at the skin still in my hands.

I blink at him. "Oh! Ohhh, you want the . . ." I look down at the skin in my hands. Kind of a weird thing to want, but . . . "I mean, I don't see why, but . . ." Tentatively, I hold out the skin to him. His gaze flickers between the skin and me.

Slowly, carefully, as though he's expecting me to try to bite him or something, he steps closer. I'm not sure if I've ever seen anyone this tense before. If he moved any stiffer, he'd be doing a total robot walk. The thought makes me smile in its absurdity, but apparently Simel didn't like that, because he draws back slightly, body still trembling like an aspen leaf.

I let the smile drop off my face. No emotion; got it. Is my smile *that* ugly? I'm pretty sure one of my classmates once told me I smile like an *ugly bastard* character, but I have no idea what she meant by it. Sure, I'm no looker, but I was decidedly *not* the product of any extramarital affair. At least, I think not . . .

As I sink into uncertainty, Simel finally comes close enough to snatch the skin from my hands, which he does with the ferocious desperation of an animal. He then scurries back to where he first started out, also much like an animal, clutching the skin to his chest.

Hm. Now that I look closer, isn't that the princess hide I got earlier?

In that case, it might actually be a good thing that he took it out of my hands—it is, after all, a limited-edition deluxe unique item. I wonder how much it might sell for in the shop? Not as much as her crown, but you know . . . Still!

On the other hand, if Simel would rather have it as a keepsake, then I can hardly refuse him. Though, frankly, I would have liked to at least hear him say a simple *Thank you*. Is that too much to ask for? No idea. His wide-eyed stare is practically begging for an explanation, though, so after pulling myself together, I try my best to give it.

I chuckle slightly and point at the skin. "Yeah, that's a bit of a long story. Now that I think about it, it was really kind of like some fairy-tale story, what with me coming to rescue the princess from the clutches of an evil witch and all that. Though, um, it didn't quite go *exactly* like that, but . . ." I try to laugh but the look in his eyes kills it before it's even left my lips. "But it doesn't matter all that much, does it?"

Suddenly, I feel a strange urge to explain why I was using the skin of a princess as a hand towel. But I can't think of any reason that doesn't describe his species as lesser, so I keep my mouth shut. Unfortunately, this has the unwanted side effect of elongating the already painful silence a few additional seconds.

I shake my head. This has gone on for long enough.

This is a weird situation, sure, but that doesn't mean we can't make the most of it, right? I mean, yeah, I kind-of-maybe-sort-of killed his fellows, but that's all in the past. Right here, right now, we can't exactly be pulling up ghosts of the past and presenting them like fresh sheets. That's not how it works. No, we need to move forward. That's right. I don't know where we'll go from here. I don't know what I'm supposed to do with Simel—if there is anything to do at all—but that will come in time. For now, I might as well get him acquainted with this place.

I clap my hands together. He jumps back like a startled squirrel. Ah. Oops. I clear my throat. "Uh, right, so . . . Yeah! You might be wondering where this is, and what I'm doing here, and that's . . ." I'm right about to launch into some sort of explanation for why I'm currently living inside the body and flesh of a living giant when I realize that, as dumb as it sounds, I actually have no idea. We're in a sooty desert, yes. But I have no idea where this desert actually, like . . . exists. Is it in a country or is it independent? No clue!

"Heh, erm . . ." I wave my hand. Yup, just going to skip that whole bit. I'm not even going to explain *why* I'm trying to kill this guy. "Right, so, this is the crib, which is inside a guy."

Simel's left eye twitches.

I open my mouth to elaborate on the *inside a guy* part, but nothing comes out. Wow. I really don't know anything, do I? Closing my mouth again, I decide to move on. Stick to what I know and all that.

"Right, so, uh, this is my combined living room, retreating room, kitchen, study . . ." I wave my hand. "You know. All of it. Yeah, it's a pretty nice place. Really good neighborhood. And the rent? Dreamy." I almost take a step toward him, but one look at the bundle of nerves that he's become dissuades me and I just stumble slightly. To make up for it, I simply point over at the carved-out piece of lung that I laid him on last night. "That's my bed. But—but, since we'll be sharing this place for a while, I guess . . ."

A patch of sweat breaks out across my back. *There's only one bed.*

I shake my head vigorously and point at the floor instead. "S—since you're the guest, you'll be sleeping on my bed, and I'll just be here on the floor. Erm, actually, fun fact, I don't technically need to sleep! And I usually don't, so I don't even really *need* a bed, it was just for the sake of it, so it's no trouble that you have it, none at all, really. Yeah. That's, uh, alright with you . . . right?"

He didn't even follow my finger to look at the floor. He's just staring at me. For some reason, though, I'm getting the feeling that maybe he isn't all that excited at the prospect of sleeping on top of a still-breathing lung. Then again, I mean . . . It's not like I want to be judgmental or anything, but it's not like he has much of a choice, right? It's lung or the soot, and unlike the soot, the lung probably won't kill him. I think.

I take a tiny, tiny step toward him. He takes a tiny step back. I shuffle closer. He shuffles away. To prove that I'm not actually trying to attack him, I hold my gaze on the farthermost wall of the crib. Once I'm close enough to actually point it out, I jerk my thumb in the direction of the door. I'm damn lucky I was able to close it properly or we might've actually died. Which, as you might expect, would have been bad.

"That," I say, waggling my thumb, "is the grand entrance and exit. It's kind of like a cloaca in terms of doors, 'cause I haven't got any back door either."

For probably the first time since our reunion, Simel's gaze leaves me for just a fraction of a second to hop down the lung-hallway to the rib-door at the end. Then he looks back at me, eyes shining with determination. He holds the princess's skin—now folded into a prim square—closer to his chest. It almost seems as though he wants something.

Oh! Maybe my explanation of the entrance was lackluster?

I step through the lung-hallway, putting my hand against the door.

"It's a very simple thing, really. See, you push here, and with a little effort, it opens as simple as . . ."

<Chain.>

I blink. Turn around.

<Chain broken.>

I have but a moment to watch as Simel darts from his place, jaw clenched, sprinting past me, leaping through the open door, and out into the sunny, sooty world. For a little magical moment, he hangs in the air, almost like he's about to fly away. And then time starts moving again and he falls down into the soot and every single instinct I've ever had flares up in high alert. "S—Simel?!" I say, scrambling to the door, my eyes anxiously searching for Simel, hoping desperately that he didn't hurt himself.

But he's okay. He didn't fall into the soot. He's on his feet, trudging, half running away from the crib.

"Simel!" I shout after him. "Simel, where are you going? You can't be out in the desert—you'll burn and die or something!"

Jumping out of the door, I move toward him. He takes one wide-eyed peek over his shoulder and then he turns back around, trying to get away even faster, pushing through the ankle-high soot like wading through BLACK snow.

Compared to his short stature, with my longer legs and stronger physiology, I have no trouble keeping pace, even as he starts trying to run, the soot whirling up around us. I don't even have to go down on all fours or anything. "Come on, Simel, stop that already! Where are you even going? You'll get yourself hurt if you continue like this!" I call after him, but as usual, he gives no response. "And, just so you know, I absolutely won't let you get hurt. Never. Not over my dead body!"

He doesn't even glance back at me. I can feel a bit of insolence bubble up in my stomach. What the heck is he doing? Where is he going? Why won't he listen to me? Gritting my teeth, I cross the distance between us in three firm strides. Without a thought, I reach out and plant my hand on his shoulder. "Come on, Simel, let's go back before—"

He slaps my hand away. I freeze in place.

Looking over his shoulder, he gives me a dark look, brimming with some unintelligible emotion I feel like I've seen before. But that's not what I get stuck on.

He redoubles his efforts.

Okay, that's far enough. Ignoring me? Sure. Not even responding? Alright. But putting himself in danger like this, simply because he won't listen to my sound advice? That's just not something I can put up with. "That's far enough, Simel. Don't say I didn't warn you!" Saying so, I take two large steps and rear up behind him, grabbing ahold of both shoulders. Maybe a little too forcefully, as he soon starts struggling, fiercely, in terror, and I—softhearted, weak little I—can't bear it. My grip weakens and he slips out, taking one step, and then another, and then no more as I finally pull myself together enough to put an end to this stupid game by tackling him.

As we both fly through the air, my brain actually kicks into gear and I remember that, oh, yeah; there's burning-hot soot beneath us.

I snake both of my arms around his midsection, twisting in midair so that it's me and my back that hits the soot instead of him. But even when we're in the soot, he still won't stop struggling, jaw clenched and his body wriggling and squirming like a worm. "Damn it, Simel," I grumble. Soot is already starting to bite into my back, and Simel isn't wearing any gloves or anything on his head. If he goes into the soot, forget mere injuries—he'll *die*.

And still, he's stupidly struggling. Does he *want* to get hurt?

"Damn it, Simel, stop struggling!" But, of course, he won't listen. He just won't listen, at all.

Really, in this kind of situation, can you fault me for what I did?

I mean, I really didn't have much of a choice. He was about to get himself burned, quite literally, and maybe even *killed*! Anyone would have done the same in my situation. It was the most logical option, and when all is said and done, it did work quite well.

I just reached out, and put my hands around his slim little neck, and put him to sleep for a while. That's all. It took a minute or so to get him out cold properly, but once it was over, he was asleep and fine.

And then I carried him back to the crib. Heck, I even let him keep his princess-binky! Isn't that nice of me? Everything considered, this was just like when your kid falls asleep in the car and you have to carry them inside and back to bed. Not that I've experienced that in either form. But now Simel has, so . . . yeah.

I carry him inside, and I put him back to bed.

There. Now he's okay.

Was that so bad?

The Right Thing to Do

He slept for a few hours.

During his sleep, careful not to repeat my earlier mistake, I kept by his side the whole time. Sometimes he'd actually make a noise—something I thought him incapable of—though this was mainly in the form of whimpers. Combined with the way his body flinched and jerked every so often, it was all too clear what kind of dream he was having.

However, as much as I wanted to rouse him out of his nightmares, I don't think he'd want to wake up to that. I mean, he got knocked out cold. When you're passed out, you probably shouldn't be awoken forcefully, right? Not that I know anything about that sort of stuff. I'm just assuming.

Still, it's far from fun to watch.

Absently, still waiting for him to wake up, I claw off a piece of my scorched-until-crispy back, bring the piece of half-charred, half-cooked, half-raw flesh to my face, and take a bite. Chomp chomp chomp.

<You have learned: Ulcer Resistance Lv.4>

Mmm, good stuff.

As I start to take a second bite, I notice a bit of movement in the edge of my vision. I glance down and find Simel staring at me, eyes wide. Huh. How long has he been doing that?

I almost take another bite of my own flesh before realizing that maybe Simel doesn't like seeing that sort of stuff, so I stick it in my inventory. Man, it's hard having to keep track of what he might or might not like. So far, it's pretty comprehensive, but if he starts to not want to see simple stuff like me dismembering things, then I might need to kindly ask him to goblin up.

Oh, yeah, he's not going to say anything. Right, I forgot that he's basically mute. Erm . . .

"So, uh, have you learned your lesson?" I try my best to talk in a reprimanding-mother voice, but it doesn't work too well. He seems neither confused nor disobedient. Just . . . resigned. He's not even trembling anymore, which would have calmed me down an hour or so ago, but now? Absolutely not. I try to steel my heart, but it's difficult. "See, the outside is . . . There's the soot, yeah, but there's also a lot of dangerous monsters that can kill you and tear you apart and eat your flesh all in no more than ten minutes."

Of course, I can do it in approximately three minutes and forty-two seconds, but I won't because Simel is my friend.

"If you go out into the desert on your own, you're going to die, Simel. Or get hurt. And I can't let that happen because you're my *friend*. And friends don't let their friends get hurt. Alright?"

He stares at me like I'm some sort of exotic predator. I don't really know what to make of his gaze, so I try to continue.

"Now, I don't know exactly *why* you thought that running out into *Death Desert the Experience* would be a good idea, but if it was purely to get your adrenaline fix, then I can't stand for it. Dying is bad, okay? It's not good to die. Only losers die, and you're not a loser, are you?" He gives me a long, unblinking stare. "Right, exactly. I mean, what were you even thinking? That you were just going to stumble out into the soot with no provisions save for that piece of royal skin to-go, and *not* die? You're lucky I was there to stop you!"

Of course, he doesn't say anything in response. Across his neck, a dark blue bruise has bloomed, suspiciously hand-shaped. I gulp and turn away, crossing my arms.

"Really, if you would just *talk* to me, then . . ."

There's a little grumble. I blink and look back at Simel. He's turned a shade paler. Wait. Is he . . . ?

"Are you hungry?" I ask, more surprised than anything. "Is that it? Did you run away to get, like, provisions or something?" Of course, he doesn't say anything or even acknowledge that I said anything at all, but the sweat beading on his forehead is all the confirmation I need. "That's it, isn't it? Oh, gosh, Simel, you didn't need to run away for *that*! If you'd just told me, I would've gone and grabbed whatever you needed!" A little thought hits me. "On the other hand, do you really need those kinds of provisions? I've got plenty of stuff on hand. I mean, take for example . . ."

Reaching out, I gouge a piece of flesh from the floor and hold it up. It twitches in my grip and I grin proudly. "The crib himself! Indeed, much like a fairy-tale gingerbread house, this spacious condo is built of one hundred percent edible materials. Amazing, right?" Smiling, I hold the piece of flesh closer to him where he lies on the lung. Like a vampire from a cross, he recoils back, eyes wide and hands trembling. The smile on my face twitches a little. "What, you don't want it?"

And for the first time since our reunion, he actually gives a response of some kind. Namely, by vigorously shaking his head back and forth like his life depended on it.

My jaw slacks open. H—he responded! That's wonderful!

Too happy to really care about the fact that his first communicative expression was staunch refusal, I quickly move on. "Okay, so no crib meat, huh? Cool, cool, very cool with me. I don't mind!" Excited for some *real* conversation, I put the piece of meat into my inventory, simultaneously pulling out close to a dozen other pieces of meat. "Okay, so, you've got basically a whole buffet of choices. We have tarantula meat, drake meat, bird meat, lizard meat, gobli—" I choke on my words. Moving on sheer instinct, I toss the piece of goblin meat back into my inventory. Nothing to see there, nope, not at all. Sure, Simel looks like someone drained all the blood from his face and replaced it with WHITE paint, but that doesn't matter. I clear my throat. "Ye—up. Lots of great, uh, choices here. I can really recommend the tarantula meat. It's basically like crab meat, but big."

He briefly looks away from my face to stare at the several meats in my hands. His body starts to tremble, and he shakes his head again, just as fiercely as before.

"Huh?" I say. "You don't want it?" He continues shaking his head, which would technically make for a double negative, creating a positive, but by reading the atmosphere, I'm able to tell that he just really, really, really, *really* doesn't want my meats. Weird. "Well, uh . . ." I frown. The meats disappear from my hands and go back into my inventory. "There's only really one kind of meat left, but . . ." Slitting a line across my forearm, I pull out my brachioradialis, presenting the lean piece of flesh like it's an unresponsive snake. "I wouldn't recommend it; my meat is really lean and stringy. Not yummy at all. Also, I think it might be slightly necrotic, so . . ."

Simel takes one look at my forearm, leans over to the side, and promptly pukes up what seems to mainly be stomach acids and little else.

"S—Simel?!" I cry, reaching out to try to help him, but he slaps my hand away.

I look at my arm. Oh, okay, I get it. I stuff the muscle back into my forearm. "Is this better?" He won't even look at me. He's just taking brief, shallow breaths. Did I do something wrong . . . ?

This feels like the perfect moment to pat him on the back or something, but I can't bring myself to. I this moment, I don't think he'd like it all that much.

I guess, in this position, the only thing you can really do is to move on and try to ignore the puddle of vomit on the pulsating floor. "Do you, uh"—my gaze briefly flickers down to the puddle—"eat meat, like . . . *at all?*"

For a second or so, he just sits there, half hunched over the side of the lung bed. Then, after some time, he shakes his head tiredly. I can feel a wave of simultaneous understanding and confusion wash over me. *He turned vegan?* No, wait, *vegetarian?* I don't know. He didn't seem too hyped to eat the tarantula meat, so maybe he's more of a vegan? I don't know. This is kind of worrying, though. I wonder what brought it on? I can remember with fairly good confidence that he ate soup with meat in it while we were in the cage, so this must've happened after that.

Unfortunately, it's not like I can actually ask him how or why, so I guess I'll just accept it. "No meat, huh . . ." This makes things just a teeny tiny bit more complicated for me. I have eaten the plants on this floor, but I didn't really make any habit of keeping them in my inventory unless they were poisonous enough to let me train my resistances. There was this one cactus that was safe to eat, unlike all the rest, but . . .

"Well, erm . . ." I scratch my neck. "Look, I could probably go get you some grub and stuff, but . . ." I pull my lips tight. How do I say this properly . . . ? I sigh. "See, I can't really go out to get you stuff to keep you alive if I can't know you'll still be here when I get back." To accentuate my point, I make a couple of nice, visible gestures. "I don't want to have to tie you down, Simel, because that just shouldn't be needed among friends, okay?" Not to mention the fact that if I were to tie him with anything, it would probably be my own intestines. Going by the way he reacted to my forearm, I can't imagine that he'd enjoy that.

His left eye twitches. Right. "I *could* bar the door somehow, but, I mean . . . That shouldn't be needed either, right? You're a smart fellow. Certainly more than me. If you know anything, it should be that the desert just isn't a place for little goblins all on their own. You'd die. And you know that, don't you?"

He looks down at his lap, eyebrows furrowing slightly in the tiniest expression of frustration.

"I don't need much, Simel. I just need you to promise not to run out and away while I'm gone. Okay? I shouldn't be gone for too long. Unlike most other things, I can't smell you. Not even your clothes. If you get lost, I can't save you." I try to catch his gaze but he won't look at me. No matter. "Can you promise me that you won't run away again?" He won't look at me. "Please. Just a single nod will do."

The corners of his lips dip into a frown. His hands curl into fists. Head hung low, I let him think—let my words sink in fully.

And, after almost a full minute of silence . . .

He gives a nod.

See, was that so hard? I almost want to make a joke about his indecisiveness, but I don't think he'd take it too well right now.

"Right! Great, thank you for agreeing. In that case, I'll get going straightaway. I'll check the camp you had, but . . . yeah. We'll see." Saying so, I head for the door. As I grab hold of its fleshy hinges, I keep my eyes on Simel. He's still looking down, periodically checking the little puddle he expelled. Right. Okay. I don't like not being able to fully trust him, but it's not like I've got any choice. I pull open the door and step out, keeping my head inside just long enough to call out, "I'll be going now—see you soon!"

And then I close the door.

Haaaah . . .

Sighing, I lean my forehead against the door. Right. Right. Okay. Yeah. Yeah . . .

I'm starting to get a feeling that the real answer to the God of Pain's question wasn't that he's gotten married recently. Maybe he's picked up an instrument? Hmm. They do say that some music is more communicative than words, so if I get him a flute or something, maybe he'll talk to me through that?

Yeah, that might work! Maybe.

Well, no use in procrastinating.

I turn away from the giant and take a deep breath through my nose. Sni—ff. Alright, the camp is that way, and if I keep the same speed as I did last time, then it shouldn't take much time at all to get there. Probably. Before I leave, I take a quick glance over my shoulder. Man, not being able to smell what he's doing is seriously messing with my brain. Is he standing up? Is he sitting down? Is he walking around? Is he lying down? I have no idea.

It feels weird, but for now, I really don't have any other choice than to trust that he'll hold true to his promise.

As I grumble and mumble, I pull a pair of snakeskins out of my inventory and tie them around my hands and arms. Now then.

Going down on my hands and feet, I start running toward the camp on all fours. At this speed, the otherwise sweltering heat of the sun and the sands becomes more of a breeze. Still horribly hot, but it feels slightly cooler than otherwise. Even better, when I'm running like this, I don't have to think so much. It's just me, and the horrible searing pain in every single one of my limbs. It's very simple, I suppose. Unlike emotional pain, physical pain is straightforward. It says, *Here's the thing that's gone wrong* and *Do something about it.*

And while you're feeling that WHITE static of burning neurons and electric impulses, nothing else really matters. The brain prioritizes and decides that the pain of my flesh being cooked alive is slightly more critical than the fact that Simel won't even talk to me.

My breathing, previously even and controlled, hitches.

Still, the pain won't entirely drown out the memory of Simel withdrawing at my touch, of his darkly burning eyes—of his strange, unreadable expression.

I bite my lip and chew straight through it, the blood distributing itself evenly between the inside of my mouth and my chin. It cools me off slightly, but even the taste of warm copper won't make me forget the thoughts bubbling to the forefront of my mind.

Simel. My good friend. My *very first* friend.

Something clawed and wrong coils around my brain and squeezes hard.

Maybe it would have been better if I never removed that hood.

My body goes cold.

My arms turn frozen and all of a sudden I can't run, so I tumble to the ground and the soot and a massive snake of some sort leaps out to constrict me. I kill it. When it's dead, I keep choking it. Once its neck goes *cra—ack*, I drop it and it falls into the sizzling soot.

Haah. Haah. Haah. Haah.

I look up. Ahead of me, just beyond a little soot dune, stands the camp. Straightening out, I walk toward it on two feet. The ground is covered in little mounds of soot. When I check inside one, I find a little goblin body, encased in ash. The body is nothing but cinders and bone. I continue.

Following the scent, I move toward one of the tents. Ignoring the one that held the prince guy, I instead head toward the other, larger one.

The entrance is slightly blocked by soot, with the fabric of the entrance held down by a few pounds of ash. I push the cloth to the side and enter. The inside is mostly unscathed from the ash storm. The main feature would be the large round table placed in the middle of the tent. There's nothing on it, though, apart from a map of some sort. The interior walls of the tent are mostly barren, though a few cupboards and similar are placed next to them. I can't smell anything normally edible inside, though, so I quickly leave.

Sniff sniff sniff. I can smell something alive. Large. Warm.

I head toward the nearby cliff. Unsurprisingly, there's a cavern in its shade. The smell is coming from inside the cavern. Mutely, I head inside.

The floor is littered with small planks of wood, ripped fabric, and bones. A few opened crates stand here and there. One of the more complete ones seems to contain a tent of some sort, made of a slick, WHITE leather. Another crate contains half-eaten dried rations. Right.

Heading deeper inside the cave, I eventually find the reason for this all.

<Woolly Drake (Lv.45)>
<Woolly Drake (Lv.19)>
<Woolly Drake (Lv.2)>

Laid atop a ripped-apart tent is a woolly drake and two smaller woolly drakes. Their blank, BLACK eyes turn to me. I kill them.

<Woolly Drake (Lv.45) Defeated.>

\<Woolly Drake (Lv.19) Defeated.\>
\<Woolly Drake (Lv.2) Defeated.\>

Since Simel is waiting for me, I disassemble them as quickly as I can. Then I leave.

No luck with the rations.

Emerging back out into the searing hot desert sun, I take a deep breath. This time, the scent of cacti hits me like a curve ball. It's a bit of a detour, but I need to do it.

I trudge into the desert and continue my sprint. Eventually I find a cactus, good and edible and decidedly non-poisonous. The kind with pink blooms. I'm just about to slice it up into nice even chunks when I realize that my hands and my claws are covered in almost a year's worth of grime. Or, well, considering Moleman's power wash, it's closer to half a year or so. Still, half a year's worth of blood and internal organs and bile and disease can't be good for you.

In that case, I'll need to . . . Or should I . . . Or would it be better if . . . ?

Damn it.

After about five minutes of grumbling, I decide to just uproot the entire thing and carry it back as is. It's not like Simel will eat the skin and inch-long barbs, so it should be fine if I touch that. The spiny needles easily stab through my hands and palms, affixing it in place. Huh. Hey, lightbulb moment! You know in cartoons how they sometimes have a guy fall into a cactus patch and then he comes up and all the cacti have gotten stuck to his back? Yeah.

I stab the cactus into my back. It's a little heavy, but my stats can handle it. Even better, it's firm enough to withstand me running with it on my back. I now have all the strats and advantages of a hedgehog, minus the spin dash.

Or do I . . . ?

Over the horizon, I spot a long-legged bipedal bird stepping carefully over the soot.

\<Altez Bird (Lv.32)\>

Target acquired. Initiating windup. Charge commencing.

Speeding up to incredible speeds, I zoom toward the road runner–looking bird. By the time it notices me, it's already too late. A leap, a roll into a ball, and then I tackle it. We both go tumbling, its startled legs kicking frantically but finding no luck. I, in a similar vein, am trying desperately to grab hold of its slim neck, but it just won't get into reach. What in the heck is—

I stand up. Oh. Suddenly, my cactus backpack feels a fair bit heavier. Looking over my shoulder, I find the answer staring back at me with BLACK, unblinking bird eyes.

Never before have I so thoroughly considered the possibility of my life and existence being a Looney Tunes sketch. For what feels like entire minutes, the both of us just stare at each other, fastened together by the spines of a cactus squeezed in the middle. Now, I don't know how you imagine my physiology to look, but I am actually—fun fact—nothing more than a man. I don't have arms on my back. My arms are also not made of rubber like a certain pirate-king-to-be.

I can't reach this damn bird.

"Squawk!"

However, its beak can reach me, and with the haughty, reckless abandon of a creature with only barely enough brain to dig worms out of sand, it attacks me, bringing its face to mine for a peck. You see where I'm going with this, right?

I bite its beak, cracking a few of my teeth in order to crush it between my molars. The bird makes some strange blubbering sound, but I don't let go, biting a hold first of its tongue and then anything else I can get into my mouth. Blood spurts, cartilage breaks, and after a bit of a tussle, it finally loses enough blood to go limp.

Good grief. Alright, then . . .

Which way was the crib now again?

Once I get back to the crib, it's been at least a couple of hours since I left. In fact, it's turned dark, and the cold is starting to creep in. I'm not exactly sure how long Simel's been on his own, but . . . Actually, let's get a specific number on that one.

<Top—Status—Community>
<00:30:10
Day 364>
<The thirteenth attempt will begin in 23:29:50>
<The Server Symposium will begin in 23:29:50.>

It's already past midnight?!

Wow. Okay, yeah, today went *fast*. Not all that strange considering just how much has happened, but still a bit of a shock. More worrying, however, would be the fact that the server symposium is literally less than a day away. I mean, considering Simel, that could be really bad, right? Not that I think he'll go get himself killed or anything. Just that, I don't know . . . I only just reunited with him, so to leave him so soon feels a bit mean. I guess.

But that's for later. Right now, I'm at the crib, and it's pretty late, so I really ought to treat Simel to some good-old fashioned *grub*!

Mustering a friendly, outgoing smile, I summon a bit of goodwill and excitement. I'm sure that now, since I've gotten him some food, he'll be much happier to see me!

Smiling, I throw the door open fully with a single, quick pull.

And out tumbles Simel, hands stretched out, eyes wide, right into my arms, almost as though he was leaning on the door for some reason and my opening it was basically like pulling the rug out from under him. Or—or something. I blink down at him. He stares up at me. I don't even know what to say right now because I'm so shocked, I mean . . . Why was he leaning on the door? Is that standard goblin behavior?

Besides, going by how he fell into my arms face first, it would almost suggest that he was pushing against the door.

My brows furrow in mild suspicion.

Below, in my arms, I see his face twist and shift in odd, unreadable ways. Even more interesting, despite the fact that I'm holding him—the both of us as close as we were when I carried him here—he isn't trembling. He's perfectly still. Not even a single movement. I'd assume he was dead if it weren't for his clothes and skin being just slightly warm.

I look down at him. The smile that was on my face before is gone. "Simel?" I ask, calmly. "What were you doing by the door?"

His jaw starts trembling, making his teeth chatter.

Since we're already touching, I guess a little more wouldn't hurt, right?

I grab a gentle hold of his jaw, making his teeth stop clacking together. "Are you alright, Simel? Are you cold?" Yes, now that I'm feeling his skin more closely, he's very cold. Almost deathly so. That isn't good. He's still young. I hope he isn't sick. I frown down at him. He twitches in my hand. And then he starts trembling. Shivering, even! Now isn't that just pitiful? Removing my hand from his cheek, I grab him closer. He trembles against my chest. "Let's go back inside, okay?"

After a second or so, his head starts to give a few curt, jerking nods. Good! Weirdly enough, his eyes look very shiny in the light of the many, many moons. But that's alright.

Still holding him closely, I step inside the crib and close the door behind us. Once the door is closed fully, I put him down. He stumbles a little, but when I try to steady him, he winces back, so . . . Yeah. Is this what it's like to have a toddler? He certainly doesn't come off as confident as he did the last time we met, but . . . Well, it's not like I can just abandon him, right? Friends change. The important thing is to remember that even if they've changed, they're still your friend in the end, no matter what.

Something itches on my back and I suddenly remember something.

"Oh!" I exclaim. He jumps back a little but that's fine. "I almost forgot! Look, Simel; I got you grub!" To show off the goods, I twist around, presenting my spiny, blood-soaked back, the cactus fastened to it, and also the large bird impaled on said cactus. Now that I think about it, that might be a slightly grisly sight, confirmed by Simel taking a couple of steps back.

Jabbing a thumb at the stuff on my back, I begin explaining. "See, I checked the camp but there wasn't anything, so I went and got this cactus! It's totally edible and not poisonous. But my fingers are covered in necrotic waste and stuff so I couldn't cut it up, but then while bringing it I found this bird, and one thing led to another, so . . ." I chuckle. "But it *is* food!" At least, I think so . . .

He stares at me. Stretching the limits of my social abilities, I spend fifteen skill points to gain the ability to read his goblin expressions. Okay, slight furrowing of the brow, uncertain shifting of the gaze, tightening of the lips . . . "What? Are you skeptical?"

He doesn't answer or anything, but I can tell what he's thinking.

"Hey! This stuff is totally safe; it just happens to be covered in a bit of blood and feathers, is all. But that's just the outside part—the inside is totally safe. See, I'll show you! I just need to—" I reach back. Or, at least, I try to.

Remember how I said my arms aren't made of rubber? That's still factual.

I freeze. Okay. Uh-huh. Um.

I reach back a little bit more. Y—eah, no, I'm not going to reach that. I glance over at Simel, putting on my best puppy-dog eyes. Without even a twitch of hesitation, he looks away. Okay, yeah, I understand that one.

Erm, alright, let's just . . .

Backing up toward one of the walls, I try to fasten the cactus to that instead. But now the bird is in the way. The spines won't go as far into the crib as they will into my own flesh. It's still primarily fastened to *me*. This is . . . quite the pickle, huh? B—but no need to fret! I'll solve this. Easy peasy! See, if I can just grab something like a long bone from my inventory, then I can use that as a poker to fix it. Easy!

Oh, wait, yeah, I don't keep the bones. I mean, it's not like I can eat them, so . . .

Okay. I've got it. Simple solution. No troubles.

I sit down on the floor and grab the knee of my left leg. Let's see, the soft spots are here, here, and here . . . I bring up my right index finger. Angling it just right, I stab it into a soft spot in between cartilage and bone. Wiggle wiggle wiggle.

<You have learned: Stab Lv.4>

I pull out my finger again. Deep RED blood starts seeping out and I put my finger against a different spot before stabbing it in again. Repeating this a few times, I'm finally left with a knee that looks almost like Swiss cheese, which is what I'm going for. To seal the deal, I bite off the last of it, accidentally scraping my teeth against the bone. One of them goes *crack*, so I pull it out and swallow it down.

And now, for the moment of truth.

Drumroll, please . . .

I wiggle my leg.

With a little tug, it comes off completely, separating by the knee.

I hold up the severed appendage by the shin and turn to Simel, grinning with pride. "Ta-da!"

I didn't notice it before, but for some reason, he's taken a seat over in the corner of the crib, hunched up with his back against the fleshy wall, knees pressed to his chest, eyes peering at me like a sailor staring out at the pitch-BLACK sea after a devastating storm. For lack of a better word, he seems completely disinterested in my wonderful solution. But I won't let that demotivate me.

Hiding my hurt, I turn the leg around and push the foot end into a part of the cactus. For a moment, I have the horrible thought that maybe this is some sort of karma, and the gods—wanting nothing less than to watch me suffer—might be so cruel as to make this not work. Maybe my foot will get stuck, and I'll have to try again with another foot, and then another foot, and by the end I'll look like a plate of finger food, but with feet instead of meats and chee—

Pop!

OhthankGodalmighty it *worked*!

The cactus, the bird, and a pretty substantial bit of the skin and flesh on my back all fall off with a thud, the spines of the cactus finding a new home in the crib's twitching flesh.

Task complete! See, was that so hard? Not at all. Simple stuff.

To show him the prickly fruits of my great labor, I turn to Simel, doing a fun little pose as I do. Unfortunately, this goes unnoticed, because Simel is currently leaning his forehead against his propped-up knees and is therefore unable to see me. Huh. W—well, it might be because the cactus is still covered in flesh and stuff, so if I just fix that, he should be okay. I think.

In silence, I pull off the flesh, mournfully munching on it as I do. As a final act, I remove the bird, leaving the cactus free of all flesh and organs and stuff. It's still a fair bit bloodied, but that's just the skin, so it should be okay, right?

I turn back to look at Simel, but he's still all curled up in a ball against the wall. His shoulders are trembling a bit, but that's nothing new.

Since he's apparently still a bit unresponsive, I guess I'll just keep going. I was going to ask him if he had a knife or something on his person, but I suppose that'll have to wait.

Bringing my index finger to my face, I give my sharp nail a scrutinizing look. After a second or so, I pop it in my mouth and try to clean it as best I can. Hmm. I wonder how much water is in my tear ducts? Or would it be cleaner to use the goop on my eyes to clean it? Argh, this is way too complicated!

When I pull my finger back out, it looks much cleaner than before.

<You have learned: Poison Protection Lv.7>

Hey, neat! Been a while since I saw that one. Doesn't bode well for the cleanliness of my finger, though . . .

Out of the corner of my eye, I catch a glimpse of the cactus's spines. At least, one of the clean ones.

Aha!

Feeling like a real clever fella for once, I snap off the little barb. If it's sharp enough to pierce my skin, then cactus skin should be no different, right? Almost cackling, I hunch down and press the sharp bit of the spine against the cactus. Carefully, carefully . . .

There!

The spine slips inside the cactus's flesh and I feel a rush of victory. So far, so good. Now, to just carefully make a longer slit . . .

After a couple of minutes of careful work, I've finally succeeded in chiseling a slit alongside the entire body of the cactus. It would've gone much faster if I'd used my claws, but things being as they are, this is the best I can do. I begin carefully stripping the thing. Halfway through removing the skin, I suddenly realize that I genuinely have no idea what to put the peeled cactus on. The skins in my inventory aren't vegan, and neither is my own skin. Simel still won't look at me, for some reason.

I eye the cactus.

Or I can just use the cactus's own skin. Yeah, that's . . . not my proudest intellectual moment.

After a few more minutes, the cactus is fully skinned and on the floor, atop a clean cactus carpet. Phew! And it only took me like an hour. Of course, had this been a goblin or something like that, I could've skinned it in a couple of minutes, tops. I really need to up my skill level in non-sentient skinning.

Turning to Simel, I give a beaming smile. He's still in the same position, but I won't let that stop me anymore. "Hey, Simel!" I call out. He twitches but doesn't move otherwise. My smile drops a little, but a shake of the head lets me regain my moxie. "I finished skinning the cactus, so now you can eat! It's kind of sour, and it doesn't taste too good, but it's got plenty of water in it, and you won't die of it, which is in clear opposition to a non-cactus diet."

He doesn't move.

Alright, now that's just rude. I've been laboring over this thing, going to get food, skinning, and everything, for *hours*, and he won't even *look at it?* My smile is soon replaced by an irritated frown and I stand up. I trudge over toward Simel. "Okay, listen, Simel . . . I've done you a huge favor here, getting you food and stuff, and it's fine if you don't want to thank me for it, that's cool, but can't you at least give it a glance? Is that so much to ask for?"

I'm standing right above him now, his hunched-over form basking in my shadow. He isn't giving a single hint of caring. Yeah, okay, that's it.

Reaching down, I grab his arm and pull him up, dragging him off the floor and into the air until his face is level with mine. I bore my eyes into his. "Well? *Is it?*"

But he still won't look at me. His eyes are focusing somewhere off in the distance, moving only slightly, and, and . . . and there's a trail of tears going down both eyes. A bit of snot is bubbling out of his nose. His mouth is open and his breath is quick.

Still holding him high in the air, I feel my heart drop and all the anger bubbling in my stomach melt away. "S—Simel?" I say. "What's wrong, Simel? What happened?"

Gently, I lower him a little, but he won't stand on both feet, and even as I lower him, his knees just buckle and I can do nothing but let him slide back down on the floor, where he curls himself up, still silently sobbing. Wh—what . . . what is . . . ?

I go down on my knees next to him. "Simel, please, what's wrong? Whatever it is, I'll put it right! Heh, you know me, Simel. If I want to do something, by God, I'll do it. You know that, so . . . So if you ask for it, I'll do it. You know that. I'm your friend. I'll do it, even if it hurts. Won't you please tell me how I can put this right, Simel? My friend?"

Face dark, eyes slightly REDdened, he slowly drags his gaze across the floor, over to me, up my bloodied body, and to my face. That unidentifiable emotion briefly surges in his eyes before dying away, replaced by dead apathy.

My chest surges with emotions of all sorts, squirming and snapping at each other like a knotted-up ball of rattlesnakes. "Is—is it something *I* did? Did I do something to you? Did I hurt you?" I almost chuckle out of pure absurdity. "I would never hurt you, Simel. Never. Is it because of the"—I can feel my own face twist like loose dough—"but that wasn't . . . Sometimes, to do the right thing, we need to do a few things that maybe don't look so good. And that's just how it is, isn't it?" I almost put my hands on him but a single glance from his dark eyes is enough to stop me. I pull back my arm and clutch my hand to my chest.

"Whatever it looks like, whatever it seems like, whatever you think . . ." I gulp. "All I've ever wanted is to—"

<A CHANGE HAS BEEN MADE.>

<TUTORIAL STAGE, HELL DIFFICULTY FIFTEENTH FLOOR: BOSS STAGE>

<[CLEAR CONDITION] DO THE RIGHT THING.>

Just Talking

I stare at the message before my eyes. It stares back at me.

What . . . ?

There's a little sound below and I look down to see Simel's face twist in pain. He gives another whimper. My mind is whirling. What? What? What? What?

Slowly, I stand up. Then I back away, over to the other wall. I sit down.

What is going on? What does that mean? What is the *right thing*? What is *right*? What is *wrong*? What does this mean? What is expected of me? I don't . . .

I don't know anything.

<THE GOD OF COWARDICE PITIES YOU.>

Uh-huh. Right. I just . . .

But I can't think anymore, because across the room, I can see Simel slowly rise from where he lies. Still hunched over, he wipes the tears from his cheeks and the snot from his lips. I watch in silence as he carefully stands up, legs wobbling slightly, and steps over to the cactus. He sits down and, without looking at me even once, grabs a piece from the cactus. He brings it to his face, takes a bite, chews, and swallows. And then another bite, and another.

I watch, enraptured, as Simel actually eats.

After a few minutes, he stops, stands up, and walks over to the lung bed. There, he lies down. The whole thing couldn't have lasted more than ten minutes, but it felt like a lifetime.

Would it be inappropriate to tell him a good-night story? How about a hug? No?

I watch him where he lies, silently, his body turned away from me. After some time, his breathing becomes slower, deeper. As quietly as humanly possible,

I stand up once more and tiptoe over to the bed. Saying nothing, thinking just as little, I remove one of the bearskins from my inventory and drape it over his form. Then I walk away, back to the other corner of the crib.

There, I sit down, cross my arms, and let myself fall into gentle meditation.

<A Canto appears to you.>

I watch the darkness in my head with curiosity. Maybe it's different? The floor clear requirement changed, so maybe, for once, the canto might actually be somewhat useful . . . ?

<[O vengeance of the Lord, how you should be dreaded by everyone who now can read whatever was made manifest to me!]>

I take it back. This isn't useful in the least. This is, miraculously enough, even more useless than the previous ones. Amazing! Stunning! I am so impressed!

Haaaah . . . What is even happening anymore . . . ?

Do the right thing. The heck does that even mean?

Without really thinking, I glance over to one of the fleshy walls.

<Giant [BOSS]>

Yeah, that's still the boss.

I turn my eyes to look at Simel where he lies on the bed.

<Simel>

I blink at the message. Hey. Whoa. That's . . . that's new. *And* weird.

An hour ago, you wanted me to put this giant out of his misery. Is that no longer on the table? Or are you just testing me to see whether I'll still kill him? Is that it? The gods seem to think he should be killed, but does that mean that it's the *right thing* to do? He doesn't have a level or anything. By that logic, killing him shouldn't even be necessary to beat the floor.

And honestly. How am I supposed to know what *the right thing* to do is? Isn't the whole not-knowing thing a huge part of moral and ethical phi-losophy? Morality is supposed to be subjective; nobody knows what's truly good or evil, or even if either one of those exists at all! Even things that seem clearly good or evil, like helping people in need or killing another human being, can become just the opposite depending on the situation. If you help someone in doing bad stuff, then what does that make you? Likewise, it isn't evil to kill someone who's trying to kill you. It's all subjective, so trying to keep track of what's right and wrong is a pointless exercise that only serves to overcomplicate the simple.

I shouldn't need to think too hard about my everyday actions. If it feels right, then it is right. You shouldn't need to ponder any further on it, because then you can easily think yourself into a corner.

Across the room, Simel whimpers in his sleep. I pause my grumbling to look at him. But he doesn't whimper again, so I guess he's fine.

Simel, huh . . . Yeah, I really have no idea.

Logically speaking, if I *did* kill the giant and it let me beat the floor, wouldn't that also be bad? I mean, that'd leave Simel in the middle of nowhere, with nothing to do but starve and die in this infernal heat. I'd basically be sentencing him to death for no reason whatsoever.

I shake my head. Yeah, no. No matter what, I can't let my goals here get Simel hurt.

<Top—Status—Community>
<03:56:10 Day 364>
<The thirteenth attempt will begin in 20:03:50>
<The Server Symposium will begin in 20:03:50.>

The server symposium, huh . . . ?

Moleman will be there. I should be able to ask him about it. He should know what the right course of action is. Sure, I'm not exactly immoral or anything like that, but in this situation, there's no way I can assume to know what the gods think is the right thing to do. Hm. Combined with the fact that I don't get taken back to the lobby with each attempt, isn't there a chance that I may be stuck on floor fifteen for months and years until I do the *right thing*?

Either that, or the *right thing* is a matter of my own mindset and not that of the gods. Who knows, really?

Since the situation is complicated enough as it is, I might as well get my thoughts off the matter by doing a little training. I'm just about to take a big bite out of my left hand when I notice Simel shifting in his sleep. Considering the way he looks at most meat, he might not want to wake up to a blood-covered floor. And, sure, it's already covered in a bit of blood, and it *is* made of meat, but . . . yeah.

Standing up, I tiptoe over to the door and creep outside, closing it behind me so gently it doesn't make a sound. The second I step outside, my breath turns to a milky WHITE and goose bumps spread across my body.

<You have learned: Cold Resistance Lv.8>

Ah, yeah, there it is. Nighttime in this desert is certainly not for the warm-blooded. You've got to have antifreeze for blood to get far. Well, either that or you could just embrace the whole my-entire-body-is-freezing-over thing. Don't people say challenges are good for building character? Yeah, exactly.

The kind of funny thing about this desert is that even though the air is as cold as the surface of Pluto, the sand below the soot is still warm. Yeah, see, the soot acts as an insulating layer, keeping the sand warm for the majority of the night. Most small creatures therefore choose to burrow down into said sand, keeping their tiny little bodies all huddled together like a group of adorable bunnies.

Or, as is common with burrowworms, they may instead seek refuge inside the flesh of the crib. I haven't cleaned them out in a couple of days, so it's really about time I gave the crib a nice de-parasite-ification.

Oh, uh, not counting myself, of course. Evicting myself would be counterintuitive to my general goals.

Now, let's see, where do we have those worms . . . Circling around to the back of the giant, I keep my back hunched and my head angled to see the underside of his flesh. Nothing, nothing, nothing . . . Oh, here we go! Almost invisible to the untrained eye, but very much visible to mine. Kneeling down, I bring my eyes level to the little hole. It's about the same diameter as a baseball, and it leads right into his flesh. The first time I met these little buggers, I was just excavating the hallway leading from the door, only to find one of these things popping up at me like a spring-loaded snake-in-a-can.

But now they're hardly a threat. Same as how I've done it every other time, I slit an incision along my palm before sticking my entire hand into the hole. No hesitation whatsoever.

The giant's bodily temperature is weird. His skin is lukewarm at most, but once you get a bit farther inside, it turns room temperature. A relaxed, lovely thirty-seven degrees. But, in reality, the burrowworms would prefer something warmer. Such as, for example, *my* blood and flesh.

Lo and behold, after less than a minute of waiting, something sharp and wet prods at my hand. I let it nibble for a few seconds, but once it takes a full-hearted bite, I grab hold of it and pull it out with all the strength and panache of a master fisher, the several-meter-long thing flailing out into the cold night air, the sheen of its blood-slick skin reflecting the light of the several moons above.

<Burrowworm (Lv.19)>

It's basically like a big pink eel but with an exceptionally toothy mouth and a bunch of insectlike grabbers by the front end. Not a pretty thing to look at, but it doesn't taste too bad.

Before it has time to try to burrow inside my arm or chest or whatever, I bring its mouth part to my face and bite off its head, swallowing it in one piece despite its tumultuous size. The body of the burroworm starts flailing frantically and without any sort of logic. To dissuade this, I bring the other end of the worm to my face and bite off the second head as well. Yeah, that's an interesting thing— it's got two heads. I have no idea if this is to make it easier to turn around, or maybe to fight predators, but it makes defeating it a two-bite deal instead of a single-bite one.

<Burroworm (Lv.19) Defeated.>
<[Level Up]>
<You have reached Level 66.>
<Agility has increased by 2.
Strength has increased by 3.
Stamina has increased by 2.
Magic Power has increased by 1.
Burn Resistance has increased by 1.
Frostbite Resistance has increased by 1.
Climb has increased by 1.>

Neato. Alright, well, I've got a whole night to waste, so I guess I might as well get to it.

By the time the sun rises once more, the giant has been almost completely cleared of his parasitic infection, and I'm feeling a fair bit rejuvenated from last night. Ahhh, is there anything better than to stand in the morning sun, with a full belly and an organic, full-body moisturizer, rich in iron, water, and RED blood cells? Absolutely not.

Unfortunately, Simel might not like my current look, as trendy and modernist as it is, so before I go back inside, I spend a while licking myself clean. Hm. Maybe I really *am* a prissy kitty after all . . .

Not a princess, though. As far as I know, I haven't got a single drop of royal blood in my body. Not that there *hasn't* been royal blood in there at some point, but that wasn't mine per se, so I don't count it.

Happy and clean, I trudge up to the door. But I hesitate a little before entering. Maybe he's leaning against the door again?

Okay, honestly, if he was leaning against the door *again*, I would probably assume it was a goblin thing and not some illogical attempt at getting out of the crib. Wherefore he would ever want to do that.

After a moment's hesitation, I pull the door open. No Simel falls out. I breathe a sigh of relief and step inside, closing the door behind me to keep out the ever-mounting heat. But when I move inside the main room of the crib, I find a startling sight.

Simel isn't awake yet.

He's still asleep, softly breathing, curled up underneath and on top of the bearskin. Well, isn't that just precious? It's almost such an adorable sight that I hesitate to enter lest my arrival might rouse him from his wonderful little dreams. Unfortunately, I've got a few appendages to regrow, and the sands and soot aren't very good for meditating on top of.

So, moving as softly and quietly as a panther, I make my way inside the room. I get halfway across the floor before I realize something.

Simel is whimpering in his sleep.

He was doing that before, sure, but it feels more frantic now. He genuinely sounds terrified, and now that I'm looking at his face, he seems scared, too. Like Scooby-Doo levels of horror.

Maybe it would be best if I just ignored it. He hasn't reacted too well to my being close during the past few hours, but watching him toss and turn like this is almost pure torture. Hrmm . . . Well, I'm sure it won't hurt if I stand just a little bit closer? And—and maybe an inch or so closer. A little bit more . . .

I stare down at him where he lies, tossing and turning. I wonder if it's comfortable sleeping in such a thick coat. If I were him, I'd probably be like a molten popsicle. Or a popsicle about to melt. Because of the heat, that is. Yeah.

Maybe the bear pelt was too much?

Bears are pretty big and need to keep really warm. How thick is that fur even? An inch? Two? No idea, but . . . Looking at the temperature in here, it's far from cold. It's kind of warm, actually. So if he's sleeping not just in his entire outfit but also beneath a thick bear blanket, then it would only be obvious he'd be way too warm. I'm sure he's sweating buckets under there.

So, considering that I was the one who covered him in said blanket, it only makes sense that I should be the one to remove it. To absolve myself of the mistake, one might say.

Yup, that makes sense.

Leaning forward, I reach out toward the blanket.

My fingers only barely have time to brush up against the hairs of the blanket before Simel's eyes suddenly flare open in wide-eyed terror, darting back and forth only to quickly fall on me, and, more importantly: my claws. At this moment mere inches from his throat.

Ah, eh, um . . . This isn't what it—

<Chain.>

Leaping out of the bed like a cat startled awake, he's somehow able to get to his feet without stumbling while also keeping all fingers on his right hand aimed at me, in a clear stay-back-or-the-girl-gets-it pose. I'm actually genuinely impressed; like, he jumped out of bed and got to a battle-ready stance faster than the pop of a cork! Going by the look on his face, he's absolutely ready, too. His hand is trembling, and so is his lower lip, but apart from that, he seems totally prepared to throw down.

How silly! And all because I accidentally woke him up! What a simple misunderstanding!

I pull up my hands in a gesture of friendly surrender.

<Chain broken.>

"Heh, uh, um," I begin, but I can't say anything else before he points at me again.

<Chain.>

Really? With this again? Gee, I almost want to roll my eyes.
"Look, Simel . . ." I shake my head.

<Chain broken.>

I barely even have time to register the pop-up before the next one shows up.

<Chain.>

My jaw snaps shut. Okay. Starting to get a bit annoying, now.
"Listen, I wasn't trying to—" I take a step toward him.

<Chain broken.>

He points at me again.

<Chain.>

I purse my lips. "Simel, I don't know if you know this, but I can see every time you do that, and it's starting to get kind of irritating, so if you do that one more time—"

<Chain broken.>

Not even a single heartbeat later,

<Chain.>

I grit my teeth. "Okay, you know what? Don't say I didn't warn you," I say, taking one big step toward him.

<Chain broken.>

He points at me again but I'm faster—*much* faster—so before he has time to do any useless magic stuff, I grab his hand, squeezing the tiny appendage within my large palm. Compared to mine, his hand is almost like that of a child. Tiny. Small. Brittle. In my grip, it trembles meekly. Thankfully for Simel, I'm not actually trying to hurt him. In fact, I'm trying to do just the opposite.

Among his fingers, I dig out his index finger. And, just as I remember it, he's wearing a little ring with a little gemstone on it. Using my sharp claws, I'm able to carefully remove the gemstone. It shines gray in the light.

With my prize in hand, I let go of him. For a second, he doesn't move at all. He just stares at me, and at the gem in my hand. And then he looks up at me, his big, fawn eyes shimmering.

"You can have it back once you promise to use it properly," I say as I stab my finger inside my shoulder. Once I've got a nice, deep hole made, I push the gemstone inside. I kind of wanted to eat it, but that'd be a bit too mean, right? Besides, if Simel can afford to have one of these on each finger, they can't be too expensive, so I should be able to have a taste at some point or another.

"As I was trying to explain," I say, looking down at him, "this was all a silly misunderstanding! I didn't really mean to wake you up. That was a mistake, okay?" I smile. He doesn't smile back, as usual. "But your reaction was completely unwarranted. Need I remind you that we have to be able to cooperate here? I'm not trying to accuse you of anything, but if we're going to share this crib, I need to be able to wake you up without getting a fistful of magic and spells. Is that so much to ask for?"

I would've liked to receive an agreeing shake of the head, but silence works just as well, I suppose.

"Yeah, exactly. How would you like it if I went all claws-first whenever you startled me? Wouldn't be very fun, would it?" Honestly, I'd like to say a few more words, but I think he's learned his lesson. And I didn't need to use any physical punishment whatsoever! I am *rocking* this assignment. As I'm mentally praising myself, a short bit of silence falls over the crib. Considering that we're standing less than a meter away from each other, the silence turns awkward remarkably fast.

"Good, good, uh . . ." I start, but I'm not sure where to take it after that, so I fall silent again. Now that I think about it, since we're standing like this anyway, I might as well explain what the day holds in store. "Okay, so, uh . . . How should I explain this, um . . ." I wave a little in the air. "Remember when we last met? After I . . . uh . . . *defeated* the king, I sort of just disappeared, right? Specifically, I guess it was five minutes *after* defeating him, but . . . I went poof. Right? You remember that?"

He doesn't nod or make any other show that he isn't both mute *and* deaf, but this is basically his standard emote by now, so I continue.

"Right. See, tonight, at midnight, in around twelve hours, I'll be doing that again." His eyes widen by a hair's breadth. "But I'll only be gone for twenty-four hours! And then I'll be right back here again, and we can figure out how to make this all work." For some inexplicable reason, this makes his ears fall a little. They've been hanging weirdly low ever since I saw him, kind of like a scared dog, but now they're even lower than that.

Maybe he's hungry? He did wake up like a minute ago, so maybe he needs some grub to get his brain going. That might not be a bad idea.

I smile at him. He flinches. "How about I explain a bit over breakfast? You still have some cactus left, so . . ." For some reason, the mention of the cactus makes him visibly pale. "Or do you not want—"

And then the most peculiar thing happens. Forget nodding or shaking his head, he actually starts communicating! Non-verbally, sure, but by God does he do it.

He gestures toward the hallway and the door and makes a movement like trying to open a door. I stare at him. Wow. I have never felt prouder of someone in my life. Can I take screenshots through the system? I *really* want to immortalize this moment.

His face twists in desperation and an orange blush spreads across his cheeks. He repeats the gesture again for my viewing pleasure. Maybe I should try drawing it? Or maybe if I describe it in a post on the forums, I can keep the memory alive for longer? Ah, that'd be something.

While I'm still thinking about such things, he grits his teeth, repeats the gesture, and then adds another one as a final addendum. He gestures down, at the front of his pants. What, did he get them dirty? Or what is he—

Oh. *Oh.*

"Ah. Uh, um . . . Y—yeah, okay, I'll open it, just give me a minute, okay? Yeah," I stammer. Moving hurriedly, I go and open the front door and hold it open for him as he quietly jumps out. I almost want to follow him outside, but . . . N—no. "Come right back after you're done, okay? Otherwise, I'll be a fair bit upset!"

I have no idea if he listened, but he waddles off somewhere I can't see and . . . Yeah.

For some reason, I keep forgetting that my body's weird. Simel's a normal creature. He needs to eat, and drink, and sleep, and . . . Yeah. All that stuff.

This might be a bit more difficult than I originally thought.

A little while later, just as I was starting to worry that he might have tried to take off, Simel returns from his break. He seems thoughtful as he trudges in through the door, but I'm just glad I didn't check up on him midway. I close the door behind him.

"Did it, um, go well?" I ask. He gives a brief glance over his shoulder but nothing more. Yeah, okay, I don't think I need to ask anything more. In a bit of a position-swap, I plod after him as he walks through the crib and back to the main area. I had hoped he would have gone for the cactus, but instead he just goes over to the farthermost corner and sits down, almost as though he doesn't want my company. But that's just speculation on my part, and I've never been that good at reading people to begin with, so assuming he doesn't want to talk to me—or, rather, have me talk to him—would be a bit silly.

Shaking off such thoughts, I trot over to him and take a seat a few meters away. And then, I just sort of watch him.

He isn't really doing much of anything. Mostly just staring out into space with an expression that might unfairly be described as *somewhat shell-shocked*, but I can't see why he would be making such an expression, so I think this is more of a meditative state. I usually close my eyes while meditating, but maybe this works better for him. He *is* a mage, after all, so there might be some difference there, too.

Meditation might not be too bad. I generally prefer meditating *after* I've accumulated some life-threatening damage, but each to his own. Crossing my legs, I sink into a gentle sort of meditation.

Do the right thing.

Do the right thing.

Do the right thing.

Eugh.

Peeking an eye open, I glance at Simel.

<Simel>

Yeah. Right.

I really need to ask Moleman about this stuff. I'm sure he'll know what the *right thing* is.

For about an hour or so, we just sit in silence. It feels like we're having some sort of moment, so I don't want to be the first to stand up, but just sitting here and doing nothing is killing me. In the end, I start passing the time by biting off my own tongue, letting it regenerate and then doing it again. It has a surprisingly chewy texture, but it isn't all that hard to bite off.

Right as I chew off tongue number twenty-seven, Simel suddenly stands up.

I blink at him. "Oh, awe you—" The second I open my lips, a mouthful of blood floods out my mouth and down my chin to splash the front of my chest and the floor. Simel, who had glanced at me, freezes in place. My eyes flash down to the front of my chest and back up to Simel. "Hey, noh, thish iwwent . . ."

Talking just makes blood splatter everywhere. Shit.

Frantically, I try to wipe the blood from my chin and chest, but it just smears it everywhere. Closing my mouth, I swallow down the blood but since my tongue is still freshly bitten, my mouth just fills back up again within seconds. Okay, this doesn't look very good. At all. Standing up as well, I hold up my hand in the universal *just one second* gesture. Okay, if I activate both regeneration meditation *and* moving meditation, then . . .

<You have learned: Moving Meditation Lv.7>

I gulp down another mouthful of blood, and after only about half a minute, the bleeding stops. My head is starting to ache a little but it's okay. I turn to Simel, rubbing the last of the blood from my chin and chest. He hasn't moved a hair in the minute or so since he stood up. If he tried to pick up a gig as one of those human statues, he could make like a million in a day, I'm sure. "Sho, uh, yeah, sowweh, I wash . . ."

His brows squeeze together ever so slightly.

I hold up my index finger. One more minute and my tongue will have regenerated enough to talk. He stares at me. A minute passes in tense silence. My tongue has mostly regenerated, though it still feels raw and other. "So, um . . ." I chance a smile. "Are you ready for lunch?"

He doesn't answer, which is just as much of an answer as anything else.

After that, I tried to get him to eat the cactus, but he didn't really want it. He seemed paler than he was yesterday. To make sure he ate anything at all, I went out hunting for fresh cacti, and since he'd need a surplus while I was at the symposium, I made sure to grab more than just one. It wasn't very easy to carry them all, but I was able to get five and after that I reached my max carry limit because my legs began to tremble and I couldn't run anymore.

I did at this point get attacked by a pack of big tarantulas, but I was able to defeat them by using my weight and the cacti to my advantage.

<Dog Spider (Lv.12) Defeated.>
<Dog Spider (Lv.9) Defeated.>

<Dog Spider (Lv.16) Defeated.>
<Dog Spider (Lv.17) Defeated.>
<Dog Spider (Lv.13) Defeated.>

"I'm back!" I shout as I enter the crib, once again giving a silent sigh of relief at Simel not trying to go get himself killed again. Striding inside the room, I dump all five cacti on the floor. "I got, like, five whole cacti! And I think I figured out how to carry them best. If you just stack them atop each other, they'll attach to each other super tightly, and everything works out!"

Hands on my hips, I turn to beam at Simel with pride. He's staring at the cacti. No, wait, I think he might be staring at the curled-up tarantulas impaled on the spikes of the cacti. "Oh, those are . . ." I purse my lips for a moment. "First, they aren't poisonous. Second, they're pretty yummy—not as yummy as gob—" I bite my tongue, thankfully not hard enough to sever it completely. Simel doesn't seem to have noticed. Phew. "Th—third, they aren't poisonous. So you can eat them. I don't know exactly what you goblins need to eat, but I doubt you'll feel very good if you eat *only* cactus. So . . . yeah."

No reaction. As usual, then. Let's see, the time is . . .

<Top—Status—Community>
<19:30:10 Day 364>
<The thirteenth attempt will begin in 04:29:50>
<The Server Symposium will begin in 04:29:50.>

Yeah, right, okay.

I crouch down next to the cacti and start peeling them. Simel's standing over my shoulder—at a safe, several-meter distance—and watching. Since it'll be awkward if neither of us says anything, I start talking, almost only to myself. "I know you've got a spell that can make a bit of fire, so you should be able to cook the tarantulas if you want them. Not that you *have* to eat them or anything. The people from where I come from usually don't eat many arachnids themselves, but there are still some places where people eat them loads, 'cause it's better than nothing."

No answer. But I feel like, maybe, just maybe, I can hear the padding of his feet, stepping just a little closer.

I keep talking. "Yeah, the planet I come from is . . . It's real big. Not sure if it's any bigger or smaller than this place, but it sure is big. The country I'm from is the best place, though. All the other places suck. Our food, especially, is the best." I gulp. I think he's standing pretty close now. If he were an enemy, I could probably grab his feet and slice his hamstrings clean off before he could react. That's how close he is. Not that I'll do that or anything. But now I've sunk into a bit of silence again, so to keep my nerves intact, I keep talking. "N—not that your food isn't good! Yeah, I, uh, I haven't really eaten a lot of your food, mostly just what, erm, your army guys gave me b—back when I was in the cage, and also a bit that this buddy of mine—Moleman—gave me a while back. Very good."

I fumble cutting one of the cacti, slicing up my palm. I wince at the blood, quickly wiping it off on my pelt to keep it from getting on the cactus.

"I'm not sure if you'll believe me, but, erm . . . I do actually think food is tastier than raw meat. Yeah, raw meat is good. It gives me resistances and all, but overall, if we're only talking taste, then . . ." I nod, mostly just to myself. "Yeah. Real food's the way to go."

As I'm mumbling about stupid inconsequential stuff, he finally moves away from my back, drawing a big circle around the pile of cacti before sitting down, cross-legged. He grabs a piece of half-peeled cactus and removes the last bit of skin before popping it in his mouth. The taste makes him cringe back but he still powers through, chewing before swallowing.

I stare at him, unblinking.

Not looking at my hands, I accidentally stab one of my claws square through the palm of my other hand. Damn it—when did I become such a klutz?

Across the pile, Simel glances at the wound before turning back to look at his food. Ignoring it fully. Considering everything, that is probably his best choice.

I frown to myself. "Sorry I keep getting RED everywhere." He doesn't answer. When I look up at him, I find his eyes trained squarely on a piece of cactus. Maybe that's for the better. I swallow. "You know, before all of this, I was pretty normal. Back in my world, people dying and animals getting killed and doing this kind of fighting wasn't normal. Least, it wasn't something you saw often. No, my world is a pretty simple sort of world . . ."

For a few hours, we simply sit around the pile of cactus. I talk. I don't know if he's listening or if he's tuning it out. After a while, I don't really care, myself. I'm just talking. And, weirdly enough, it feels good to just talk. I talk about the world I came from. The kind of person I was. What I did to pass the time. The people I knew. Anything and everything.

But the world works in specific ways, and that was clear as a certain message popped up.

<The Server Symposium will begin in 0:00:00.>
<The Server Symposium has begun. You will be automatically summoned in 00:10.>

Over a Cup of Tea

I blink at the message. The next words I was about to say die on my tongue.

"Oh, shoot, um, I'm about to disappear, but like I said, I'll be back in twenty-four hours, so just sit tight, and try not to get yourself kille—"

The last thing I have time to see before the summoning teleports me away is the bewildered look on Simel's face.

And then, in a flash, I'm gone.

My vision is BLACK for all but a moment before I reappear, falling square on my ass in a room I'm very familiar with. Oww. It feels like my tailbone snapped, but I'm sure it was nothing.

"K—Kitty?" someone says—Virgil, I think. I look up to find her hurrying over to me, looking as worried as she sounds. "Are you okay?"

I leap to my feet, automatically sinking into a crouched, ready stance. But then I remember that I'm among human people and I slowly straighten out. It feels just as uncomfortable as ever, but I don't have much of a choice. I turn to look at her. For a moment, the fact that I've only seen her so far gives me the lighthearted thought that maybe Almos went and died. Then I wouldn't have to bother with his puppy antics. On the other hand, if Almos were dead, then Virgil would be sad, and that wouldn't be good either, so . . .

"You really are as agile as a cat, huh?" Almos says from the other side of the room. I look at him with a mixture of relief and annoyance. He smiles at me brightly. Eugh. "Say, that wouldn't be from the stats and the levels, right? Or do you have some specific skill?"

I *really* don't like the way his eyes are shining. I glance over at Virgil. She doesn't seem to mind what he's asking about in the least.

I don't have time for this, though. I have my goal, and being the third wheel to these two isn't part of it. "Okay yeah uh I'm going to go now shame you couldn't convince more people good luck next time I guess also levels don't do all that much honestly okay bye gotta go," I say, and before either of them can respond, I toss myself out the door and into the hallway. Phew. Okay, time to make a run for it—

"Geez, he sure is quick to leave . . ."

I freeze in my step.

"Do you think he hates me?" Almos says quietly.

"No, he doesn't hate you," Virgil says back, her voice just as low. I'm only barely able to make out their words thanks to my enhanced hearing. "He just . . ." She heaves a sigh. "I think he has trouble being close to people. Not just you."

"Do you think he'll be at the party tonight? I *really* want to show him what I can do with my bagpipe." I can hear the smile in his voice. "I mean, we've been practicing the whole past attempt to join in on the music, so it'd be a shame if he wasn't around to hear it."

"I hope he'll be there too, but some people just don't like crowds."

"Right. Of course . . ."

I draw away from the Hell Lobby. But I can't bring myself to fully run away. My head feels weird again.

Why?

Why are they . . . what did they mean by that? That was . . .

I bite my lip. I shouldn't have stopped. Eavesdropping never does you any good. It's always bad. People don't say nice things behind people's backs. Only mean things. That's how it is. And this wasn't nice. But it wasn't mean, either. I don't know what it was.

I continue trudging through the hallway, my brow low and furrowed, barely even heading toward any specific place. The Hell Lobby is pretty far away from the main parts of the castle, leaving the hallways mostly deserted, allowing me to grumble in peace.

There's going to be another party tonight? I mean, I assumed as much, but . . . I don't think I've ever heard anyone say they wanted to see me at such an event. It's usually *Yeah, but I hope Fennrick doesn't show up, he's really creepy* and *LOL yeah I bet he'd try to film us dancing or take upskirt pics or some gross shit like that* and then I just wouldn't show up. Simple. Easy. Predictable.

This? Not so much.

But maybe they didn't mean it in . . . *that* way. Maybe they knew I'd hear them and they wanted me too embarrassed to join in. Or they wanted me to stay longer so they could . . . could . . .

I feel myself frown. My brain feels way too cluttered. One moment I knew exactly what I was going to do, and now I'm just . . . Argh!

Grabbing hold of the nearest stone wall, I bash my face into it as hard as I can, feeling my nose crunch and my jaw snap in two like a wishbone. Intoxicating

WHITE pain flashes across my vision and my brain and for a single moment I don't think about anything at all anymore. Then the moment passes and the muddy BLACK thoughts rush back in, drowning my brain with horrible cruel uncertainty.

O—kay, one bash didn't do it; let's go number two!

Bonk!

Ah, that didn't do it either. Let's see number three!

Crash! Bang! Smack! Crunch! Splat!

<You have learned: Concussion Resistance Lv. 7>

I pause my bashing to regard the message. Hmm. Not too bad! Alright, back to i—

"K—Kitty?"

Was that a real voice or did I just hallucinate? Let's find out. My neck is kind of creaky right now, so I put both hands on either side of my head and turn it. Oh, hey, it's Moleman! Since we're good friends, I smile and wave at him. Hello, Moleman!

He hurries closer to me, lifting his fancy WHITE robe to take longer steps like a dainty maiden. "Kitty, what happened? Did someone attack you? You look horrible!"

And that's somehow different from my regular state? Turning the rest of my body toward him, I wipe at my nose, which actually just dislodges the entire organ from my face. Though, since it's honestly just cartilage and mush, there's not much of it. I stick it in my mouth, chew, and swallow. Oh, hey, Moleman is making the same face as Simel usually does! This is a perfect moment to make a few inquiries. "Hey, Moweman, whass ub wivv . . ."

Apparently, my lack of all front teeth was insulting enough for Moleman to point his middle finger at me, effectively flipping me off. Did I perhaps misjudge our relationshi—

<Recover.>

A wave of gentle warmth rolls over me before assaulting my nose and face, turning it to fire and giving me the genuine feeling of flaming hot coals being pressed to my face. I almost want to ask Moleman what he's doing to me when the pain abruptly recedes, and in its place is a face that feels as soft and tender as an infant's bottom, my teeth all returned and my nose firm and perky like usual. I carefully touch my hand to my face. Wow, it's all healed! That was *fast*.

"Are you feeling better?" Moleman asks. I nod at him. He gives a chuckle. "I'd be impressed you didn't scream if it hadn't been, well, *you*."

Putting a hand to my jaw, I move it back and forth a little. Wow, it even merged my jawbone back together! Rubbing my chin, I squint at Moleman. I wonder what his current level is . . . ?

"Hey, Moleman?" I say.

"What is it?"

I open my mouth but close it again. A completely different little thought has suddenly nudged its way inside my head, and although it's probably just me being paranoid, I look Moleman up and down with a heavy ounce of suspicion. All the way from his leather boots to his WHITE embroidered wizard's tunic to the strange shiny headband he's wearing. "How'd you get to me so fast?"

I hadn't even been heading toward him all that fast, and then I got stuck, and then he appeared out of nowhere. Does that make sense? Kind of. But not completely.

He blinks at me. Then his eyes widen. "Oh! That's . . . Heh, now that I think about it, I really should have asked you about it before I just went ahead and . . ." Smiling meekly, he begins digging around in his pockets, eventually fishing out a little silver thing that looks sort of like a pocket watch, or one of those round makeup containers my sister used to have. He holds it out to me, and at the press of a small button on the side, the lid pops open, showing that it contains neither a watch nor powder, but rather a little compass. Apparently, according to this thing, I'm standing right to the north of Moleman. Interesting.

"This," Moleman says, "is a silver compass. The name is a little deceitful as it's really not a compass at all." Flipping it over, he shows me the lower bit. Pressing another tiny, invisible button, he opens a small compartment on the back, which seems to contain a small vial of . . . something RED? It's encased in glass so I can't smell it, but going by sight alone, it seems to be blood. How grisly. While holding it up, he opens a flap on his satchel and pulls out a little case. Having only one hand, it becomes a bit difficult for him to hold both, so I helpfully take hold of the silver compass. "Oh, thanks," Moleman says.

Opening the case, he reveals it to contain six other small vials of blood, each helpfully labeled with a pair of initials, like *B* or *P*. Removing the vial already in the compass, he replaces it with the one labeled *B*, putting the old vial in the slot labeled *K*.

And when he then closes the compartment and turns the compass back around, it's no longer pointing at me. Weird . . .

"See? Now it points at Bach instead, so if you just follow the arrow, you'll get to her eventually," he says, smiling. Okay, so if I understood this right, it lets the user follow someone's blood to get to the person? That's metal!

Wait a second.

"Yeah, uh, I got some of your blood after the meeting at the last symposium. I went back to help clean it up, and then I thought, *What the heck?* and I scooped up a little bit, just in case." In case of what, exactly? To that, he says nothing. Probably because I didn't vocalize my thoughts. Nevertheless, it's not like it's a bad thing if he can find me at any time. If anything, it levels the playing field between us. I can find him by scent; he can find me by using a blood-fueled compass . . . Makes sense! "You aren't mad, are you?"

Now it's my turn to blink at him. "Huh? No, not at all! Really, if you ever need more blood, all you have to do is ask. I've got a ton. My bleeding protection is also, like, really high, so I can bleed buckets—no sweat."

He makes that typical conflicted Simel expression. "You know, it's not actually very fun to see you hurt, right?"

I wave in the air. "That's only if I'm *really* hurt, though." He doesn't look like he agrees much. "Th—that's how it works, right?"

Moleman pulls his lips tight. "Listen, Kitty . . . If you accidentally see a guy stub his toe, that's a bit upsetting even if he didn't *really* get hurt, right?"

"I, well, uh . . . I suppose so?"

"It's the same with you. Even though I know you'll make it out of it just fine, seeing you a gory mess isn't a pretty sight, even if you don't mind it yourself."

"So, what you're saying is . . ." To give me enough time to pull my thoughts together, I speak slowly. "I shouldn't show you my RED?"

It takes him a second or so to digest what I just said. "Erm . . . pretty much?"

I nod gravely. Okay. So the no-RED rule also applies to Moleman. Right, got it. Speaking of no RED . . . I lock my eyes onto Moleman's. "Moleman, I need your advice."

He scratches his chin. "How about we take it over a cup of honey water?"

I stare at him.

Honey water?

My mouth begins to drool. "Yes," I say breathily. "I would *love* a cup of honey water."

He smiles at me and starts walking. It takes me almost a full second to realize the social implications of this, which is just as much time as it takes for me to scramble to catch up with him. Thankfully, he didn't notice my mistake. As he walks, bringing me up a nearby stairwell, he starts talking. "I forgot to tell you earlier, but I've actually almost finished the Purgatory section."

I stumble on a slightly raised bit of stone but catch myself before I fall. "Y—you have?"

His chest puffs out a little. "Purgatory is really different. And, honestly? I've come to enjoy it. Maybe that's a bit ridiculous to say considering the position we're both in, but being in Purgatory has genuinely been fun at times. Camping with friends, meeting new people, exploring undiscovered cultures . . . It's like being a true explorer!" The excitement in his voice is palpable. "It took a while, but I'm actually starting to learn proper goblin-speak. They have a lot of different accents, and some dialects are near incomprehensible, but it's still satisfying to be able to finally understand what someone is saying, and to have a real conversation."

I lumber after him, hunched down, looking up at him through furrowed brows.

"The last town we were in was this desert city. We had trouble finding an inn at first—most places won't accept humans as patrons—but we eventually found a room living with an acquaintance of a man whose life we saved a while back. It's funny; the world they live in feels so small. You'd think they wouldn't be so connected, what with the lack of modern technology, but they make do. I've been keeping a notebook on all the noble lineages and aristocrat houses and whatnot we've come across. There's so much to know. So many intricate rivalships and alliances and everything . . ." His voice is so wistful talking about it all. Dreaming. "It's really interesting."

"Right," I mumble.

Stepping out of the stairwell, he pauses for just a moment. I only notice it when I bump into his back, making the strap around his folded-back arm loosen. He doesn't notice. Rather, he turns around to look at me. "I'm not sure if you want to hear this, but . . ." He compresses his lips into a tight line. "I looked a bit into the Shore City of Acheron."

I freeze where I stand. "You did?"

He turns away from me again. Facing the dark corridor ahead, he gives a small, almost unnoticeable nod.

I take a small step back. "What did you find?"

He takes a step forward, then another, eventually finding his way over to a nearby glassless window, overlooking the court outside. I slide up to him, taking my place at his side. Down in the courtyard, there's a fair bit of activity. A group of challengers are standing off to the side, playing music. A larger group is gathered nearby, dancing together, some coordinated, some moving by feeling alone. On the other side are a few groups dueling, testing their skills, challenging each other. Yet more are simply sitting on little blankets on the grass, eating good food and sharing words and laughter.

My grip tightens on the stone window.

"There wasn't much left," Moleman says, his voice neutral, as though he's giving a report. "Mostly ash and BLACKened rocks. The castle was the only part still standing, with all the towers and the . . . the *bodies* intact."

"I never lied," I say sharply, my head whipping to face him. "I never said a single lie—you know that, right?" I try to swallow to make my mouth and throat feel less dry. "I would never lie to you."

He continues without turning away from the courtyard. "When I went there myself, they'd already rebuilt most of the capital, and the streets had been cleaned. But it still reeked something foul, even months later." His eyes flutter closed for a few seconds. I want to say something, but I don't know what. I don't think there's anything I *can* say. He lets out a long breath and I wonder if he'll say anything more. He meets my gaze.

His eyes aren't like Simel's. There's no BLACKness in them. No firm repulsion. No terror. Just a shimmering little gleam of pity that I somehow vastly prefer to the aforementioned. "You did what you thought was the right thing to do."

"I did?"

He takes a hold of my shoulder and his eyes grow harder. "*You did.* You didn't think you had any other choice. The system told you to do it." His eyes, firm as those of a lawmaker, shine oddly in the light. Something deep inside, some little part of him I couldn't remember seeing before, trembles. "That's how it was, right?" I stare at him, helpless. "Because if that wasn't how it was, then . . ." His lower lip trembles.

Reflexively, my head begins to nod, up and down, quickly. "Y—yeah," I say, "that's how it was." I gulp. "That's *exactly* how it was."

I feel his hand squeeze my shoulder tighter and for a second, he just stares at me, his eyes penetrating deep into my soul. I want to look away, but I keep my gaze steady. And after a second or two, he lets me go, turning back to look down at the courtyard. "Good," he sighs. "In that case . . ." With a wave of his hand, a pair of crystal cups alongside a glass pitcher of water and a small jar of suspiciously brown honey appear, all of which he places on the windowsill. Then, with another movement, he brings out a pair of small spoons and a tiny plate of what appears to be cookies.

My previously dry mouth instantly fills with drool, and I stare wide-eyed at the stuff presented. Some water would be *very nice* right about now, *thankyouverymu—*

He effortlessly stops my hand midsnatch. I resist the urge to growl at him.

Like the tease he is, Moleman waggles his finger at me, which does not douse my bestial instincts. "Have some patience, Kitty. Don't you want to enjoy this like a proper human?"

My scowl recedes. Slowly, I cross my arms. "I suppose I do."

Saying nothing, he gives a temperate smile and reaches for the pitcher. First, he pours us each a cup of water, which by itself looks so yummy I'm left to drool. Now that I think about it, when was the last time I drank something that wasn't blood? Follow-up question, does the soup I got on the third floor count? I can feel my brows furrow again. Is soup a drink or an eat . . . ?

While I descend into such madness-inducing pits of thought, Moleman grabs the little jar of brownish honey, humming as he does. Surprisingly, when he opens the lid, what erupts isn't merely the scent of honey but also that of numerous other spices as well. It smells vaguely cinnamon-ish, but not quite.

Curious, I lean closer, sniffing as I go. It smells of spices, but without any truly recognizable smells.

No, that isn't quite true. I do recognize the smells just a little. However, not from my time on Earth. Rather, it smells like the aforementioned stews and soups the goblin soldiers served me. That's kind of what it smells like.

Since I'm basically inches from the cups and honey, it's no surprise when Moleman notices me and gives a little chuckle.

"You noticed it, huh?" In response to his words, I perk an eyebrow. He holds the little jar higher so I can see it better. It's made of uneven glass and is unlabeled, with the lid being made of some sort of ground-up wood cork substitute. "I got it from a villager we happened to save. I couldn't understand the word she called it, but I understood what it was by the description." As he explains, his voice becomes distant and wistful again, like a real adventurer. "It's not quite honey, but it is made by the same sort of process, though by birds rather than bees."

"Birds?" I repeat, stunned.

"Yeah, birds!" he says, voice perking up. "Little hummingbird-like things that made nectar into honey to feed their young and to store during the winters in the stems of trees. So, they'd bore holes, regurgitate the nectar . . . Pretty much like bees." Swiveling the jar, he makes the "honey" go around and around, glimmering deep amber in the outside light. "This is actually not honey alone, though. It also contains a few spices that were boiled in the honey to season it." Grabbing one of the spoons, he carefully pours a little dollop into each of the two glasses. "Which means that, technically speaking," he says, stirring both glasses, making the water as a whole take on a slightly orange-ish color, "it's actually clarea of water—not honey water." He hands me one of the glasses and smiles. "Personally, I prefer this a lot better."

I accept it. Looking down into it, I see my own deeply skeptical face reflected in the surface of the clarea. "A bird barfed this up?"

"Pretty much."

"This is bird barf?"

"Yup."

I look at Moleman. I look down at the amber water. Well, if it's bird barf, it should give me at least a few resistances, right?

He holds out his glass to me. I put the rim of mine to his and clink it.

Bottoms up!

Though, of course, since it would be rude to chug the clearly expensive drink, I just take a sip. The status messages will be sure to roll in any second no—

Hang on a second. This is . . .

Moleman grins at me. "It's good, isn't it?"

Good? This, *good*?

I bring the glass to my lips and take a full swig. Flavor and sweetness and mellow aromas explode across my tongue. Spices! Spices! Spices! But the second I swallow down half a mouthful I stop myself, my throat wringing itself shut. No, I can't drink this too quickly! I have one glass and that's it—I need to be frugal! I can't allow myself to just drink this all down in my greedy carelessness! I have to—

But that half a mouthful was my downfall. My throat is flooded with yummy yummy yummy yummy delicious honey water that suddenly can't go down my esophagus, and with no other road ahead, it obviously goes down into my lungs where I'm promptly choked and/or drowned. Pain blossoms through my chest as I clutch the glass with trembling hands, desperately trying to keep it steady as I cough my lungs out. *COUGH COUGH COUGH COUGH—*

<You have learned: Drowning Resistance Lv.4>

"H—hey, Kitty, calm down!"

In some attempt to help me, Moleman starts slapping my back something fierce in an attempt to dispel the demons, which is silly because he literally has supernatural abilities of healing, something he himself realized after pounding my back a couple of times. "Hang on just a second—"

<Recover.>

If the pain was flower blossoms before, it now explodes into full-on rose-bushes, granting a sensation closest compared to that of my rib cage being cracked open from the inside. The pain only lasts for a moment, though, before instantly receding, leaving my chest warm and clear, and I take a deep gasping breath, my airways cleared and open. "Haah, haah, haah . . ."

Moleman pats me on the back, this time clearly as emotional support rather than physical. "You alright there, Kitty?"

I nod at him. "Yeah, I'm okay. I just got a bit of hubris is all." My voice is a little hoarse but it's okay. I'm good now. No more problems. Now I'll be fine.

My gaze surreptitiously slides over to the half-emptied glass of honey water. I glance up at Moleman. He doesn't say anything, instead letting his actions speak for him by reaching out, grabbing my glass, and holding it out to me. I reach for it, but he pulls it out of reach at the last second. I glare at him. "Only," he says, "if you drink it slowly. And don't choke on it. Hanging around you is really starting to drain my recovery crystals."

I look at him, and then at the glass of auburn water, and then back to him again. I put on the face of a soldier going to war. "I swear I won't drown on it again."

He holds my gaze for a second before finally capitulating and handing me the glass. Living up to my username, I snatch the glass from him like a greedy little cat, almost spilling a few drops. I put the glass to my face and take a careful, tempered sip. Ahhh. Oh, that *is* good. More than good. Absolutely yummilicious.

For a few seconds, Moleman watches me carefully, like I'm some unlucky kitty who always gets caught in the clothesline when his back's turned. Eventually, though, he grabs his own cup and takes a sip. When he puts the cup down, he turns to me, looks me up and down, and asks, "So, what did you want my advice for?"

I gulp down a mouthful of the tastiest liquid I've ever had. "Advice?" He stares at me. I stare at him. Realization flashes through my head like a lightning bolt. "Oh! Advice, yeah, okay, you're right, um . . ." To stall for time while I let my thoughts spin in their hamster wheels, I wave my hands a little. "So, okay, to make a long story short, it kind of started when I reached the boss of floor fourteen . . .

"And now I'm not totally sure what to do. I *want* to help Simel, but I don't even know how I'd do that, or if that's even what the gods want me to do, and for that matter, do I even care about what the gods want me to do when Simel's life is at stake?" With that, I finally turn my gaze back to Moleman. He hasn't stopped staring at me since I opened my mouth. There's a weird look in his eye, which might be attributed to the non-specificity of my question. "So, uh . . . yeah. What should I do?"

His face tightens just a smidge. He's been holding the cup during my whole explanation, but it's still mostly full. For some reason, he seems a bit reluctant to say anything. "Do you really want to hear what I think you should do?"

I hope my face is as firm as my heart is. "Yes," I say. "If there's anyone's advice I trust, it's yours."

That seems to put him a bit at ease, as the tension melts from his face a little. "Right. Okay. In that case, I really think you should

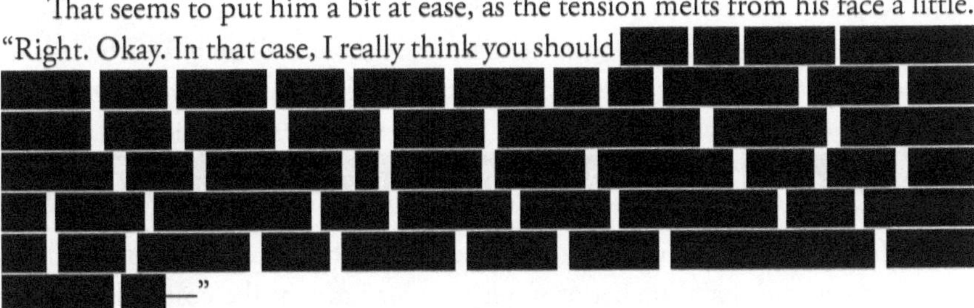

—"

"H—hang on a moment," I say, interrupting him mid-sentence. If that can even be *called* a sentence to begin with.

He turns to me, a sympathetic look on his face. "I know it'll be hard, but—"

"No, no, that isn't it. What you just said, uh . . ."

His heavyset brows furrow. "What's wrong? It might not be what you'd like to hear; however, I think that —"

"There it is again!" I cry. "It's like—it's like you're cussing up a storm and the censors are bleeping out every single word you say!"

"B—bleeping?" Moleman repeats. "I'm being bleeped out?" His lips form into a little frown. "Are you sure you're not just—"

"No, I am *not* hallucinating this. Something is making it so you just sound like one long bleep instead of actual words." A little thought strikes me. It's so logical it makes me grind my teeth. "And I know just who and why."

Moleman looks skeptical at best. "And who and why is tha—"

"Those damn gods!" I blurt out. "They don't want me getting pro gamer advice, so they're messing with my head so I can't even hear what you're saying! Argh, those damn hacks . . . !" I gnash my teeth and scowl at the empty air around us. I'm sure those damn gods are around here, watching—waiting . . . !

Moleman lifts his hand and almost says something before closing it again, rubbing his chin in thought, and then finally admitting, "Honestly, I wouldn't be too surprised. Going by what you've explained before, they seem to really have it out for you. I mean—forcing you to decide for yourself what the *right thing* is? Clearly, they're testing the merit of your morality."

"For what, though?" I grumble.

He shrugs. "That's the question, friend. Maybe, if you do what they think is *right*, they'll be nicer to you? Maybe even remove your debt and let you buy armor and food?" His words make me rub my chin. Hmm. That's possible . . . "Personally, though, I'd bet they just want to see if you'll ██████ ██████ ██████ ██████ ██ ██ ████ or if—"

"Stop, stop!" I say, waving my hands at him. "Just—stop making that damn bleeping, okay? It is *really* getting on my nerves."

For a moment, he's actually quiet. But then I see something develop inside him. Something I have only ever seen in my sister. Something that now takes form with such power and vengeance that we might as well be related by blood.

He grins at me like a brother just about to do the one thing his brother told him specifically not to do. "Or what, Kitty? You'll make the right choice and ██████ ██████ ██████ ██████ ████████ ██ ██ ██████—"

"*Stooooooopppppppp!*"

Suffice it to say, after that, I did not receive much future advice for the floor. But I *did* get to dunk a pitcher of water over his head, at the cost of him using magic to dangle me over the drop outside the window. In the end, though, we were able to find a common ground in the desire to neither drop nor sully the cookies, so the final few minutes of our chat were spent calmly and not at all in tense expectation of the second shoe to drop.

After that, I accidentally mentioned the fact that I couldn't get the whole magic thing to work, which surprised Moleman enough to decide to try to teach me magic himself. I would show that progress in more detail if it hadn't been composed solely of me failing and of Moleman proving himself somehow even more patient than I had previously believed.

By the time the sun went down, I had learned more theory behind the magic and why it *should* work, but actually having the magic take form inside me was something completely different. It just wouldn't happen. In the end, Moleman swore that he would try to find the reason behind it, despite my objections.

Once the huge, serverwide New Year's Eve party was going full blast in the main hall of the castle, we both agreed to simply leave and take our places on the dance floor.

I couldn't enjoy it, though. Not really. The fun little tussle and the magic teaching had distracted me from the real thoughts at play.

The only one who could tell me what the right thing to do was me.

The gods didn't want me to do the *right thing*. That wasn't their goal here. They couldn't care less if I killed the giant or saved Simel or ended world hunger. What they really wanted to see, what they really wanted to know, was what *I* considered to be the right thing. And if that thing just happened to be what they would consider the *wrong thing*, then . . .

Then what?

I don't know. I can't know. That's in the future. A future I don't know. One I can never know.

The room is thumping with music and stomping feet and the air is thick with breathing and alcohol. I don't really want to be here. But I don't want to think, either. And when I weigh them against each other—thinking or drinking—one's clearly the winner.

I look across the dance floor. Over by the group of musicians stand Virgil and Almos. They smile and wave at me and I wave back. I take a swig of the bottle in my hand, though I'm not sure what it is. The sting of alcohol burns a track down my throat and I take another. The world seems to slow down around me, and I stumble out onto the dance floor.

After that, I don't remember much.

Off to the Empire, I Guess

. . .

. . .

Hm? Where . . . where am I . . . ?

I pry open my crusty eyes. Oh, hey, it's the crib! That makes sense. Yup. Total sense. Ah, my body feels a bit weird . . . As I move to a sitting position, a little prick of pain rings out from my left shoulder. Hm? What's this . . . ?

I blink at the thick cactus needle stabbed deep inside my shoulder. Huh. That's kind of weird. I can't remember wrestling a cactus . . .

Pulling out the needle, I toss it to the side. Still, that's pretty weird. Normally if you step on a cactus, you'd get more needles in you than just one. Odd. It's almost like someone purposefully stabbed that in there, but I can't imagine who'd do that, so . . . Yeah. Must've been the wind or something.

With the needle removed, I sit up fully. The first thing that alerts me to the fact that things are not as they maybe should be is the frankly unholy amount of gore littering the room. Most of it is concentrated in a huge pile in the middle of the place, but a fair bit has splattered the walls, and the roof, and pretty much any place where a bit of blood and organ mush might be able to get in. It is, frankly speaking, enough gore for at least three full humans.

And surrounding this pile, like the candles around some unholy ritual, are what appears to be five empty bottles of vodka.

I feel like there's a story to be read here. Unfortunately, I am currently illiterate.

Standing up, I walk over to the pile. It's very fresh, without a single sign of being spoiled. What exactly could have made this much raw meat and organs? Did some animal die here? No, the intestines are too small. In that case, gobli—

My heart rears in my chest and I start digging through the pile like a madman.

Simel? Simel?! Oh, God, please, don't tell me I—

There's a tiny movement in the edge of my vision and my head flashes to face it. On the other side of the room, as far away as physically possible, I see clearly as Simel squeezes himself closer to the wall. He's covered in blood. Huh. Now that I look at myself, I'm also covered in blood, a lot of it dried. It's clearly from before my current dig. I look back up at Simel. He draws back in animalistic terror. Hm.

Returning my gaze to the pile of organs, I allow myself to notice a little detail. You know, these intestines are quite similar to the ones I have in my stomach. Same shape and everything. And if I take a bite . . .

Yup, that's my own spleen.

Okay, so, to summarize what may have happened here . . . I was probably still pretty drunk when I came back from the symposium. In my non-sane state, I decided that the best way to spend my night was to train my evisceration resistance. Right. Okay, yeah. That feels like something my drunk self could have done. Still, that doesn't explain the cactus barb in my shoulder, or why Simel is *also* covered in blood. Hmmm . . .

Well, we're both alive and okay, so it doesn't matter what happened.

Sitting down, I try to make sense of what the best future course of action is. I can't exactly *keep* this pile of rotting organs. Eating it would be fine, but I don't think that that's something Simel would like to see. In that case, putting it into my inventory . . .

As I furrow my brow in thought, I suddenly notice the sound of gentle footsteps moving over the soggy floor with quiet squelches. I look up at Simel. He jerks back in fear, but after a second or two of trembling, he's able to pull himself together, taking long, deep breaths. With his whole body shivering, he steps closer to me. Our eyes meet. He slowly points a trembling finger toward the door.

"Do you need to—?" He doesn't nod or shake his head, but I can pretty much understand what he means. "Yeah, okay, let me just put on some sort of shoes . . ." I'm just about to reach into my inventory when I notice a large patch of skin in the pile of gore. The cogs of creativity slowly start moving in my head once again. If I took . . . and then . . . Could I . . . ?

Creativity turns to inspiration. I grab the patch of skin and start cutting it into shapes using my sharp nails, pulling on all my technological this-is-how-shoes-look knowledge to cut out soles and insoles and everything else. I fasten the soles and the leather and everything else by using some of the snapped-off teeth and claws in the pile. Then, as a final touch, I thread the inside of the human leather boot with my own large intestine, giving it insulation and softness.

It's crude. It's novice. It's probably a little disturbing. But it *is* the first proper piece of clothing I've worn in almost a full year.

I pull on the pair of boots. They aren't the same length and they feel grossly squishy, but by God is it a pair of boots. Instead of a pro gamer, should I have become a cobbler . . . ?

Oh, Mother, Father . . . Your son has finally found his calling in life.

I turn to Simel. "I'm ready," I say with all the pride of a real American cowboy. "Let's go."

It surprises me slightly to see his facial expression not having changed a twitch from when he first stepped up to me. Is this a good or a bad thing? No idea. Doesn't matter.

Since time is of the essence in moments like these, I head for the door, glancing back periodically to make sure Simel is still following along. For some reason, there's a really haunted look in his eyes that wasn't there just before I left. Keeping an eye over my shoulder, I push open the door and jump out. My thigh-high human leather boots are working great. I'll need to look into how to tan leather properly, though, since this is really just fresh skin. Maybe Simel knows more about that stuff?

I turn to look at Simel. He's also standing outside the crib, in the ankle-high soot. But he isn't moving. He's rooted in place. I tilt my head at him. "What's up?"

Keeping his eyes glued to mine, he slowly reaches up and touches a hand to the crest on his chest. I look down at the crest. It's kind of hard to discern because of all the RED on it, but it seems to be a picture of a city on fire with the flames forming a phoenix. I look back at him. "Yup, pretty cool crest."

His left eye twitches. He touches his hand to the crest again.

I nod. "Yeah. Maybe not my personal style—I personally prefer dragons—but I respect it. Phoenixes are cool. Can't say I'd want to be one or have it represent my country, but I can see the appeal."

Not swayed, he pokes his crest again. I furrow my brows. How do I politely tell him that I'm not psychic? And, furthermore, that if I did have such powers, I would probably avoid using them to invade his privacy?

But apparently, he can read the confusion on me, because he suddenly points out toward the horizon and the gently rising sun. Then he pokes his crest again before pointing at himself, me, and the horizon one more time.

I blink at him, slowly. Wait a second . . .

Me. Him. Go to place. Go to . . . crest. Crest—army. We go to army. Army *encampment.*

"You . . . want to go back to the camp? Where I . . . where we met?"

He nods at me.

Maybe I'm more psychically gifted than I thought? Still . . . "Are you sure? It's not exactly . . . There's not much left, you know. I checked for food, and most of it was spoiled or eaten by animals, so I don't think . . ."

He shakes his head firmly. His eyes, although as dark with fear as before, shine with determination. He means business. I gulp and look away. "Well, uh, okay, but . . . Don't say I didn't warn you, okay?" Not that he'll say *anything*, but what matters is that the message got across. Turning away from him, I close my eyes, stick my nose in the air, and take a deep breath. Soot. Soot. Soot. And, a fair bit away . . . Leather. Cloth. Wood. Dried skin and exposed bone. Moisture. I open my eyes again and point toward the encampment, which just happens to be in the opposite direction from Simel pointed in. "Over there," I say. "That's where it is."

He doesn't turn his eyes away from me. It's like he expects me to teleport closer when he looks away. I meet his gaze and he flinches. I pull my lips tight. "So, uh . . ." I scratch my neck. "How do you want us to do this? If you want, I could carry you there, just like last time, but . . ."

Not waiting for me to finish my sentence, he starts walking in the direction I pointed, trudging through the soot with big, heavy steps.

"That works," I mumble after him. I follow.

Normally, getting to the encampment would only take around ten minutes of running. But, like this, it took over half an hour to get there. By the end of it, Simel was dragging his feet and panting, but whenever I tried to help him, he'd slap my hand away as though it were poisonous. Still, we were able to get there in one piece, and by that time, my boots were starting to crack a fair bit. At some point I think a tooth went through my sole and into my foot, but I didn't want to bother Simel, so I kept it to myself.

<Top—Status—Community>
<07:03:10 Day 366>
<The fourteenth attempt will begin in 29:16:56:50>

By the time we arrive, the sun has risen fully, banishing any former tendrils of the night's cold. In the dry heat of the sun, the encampment doesn't look like much of anything. There's a big pile of ash encasing the woolly drake I killed, and then there are the two tents in the distance, next to the cave. Everything else is covered in soot.

I pause in my step once we're here, but Simel moves on ahead with brisk strides.

Only to moments later step on a minute raise in the soot, his foot going right into something soft and crunchy, making him lose his footing and fall. But before he can fall headfirst into the burning hot ash, I've leapt out to put my body below his, catching him just before he can scald his face and hands on the stuff below. With his body atop mine, I can feel closely how the stuff below the soot isn't just sand anymore, but also hard, dry things that still wear clothes without needing them.

Standing up, I lift him along with me, only letting go of him once he's upright and standing fast. "You alright?" I ask him. He gives a short nod and I sigh in relief. I look out toward the tents. "We'll need to be careful," I say. "You can't really see it, but below the soot . . ." I frown and reach up to my shoulder, peeling off a bit of the soot that got branded onto it alongside some skin. Trying to scoot around the real subject at hand, I point toward a nearby bump of soot. "Avoid those. Stick to where it's even." I try to give him a look that shows my worry properly, alongside how grave this really is. "If you trip, and I'm not there to catch you . . ." I swallow. "You might not die, but you may certainly wish you did."

He looks at me, then follows my finger over to the protrusion. Slowly, he turns his eyes down to the soot as a whole, searching for bumps—for the unmarked graves of his men. I watch him carefully. At least he understands how dangerous this is. For him, that is.

Carefully, Simel steps forward, his eyes glued to the ground, each step large and meticulous. It's not quite a minefield, but by the number of soldiers lying here, you could almost assume that that's what it was.

Following Simel, I keep my eye on him. It's times like these when I'm almost glad he doesn't speak.

It takes some time to move across the battlefield fully, but we eventually reach the tents. I had expected him to go into his own tent, and he was almost about to do so, too, before he suddenly veered away and went toward the prince's tent.

His body is still sitting in the same place, wearing the same things. However, as happens with fresh meat left in the open, a number of animals had clearly made a feast of the place. The skin and flesh on his thin arms and face remained, though it had dried to the point of mummification, but almost everything else had been taken. His chest was just one big open cavity with only skin and bones remaining. His eyes, lips, and tongue had also been removed, making him a pretty grisly sight. Though, since he didn't smell like much of anything, it wasn't that bad.

Simel seemed to think otherwise.

Removing the hood from his head, he put his hand to his chest—to the emblem—and gave a deep bow to the prince's remains. And then, once he'd straightened back out, he started looking for something. At first with mere interest, and then as frantically as a mother of three who can't find the car keys on an early Monday morning.

Humming, I rub my chin at the sight. Maybe . . . ?

Reaching into my inventory, I pull out one of the few things that is neither hide nor meat. The little crown glimmers with regal authority in my hand. "Hey, Simel, is this—" And that's about all I have time to say before he notices what I'm holding and snatches it out of my hand, simultaneously casting Chain as he does.

<Chain.>

I'd almost be impressed if I hadn't expected it. I shrug it off.

<Chain broken.>

"You didn't need to rip it out of my hands, you know? I *was* giving it to you."

But he's clutching it to his chest like a mother cat with its kitten, so there's nothing left for me to do. I sigh a little. "Was that all you came here to do? I could've given you that at the crib," I say. *If you'd asked for it, that is.*

He can't hear that last part, though, so my thoughts join the air.

"So, are we going back now, or . . ." Going by the look he gives me, he's still got stuff to do. It's not like I *want* to go back to the crib and clean up everything. It's just that it feels vaguely nostalgic in a bad way to be dragged around without knowing exactly what it is we're looking for. If I knew what he wanted to find, I could get it super easily! Because, as you know, I got a *really* good sense of smell. A god-given one, you might say.

Turning his back on the prince, he exits the tent. I follow.

The second I exit the tent my instincts flare up and alarm bells explode through my brain, but I don't have time to dodge as a massive steel beam of a tail smashes into me, sending me flying back into the tent, a crunching in my chest making me all too aware of the ribs broken. The second I touch ground, I instinctually pull myself into the fetal position, falling into a roll to spin back around to leap out of the tent, claws ready and back hunched.

<Royal Drake (Lv.28)>

It's a drake. But it looks really weird.

Much like the sprint drakes, it stands on both hind legs, with short front arms and powerful legs. But the legs are, like, beyond that. They're downright chunky, the most curious aspect being the ankle parts, which are extremely thick to the point of being blubbery, as stout as the foot of an elephant. With the rest of the leg being muscular, this makes the ankle look kind of like the pom-pom feet of a poodle. Its tail is also as girthy as a log, though not all of it is mere muscle. Still, considering the way it broke my ribs, it's more muscle than fat.

The rest of its body is slim, with an intelligent pair of eyes glaring down at me. Aside from the lower part of the legs and arms, it's covered with long, silky WHITE hairs, though the underbelly is smooth. It looks as though it was made for an arctic climate, but that isn't what startles me too much to attack properly.

After all, in its arms, held in the same way a child holds its teddy bear, is Simel.

My mind splits into several different directions. What? Where did this thing come from? Why is it holding Simel so protectively? Why isn't Simel fighting at all? No, now that I look at him, if anything, he seems gently worried rather than scared. Why? What does that mean?

I hunch down farther. It doesn't matter. For now, the safest option is clear. I'll fight.

The second I fall down into a crouch, claws bared, teeth snarling and visible— the drake following suit by turning sideways, angling Simel away from me—the whole game is suddenly flipped on its head as Simel almost effortlessly wrestles out of the drake's grip, leaping to the ground with a slight stumble. I watch him, stunned, as he regains his footing and hurries to take a stand right between me and the drake, one hand raised to hold each of us back. For a moment, all that can be heard is Simel's panting.

"S—Simel?" I ask, tentatively straightening out just a little. "What are you trying to . . . ?"

He looks at me, eyes boring into me, telling me with words even I can under-stand, *Don't move.* I obey. Slowly, moving with measured steps, still keeping his eyes on me, he approaches the drake. The drake simply watches his approach, the only sound it makes being a gentle murmuring. I want to tell Simel to be careful, but I can't bring myself to speak. Even when he's right next to the drake, Simel doesn't seem even slightly afraid to touch it, pushing some of the hairs on its back aside to show what is clearly a brand. A brand of a city on fire. The fire being in the form of a phoenix.

"Is that . . ." I say, "your *mount?*"

Simel nods at me.

I look up at the drake and whistle. "Not a bad-looking thing," I say. "Not bad at all." Stepping closer, I briefly pause as it hisses at me. I bare my teeth at it. "Some attitude problems, but if we skin it, I'm sure it'll make for a great coat." That little expression is enough to get Simel to glare at me, too. "What?" I say. "You can't expect me to let you *keep* that thing."

Ignoring me, Simel leads the drake toward the other tent. Right. Great. The second I get my chance I am going to kill that thing. My ribs aren't going to heal for at least an hour! Oh, but I can't complain about that, because he's obviously got to keep his precious oversized lizard. Of course.

As I trudge after them, silently seething, Simel stops outside the second tent. He looks up at the lizard, before making some little hand gesture that I can only imagine means something like *Stay*. He enters inside and I follow, the lizard growling at me as I pass by. I growl back at it.

Inside the tent, the first thing Simel does is rummage through the crates until he finds a couple of reins and a saddle of some sort. It's a pretty big saddle, though, so although he can pull it out, he can't really carry it. He looks over at me. I almost want to let him struggle for the sake of his precious lizard, but that wouldn't be very friendlike, so after grumbling for a second, I finally assist him, grabbing the saddle. As expected, he then makes me also put the thing on the lizard, the lizard being almost as unhappy as me about it. In the end, though, after only a few minutes, the lizard is fully ready, with everything any sort of steed might need.

Right as I start thinking that this might be the last thing we need to do, Simel heads back inside the tent. I follow.

"Simel, I really don't know what it is you want to do with that lizard, but I think we should do away with it. It is clearly feral. Totally untrustworthy." Mumbling such things, I watch Simel as he rummages through the things in the tent, eventually finding a small knapsack. He looks inside it, and I only barely catch a glimpse of its contents—a pair of small books, a quill and ink, a bundle of herbs, a few pouches, a pair of crowns, a bit of jewelry, a sealed envelope—before he fishes out a single item and closes it again, hanging the knapsack over his shoulder.

As I inch closer, my eye falls on the item in his hand. "Oh, hey, I know what that is!"

At my voice, Simel jerks, head swiveling to look at me in terror. I point at the little silver thing in his hand. "That's a silver compass, right? My other friend told me all about it! Very cool thing. Is it expensive?" Simel doesn't answer me. Standing up, he pushes past me and over to the large table in the middle of the room, which is still covered in a really large map. The map is seriously big enough to cover the whole table, and since the table is quite big, that's a feat.

I wish I could understand the map, but I really can't. All I know is that it's a big map, showing cities and oceans and mountains and forests. Oh, and also a big BLACK splotch. There are a few little figurines on top of it, but they're all toppled over, so I don't know if they mean anything.

Simel frowns at the little figures and picks up one of them, showing a crowned phoenix. He puts the figurine in the big BLACK area, which I presume to be the desert we're currently in. I'd be genuinely surprised if there were more than one soot desert in this world.

Moving with the knowledge of an expert, he grabs the other figurines as well, putting them across the map, some in cities, others in forests. And then he holds a final one. It's fleshy and tainted with RED and looks like a tall, hairless wendigo of some sort, with long claws and teeth and carved flames at its feet. It actually looks pretty cool, but I really wouldn't want to meet it if it was real. Hmm. Might as well ask just in case. "Hey, Simel. That thing doesn't exist for real, right?"

He gives me a look that says a thousand words I can't read. Then he puts it next to the crowned phoenix. Interesting. The craftsmanship on these is really quite something . . .

I reach out to look at the phoenix closer, but he slaps my hand away. "Fine, fine," I mumble at him.

Ignoring me, Simel places the silver compass on the map. When he flips open the lid, I find the little RED arrow pointing at me. Heh, uh, that's quite the coincidence. I must just be standing in the way, I guess. But when I cha-cha slide to the left, the arrow follows me. Huh. That would suggest that . . . But I don't really . . .

Why would Simel be following me?

My brows furrow.

And with an *army*, to boot. Glancing across the table, I watch as Simel removes the RED vial from inside the compass and replaces it with another. Going by the way the map is placed, it's pointing to the non-hypothetical, literal east. Grabbing a pencil and a long tool of some sort, Simel draws a line along the map from one of the little figurines toward the phoenix and the hairless wendigo.

I shake my head. No, I mean . . . They had the prince, right? Yeah. In that case, he could very well have told them about what happened in the forest—about how I killed the witch and saved the . . . Well, I didn't save her exactly, but I did save *him* by proxy, so I still saved a royal. And then I killed him a while later. Eh, you win some, you lose some. What's important is that Simel marched an army to the witch for whatever reason—maybe even to rescue the princess, and then instantly started marching toward me presumably once they'd heard the prince's story.

In that case, that would suggest . . .

Scratching my chin, I silently watch how Simel repeats his process with a few other vials and figurines, forming lines and slowly triangulating our position based on our position relative to them. He's clever, alright.

I mean, everything considered . . . Isn't there a chance that he wanted to come visit me? Or—or maybe the prince wanted to thank me for saving him. Maybe they were even going to bring me back to that empire place to let me have the princess's hand in marriage!

Oh, wait, I killed her. Shoot.

Still, some sort of reward wouldn't be out of place, no?

I can't imagine any other good reason for them to come after me with an army. It makes no sense. I wish I could ask Simel, but he's kind of mute, so I'd need to do it in yes-or-no questions, and even then he might just refuse to answer at all. Damn it. Why does life have to be so complicated?

Anyhow, while I've been mulling over these important things, Simel has apparently finished triangulating our current position. Looking at the map, it seems we are . . . right in the middle of the BLACK desert. Unsurprising, but okay. Also, looking at the name of the desert, it seems that it's actually called . . .

The desert desert.

Excuse me?

I rub my eyes. Yeah, no, that's still what it says. The written words get automatically translated into Swedish in my head, and the translation leaves it at desert desert. *The* desert desert.

Oh, but if I look at the subheading, there's another name! Let's see here . . . The Desert Desert of BLACK Sand. Uh-huh. Wow, that's . . . That's really what it's called? Interesting.

Anyhow, the desert is quite expansive, even more than I'd thought myself. No wonder it took them a month to get all the way here, from . . . Over there! The witch's tower and her wailing forest is still on the map, with all the harpies drawn in and everything. It's really detailed, huh? Still, I'm kind of surprised to see it so close to the desert. I mean, there's even a little river going from the tower into the desert! I wonder why it's RED, though. Reminds me of the twelfth floor, but that can't be, can it? Hm. Weird.

Nevertheless, we're apparently almost in the perfect epicenter of the desert, so it would take at least a month no matter which direction you went in. As I stare at the map, Simel suddenly points at something in a way that's clearly for me to see. Hm? What's that? Oh, it's a little city! It's on the outskirts of the desert, but it's absolutely meant to be a city.

While I look down at the city, Simel draws a line from where our little figurines are all the way over to the desert city, and then . . .

And then he draws a long, swirling, twisting line all the way over to a spot on the very other side of the table, where it ends at a large city. A city close to the border, but still within a massive country whose name I surprisingly enough recognize.

The Split Horizon Empire.

The city Simel is now pointing to is dubbed *Crown of the Country*. Weird name for a city. Nevertheless, I know what he's saying, and I know what he's trying to express.

"You want us to go to the empire?" I ask with no little amount of skepticism. He nods at me, which is nice, because I would like to not have to go halfway across the world because he made a joke. I look back down at the map, at the line snaking between mountains and across a sea and through cities. "I don't know, isn't that, maybe . . . a bit far?"

He stares at me. I huff. "I mean, I'll still do it if it helps you get somewhere safe, but . . ." Searching the map, I quickly find what I'm looking for. I point at the little, RED-colored city. "Wouldn't you rather get here? To the Shore City of Acheron?" His gaze doesn't shift an inch. To dispel the tension at least slightly, I give a nervous chuckle. "Heh, I just . . . Or maybe that's where you live now? The empire?"

But the crests don't match up, so I doubt it. The empire's crest is a RED sun split by a blade. That's not the crest Simel wears. Besides, the Shore City of Acheron is much closer. Still over a month's trek, but not nearly as daunting as the empire.

Simel's gaze burns into me. I try to swallow down my fears. "Honestly, I'm a bit . . . You know when we met? When—when we were in the prince's tent? I didn't say it then, but I kind of . . . I defeated him." His expression doesn't show the slightest hint of change. As a matter of fact, he seems thoroughly unsurprised. Sighing, I raise my hands in surrender. "What I'm *trying* to say is that those empire guys might not be too hot on me being there."

I look up. And into his eyes. His eyes that shine with a demand. A demand that echoes through my mind. Four simple words.

Do the right thing.

My hands twist into fists. "But I'll still do it," I say, defeated. I look up at him. "I'll take you there. Even if it's the last thing I do."

That's what he wanted to hear.

With my agreement, Simel removes the silver compass from the table and packs it into his knapsack, alongside a few other things. He was even able to somehow find a pair of bags to go on the lizard's saddle. He packs these with various things, including the map and the little figurines. Within only a few minutes—the majority of which I spent just looking at him—he's fully packed.

And I'm standing without a single thing in my hands.

So . . . this is it? We're leaving straight-away? Not even going to stop by the crib for provisions? Well, anything still in there is tainted by gore, and it's not like Simel eats meat anyway, and I don't need to eat to begin with, so I guess there's no real need to return there.

But it still doesn't feel right. Shouldn't I at least be able to bid the crib adieu? Is that so bad? Apparently so.

Since Simel is too weak to carry his bags properly, I grab the saddle ones for him. I also hoist them onto the lizard's back, despite its attempts to protest. Simel easily calms it down, though.

In that case, we have pretty much all we need.

Simel is trying to use a regular compass, but I stop him. He looks at me. "I don't need a compass, Simel. If it's where I want to go, I'll be able to get there." Which obviously confuses the shit out of him, but it was a funny line, so I won't explain it to him.

Sticking my nose in the air, I take a deep whiff. Since I want to get to the empire, that's what I'll smell. But first, we need to get to that one city he pointed out. So that's what I try to focus on. Sniff sniff sniff. Sni—iff.

I turn toward where the sun is rising. "Yup, that's the way." I turn back to Simel only to find him already steering the lizard.

I'm just about to jump up next to him when the lizard hisses and I remember that this feral creature illogically has it out for me. Oh, you don't want me to ride you? Fine! I'll just walk right next to you. How's that, huh? And if we get attacked, you're the one going down first, punk!

The lizard, of course, doesn't understand anything I think. But I still got my anger out there, so while still seething a little, we set out into the deep desert.

IX

Desert Travels

It starts out pretty okay. We walk at a calm pace, only pausing to fight off the local wildlife or to pick up some cacti here and there. My human-leather thigh-high boots broke after only a few hours, though I easily substituted them with some snakeskin. And then the trek continued.

We took a break around midday to eat. It was mainly for Simel's sake, though. I ate some random flesh from my inventory, Simel ate cactus, and the lizard ate some of the flesh harvested earlier today. With that concluded, we continue walking.

The sun is relentless. I'm covered in a sheen of sweat at all times, and Simel sits atop the lizard slightly hunched over, his hood drawn and a book in his lap. He scribbles something into it. We continue walking.

Something bites onto my foot deep in the soot and I'm pulled under, but it's just one of those anacondas, so after a few seconds of grappling I'm able to grab its neck and snap it in half. The rest of its body clenches, twitches, and writhes before dying. I stand up, skin the snake, and tie the leather around my feet before throwing the rest at the lizard. It grabs the meat in midair with its jaws before throwing it back at me. I'm almost about to try to tie the snake into a noose for that damn reptile when I notice the way Simel looks at me. Grumbling, I slice the snake in half and stick it in my inventory. We continue walking.

One of my snakeskin wraps fell off but I didn't notice until my foot was beyond merely well done. By tying a few skins around my hands, I walk on my hands and one foot until the other foot heals enough to walk on. We continue walking.

During a small break spent in the shade of a cavern, we watch as the sun begins to set. We eat dinner and then we continue walking.

We continue walking until the air is so cold Simel's breath becomes milky WHITE, at which point I thread a bearskin over him. We continue walking.

At midnight, we finally decide to set up camp for the night once we find a suitable cavern. It had a few inhabitants, but I took care of them rather easily. I almost expected the lizard to help, but it was clearly used to being a steed and nothing more. Since Simel was still asleep, I removed the baggage and things from the lizard myself, only having to avoid its snapping jaws a few times for it to finally accept my proximity. Once it was fully unloaded, I woke Simel by gently tapping him on the shoulder. It still startled him to the point of almost falling off, but it did awaken him.

We remove the saddle together. Simel seems uncertain, so I set his mind at ease. "I don't need to sleep," I say. "So I'll keep guard during the night. You can sleep easy." I smile at him. "With me around, you have nothing to fear!"

For some reason, he doesn't seem to trust my words, but he still goes to sleep. Good enough for me, I guess. Apparently, he did seriously bring an entire sleeping ensemble, complete with a rolled-up mattress of some sort, a thick cover, and a pillow. All of this he lays out on the floor in the innermost part of the cave. Before he tries to go to sleep, though, he does some weird prayer thing by kneeling down and putting one hand to his chest and the other to his forehead. I have no idea if he actually said anything, though. If he did, it must have been so hushed that even I couldn't hear it. Nevertheless, with this done, he finally lies down, pulls up the covers—mind you, he is *not* wearing any pajamas—and pretends to go to sleep.

I watch him from the mouth of the cave. I am absolutely certain that he did not fall asleep straightaway. His breathing was too quick. If I'd been closer, I'm sure I would've been able to hear his heart beating just a little too fast, too.

Is there anything I can do for him? Maybe a night meal? Bedtime story? Good-night hug?

Before my thoughts can go any further, he abruptly sits up, reaches for the bearskin lying a foot or two away, and suddenly notices the lizard. The lizard, for its own part, is silently curled up across from Simel. At Simel's gaze, the lizard's head slowly rises, like a curious dog. Following with the analogy, Simel silently pats a spot next to him. The lizard perks up, gets to its feet, and practically skips over to where Simel is to lie down next to him, curling up and placing its head across Simel's chest. Then Simel pulls up the bearskin to cover them both. Since the lizard is slightly bigger than a bear, the skin doesn't cover it entirely, but it doesn't seem to mind.

And just like that, Simel falls asleep. I can tell it instantly. His hand is on the lizard's back and the lizard's tail is curled around them both.

Bundled up like that, they sleep soundly, both taking slow, calm breaths, not even stirring to shift in their sleep.

And I have never before felt such a strong urge to—

The lizard's eyes suddenly snap open and its head lifts from Simel's chest but I've turned away from them, and after a second or so of feeling its reptilian gaze burn into the back of my head, I can smell it lie down again, calming down as Simel gently pets its head. They both fall asleep once more.

When a long-legged wolflike creature later wanders by, I almost feel glad, because it gives me a distraction from how horribly quaint the cave became all of a sudden. Ripping it apart limb by limb was an excellent bit of stress relief.

<Top—Status—Community>
<04:31:33 Day 367>
<The fourteenth attempt will begin in 28:19:29:27>

I give them about six hours of sleep and then I wake them up. The lizard is easily awoken by stabbing my finger into its behind. Simel is then consequently brought back to the land of the living by the lizard flying away from atop him. For some reason, he doesn't seem too happy to see me.

We spend half an hour or so repacking everything and eating breakfast, and then we head out.

The day happens like yesterday.

For the evening, we find some place to rest, and Simel and the lizard sleep.

We wake up and head out again.

The day happens like yesterday.

Simel and the lizard sleep.

We wake up and head out again.

The day happens like yesterday.

The day happens like yesterday.

The day happens like yesterday.

The day happens like yesterday.

And before I knew it, a week had passed in mindless droning desert desert desert desert.

Sometimes it would rain soot, and we would take cover.

Sometimes we would meet animals and I would kill them.

Sometimes, to relieve myself of the endless dull monotony, I would specifically seek out animals to kill. Not to eat—just to have something to do.

Sometimes I would look at Simel and at the lizard and wonder how fast I could skin them if I really tried. But skinning Simel is a *bad bad bad not good* thought, so I stop and don't.

Sometimes I consider turning back around and killing the giant and finishing this damn floor already.

But the day would always end eventually and I'd sit down for a few hours and I'd be left with the BLACK soot inside my head, the dark ashes that burn through my skull and cook my thoughts until they're nothing but charred guilt.

And then the sun dawns and we head out again.

Dull. Dull. Dull. Dull. Dull. Dull. Dull. Dull. Dull.

I decide in my head at some point when my thoughts are the most charred and the heartbeats of Simel and the lizard are the most synced that I am going to find any excuse necessary to kill the lizard. It needs to die. I must kill it. I just can't stand it anymore. The way it looks at me. The way it snarls. The way it lies curled up like a happy dog.

It must end.

The opportunity arrives with the sootfall. The ever-blue sky is covered up by BLACK. I could smell it miles away, but I let it gather. I let it form. Because now, we're in the middle of the desert, and there isn't a single piece of cover nearby. Not an inch. No caves, nothing at all. Nothing, save for one, single creature.

I turn to Simel and the lizard, my smile betraying my true feelings as I say, "Sorry, Simel, but I think that"—and I lick my lips—"we might need to find cover. And we don't have time to find a cave." I look up at him and I think he might have been able to see the glee in my eyes because he jerks back, eyes wide in fear. I wipe some sweat from my brow. "I'm really sorry," I lie. "You know I hate to say this, but this lizard . . . He's our only chance. You understand that, right? I'll make it gentle. He won't even know what happened. Isn't that good? It's good, isn't it?"

He's pale. I can see the WHITEs of his eyes. He slowly reaches down to take the reins of the lizard but I'm faster—much, *much* faster.

I cross the small distance between us and put my right hand on the lizard's forehead.

<[Touch of Reversed Stroke Resistance (Lv.2)]>
<[Touch of Reversed Organ Failure Resistance (Lv.2)]>
<[Touch of Reversed Brain Damage Resistance (Lv.2)]>

It drops with a dead thud.

Simel cries. I have to pry him away from the lizard's empty-eyed body. Getting him into the empty cavity I made of the lizard's abdomen is even harder. By the time I climb in as well—the only bit of Simel's possessions I was able to bring along being his satchel—Simel's curled up into a little ball, sobbing.

But we survive the sootfall. That's good, isn't it? I think so.

It took a bit of effort to dig us out of the caked soot, but it all worked out. Simel didn't want to leave the lizard's body, but I was able to drag him away. He didn't want to walk, either, but I was able to pull him along. All he did was stumble, hiccuping between heaving breaths. Telling him to get himself together didn't help. I guess, if he wants to mourn some stupid overgrown lizard, that's his choice.

We continue walking.

Since Simel has to walk with his own legs now, we have to take more breaks. More rest time. But that's okay.

Toward the end of the day, I have to carry him on my back. He feels hot and cold both at once, and while I'm carrying him, I can feel him sob into my back, leaving wet stains on my pelt and my neck. Eventually, we reach a small cave. The only inhabitants were a small family of tarantulas, but I take care of them. Halfway through the battle, Simel stumbles right into it, right in front of them, but I act quickly enough to throw myself between him and the tarantula's fangs. Then I kill the rest of them.

"That was dangerous, Simel! You could've *died*!" I scold him, but of course, he doesn't listen in the least. All he does is stare into the lifeless eyes of the tarantula I just killed. And then, while I'm still dissecting the thing, he turns around and vomits in a corner of the cave, which is very unhygienic. He's had a long day as it is, though, so even if I want to tell him not to do that again, I restrain myself.

Since we had to leave most of the packed stuff behind, Simel's forced to sleep on my bearskin, which shouldn't be too bad, but he still seems really uncomfortable. For some reason he shivers all night as though cold, even after I gave him two additional hides.

Even more worrying, he woke up several times during the night, usually after whimpering and groaning. Probably nightmares.

Each time he woke up, his eyes would flare open, searching for something only to suddenly stop, and then his face would slowly move over to look at me, and even though I took care not to look at him, I could feel just how intense his gaze was, burning with some emotion I couldn't discern. But then he'd turn over and go back to sleep again. And just like that, the night passed rather uneventfully.

In the morning, I noticed a little patch of what seemed like BLACK mold, growing around the area where the tarantula had bitten me. The bite itself had already healed, but the BLACK stuff was growing strong regardless.

<You have learned: Lichen Tolerance Lv.1>

Lichen? That's new. If I'm not misremembering, lichen is some sort of cross between fungus and algae and plant, right? Or is it just plant and algae? No, hang on, isn't algae already a cross between fungus and plant . . . ? Okay, I honestly have no idea. Still, it's a new type of tolerance, so I think I'd best let it grow a bit to really milk the levels I can get from it.

With the dawn arriving, we head out again.

About halfway through the day, I feed Simel the last bit of cactus I had in my inventory. I try to find more, but I can't smell any nearby, or even in the direction we're heading. With Simel upset enough as he is, I don't really want to force him to do anything, but soon enough I might not have any choice myself.

As we take a small break in a cave, I sit him down to have the talk.

I take a deep breath. "Simel, I really don't like saying this, but from here on out, you might need to eat, like, meat and stuff." Until now, Simel had been sitting hunched over, gripping his stomach, staring blankly at a patch of sand. But at my words, his eyes blink and his head snaps up to face me, his head already shaking back and forth. I frown at him. "Look, I know you're a vegetarian or a vegan or whatever, but . . . if you don't eat meat, I don't think you'll be able to make it going forward. Don't you want to survive to get to that city place?"

I can see the muscles in his jaw working.

"It's not like I'll force you to . . . Well, if you refuse to eat *anything* I'll probably make you eat, but it shouldn't get to that point. We're *friends*, remember? Friends don't let their friends kill themselves." I almost reach out to pat him calmingly, but he jerks back before I can get close. I pull my hand back. "R— right. Yeah. So, uh . . ." I wave my hand in the air, trying to bring the conversation elsewhere. "You know, I've been thinking, but . . . Goblins do need water, right? That should be—" He glares at me. "Yeah. Yeah, I was just . . . Um. So, I've been thinking of a way to get water. So far, I haven't seen a single oasis in this entire damn desert, and even if there *was* one, I'm pretty sure it'd be covered in soot, so that's busted from the get-go. But I've been thinking . . . See, if we . . ."

Going just by the look on his face, I don't think Simel's entirely recovered from the whole *you'll probably need to eat flesh* situation. In that sense, I don't know if this is the perfect or the worst possible moment to mention this.

"See, my body's kind of weird, so if we just did a bit of bloodletting, and then distilled the blood to get water, I think that . . ."

I don't have time to say any more before Simel's hands shoot up and clasp over his big pointy ears, pressing them to the side of his head.

I stare at him where he sits hunched over like a stubborn toddler. Okay, that is actually *very* rude. He can't seriously believe that that's any way to act in a civilized conversation, can he? Why, if I were any less patient, I might just . . . But I wouldn't, and I won't. Instead, I just mutter, "Well, okay, if that's how you want to be . . ." and cross my arms. You know. Like a sensible almost-adult.

And to make matters worse, later on when we set out again, he seriously expects me to carry him. Isn't that just the height of entitlement? Of course, I do still carry him, but certainly not because he asked so nicely, because—as you may or may not remember—this guy doesn't exactly talk, much less ask for *anything*. So, yeah.

We continue walking. As we go, I rack my brains over what kind of meat would be best for Simel.

The stuff kept in my inventory is almost all spoiled, so that's a no-go. I'd need to get fresh stuff. I almost feel tempted to give him my own meat if I didn't know it was all diseased and gross. If Simel's going to eat anything, it has to be high-class, right? I mean, from what I've seen, this man is basically a commander-type guy. Leadership position and all that. So he needs good food. Furthermore, since he hasn't eaten actual meat in a good while, it might do best to start out small, like tarantula meat or bird flesh. Hmm. Now that I think about it, tarantula would probably be best. It isn't poisonous, it tastes pretty good, and it only gave me a few levels in ulcer resistance.

For Simel's sake, I should probably try to cook it somehow. It's basically just land lobster, so I feel like it ought to be boiled. However, water is not something that we currently have access to, and I really don't think Simel would like to be fed something boiled in blood. Now that I think about it, would that even be tasty? I know blood soup is a thing, but this would be something different. Also, blood soup contains more than just blood, so I don't think I could make it right here and now.

Yeah, all things considered, it'd be best to stick to the basics. Seared meat would be best, no doubt.

Keeping my eyes open, I eventually find some tarantulas, which I kill with ease, disassembling them on the spot to put in my inventory. When I go to pick Simel back up, he practically collapses onto my back. That's probably not good.

Now that I think about it, if I had been in favor with the gods, couldn't I have used my points to buy water and food right here? I could, couldn't I?

Life is so unfair. But that doesn't mean I can just stop going.

So we continue. Before the sun has even set, I find us a little cave to take up residence in. There were a few animals in there, but I take care of them. Before I kill them, though, I pull out a few of the empty vodka bottles I kept and drain the blood into them, though it was only enough to fill a few. I'm actually surprised to find more bottles in my inventory than previously expected. I mean, there's enough in here to contain enough blood for three whole Fennricks! That's a bit too much, if you ask me.

At this moment, it'll be more than enough for my goals.

Before I start doing any of that, though, I pull out the tarantula meat and put it on top of one of my many hides. Then I spy toward the entrance of the cave. See, I chose this one for a reason. Out here, right beside the mouth of the cave, is one of those little kowtowing goblins covered in soot. Strolling outside, I casually clean the top of it, removing the flaky ash covering its hunched back. You should remember this, but I'll repeat it regardless—these goblins are *alive*. And you know what that means?

Once the back is uncovered, I touch my hand to it.

<[Touch of Reversed Dehydration Resistance (Lv.2)]>
<[Touch of Reversed Heat Resistance (Lv.2)]>
<[Touch of Reversed Burn Resistance (Lv.2)]>

And, just like that, the goblin bursts into flame. But not like a wild, all-eating fire. No, this is a more subdued one, contained within the ribs of the goblin, eating at its still-beating heart, carefully swallowing it from the inside. It's a slow process, and one that is perfect for my intentions.

Because, like this, in just a few minutes, we'll have the perfect barbecue grilling embers.

I take a deep whiff. Ahhh, now *there's* a nostalgic smell . . . "Hey, Simel, are you excited for some barbe—" My words die on my tongue as I turn around and find Simel curled up in the depths of the cave, both hands squeezing his nose and mouth shut, eyes wide and glistening. I blink at him. When—why did this happen? What the heck did I do now? "Simel?" I call out, turning to walk toward him. "Is everything . . . are you alright?"

He points his left hand at me.

<Cold.>
<Cold.>
<Char.>
<Cold.>
<Crackle.>
<Cold.>
<Char.>
<Char.>
<Char.>

I stare at him, more confused than anything. "Simel, what the heck are you doing?"

His chest spasms up and down, anxious little breaths hopping out of his throat. His eyes tremble, never leaving me for a moment. Somehow, it doesn't even feel like he's looking at *me*, but rather at something that just happens to be where I am.

Frowning at him, I put my hands on my hips. "I'm not entirely sure what you're trying to pull here, but when you snap out of it, I'll be over here making you food and water, okay? And I'm not trying to stress you here or anything, but I suggest you get your marbles in order within the hour or the food will go cold."

Still basically gasping, he keeps watching me even as I turn around to go get the food ready. Maybe, when this is all over, he might actually appreciate all of this? Ahh, who knows.

Grumbling to myself, I pull a few clean bones from my inventory and lay them atop the perfect goblin grill coals. After shuffling them around a little, I remove the tarantula legs from my inventory. I usually crack these things open and slurp out the meat raw, but since I'll be cooking them, I've elected to keep the meat inside the legs, only altering them by shearing off the thick bristles covering them. Now, how many of these might Simel reasonably eat . . . ?

I glance over at where he sits in the back of the cave, head in hands, breathing sharply.

He's a growing boy. He should be able to eat a couple, right?

I put three tarantula legs on the grill. Hmm. Now that I think about it, I actually have no idea how old Simel is. How old do goblins get, anyway? In games and stuff, goblins are usually shown as fast-aging things, but that doesn't necessarily hold true for the real-life variants. Really, since this seems to be a completely different kind of situation, these goblins might age even slower than humans. Going by that logic, there's a fair chance that Simel is way older than me, maybe even by hundreds of years.

I glance back at Simel where he sits hyperventilating.

Yeah, no. He's probably around my age at most. Maybe even—

POP!

I whirl around to look at the tarantula legs. One has literally exploded. Oo—kay.

Removing a clean bit of tarantula hide from my inventory, I put the other legs on top of it. They look a little dangerous, but I'm sure it's fine. Carrying the plate, I reenter the cave. Simel is still deep inside, curled up and everything. Geez. Since he might inadvertently use magic on the plate, I stop a fair bit away, putting down the food in his field of vision. "Here you go," I say, standing back up. "Cooked tarantula legs, just for you."

He doesn't look up from where he sits. Alright.

Leaning down again, I crack open the legs, scalding my hands as I do. The inside is filled with rich steam, and it honestly doesn't smell all that bad. "There. How's that? I know it isn't gourmet, and I didn't exactly have anything to season it with, but it's better than starving by far." I stare at him for a moment. He doesn't budge. I sigh. "I'll leave you to it, then."

I wander back to the grill. There's still some tarantula splattered here and there. I take a piece and taste it. Very bland, but it *is* food. Personally, I prefer the texture of the raw variant, but this is fine, too.

While the grill is still hot, I start enacting my latest and greatest plan.

For this, you'll need four items: an empty vodka bottle, a cleaned-out small intestine, a few pieces of hair, and a snake fang.

Step one is to grab the small intestine, and if it isn't clean, you clean it using your mouth. Once you can't taste any flavor on it, you loop one end over the mouth of the empty vodka bottle, fastening it in place with some long hairs. Then you secure the other end of the intestine around the snake fang, making sure that the sharp tip is pointing outward. And just like that, you've got yourself an impromptu bloodletter!

With that done, you just take the snake fang part, find yourself a good vein, and pop it right in. I decided to go with that one vein in your armpit that all the druggies use in the movies. I had to dig around a bit to find it, but once I got the vein, the blood went into the snake fang and through the intestine and into the vodka bottle. Success!

It takes around half an hour for the entire bottle to be filled up, at which point I've already started considering using my jugular vein next time. That might actually kill me, though, so I think I'll abstain.

I repeat the process for a few more bottles until I've got a total of eight bottles of both my own blood and animal blood. I feel a little woozy, but that'll pass soon enough.

Now I can move on to the true science part of this.

First, though, I need to make sure the grill is still going strong, which it thankfully is. Great. Okay, so, now, we'll do something a little funky. Taking the used small intestine, we clean out the blood first before fastening one end to a bottle of blood and the other to an empty bottle of vodka. And then, we just put the bottle of blood over the fire and watch the magic happen!

Any time now. Aaaaaaany time now. Any . . . time . . . now . . .

I sit and stare at the bottle of blood. Did I mess up somewhere . . . ?

As I watch the two bottles with due suspicion, the whole thing being a caveman's science experiment at best, a change suddenly occurs. A little bit of steam seems to be rising from the blood! Scootching closer, I watch with interest as the tawny bit of steam crawls upward in little WHITE wisps of oxidized water, trailing through the smaller intestine to condense in the uppermost bendy part before turning into just the smallest droplets of water. The teeny-tiny droplets slowly inch down the throat of the bottle before sliding down the sides and gathering at the bottom.

Success! Hah, and my biology teacher always told me I'd never become anything worthwhile! Well, not that he was wrong, but he was *absolutely* wrong to fail me in science, that's for sure.

Giddy, I watch the little experiment take form. Soon, the blood is bubblin' and the steam is flowin'. I take a deep whiff. Ahhh, is this the scent of victory? Technically speaking, if it's a battlefield victory, then it should logically follow that said victory would smell like blood. But this is a different type of victory, so the scent isn't as set in stone.

One thing that worries me a little, though, is that the small intestine is sort of, I don't know . . . ballooning? I don't know how else to describe it, but it's simultaneously being cooked while also getting filled up with steam. Right now, it's starting to look an awful lot like a snake being inflated. You know, like that one scene in the animated hit movie *Shre—*

POP!

With an almost melodious *pop*, the small intestine finally gives out, the middle part of it rupturing and the steam held within flying out in a big WHITE puff.

H—hey, wait, no! *My steam!*

Grabbing hold of the intestine, I wedge it shut, ignoring the way it scalds my hands. Okay, okay, I forgot the basics of how steam engines work, but that's fine, we can still make this work, I just need to—

POP!

The intestine had other plans, as the part I held shut pops once more, startling me enough to not care to grab the loosened end again. And for just a moment, I stare at the bottle where it sits atop the perfect barbecue coals bubbling silently, wondering where my life went wrong.

I look over at the vodka bottle with water in it. There's maybe a deciliter or so of water in there. Closing my eyes, I take a measured breath. If I replace the small intestine every now and again . . . it's doable. It'll take a lot of patience—something I don't exactly have in spades—but I can do it.

For Simel's sake.

So, even though it hurts, I keep going. I put more stuff on the fire to keep it going all through the night. I learn how to make the process more effective by lengthening the intestine and letting the steam cool down every now and again. And by the end of it all, I was able to distill the blood into three bottles of water. The water is kind of murky and I should probably try to refine it somehow, but I don't trust my process—if you can even call it that—to be anywhere near good enough to do so properly.

I've even tasted it, and although it wasn't exactly tasteless, it didn't give me any levels in any tolerances or resistances. In other words, it's good enough. Better than dying, at least.

<Top—Status—Community>
<03:01:54 Day 377>
<The fourteenth attempt will begin in 18:20:58:6>

It's early in the morning, but my excitement is too great to stop myself. Sneaking inside the depths of the cave, I shake Simel awake. "Simel, Simel," I whisper-shout. "Hey, Simel, wake up. I got you something!"

He awakens with a startle, drawing back in fear at seeing me so close. I hold up my hands placatingly, simultaneously presenting one of the bottles. The two other bottles are in my inventory, corked and safe. "Look!" I say, boastfully shoving the bottle toward him. "I did it, Simel! *I got you water!*"

He looks at the bottle in my hands as though he expects it to contain nothing but one hundred percent pure distilled snake venom. I chuckle at him. "Yeah, it doesn't look too good, but it'll keep you alive. I mean, when was the last time you drank proper water?" He doesn't really answer that one, so I can assume it's been a while. I push the bottle closer to him. "Here, drink. Drink as much as you'd like!" But for some reason, he draws back further. My smile feels strained. "Come on, Simel, don't be like that. It's not unsafe, I promise! No more than drying out, that's for sure."

He still doesn't seem keen on so much as having a taste.

Unfortunately, at this moment, I can tell that he needs this water more than basically anything. His cheeks and eyes are far more sunken in than they were before our travels. The skin around his ears is dry and cracking in places. He needs water. Knowing my inventory and the state of this water, I can't be certain that this water won't spoil.

So, even though I hate to do it, I force him to drink. It's true—I do. I had to. You understand, don't you? I didn't have any choice!

The taste made him puke a few times, but I still made him drink. Until he no longer puked and he still had water in his stomach, I forced him. I didn't like doing it. It hurt. But it had to be done.

I didn't have any choice.

After such a night, I wanted to let Simel sleep. But he didn't want to sleep. He just kept awake, curled up, hiding inside a cocoon of bear pelts. So, to avoid wasting the hours, I decide to set out again.

<You have learned: Lichen Tolerance Lv.4>

I absently scratch the spot on my right arm where the tarantula bit me. The BLACK lichen is spreading well. A little too well, maybe. My other resistances don't seem to be hindering it in the least, which confirms the slightly worrying theory that resistances are mainly very specific instruments and useless against other stuff. Interesting. I think I'll let this lichen stuff keep going until I get to resistance, but at that point my body might fight it off on its own, so it should be fine.

We continue going. Simel only has the energy to walk for about an hour before he collapses, only avoiding a faceful of burning soot because I was fast enough to catch him. The thing is, I know exactly why.

He didn't eat anything last night. I was able to force the water down his throat, but he left the tarantula completely untouched. In the end, I was left to use the legs as bait to catch a few more creatures.

He needs to eat. He needs to drink. He needs to sleep.

I can't let him kill himself.

Around midday, we take a break, and I use the sun and the hot soot to cook a few more tarantula legs. I try to give them to Simel. He doesn't even look at them.

Maybe someday in the future, he'll understand why I'm doing what I'm doing. But for now, I'll just have to do what needs to be done.

Once the legs have cooled down, I crack them open, pull out the flesh, and do what needs to be done. I hate doing it, but it needs to be done. So I hold him down. I force him to the floor and I ignore the magic he tries to use against me and the kicking of his legs and the pressing of his arms. I hold him down, one knee on his chest, mumbling, "I'm sorry, I'm sorry," and then I pry open his mouth and force the meat inside. I move his jaw for him. "I'm sorry, I'm sorry, I'm sorry," I continue. "Please, swallow, please, Simel," and I hold his mouth and his nose shut. I know it's bad. I know it's not good. But he needs to eat.

Eventually, forced to breathe, he swallows it down. I loosen my grip on his face and he takes a few panting, gasping breaths, snot running down his nose and his eyes RED. Then I feel his stomach and chest spasm beneath me, so I hold his nose and mouth closed. Stomach acids are important liquids. "I'm sorry, I'm sorry, I'm sorry," I mumble down at him as he spasms and his eyes bulge but after a few seconds he finally swallows it back down. I let go of his face again.

And for just a minute or so, I keep him beneath me, pinned down. But he just lies there, breathing heavily, precious tears rolling down his cheeks. I remove my knee from him and step off.

As I watch in silence, he crawls up into a little ball, hugging his knees to his chest.

I glance over at the other two cooked tarantula legs. Something in my heart clenches painfully and I look back at Simel. "Please don't make me do that again," I say to him. I don't know if he heard me or not, but I'm not going to repeat myself.

I don't want to do that again, but if he gives me no other choice, then what else is there for me to do?

While he's still lying there, I put a bottle of water and the other two tarantula legs next to him. Then I move over to the mouth of the cave. I sit there for around an hour. That's more than we usually take for lunch break, but I can tell he needs it right now. In the meantime, I just sit at the entrance, staring out across the sands and the soot.

After a while, I decide that enough is enough and stand up, turning around toward Simel. "Alright, let's head back ou—" I freeze midturn. Simel is still curled up, but the water in the bottle is gone and the tarantula legs have been emptied and lie tossed to the side. I blink at the sight. Something warm wells up to my cheeks and I wipe at my eyes. I gulp down a lump in my throat and walk closer, plucking the empty bottle from the floor. Hunching down, I put a hand on Simel's back, as gently as I possibly can. "Thank you," I whisper at him, my voice trembling only a little. "Thank you, my friend."

I bring him to his feet and we head back out.

In the evening, I do some more bloodletting and distillation. I don't know how much Simel needs to drink on the daily, but I think it's better to have too much than too little water. I cook some tarantula legs for him, alongside some bird legs. I'm beyond relieved to see him actually eat them, though he did almost vomit twice. I gave him some water and he drank it. During the night, while he slept, I continued distilling more water.

And, for once, when morning arose, I felt a strange sense of hopefulness for the future.

During the coming days, Simel both ate and drank. His cheeks slowly regained color, and his eyes weren't quite so sunken in, and he could walk farther every day. For my own part, I was also doing pretty well. The lichen thing was spreading more and more, and it was starting to itch to high hell, but that just meant my tolerances were increasing.

After a couple of days, I started feeling oddly tired. While bloodletting, I would at times suddenly BLACK out, only waking up a couple of minutes later, with no idea what did it. At one point, this BLACKout even lasted a full hour. That wouldn't normally have been the last drop but combined with the fact that I always felt tired and weak, I decided to do away with the lichen. So I sat down one evening, poked a few holes around the area covered in the BLACK, crusty lichen, and then I just cut it out in one big flap. When I did, I found a bunch of stringy things inside my flesh, which is . . . maybe not good? I don't know.

I'm more worried because the wound won't stop bleeding.

Not that my wounds bleeding a lot is anything new. No, it's just that for some reason, my regeneration meditation isn't helping, nor is my moving meditation or anything like that. It won't heal, and it won't stop bleeding. In what was absolutely not pure desperation and a dash of panic, I took some skin and hides and hair and whatnot from my inventory and used it to tie a tight gauze around the wound on my arm. I can't really afford to spend too much time and effort on a simple flesh wound.

The next day, when I give it another look to check if it's still bleeding, I find that not only is it still open, but the flesh itself is starting to grow BLACK spots of lichen. Uh-huh. Yeah. Uh. Okay, that might not be all that good. My arm is starting to feel worryingly cold, too. With it being my right arm, losing it would be detrimental at best.

Redoing the gauze, I decide to just not think about it. Once my resistance catches up, it'll heal in no time!

After about a week more, I decide to amputate it.

We continue.

Leaning down, I poke Simel. "Hey, Simel," I whisper. My throat hurts. "Simel, we need to go. Wake up." He doesn't move. I poke him again. "Simel," I say. "Simel, wake up." His face, pale and dry and stale, twitches. His eyes, set within deep, dark eyeholes, slowly flutter open and he stares up at me, at some little point behind me. He doesn't move any more. But he's awake. Just like the day before, and just like the day before that, and the day before that, I take his skeletal hand in mine and pull him up so that he sits. I have to hold his shoulder in place so he doesn't fall. "Here, let's go," I whisper. His hands slowly move, his arms trembling as he lifts them above my shoulders. I let go of his shoulder and put my only hand beneath him, hoisting him up on my back.

I put his sleeping things into my inventory. Then I carefully stand up, stumbling only once, twice, before righting myself. Simel's head rests against the back of mine, his slow, shallow breaths, as raspy as sandpaper, meeting my ears. That means he's still alive.

Even after a month on these BLACK dunes, he's still alive.

I head out.

As I walk, I take slow, shallow breaths. Everything smells like soot and death and cold bone. But I can smell it. A city. Distant but closer with each staggering step I take. It smells like spices and living skin and dusty clothes. Like greasy hair and polished sandstone and milk. Like people, living and existing together. Children and adults and elders and the rich and the poor and the beggars and the believers. I smell them. Their collective breath carried on the dry wind. Close. Nearby.

I pass by a little cave. I can smell the things living there, hungry and dry and starved. I pay them little more than a glancing thought as I continue walking, wading through the ankle-high soot.

I'm thirsty. I'm hungry. I'm hot and I'm cold and I almost feel like I'm already dead. I can't feel my feet but I can feel the lack of my right arm. It's healed into a stump but it's still useless. But I'm close now. *We're* close. I can smell it. Closer, closer.

The sun begins to set.

I can feel Simel's heartbeat against my back. Weak. Gentle. Slow. When was the last time he ate? He hasn't been able to keep anything down for the past week.

I forced water down his throat but it didn't help. He's still so weak. He can't even muster the energy to stand, or to sit, or to look at me with any emotion but bland apathy.

He's dying. Simel is dying. I can't stop. If I stop, I don't know if it'll be the last time I lay him down on a bear's hide to sleep. I can't tell if this is his last day. I can't let him die. He's depending on me. If he dies, what kind of friend does that make me?

I keep walking. The sun is down. The cold is starting to claw its way up through the sand and the soot, freezing my breath WHITE, leaving my jaw to chitter and chatter. I only pause to pull the bear hide out of my inventory to cover Simel. Then I keep walking.

His breath is so slow. His heart, too. I can hear it. As soft as a dying clock.

I can usually smell when something is dead before the light leaves its eyes. But I can't smell Simel at all. Never could, never can. I wonder if he's already dead, and I've only been carrying his corpse with me these past few days. I can't know. I can't know.

I pass over a hill and freeze in place, the only movement I can muster being the beating of my heart, the breathing of my lungs, and the trembling in my jaw as I finally lay eyes on something that is neither soot nor sand nor rock nor cave.

Before me, just down the hill, lies a city.

We Made It

"Simel!" The word erupts joyously from my throat, and I turn my head to look at his face. "Simel, we're here! We made it! Simel, the city, it's—" He doesn't react. His face is slumped over across my back, eyes closed, mouth slightly open, ears drooping. I can feel my chest rising and falling. "S—Simel . . . ?"

The world stops turning. The wind stops howling. My heart no longer beats, and my lungs no longer breathe as I stare at the silent, lifeless face slung over my shoulder.

And then a tiny, almost unnoticeable wisp of WHITE air leaves his lips, and the world returns to color.

He's alive. He's alive. He's alive.

He isn't dead.

But I don't have any more time.

Feet wheeling beneath me, I practically throw myself down the hill, heart in my throat, speeding as fast as I can, not caring about the hides around my legs falling off in my mad dash toward the city. Mind reeling, I sprint for it, not stopping when my feet connect with sand rather than soot, continuing even when said sand becomes firm and trampled. I run inside the city, through the simple road and passing by the small, blocky houses without any mind for anything.

Where—where—where can I take him? Who will help? I'm not wearing any disguise. No one would help me, looking like this. What does he need? Food, shelter, drink . . .

Throat burning with each panting breath I take, I abruptly stop in my tracks right outside one of the many, many houses lining the simple road. The inside is dark. The windows are little more than openings along the top of the wall. The door is made of wood. The inside is dark. Breathing heavily, I step closer to the door. I knock on the door using my forehead. There's no response. But the door is locked. So I knock again. *Knock knock.*

Standing out here, in the horrible cold, with Simel on my back, the both of us covered partially by a bearskin, I wait for a response. I shuffle a little. Looking down, I notice that I'm missing a couple of toes, but that's okay. I can make do. I'm okay. I just need—

I smell someone awake. I hear movement inside the house. Someone steps down the stairs. The door is smaller than my own frame, so I take a step back once I hear the movement just behind it. Someone fiddles with what I assume is a lock and the door slowly opens, a head peeking out from within. "Hello? What do you want?" His yellow eyes fall on Simel, and they widen, the door opening a bit more, too. "Is he alright? Would you like to come—"

Leaning forward, I carry Simel's weight on mostly my back as my left hand, my only hand, flashes out and gouges a deep slash across his throat. He stumbles back, eyes wide, mouth moving. I step closer, pulling the door open fully and closing it behind me as the goblin—a strangely yellow one—falls over and bleeds out on the floor.

<Goblin (Lv.10) Defeated.>

Let's see, how do you lock this thing? Well, since it opened inward, it can be blocked somewhat easily. Using my feet, I push the yellow goblin over to the door, holding it closed that way.

I take a deep breath through my nose, breathing in the layout of the house. The master bedroom is upstairs. That's my goal, then.

Huffing, almost gasping, I drag the two of us upstairs, up the coarse stone stairs, into a little hallway and then into a room to the side. There's a little mound on the bed. No, not a mound. Another goblin. It looks at me, eyes wide, instinctually backing up atop the bed. "Wh—who—"

I cross the room in three even strides, grab it by the throat, and crush its neck in my hand as I simultaneously toss it to the side. It lands on the other side of the room with a dull thud.

<Goblin (Lv.8) Defeated.>
<You have learned: Crush Lv.6>

Bed. Bed. Bed is good. That's what he needs.

Moving gently, more gently than I would move even a sleeping infant, I remove Simel from my back and lower him onto the bed, making sure his head finds rest atop the pillow. A proper pillow. A real pillow. And real bedsheets, too! But he can't sleep in his uniform. Not anymore. He's safe now, in a cool and warm and cozy bed. He needs to be wearing proper pajamas. Now, where would I find some of those?

I hear small footsteps outside the doorway.

"Mother?" a little voice says. "Mother, is everythin—" Moving swiftly, I grab it by the throat. Pajamas. Most households of any repute should have pajamas, right? That's only standard. The thing in my hand squirms and kicks at me so I clench and feel how its throat gets crushed in my hand.

<Gobling (Lv.2) Defeated.>

A thought strikes me and I look down. However, the gobling—despite wearing pajamas—is not wearing Simel's size. It's too small.

I look back up and find another one in the doorway. "A—ah . . ."

<Gobling Lv.1>

My eyes fall on its sleepwear. Decidedly not Simel's size. It's even smaller than the one I'm still holding. Since I don't have much use for it anymore, I toss the one in my hand to the side and move for the second one. As I walk toward it, it spins on its heel and sprints down the stairwell, tripping across its own tiny feet to tumble down the stairs, crashing into a heap at the end of the stairs. I hear a little crack as its ankle bends the wrong way. I calmly follow. Pajamas. Maybe they have some in the cupboards? I'll have to check later.

The tiny thing is now dragging itself toward the door, though its advance is soon hindered by the one I left there as a doorstop. It gives a whimper and tries to grab hold of what I assume to be its father's shoulder, shaking him and trying to pull him back to consciousness, which obviously doesn't work since that goblin is very much expired by this point.

I step close enough to where my shadow falls across its tiny body. It looks up at me, eyes glistening and a dark look much like Simel's burning into me. I blink down at it. Then I put my foot atop its back, pressing it in place with only a fraction of my body weight, which in this case is apparently enough to crack a few of its matchstick-thin ribs. While I'm holding it in place, I bend down and pluck its father from the ground. Lo and behold—he's wearing pajamas! Unfortunately, though, the entire front part is drenched in blood, something I know Simel isn't a big fan of. Darn it. Should've killed him in a less creative way, I suppose.

Something suddenly bites into my foot and I look down to find the little gobling desperately gnawing on my sole, eyes burning with dark tears.

I toss its father to the side and lean down, picking it up with routine ease. It practically growls at me, like some sort of misshapen beast.

"L—let go of me!" it cries. "You—you demon! You killed my—"

Ah, oops, my finger slipped. With just a flick of my long claws, the little thing's head goes rolling. I throw the rest of it to the side and trudge upstairs. Pajamas, pajamas . . . I root through the cabinets and cupboards for a minute or so.

Oh, here's a set! It's basically just a tunic made of some thin, coarse fabric, but it is certainly better than whatever it is he's wearing right now. I think these would be the right size. I pick a set that's a bit large just in case. If he doesn't like them, he can always get changed once he wakes up. Yup, yup.

With my prize in hand, I move back over to the bed. For a second, I imagine that he's breathed his last, that his heart isn't beating anymore, that he's finally been laid to rest. But those horrible thoughts are gone once I notice his chest slowly rising again. *Phew.* Scared me there . . .

Now, it isn't exactly polite of me, but to put him in pajamas, I first need to remove, you know . . . all the rest. I'm sure he'll understand why I had to do this once he wakes up in his super comfy and airy pajamas, hehehe.

Trying not to think about the implications of this or really anything else for that matter, I undo the buttons of his jacket, remove the undershirt, the chain mail that can't possibly have been comfortable, a bit of this, a bit of that . . . And then, his shoes. Or, at least, I *try* to remove his thigh-high boots. Even when I had the straps undone, they barely budged. Only by using a bit of good ol'-fashioned violence was I able to finally get them off. And then I understood why he didn't much like walking.

The entire inside of the boot is covered in a thick crust of dried blood. His feet are covered in loosened bandages and more RED than green. He was wearing a thin pair of socks, but they hadn't done him any good. The socks themselves are so entrenched in dried blood and sweat that once I pried them off his feet, they could stand straight up on their own, not to mention that I seemed to also peel off a layer of pale, loosened skin. I can't imagine what the socks' original color was, but right now they are a dark, brownish BLACK.

Silently, I remove the rest of his clothing and put him in the pajamas.

Then I search around the house a bit before finding a well. I draw a bucket of water, checking its cleanliness before carrying it up to Simel. Using a bit of the cloth in the cupboards, I clean his feet, drying off the blood and the grime and the dirt. I wash the bandages he wore and replace them around his feet, making sure to wash my hands before doing so. His ankles felt weirdly swollen. I don't think he'll be able to walk for a while, but it's not like this floor has a time limit, right? We can take our time.

I draw the covers over him, as well as a bearskin. And for a minute or two, I just sit at his side, watching him, making sure he won't suddenly die or something. I glance up at the screen above his head.

<Simel>

I look back down at his face. He doesn't seem so pained now. In the morning, I'll be sure to feed him vegetarian food. Healthy stuff. Things he'll be able to keep down. And then, he'll get better. I know he will.

I will not let him die.

In the middle of the night, while Simel is still sleeping, I grab all of the bodies and put them in this one room, off to the side. I'm not sure exactly what kind of room it was originally, but like the front door, it was one of a few rooms protected by both a door and a lock, said lock actually having a key to it. The key is small and made of what I think is brass. After locking the door, I put the key in my inventory.

And then I return to my seat next to Simel and wait for morning to arrive.

I know I should probably have spent this time scouting out the house, or searching the city for more materials, or something like that, but I just can't bring myself to leave his side. I mean, what if he were to up and croak while I was away getting berries or whatever it is they have here? I'd never forgive myself!

Crossing my arms, I lean farther back in the little chair I dragged over to be by the bed. It isn't exactly as small as one of those toddler chairs, but it isn't quite normal-sized either. I'd say it's about seventy percent the size of a normal chair. In other words, I can sit on it in relative comfort, but it still leaves my knees only slightly too bent, which is a little straining. It's the best option I have apart from sitting on top of the bed next to him, though, so this will simply have to do.

Regardless, I can't bring myself to feel fully relaxed.

I let my eyes wander over the room. It's mainly made of a semi-WHITE sort of stone, with a coarse, rough exterior that would probably leave your feet calloused if you walked on it too much. The room itself is sparsely decorated, with only a cupboard and nightstand for furniture. In terms of decorations, it's even less interesting, with the only real things I can notice being a tiny statue and a small, crude tapestry on the wall adjacent to the bed. It looks almost as if a child made it, though. Then again, the little bamboolike statue on the nightstand also seems like it was made by an unskilled maker, so it might just be that goblins aren't very good artists. Maybe. What do I know?

And then my eyes fall on the big, random pile of clothes on the floor. Simel's clothes. The ones I just haphazardly threw there. His socks are still standing tall.

Okay, that's just not a good thing to wake up to. I don't know if I'll be able to wash them, but I should at the very least be able to not leave them in the middle of the room. Leaning down, I scoop up the whole pile. Besides, if I'm just putting away a bit of clothes, it's not like I'll be gone for that long, so . . .

Something slips out of the jacket before fluttering down to settle on the floor.

I freeze in my step. Then I slowly turn to look at the thing on the floor. Small. WHITE. Rectangular. I squat down and pick it up.

It's a sealed envelope. Or, no, on closer inspection, it has been unsealed, but the little purple wax seal remains. Huh.

And at this point, my whole only-having-one-arm deal becomes too much and I drop all of the clothes. Argh, darn it!

I lean down to pick it all back up, but I stop midhunch, noticing the letter yet again. The writing on the front is in such an obnoxious cursive that I can't make it out even with my language skill, but I can still recognize the sigil in the corner, and the title written above it.

Emperor of the Sun.

To heck with the laundry.

Shooting a glance at Simel, I push the laundry outside the door with my foot, following suit myself. Standing just outside the door, I look down at the letter pinched between my bloodied fingers. My hand is trembling just a little.

I shake my head.

I shouldn't. But . . . I take a deep breath.

Considering that Simel can't speak for himself to make his own case, information is of vital essence right now. I can't say that I like prying and snooping, but . . . This is *clearly* a main quest clue, right? I can't just *not* check it out. I don't have any choice. I have to do it. Yeah. That's why.

Gulping, I flip open the letter and pull out the contents. It's plenty crumpled, though, so it would be fair to assume that Simel has reread it at least a couple of times. Taking another peek inside the bedroom, I ensure that Simel is still fully asleep and decidedly not dead. Since that appears to be the case, I return my attention to the letter. I unfold it.

It's only a single piece of paper, well-printed and crisply WHITE. It's so WHITE it almost feels unreal. The writing on it, however, is done in not BLACK but a deep purple ink, one that somehow shimmers half-blue in the tawny moonlight. More importantly, though, the handwriting is atrocious. Sure, it's legible, but every single stroke has been done with such violence that the ink has splattered everywhere. I can practically taste the animosity emanating from the letter. A simple skim through its contents is enough to give that very same impression.

Dear INGRATE

Or as your dear devotees call you, Simel the Survivor. Ask Grand Myself, it's Simel the Coward!

I have received your letter, granted by way of flapping fiend. Bravo, you rescued my son. Fifteen pardons if the following statement should be deemed incorrect—but you mean to tell this Grand Myself that my son's wife Swee-whatsherface was turned into a beast and eaten by that spook of a Tallthing you've been chasing? Are you aware of how the Queen of Ret-inn will take this? It may mean war!

Again, as said in my previous letter, I DEMAND that you return immediately, WITH my son. My other sons are all soiled eggs. If you should ignore this letter, I will burn that half-charred lump of coals and bones you call your city to the ground. And unlike that Tallthing you speak of, I assure you my finely trained army will make sure to leave NO survivors NOR any castle to stand in its wake. There shall be no ground to rebuild upon and no soil in which to plant crops anew.

This is not a threat, but rather a simple prognosis of what is to happen if you refuse to do the one thing this Grand Myself sent you out to do.

If I do not see you soon you will be sorry.
Emperor of the Sun,
Blind of Seventh Heaven.

I blink down at the paper in my hands. I turn it over, but there's nothing on the back except traces of the ink bleeding through. I turn it back over and read through it one more time. And then, when I'm done again, I read it yet another time, just to really get a sense of what this actually says.

What the fuck?

No, seriously. What does this even mean?

Okay, well, first up—what a douche! Who refers to himself as *this Grand Myself*? What a prick. And the way he insulted Simel, too? Threatening his city? Nuh-uh. No way. That's just . . . Totally mean. I mean, he practically told him that Simel alone was to blame for some war that's probably not even going to happen! That's just cruel, I'd say.

And then to say that the whole business *isn't a threat*? Bah! Humbug!

This sun emperor fella is really grinding my gears, that's for sure.

So why the heck does Simel want us to go to the empire? If we go there, and Simel somehow tells them nonverbally that the prince is also dead . . . I don't know about you, but from what I've read from this emperor guy, I don't think he'd be all that merciful. Just the opposite, as a matter of fact.

So again . . . Why are we heading toward a guy that absolutely wants us dead? Is it . . . could it be . . . ?

I take a glance inside the bedroom, at Simel's sleeping silhouette in the moonlight.

He knows me better than I thought, huh?

A chuckle tumbles from my lips. Yeah, he's right. If he asked me to my face, I'm not sure I'd agree to such an insane plan. I mean, who would? The fact that he didn't ask me directly tells me a fair bit about him, though. I assume his plan is just for us to get there, get in trouble, and once the emperor predictably sentences the both of us to execution without the possibility of parole, I'll strike.

After all, he can't want us dead if *he's* dead, can he?

It's clever. It's ruthless. It's simple and it makes sense.

Chop off the head of the snake and the tail dies. Kill the emperor and the soldier ants left will be too busy scrambling to survive to care about a measly little goblin and his human companion. Furthermore, if there's already a war with some completely unrelated kingdom on the horizon, then the lack of a competent leader will be even more damning.

I really underestimated Simel. And here I was, thinking he just wanted to get to the empire because, well . . . fulfilling his obligations, or whatever.

Honestly, I never thought much about it. The fact that Simel wanted a thing mattered more to me than *why* he might want said thing. In hindsight, that was narrow-minded of me. A friend needs to be able to give their beloved companions not merely what they *want*, but also what they *need*. I've already been doing that, but I need to zoom out. Get a bigger perspective and all that.

At this moment, I'm very lucky, because what he wants and what he needs seem to align perfectly in me killing the emperor.

How simple! How easy! How quaint!

Finally, after so long, I am entirely certain of what the right thing to do is.

And it wasn't even all that far off from my original plan.

Simel's Lament

Simel of Acheron—also called *Simel the Survivor* by those his ruling entailed—awoke from his deep sleep sometime in the early afternoon. He found himself inside a bedroom he had never seen before, with walls of yellowstone and furniture of thickreeds.

It was a simple room, one that in many ways resembled that of the inn he had resided in before their disastrous pursuit into the desert of ash. At that time, he had wanted to remain with his soldiers, sleeping in their simple tents on top of their simple mats. However, that would not do for a man of his class. Regardless, he had refused the more expensive inns their guide had suggested. Instead, he had chosen a simpler one, one he could remember his uncle suggesting many years ago, before he had been swallowed by a desert crawler. He had always been the explorer of the family. If, by the grace of the God of Endings, he saw Simel now, he must have been having quite a laugh.

The thought almost brought a smile to Simel's cracked lips.

This bedroom was not like that of his inn, though. This room didn't have a bed of wool, or a pillow of feathers, or a finely woven blanket. No plants decorated the windowsill, and the walls were mostly bare apart from a single tapestry. The moment his eyes fell on it, Simel froze where he sat half-righted in the bed. He almost wanted to step out of bed to get a closer look, but a twinge of pain in his feet killed any such thoughts. All he could do was to sit there, staring across the room, at the little hand-painted tapestry portraying a small family of four. Mother, father, daughter, son. Four.

By the standards of the upper kingdoms, having merely two children was almost unheard of. But Simel knew that things were different down here. Still, the sight of the tapestry did anything but calm him.

It should have brought him relief. He knew of only two explanations for it, and one of them—although equally despair-inducing—would still have been far preferable to the other.

But would he truly allow himself to hope that he had been rescued by a loving little family of four? That the demon plaguing his life had drawn its final breath in that desert, and that instead of dying a drake's death beside it, Simel had been rescued? It was too good to be true. Not to mention that the only other option would have been so much worse.

Slowly, Simel clasped his hands, pressing the fingertips of each hand to those of the other. *By the grace of the God of Curiosity, I ask for strength in these trying times. I ask that my people are given solace in their times of weakness, and that the Emperor of the Sun should show mercy and benevolence toward myself and my people. So, too, do I ask that—*

Footsteps. Simel's thoughts jerked to an instant standstill as he froze atop the bed, hands still clasped, tighter and tighter as a bead of sweat rolled down his forehead and across the side of his face.

Soft, gentle padding. Like that of a Paarthen wildcat. Almost inaudible, had Simel not recognized that sound more than he would his own mother's voice.

In silent, wide-eyed terror, Simel turned toward the open doorway. It was dark out there in the hallway. Simply knowing that that creature was out there was enough to make the darkness all the deeper. In the brief stillness, that liminal moment before he once more came face-to-face with that Hoeksak, Simel let a tiny prayer shoot through his mind.

And then the creature stepped out of the darkness and into the light.

For just a moment, it stood there, midway between the room and the corridor, staring inside with intense orbs of yellow and black. Its eyes, small and deformed, peered into the middle of the room. Not at Simel. Not at first. Only after a moment did its beasty eyes slide down, down to look him in the eye. Simel couldn't repress the instinctual twitch or terror that ran through his body.

"Ah," the creature said, "you're awake!"

Its voice was a terrible thing. To any refined audiophile, its voice would have been an effective weapon. Nasal; neither high nor low but rather some horrible middle-thing. It cracked at times, suggesting to the scientifically inclined Simel that this creature, as ungoblic as it was, was not even a fully grown adult. Not to mention that no matter what it said, it never seemed to hold the slightest twinge of emotion any which way. It spoke as though the world was a specimen to be observed and analytically commented on. The only times Simel had ever heard any true emotion in what that thing said were during moments he would rather forget.

With those words, the creature's face twisted, upper lip furling to show its horrible teeth in what might by itself be called a smile. Then it lurched inside.

Saying that it *walked* would be an insult to all bipedal creatures under the grace of the Gods.

Its gangly, bonelike legs brought it closer.

Some childish instinct deep inside Simel's mind wanted to try to move away, toward the window, away from that horrible thing. But adult logic spoke louder, firmly—*There is no escape*. Mentally, he chanted that mantra, two, three times as the creature stalked up close enough to the bed to be able to kill or restrain Simel without having to step any closer. Even though it only had one arm, that would be enough. Simel had seen it tear apart creatures capable of taking out entire villages with one arm alone. A single goblin would be nothing.

His hand trembled as the creature looked down at him, eyes shining like starving fire, and he clenched his hands to keep himself still. Showing his fear did no good. Not to this creature of no pity. It was the same as surrendering to a bear. *There is no escape.*

For a moment, the creature stood there, hunched as it always was, eyes moving about erratically before finally settling on Simel once more. Not for the first time, Simel made note of how he could not hear the creature's breathing.

It sat down. Tall as it was, it almost seemed comical where it sat in the chair. It made another facial expression. Simel couldn't imagine what it was supposed to mean. He didn't want to know, either.

"So," the creature said. Its face split into a sort of grin and its eyes flashed. "We made it!" Triumphantly, it raised its arm, its clawed, bonelike fingers spreading wide. When had its hand become reddened again? It was fresh. Fresh blood. Simel may only barely have been able to remember the past days, but he could recall this creature being able to make it two days without killing anything. Now it had killed again.

Killer. Killer. Killer. Always killing. Horrible thing. Never before had Simel seen such death.

Its triumph was not reciprocated; the creature slumped a little where it sat. "That is, we made it to the city. You know—the one you told me to bring you to? Yeah. We're here! Great, huh?"

Although he hated to take his eyes from this creature that killed without a moment's hesitation, Simel turned to look out the window. He could see a street, and people, and houses. It was as the creature said—they had indeed arrived at Sandshore.

He turned to look back at the creature. It stared at him with eyes that begged for praise. Simel gave it nothing.

By the way it looked down and away, Simel could fairly assume it was disappointed.

"Well, uh . . ." The creature looked up again, into a patch of air, focusing on something that wasn't there, its dark pupils moving back and forth as though reading. "Since it might, um, interest you, we were actually walking through that desert for almost exactly thirty days! Meaning that I am now on the fourteenth attempt." Its thin, scabby eyebrows squashed together in thought and Simel let a prayer rattle through his mind, hoping that the creature wasn't thinking of causing any more bloodshed. The creature burst into a smile. Simel's heart dropped. "That means it's almost been a whole year since we first met! Isn't that lovely?"

The words sent a shock wave of memories, each more horrible than the last, flying through Simel's mind, all of them as burning and terrible as a four-winged dragon. Only a few memories weren't scalding to touch, but all they did was bring to mind the bitterness he had felt so long ago. It had almost been a year since it all happened—since his world ended.

The creature smiled at him expectantly as it always did whenever it said anything. And, as always, Simel said nothing. Its smile twitched. "Of course, for now, we're kind of stuck here. Oh, yeah, I should've . . ." Thinking of nothing and everything, the creature began to absently claw at the flesh of its thigh, tearing deep, gouging lines that spewed blood liberally. "See, you're kind of . . . your feet are all messed up, and my arm still hasn't fully grown back, so we'll have to stay in this city for a little while. At least until you've recovered. 'Cause, you know . . . I can make do with one arm, but you without feet would be pretty bad, I think."

Stay in the city. Stay in *a city*. The killer of cities, in a city? Simel bristled.

He turned to look at the creature, hoping a fraction of the overwhelming emotions he felt could possibly be interpreted by the creature—that it might for once understand something that wasn't itself.

The creature blinked at him. "What, you don't want to stay?"

Simel clenched his hands into fists.

The creature's little eyes squinted. "You don't want . . . *me* to stay?" And then the eyes flared open, and its face twisted again, like clay being re-formed, and it made an expression like a jesting drake. "Oh, you don't have to worry! I'm . . . Well, I mean . . ." It sank back into thought. Simel couldn't tell if he was breathing anymore. It sat there, relaxed, its eyes calm as it muttered to itself, "I mean, this *is* technically a floor, so . . . does this city count as part of it? The goblins have levels, so they should be enemies, which would mean that . . ." Simel could barely even hear its terrible words above the hammering of his own heart.

As casually as a farmer discussing the weather, it raised its eyes to Simel and said, in that terrible voice, "If we're staying a while, I should have enough time to—"

Its jaw suddenly snapped shut. The sound startled Simel to the point of twitching. Now it wasn't looking at him anymore. It was looking at the empty air again, reading invisible words, its wax-pale forehead furrowing in thought. "It . . . I . . ." Its mouth closed again, and its eyes gained focus, turning to Simel.

"Sorry, but I just got a message from the God of Pain that I apparently don't need to defeat every single enemy to completely clear this floor—just the relevant ones." A smile. "So, uh, for now, you shouldn't need to worry."

Even after Simel heard that, the panic still gripping his heart like a vise would not fade.

The creature absently scratched at some spot behind its head; then, when its hand returned red, licked off the blood. It glanced into the air once before returning its eyes to Simel. "By the way—great news! I've got food, and water, and whatever else you may want. Now, I don't know exactly what you want—I still haven't received any telepathy skill—but I'll try to get what you need. As a matter of fact, I've currently got a pot of vegetable soup bubbling! And whenever we need more food, I can just go out and get more, easy peasy. I can probably find almost anything else as long as it's inside the city borders, so if you just tell me what you want, I'll get it for you. *Anything.*"

And it looked at him like that again. Like a drakeling wanting a treat for being such a good boy. Obedient. Simel didn't have a single doubt in his mind that the creature was absolutely serious. And still, in the city, there was nothing he wanted. No physical item could fill the hole in his soul, nor could it complete the divine task he was set upon.

Deep inside his heart, spoken loud and clear through his eyes, as obvious as a cry, Simel thought, *Please turn yourself in and let the due course of justice be done.*

Please let the Goddess of Law judge your soul.

Please let the God of Truth lead Her hand just.

Please let the God of Repentance blind the eyes of the Goddess of Forgiveness.

And let the world find peace in your due penance—blood for blood.

But, of course, this blind creature of deaf cruelty heard none of this.

"So yeah. For now, how about I go get you a bowl of that soup I mentioned? That'd be nice, wouldn't it? And, just so you know, there's *no* meat in it whatsoever, and the broth wasn't distilled from any blood, so it's totally pure and fresh and healthy and all-organic." Saying so, the creature stood up. "Just sit tight and I'll be right back, yeah?"

There is no escape.

As though Simel could leave.

With that promise of return, the creature left, and for the first time in many minutes, Simel could breathe again. For a few seconds, he simply sat there, breathing, letting the beating of his heart slow down.

He had survived. Again. Would the Gods ever let him rest?

No. As they had a plan for that creature, they had a plan for him, too. He could not escape his purpose. Gritting his teeth, Simel leaned down, lowering his head. He should have died. But before his thoughts could devolve further, he noticed how he was no longer wearing his uniform, and his boots weren't on his feet, and his satchel was gone, too.

An arrow of panic pierced his chest and he frantically removed the blanket, finding himself dressed in a simple, coarse tunic that went below his knees. Had the creature dressed him in this? Why? *To weaken me? To make me easier to do away with when it no longer cared for me?* No. No, that wasn't it. No cloth or armor could hinder that beast any more than paper would hinder a spear. Then . . . why?

With his body uncovered, Simel could see his feet. They had been gently washed and wrapped in clean, tightly fitting bandages.

The soft padding of feet in the doorway alerted Simel and he quickly covered himself in the blanket once more.

"Here you go!" the creature said as it strutted inside, holding a tray containing a bowl and a cup of water. He set it down atop Simel's lap. The bowl of soup was still steaming—still warm. Warm like flesh scorched upon the burning body of the desert's faithful. The memory made Simel feel bile rise to the back of his throat, but he couldn't let himself puke. He could never puke again.

As expected, the creature wasted no time sitting down next to him, watching—waiting for him to appreciate all its hard efforts. Simel stared down into the bowl. It was a simple soup. That was all it was.

His gaze slowly slid up, eventually finding the tapestry on the opposite side of the room. Two children, mother, father. Simel turned to look at the creature again. It smiled back at him.

Trying to hold back everything he didn't want to think about and everything he didn't want to remember, Simel picked up the spoon, put it in the soup, and brought it to his lips.

He ate, he drank, and that was all he did.

Afterward, he was glad to see the creature leave him. He was less happy to hear it explain in excited tones that it would be heading out to "scout the place." Nevertheless, this left Simel alone for a little while.

He found his satchel on the floor, next to the bed he was on. For a moment, he took out the old king of Acheron's crown, held it in his hands, and gave a prayer—the latest of many—promising justice to the creature that had ended his reign. Then he put it back into his satchel and removed his simple diary and his spellbook. For the remainder of the evening, he took notes of the events surrounding himself, the latest crimes of the creature whose unwilling guest he remained, and where the future might be headed.

The day passed.

The creature returned in the evening, bringing a little bag of sweets. Stolen. Maybe robbed. Possibly worse.

Then, dinner. Soup again. Once the sun went down, it seemed the creature expected him to somehow be able to sleep. Even worse, with the past few days being what they were, that was exactly what Simel did.

The next day, the creature woke him up with breakfast, cleaned the wounds on his feet, replaced the bandages, put him in a new tunic, and gave him warm water with bark syrup to drink. It took care of him—nursing him, caring for him as a mother cares for her child.

Simel endured.

After a few days, Simel could finally stand without it being unbearably painful. He could have quickened the healing by using Cure, but low-level healing spells of that type would often cause unintended complications when used too often or carelessly, so he refrained. Still, to recover, he chose not to walk too often. More importantly, he didn't let the creature see how much he'd recovered.

At this point, Simel had decided that in order to bring the creature to justice, he would need to contact the arch judge of Sandshore.

They would listen to him. They knew of his quest and had already agreed to assist in restraining the creature and holding it captive when the time came. Arch Judge Gant would know his face. He would know how to handle this.

If Simel had continued his previous plan of bringing the creature before the Emperor of the Sun himself, he was no longer certain that he would survive the journey.

The creature would keep him alive. He knew that. That wasn't the issue. The issue lay in his own strength of will. Could he bear to see the cruelty of this creature during the course of the months it would take to reach the empire? Would he not choose to cut the journey short? He could not know. A month ago, he'd believed himself strong enough to see anything this demon was capable of. Had he not already seen the deepest depths that these beings called *humans* could achieve? Their depravity?

That was not the case.

It had been a week since they reached the city. And for the first time in a week, Simel heard a voice downstairs that was not that of the creature. A thick accent, so heavy it might almost have been a different language. The voice itself was deep and brassy, nothing like that of the creature. It was a real person. An actual goblin.

Not thinking, Simel stepped out of bed, wincing at the pain in his soles before pulling himself to his feet and tiptoeing over to the doorway, his eyes moving down the stairs to the front door entrance.

There were two goblins, one inside the house, the other outside. The creature was nowhere to be seen. Simel gripped the doorframe tighter.

"Ar ya shure yer okay? Plenty a' lads go ta work even wiff a sickly wife an' kids in da house. Ain't no shame ta go an' provide if ya get what ah'm sayin'," the baritone voice said loudly. Through the gap beside the goblin inside the house, Simel could see what kind of man this goblin was. Large. Burly. Yellow skin, with deep orange freckles. A standard Sandshore resident, built for heavy manual labor. "Ya get me?"

"Huh? Oh, uh, yeah, shore," the other goblin said. But it wasn't right. The goblin's voice was familiar. Too familiar. It was tall, too. Far too tall to be any goblin. And still, it felt as though Simel saw double, both the goblin that couldn't be a goblin, and also a completely regular man, just standing there. Speaking with a clearly faked accent. "But, uh, one problemo, um, she's got . . . The missy's got AIDS. Yup. Real tragic story ther', tha'ss for sure. Shore. Ya get me?"

". . . Aides?"

The goblin waved an arm. His left arm. The other arm hung limply like the empty arm of a shirt. "Yup. AIDS. Stands fer, uh . . . Absolute Insufferable Dumbo Syndrome. Super infectious. Yea, just openin' the door like this might be gettin' particles all over the street. Why, right now, you could have AIDS and you wouldn't even know!"

The goblin outside the door visibly paled. "Is—izzat so? Well, heh, erm . . . In that case, I s'pose I'll just . . . Leave ya to it, then."

"Thanks fer visitin', Tromb."

Without replying, the other goblin hurried away. The goblin inside the door closed it and gave a deep sigh. "Whew, what a wet-nose . . ." And then, he turned around. *It* turned around. A goblin. Not a goblin. Something else. Something that was too big for the skin it wore, with thin, gangly legs that pulled the skin tight and a head that was a little too big. The face was stretched across the skull like leather out for tanning.

And from within the sockets of what had once been a face, two dark eyes peered out, and up, and right at Simel.

"Oh, hey, Simel!" it said. "How come you aren't in bed? Your feet are still hurt, so you really should be taking it easy." But Simel couldn't move. He couldn't even muster a horrified tremble. The eyes within eyes blinked up at him, and a mouth within a mouth twisted into an amused smirk. "Oh, you don't recognize me, do you? Well, heh . . . Maybe *this'll* help!"

It grasped at an open part of its throat and pulled up, skinning itself, removing the face from the face and revealing that horrible ash-pale face of the creature, looking as proud as though it had won a war. "See? It's just me—Fennrick!"

And that it was. Wearing the skin of a dead man.

The world spun and Simel could feel whatever he ate last pushing its way back up, but he couldn't allow himself to puke, not anymore. Fighting the urge with every instinct in his body, he staggered back into the bedroom and collapsed onto the bed. The room was still spinning. The padding of soft feet made the world freeze, still upside-down.

"Everything alright, Simel? You look like you've seen a ghost, haha!" A pause. "Sorry, I just . . . I've always wanted to pull that one, you know? You understand, don't you?" Silence. Then, after a while, "But, uh . . . I didn't know you could walk. Which, you know, heh, nothing wrong with being able to get out of bed, but . . ." A pair of cat-yellow eyes stared down at him. Unblinking. "You really should stay in bed. There's a lot of things in this house you maybe shouldn't see. You understand that, right? I'm just trying to do what's best for you, so . . ." It ran its tongue across its front teeth. "Even if you smell something rotting, don't go in there."

With that, it left, leaving behind a cold that left Simel with goose bumps.

That night, Simel decided to escape to get in contact with the arch judge.

The room was not quite dark. In these places, the night was never entirely dark. Not like at home, where night held its rule for all hours of the night, only unwillingly banished once the sun took her throne. Down here, the moons seemed so much brighter, and the stars were so many.

The night air was cold. It streamed gently through the window, alongside the little wisps of moonlight. As Simel stood by the window, he put one hand to his heart and the other to his mind and gave a short prayer to his devotion, the God of Knowledge.

He prayed for strength.

He prayed for mercy.

And most of all, he prayed for guidance.

And with that, he was ready. As ready as he ever would be. He had wanted to wear his uniform, or to bring his satchel, but he couldn't risk making any noise on the way down. That beast could hear a mouse sneak. The arch judge would recognize him anyhow. If he did this right, they would have the beast restrained and in cuffs before it ever realized Simel had left.

It would have to work. There was no other choice.

Steeling his heart, Simel turned away from the window and toward the open doorway, into the thick darkness of the hallway outside. He moved softly, walking barefoot on the yellowstone floors. Without hurrying, he arrived at the doorway. The hallway was darker than the night sky. It was almost pitch-black. The color reminded him only of the sea of tar and its dark waves. The way the pitch would cling to you like the damned souls of those in the underworld.

Simel didn't dare try to swallow down the lump in his throat. What if the creature heard him? That thing could hear the beating of hearts. He wished he'd kept his ring of cover. Though, with the way the creature had changed, he doubted it'd be of any help.

Gritting his teeth, Simel stepped out into the hallway. Never before had he listened with such intensity.

The whistle of the wind. The creaking of a neighbor's door. The howling of a yipdog.

Not a sound from the creature.

He knew it did not sleep. Never had he seen it sleep, not even when they first met. It seemed unbound by such simple goblic needs. It didn't *need* to eat, it didn't *need* to drink, and it didn't *need* to sleep. Yet it still ate flesh, and it still drank blood. But in terms of sleeping, the closest it approached such basic needs was meditation.

It did that often. It sat still—as still as a propped-up corpse—and it held its eyes shut, and then it would not move for hours at a time. Simel was certain it could sit unmoving for days if it so desired. At night, although it did not sleep, it would often meditate. Simel knew this. He had been keeping watch. He knew that the thing would spend its nights in a room, just off to the side, sitting as still as a corpse. Meditating.

This was the spider that wove his plan. With the creature in dead meditation, Simel would be able to effortlessly tiptoe down the stairs, slipping out of the door with ease and into the night. And that would be it. Then it would all be done and over with. He would no longer feel any need to rule Acheron. They could find some other king for all he cared. He just wanted this all to be over with.

But as he moved through the hallway, as silent as a chapel mouse, he was struck by a scent he hadn't felt that morning.

A faint odor, like that of rotting meat.

He hadn't noticed it before, not in his bed nor earlier that day, but now that he noticed it, it was all he could think of. Rotting meat. Decaying flesh. Death. Slowly, he turned toward a little door across from the bedroom—the only room in the small house that seemed to have a lock on it.

He knew he shouldn't have. He should've just run for it, leaving everything and everyone else behind to finally bring this creature to justice. To finally put it on trial for all the pain it caused. To be fairly judged, and not simply escape through the coward's repentance.

But the smell . . . It lured him. It crawled in through his nose and up into his brain, where it begged and pleaded not for mercy but for recognition.

His feet moved without conscious thought, bringing him to the door.

It was worse now. Meat, festering. An irritating sting of bile in his eye. Decomposition. Smells that reminded him of the creature, of its eating habits, of what it made and what it did.

Of the tapestry in the bedroom.

His hand fell on the knob, but as expected, it was locked.

Breathing shallowly, he turned around once more, his eyes moving down the hallway, passing by the stairs leading down and to freedom, and instead finding themselves at the open doorway to the room he knew the creature was in.

He shouldn't. He couldn't. It was idiotic. It was a fool's mission. He knew already. He didn't need to confirm it.

But he had to be certain.

He moved like a golem, one foot in front of the next, soft flesh on harsh yellowstone, closer, closer, toward the room, passing by the stairwell and moving farther beyond, over to the open doorway. Slowly, he moved to look inside.

In the light of the moons, sitting atop a table, was the creature. It sat with its legs crossed, eyes closed, face as motionless and blank as a frozen carcass out for display. But Simel wasn't looking at that. He saw something better. On a small nightstand, barely in arm's reach of the creature, clearly visible in the light of the moons, was a tiny brass key. It glinted alluringly in the light. The way it was placed reminded Simel of a spider-trap, with the bait ready and the trap just beside it, waiting for someone to take it.

Only a fool would head into such a trap headfirst and willing.

For the first time in his life, Simel fully considered himself more of a fool than an intellectual.

He crept inside. His eyes were in a constant state of movement, hopping from the beast to the key as though either of them could at any point leap up and strike him. Nevertheless, he held his composure with a steady hand. He slid through the room like a shadow, exhibiting a deftness unbecoming of a scholar. Every single sense he had was on full alert.

He was close now. The brass key was in reach, and so was the creature. Slowly, with trembling hands, Simel reached out, his hand hovering just above the key, shaking only slightly, a bead of sweat rolling down his forehead, and as he let his hands fall, his fingers touching the cold metal of the brass key, one hooking around its smooth eye . . .

His fingers slipped.

Clink.

There was a sharp inhale. Simel froze. His eyes jerked to look at the creature. Its eyes remained closed. But it knew. He could tell. Its nose wrinkled. Its nostrils flared. And then it took a deep, long, calculated breath through its nose. *Sni—iff.* A bead of Simel's sweat rolled down his cheek and dropped to the floor. His body was shock still. He was as motionless as the air around him. He didn't breathe. His heart didn't beat. He was nothing.

The beast sniffed again, brief, sharp inhales through its nose, like a drake smelling for prey. *Sniff sniff sniff. Sni—iff.*

And then . . .

Its body relaxed once more, back hunching and face falling back into dead apathy.

He had been spared.

Plucking the key from its place, Simel quickly stepped out of the room, suppressing his need to breathe until he was beyond the stairwell and back by the locked door. But when he then drew in a deep breath, he found it putrid and disgusting. The rot was there. He had no time to hesitate. The door loomed before him, almost as tall as the creature. Earlier that evening, the creature had spoken to him in some attempt to convince him not to suspect anything.

I think something crawled into one of the walls and died, it had said. *Some little animal or whatever."*

Simel hadn't believed him. Still didn't.

His hands were gripping the brass key so hard his knuckles whitened. Hoping the beating of his heart wasn't as loud as it felt, he moved closer. The brass key fit snugly inside the keyhole, giving the tiniest sounds as it settled in. As he turned it, each little click and clack felt like the slamming of massive instruments. Every little sound felt louder than a full war orchestra. He turned it as slowly as he possibly could, but the sounds could not be suppressed. Not fully.

Finally, with the tiniest little click, the door unlocked. Simel pulled it open.

A waft of horrid, putrid rotten-meat stench hit him before anything else. Ruptured bowels. Half-necrotic organs. Liquefied tissue. Death and decay. Worse than any sewer or butcher's back alley. There, inside, lay four bloated figures, flayed, dismembered, disassembled, skinned, half-eaten, pulled apart at the seams, ripped into pieces, the only untouched pieces being the staring, lifeless heads, all sitting in a neat row, ears drooping and eye holes filled with squirming, crawling maggots. Mother, father, daughter, son. Blackened, rotting flesh. Bloated, distended abdomens. A smell more putrid than a morgue. Bite marks on the mother, the father fully skinned, the daughter curled up in a ball, the son almost fully eaten.

Simel buckled over and released what little he had been able to force down during the day. The stench stung in his eyes and burned down his throat and even in the darkness of the hallway and the room he could see the four of them with perfect clarity in all of their rancid tragedy.

All he could see was them.

All he could smell was them.

All he could taste was them.

All he could feel was the cold stone beneath his hands and feet.

All he could hear was the sound of his own throat retching, trying to force more up, trying to break his own promise again.

In the empty silence, he heard the soft padding of footsteps.

"Simel?" a voice said. The beast that speaks. "Simel, what are you doing up this late? You'll catch a cold! You need to get some rest, so—"

The voice stopped. Its owner saw. Its owner knew.

"Um, well, uh . . ." The voice was worse than the stench. "You weren't supposed to see that."

He was on his hands and knees but at that moment it didn't matter as Simel threw himself to his feet, flying past the outstretched hand of the creature, ignoring its cries of "Wait, Simel, I can explain!" and "It's really not that bad, I promise!" to willingly toss himself down the stairs, not caring as his battered and busted ankle gave out, leading him to tumble all the way down to fall into a heap on the floor, a heap that for some reason startled the creature, as it said nothing and did not pursue long enough for Simel to pull himself back to his aching, burning feet, unlocking the door and casting himself into the cold night air.

His throat burned. Their putrid stench clung to his nose. His feet felt like they were simultaneously freezing and burning all at once. As he ran down the barren street, he left bloody footprints.

He had to get help. He had to find someone. *Anyone.*

Someone to save him, to bring justice, to—*anything.*

Down an alley, he caught sight of someone. A group of five guards, each bearing the city crest. Hope reared in his heart like a long-forgotten love and he bounded down the alley, panting and gasping for air. The five turned toward him as one, suspicion and concern painting their faces in equal measure.

"Is everything alright?" one of them asked.

"Do you need help?"

"Are you being chased?"

Putting his hands on his knees, Simel let the relief of finally finding help wash over him, allowing him to take just a single breather. He had been running for so long. Pursued by death itself, he could allow himself to breathe for once, could he not?

Once he'd gathered his scattered composure, he straightened back out, allowed himself to regain the countenance of a ruler, opened his mouth to speak, and watched as a long-limbed pale creature dropped down from above, right atop one of the guard's heads and shoulders. The guard only barely had time to register the intruder's presence, stumbling once as the weight of it settled, and then it was already over. With a single stroke of its one arm, the creature pulled the tongue of the guard clean from his open mouth, as easily as one plucks the petals from a flower.

Only when the severed tongue hit the ground did the other guards recognize what was happening, but by that point, it might as well have been over already.

One arm, two legs, and a pair of jaws was all it needed.

It was a flurry of death and blood, slices of flesh dancing through the air as it effortlessly dodged, parried, or took the guards' panicked strikes head-on. In the light of the moons, it almost seemed like a southern dancer, the way it leapt and threaded on the moonbeams in the air. Graceful.

It was not cruel in the way that dragons were, with their hatred and their pride. This was a different sort entirely.

When all the guards lay dead at its feet, and all that showed on its face was a vague touch of disinterest, Simel understood exactly what this cruelty was.

Mere apathy.

And against such cruelty, a simple city would never be enough. A single army could never do away with it. Simel had been naive to think it could be defeated so easily. No, as he watched the creature stand tall and gangly and glimmering with red in the moonlight, Simel understood that the only way to defeat such cruelty was with the cruelty of the arrogant.

The empire was his only choice.

The Journey Begins

I put my hands on my hips, hopefully only resembling a disappointed mother by coincidence. "Now, why would you go and do that?" He stares up at me with the same kind of look he's had the past couple of days. I heave a sigh, mostly just to show him how I really thought better of him. I mean, *come on!* "You're lucky I went running after you or these armed hoodlums would've had their way with you. Can you imagine that? I mean, this guy was carrying an entire halberd, for crying out loud! Do you really think they'd stop at just mugging you?"

And, of course, as usual, he gives no response. He could've *died* and he doesn't seem to care in the least! One of these days I really ought to hammer into him the importance of staying alive and not giving up hope for the future. Only losers die, and I like to think that Simel, should he have been born human, would have been a certified gamer much like myself.

Not that I don't understand him just a little, though. I mean, he must have had quite a spook, seeing my personal pantry in that state. I knew I should've tidied it up a little.

Pinching the bridge of my nose, I look down at him. He's staring up at me. "What?" I say. As usual—as always—he says nothing. Is it too much to ask for a little communication here? I draw in a sharp breath. It only takes two broad steps to bring myself to him. Crouching down a little, I lower my face to his level. "You've had a big scare. I get that. But we need to get back to the house now, okay?" His head is shaking back and forth. Oh, *now* he'll communicate. Of course. I roll my eyes and put my hand on his shoulder. "It's not a question, Simel. We need to go."

If these hoodlums were able to get to him within, like, a single minute of him leaving the house, I can't imagine how many more could be hanging around. I kind of want to loot the guys who are left, but Simel *really* needs to get back to bed.

I grab him and hoist his stiff body onto my back. He doesn't fight it in the least, which is good. My eyes fall on one of his feet. His bandages have all been ripped up by his running and a bunch of his wounds have been torn open again, his whole sole covered in blood. "See this?" I say, grabbing one of his feet. "You're bleeding everywhere now! What were you even thinking?"

Though, of course, if he hadn't left splotches of blood everywhere he went, I wouldn't have been able to find him since I can't smell him. Also, apparently, he's way quieter than I thought.

As I walk back to the house, following the RED footprints, I mumble to myself, "Besides, that key was just to lure any snooping burglars close enough to handle. You weren't supposed to take the bait yourself..."

We walk back to the house. Or, I guess, I carry him back. Hopefully the bloody footprints going from the house down the street won't be any issue, considering that Simel will need a fair bit longer now to recover, not to mention that my arm still refuses to regrow with any real speed. Well, all in its due time. For now, I'll just try to make the best of it.

It only takes a minute or so to get back to the house. I lock the door behind us, take Simel back upstairs, pass by the no-longer-locked room, and put him back to bed.

"Try to get back to sleep, okay? I know we've both had a kind of weird night, but you still need the rest." He looks up at me. I look down at him. Sighing, I avert my eyes. "You want me to explain myself? Is that it?" His gaze doesn't waver. I can feel my lips twist into a frown and I turn back to him, hand clenched and jaw set. "Well, there isn't any. I did what had to be done. That's obvious, isn't it? We needed a place to stay, so I got us one. So why—"

Why are you still looking at me like that?

I can feel my breath rattling through my throat. My hand clenches and unclenches. Claws prickling against my palm. My eyes briefly drop down to look at his slim throat. But then I notice the marks—still lingering, even after a month—and everything in my chest melts away, draining through my rib cage, down my spine. "Okay," I hear myself say. "You don't like that. I get it." My eyes fall down to look at the floor, at my REDdened feet. "You don't . . . want me to do that, do you?" My voice is a whisper.

His eyes speak. I can read them. I know exactly what he's saying, but I don't want to hear it.

That anger wells up again, burning, like flaming boiling tar building up all the way to my eyeballs. "How do you expect me to do this, then? I know what you want—you really think we can get there without a little bloodshed? Are you really *that* naive, Simel?" My voice isn't mine anymore, but his eyes are his and I can't stop looking at him. He isn't trembling. He isn't sweating. He isn't scared. He sees me, but I don't want to be seen.

I feel like a misbehaving kid. But I didn't do anything wrong! Haven't I always done the right thing?

I turn away from him, toward the doorway. "I'm going back to meditating," I say. "If you try to do something like this again, I . . ." I choke down what I was about to say. Some of the tension roils off my shoulders. "Just . . . stay here. Don't be an idiot."

I leave him. His eyes scald me as I go out into the corridor but I can't turn around anymore. I'm just not strong enough.

Returning to my little room, and to my little table, I sit back down again. But I can't bring myself to meditate. My head feels like a big wasps' nest, buzzing and chittering and stinging with it all.

Does he seriously think we can travel across the continent without getting our hands dirty? I knew he wasn't exactly trigger-happy, but this is too far in the other direction. I mean, really? Ugh, my head is starting to hurt . . . Okay, okay. Let's think about this rationally. I can't exactly compromise on my actions just to satiate his apparent need for a clean conscience. But I also really don't want him to glare at me for the entire trip. The way he looks at me normally is bad enough.

Luckily enough, I have a perfectly reasonable compromise where we're both content and neither of us has to go unhappy.

Once morning dawns and I bring Simel his breakfast of totally-not-stolen fruits and totally-not-robbed flatbread and totally-not-looted jam, I tell him my thoughts.

"Simel," I say, putting as much regret as I can muster into my voice, "I've had a change of heart. It took the whole night to understand what you were truly try-ing to say, and now I get it." A nod for effect. "You're right. Defeating goblins too liberally will totally alert the empire to our mischief before the intended time. If we want to get there safely, we'll need to keep a low profile, so"—I glance away, speaking through my teeth—"to do so, I'll keep the defeating on the down low."

He blinks at me.

"What?" I snap at him. "Is it that surprising for a man to change his mind?" He looks away. Yeah, that's what I thought. I gulp. "So, from now on . . . I'll keep it to a minimum. Or something."

He seems genuinely shocked, and not in an entirely bad way. My gaze falls to my feet again. His eyes, suddenly bereft of that scalding fire, bring me nothing but BLACK cold shame. Why? Well . . .

Almost everything I just told him was total horseshit.

I'll keep it on the down low, but only insofar as he can't see it.

I'll keep it to a minimum, which I was already doing.

I'll keep a low profile, like usual.

That's what I say, and that's what I'll do. So the fact that he's suddenly looking at me *like that*, like I'm a person and not a beast, feels wrong. Unearned. Bad. Not good. But the words have already been said. I can't take them back. Not without losing the little trust I seem to have stolen.

He eats. I watch him for a few seconds before leaving him.

Putting on the father's skin, I head out into the streets.

"Hey, Teff! Wife's still sick and all?"

"Are you sure you should be out and about, Teff?"

"Have a taste of the sootpears, Teff!"

I pass them by. Down the street lies a little grocery shop that's been *closed due to sickness* for a few days now. Another necessary defeat, of course. I mean, it's not like I have any money, so . . .

"Excuse me—Teff?"

It takes me a moment or so to recognize that the words are for me. I turn around.

<You have learned: Impersonate Lv.6>

A ruffian looks at me. Hoodlum. I frown at him. "How can I help you?"

The ruffian seems shocked somehow by the way I address him. "I've been looking for you. There have been complaints, Teff. First regarding a stink, and now . . ." His eyebrows squash together. "There was a strange incident last night. Five guards killed most ruthlessly, with the only traces being a pair of bloody footprints leading from your house. I was just on my way to speak with you personally since we used to work together and all."

I blink at him. Huh. Ah. Hm. I flex my fingers within the skin I wear. My eyes dart down to his throat and then back up to his face.

But could I get away with it? We're in the middle of a busy marketplace. It's practically bustling. No, if I did away with him here and now, everyone would know, and it would become a huge thing. I could probably escape if I were alone, but I'm not. I need time to get Simel away from here. Slowly, I let my hand relax once more. I chance a smile. The guard—as this apparently is—reacts favorably. "Sorry," I say, "that was just my wife. She's delusional, because of the sickness. She must have snuck out, found the poor dead guards, and came back in a hurry. Sorry about the inconvenience."

His face loosens a little. "Really, now? That's a relief. The honorable arch judge was considering pulling you down to the court of truth, so your words bring me quite a bit of relief." He gives a pause, his eyes narrowing a little. "However, the bloody footprints were leading *away* from your house. Why could that be?"

Ah. He got me.

I make a show of shock. "Oh, that's true! Why, I didn't even—how silly of me!" I smile coldly at him. "You know, being an officer of the law, how about I just bring you to my house and you can ask her yourself? I'm no deductor, so I'm sure you could make much more sense of it than myself."

The guard nods slowly before laughing tentatively. "Haha, well, I suppose you're right, Teff. Knowing her, I'm sure this is all just a big misunderstanding."

I twist my lips into a smile. "Yes," I say. "I'm sure."

I lead him back to the house and inside. He stops right in the mouth of the door, eyes falling to the puddle left from the father of the house. "Might this have . . . ? No, this is much older. Did something happen here?" He seems surprised and concerned in equal parts. Oh, well. I close the door, bringing him inside. He stops right in the entrance, taking a few breaths before plugging his nose. "Whew, it reeks in here. Those reports were more than right. Did something die in here or—"

I stab my hand straight through his chest.

He blinks down at my bloodied hand. "Wh—what . . . ?"

Then he slides off my hand to collapse onto the floor. I step over his still-moving body, climbing the stairs two steps at a time and practically bursting into the bedroom where Simel lies writing something in his little diary.

"Simel, we need to go—*stat!*"

And, like that, we left the city of . . . what was it called? Standsore? Something like that.

Before we left fully, though, I stopped by a little shop and, uh, "borrowed" a map. See, we're here, and to get to the empire, we'll need to pass through a couple of cities, a number of forests, a mountain range, across a sea, and . . . Yeah, it's a bit of a distance. But that's nothing the dynamic duo of Fennrick and Simel can't achieve!

Why, on our first day alone, we were able to leave the desert fully, make it across someone's field without getting attacked by their no-horn bison, and sneak inside a forest all calmlike.

I did make sure to grab as much water as I could get my hands on to put in my inventory, but the problem lies in vegetables. My inventory doesn't keep things fresh. It isn't even like a refrigerator either—I think it has the same temperature I'm currently in, so things go bad *really* fast.

Until we reached the next village in our path, my main strategy was to just bite every single bit of floral wildlife I came across, and if it didn't have any bad effect, I'd show it to Simel to get a second opinion. Depending on his reaction, I'd either cook it for him or eat the rest myself. Things would, of course, be way easier if he ate meat, but now that we have access to actual greenery, I won't force him.

Most of our trek is through forests, across dry lands, or by farmland. The place we're heading for—some tiny village called Throughwalk—is luckily connected to that city we came from by a pretty well-used path. Actually, almost all of the places we'll be going to are shown on the map as having roads, so braving the wilderness is completely optional. I still do it, of course, but I could at any time choose not to.

It takes us five days or so to reach the village, and we arrive just at nightfall.

I'm just about to scout out a proper house to "borrow" for the night when I notice Simel's gaze. Judging. Knowing. "I—I was just . . ." Not letting me finish the sentence, Simel confidently strides ahead. The village would be called big if you compared it favorably to a shoebox. It's basically just a bunch of farmhouses spread out, a church of some sort in the middle of the village, and a couple of non-farmhouses close to said church. Simel is confidently heading toward one of those houses, and I can't exactly do much other than follow.

I realize only when we're at the door of the house that I'm not wearing any disguise. "W—wait, Simel, hang on, I need to—" I can't say any more before he abruptly pulls the door open and slips inside to the sound of a gentle bell. Damn it, Simel!

I hesitate at the door for a second. Disguise or Simel? I grit my teeth. If need be, I can do away with whoever's in there.

Grumbling a few curses under my breath, I step inside.

Warmth hits me alongside the smell of freshly baked bread and bubbling stew.

"Why, it really has been a while, Your Grace! I can't say I haven't been expecting you, but seeing you like this is still a bit shocking. Though, I must ask—pardon my curiosity—but did you ever find that Tallthi—" Her eyes fall on me. I stare at her.

This place is . . . an inn, I think? It's warm. It smells like food. There's a stout goblin woman standing behind a counter, previously conversing with Simel, now looking at me.

She blinks at me. I consider how fast I can leap across the room.

Her fat face twists in delight. "Why, would you look at that!" I freeze in place. She steps around the counter, hips swaying as she boldly steps up to me. She's somehow even shorter than Simel, but she makes up for it in confidence as she looks up at me, smiling, her ears wiggling. "So, you're what's called a human, eh?"

I take a little step back. She advances on me. "I am," I say, to her obvious delight. "What's it to you?"

She grins. "Oh, nothin'. It's just I've heard so much talk of you humans as of late. Human this, human that, Tallthing here, Tallthing there. I've always been fascinated by wolf stories, so those bard's tales about your sort . . . Very fascinating." She puts her hands on her hips. "Now, is it true what they say, what with your sort eating babies and all that?"

I open my mouth, and then I close it again. I swallow down a bit of drool. "Not all of us, no."

And for some reason, that gets her crestfallen. "Oh, I see . . ." Thankfully, it also makes her step back a little. I let out a breath. "Well, as I told His Grace, we are unfortunately fully booked for the night. Lots of strange happenings going on over in Sandshore. Of course, knowing it's His Grace and his . . . *human* companion, I'd love to offer you our finest rooms. Best we've got right now is the stables, but I can't exactly let His Grace sleep with the farm animals, so . . ."

"No, no," I say, quickly cutting her off before she can continue. "The stables would be great. Really, we're thankful to sleep in any place where we might be able to rest our weary legs."

She puffs up at my words, an amused glint in her eye. "My, haven't you got some manners? And here I thought your kind was all about bloodshed and killing demons and what's-it-to-ya. You really can't trust everything they say through the lyrevine, isn't that right?" She gives a little harpy laugh and I'm somehow able to muster a laughter to match hers. "Well, if it's acceptable to His Grace, I haven't got any issue with it. I can't speak for the animals, but I couldn't imagine they'd object to such high-class company."

"Yeah," I say. "Sure."

Before we head off to sleep, she actually lets us eat our fill of stew and bread, which was . . . Let's just say I absolutely did not cry, because crying isn't my style, and besides, who cries over *bread*? No matter how freshly baked it is, that's just lame. Besides, if you cry *onto* the bread, the bread gets soggy, so, yeah.

We went to the stables. There were mostly just a bunch of tied-up drakes, but there was also some lunatic that had brought an entire damn snake? For some reason, the drakes didn't like me looking at them, so we were able to procure a pretty good spot, with the drakes seemingly fully intent on staying as far away as possible. Interesting.

I put Simel to sleep, and then I contemplate sitting next to him. But I don't want the night to go to waste when I'm in such an interesting place. I have a few things I want to do while the sun is down.

I give the drakes a few suspicious looks. They somehow retreat farther away, straining their tethers and whimpering in their mouthguards. Okay, yeah, Simel should be alright. I'll know if they get close to him. Still, if only to prove a point, I grab one of the thin-necked sprint drakes, twist its neck, and disassemble it so fast the flesh didn't even have time to go cold. Once I've put all of it into my inventory and licked the blood from the floor, there isn't even a sign left that it was ever there to begin with. The drakes stare at me. I glare at them.

Got that?

Going by the looks in their eyes, they probably get it.

And so I sneak out. The night air is cool and for just a moment I let my eyes linger on the seemingly endless starry sky, and the moons and the constellations. I take a deep breath through my nose, taking in the exact position of every single warehouse and pantry in the village, alongside what they contain. I've been in this world enough to know what's normally eaten. Alright, time to head out and get Simel some grub!

I head toward the farthermost place purely by instinct.

The farm is basically just three houses, each placed at an angle from the others to form a courtyard in the middle. This also happens to be what almost every other farm I've seen so far has looked like, so I'm not surprised. One of the houses is a stable for the thick, stubby drakes they use to pull their hoes and things, the other is the house that the family itself lives in, and then we have the storage house. Fun fact! For some reason, there are some goblins that also sleep in the stable. No idea what they're doing in there.

Also, this is probably one of the two biggest farms in the village. The smaller farms don't have their own stalls and storage houses, but this one does, so here we are.

The storage house is locked, but that's nothing my claws can't help against. Of course, it's not like I can cut through iron, but if I just shove my nails in the hole and jimmy them around just a little, then . . .

Click!

As easy as that. Smiling to myself, I head inside. Alright, we've got a bunch of grains, some pea-like stuff, a bit of dried meat and some salted meats . . . I drool a little.

I start shoving things into my inventory. I don't think Simel would be too interested in eating the salted meats, but they'll last for way longer than raw meat, so it's worth it to grab them anyway. And then some grain, and some of this, and some of that, hehehehe, now *this* is the true meaning of looting! Ah, I miss playing video games. But this is almost as good! It might actually be a little bit—

"Wh—who's there?"

I freeze in place. Sniff sniff. I turn toward the open door.

<Goblin (Lv.7)>

It's a young woman. Goblin. A young *goblin*. It's holding a little candle, dressed in a dress that's too big on it. I usually can't tell the ages of these things, but this one is clearly young.

And it's just caught me in a pretty bad situation.

I stand up properly. I begin to walk toward it. It takes a few steps back, but it isn't enough.

"P—please, what . . ." Its yellow eyes flash in the moonlight and it sees me. Of course, by that point, it's already too late.

I do what has to be done.

"Did you hear what happened last night? Nasty business!" the innkeeper says in greeting as I step up to the counter. A number of goblins are already seated in the dining room, not a few of them giving me looks that can, at best, be described as unsavory. They're looking at me in the same way you'd look at a loosed tiger. *Suspicion.* That's it.

"What business?" I say, somehow managing to not stammer. From the corner of my eye, I notice a few of the patrons' eyes widening a little at my fluent speech.

She shakes her head, handing me a pitcher of beer. For breakfast. Excuse me?

"Oh, it's a right story. Old Tiller's serf—this young, pretty lass—went missing. Took a good lot of his harvest, too. And to make things worse, she even went and stole one of my patron's sprinters to get away as well! Can you believe it? And I always thought her a mature, well-bred girl." Her eyes gleam, turning to look at me. "You didn't happen to notice anyone enter the stables, Sir Tallthing?"

I glance away. "Eh, uh . . . Nope. Nothing like that."

The smile slips off her face. "Oh, well. I suppose a lassie running off with a bunch of crops isn't an inch as interesting as whatever you've seen."

Maybe not. Taking the brew, I head off to the table Simel's sitting at. His wooden bowl is filled with mainly stew, alongside a piece of bread. Same as my own breakfast, that is. I sit down across from him, putting my large mug of beer next to the one he has. He's already half emptied his own, though. And he's made good progress on the little bowl of brandy the innkeeper brought us. It's not something I've seen before, but it's basically just a small bowl of what seems to be brandy with a single spoon in it. Going by how Simel uses it, you're meant to just take a spoonful, drink it, and then put the spoon back in the bowl.

Uh, yeah, I'm not doing that. Even drinking an entire mug of beer first thing in the morning is a bit . . .

Then again, technically speaking, this isn't even beer, because it isn't made with malt or wheat or anything like that. It's just that the process is basically the same, and the taste is very similar, so that's what I'm calling it. Same with the brandy.

I look at Simel. He doesn't look up at me. "So, uh," I say. "Did you hear about that nasty business with the—the . . . serf?"

He takes a shot of brandy, wipes his mouth on his shirt, and gives me a look that shuts me up in an instant. I look away from him, accidentally meeting the eyes of one of the goblins in the inn. They look away. When I look at another one, it doesn't want to make eye contact either.

Right. R—right.

We finish breakfast, returning the bowls and things to the innkeeper. Simel was able to fully empty the brandy bowl, all on his own. It feels good to return nothing but empty bowls and mugs, but I'm still a little worried about Simel.

I clear my throat and glance at Simel. "Now, I'm not sure if we have money, but . . ."

"Oh, don't you worry about that, dearie!" she says, beaming. What the heck did she just call me? "Just being able to meet a *human* is payment enough. Besides, it's not often you get to lodge a man like His Grace in our stable, of all places." She gives a wink. "When the bards come asking for all the details to tell your tales, I'll be sure to tell them all about it—you've got my word!"

"Okay?" Since I don't really know what else to say, I thank her for the lodging, and then we head out again.

The next time we get to a village, Simel doesn't want to enter it. Rather, he makes us walk in a wide arc around it. Or, well, he makes *me* walk it, since he's still too hurt to walk on his own. He also refused to eat the grains I presented him with. Sometimes I really don't understand this man.

We make it along pretty well, though. When he doesn't see it, I often sneak back to steal a bit of food and grain from the villages we pass.

Eventually, we reach the next city. This time, Simel is okay with us entering it, but he gives me a long look before we do. Also, unlike the last time, I put on a proper disguise before we enter. For some reason, being recognized as a human felt weird. I'm much more used to this, although Simel didn't seem to like me wearing it. We spent a day or two in the city, and then Simel insisted on us leaving again.

And that's how it went, mostly. We avoided villages, spent only a brief time in cities, and then continued. And just like that, three months passed.

It would probably have gone a lot faster if we'd "borrowed" a drake or hitched a ride on a caravan or whatever, but Simel always seemed against it. Nevertheless, I didn't really have anything against carrying him much of the way, so it was alright.

Three months, and we have finally reached the port city of Ullum.

"You mean to tell me that the next boat to Yattisbay leaves in two *weeks*?"

The guy on the pier—some old sailor-looking dude currently scamming us—merely shrugs. "That's the best you'll get at this time a' year. Frankly, lad, you're lucky any boat's leaving at all, what with the whole war business brewing." He takes a puff of some sort of glass pipe I still haven't gotten a proper explanation of. "Nothing's stopping you from going there by carriage. Shouldn't take more than a month or so to travel there by land."

I wipe my face, unfortunately only wiping at the face I'm wearing. "Okay, listen. I'll get you twice the money if you take us there, like, today. You need vira?

We've got vira aplenty. That not good enough for you? I've got plenty! I've got lent, ore, fra, holdings . . . name your price. Come on."

He looks me up and down, his thick eyebrows quirking a little. "You've been places, haven't you?"

Okay, that's it. That's it. I can't—

Simel glances at me. I return his look. Seriously? Ugh, okay, okay, *fine*. I turn back to the old sailor. "Fine. Okay. We'll go when you go. How much are you asking for?" He holds up his hand, showing four green fingers. "What, four vira?" He shakes his head. No way. "You can't seriously expect me to pay four vire for a simple boat ride." He shakes his head again. I can feel my eye twitching. "Now just you hold on. Viru? Are you serious? Four *viru*?"

"Do you know any other boats leaving for Yattisbay?"

Oh. Oh. Is that how he wants to play? Is that it? Oh, I'll—

Simel shakes his head at me. Damn it. Every time. Leaning down, I turn to him. "Listen, four viru is enough to get us to the other side of the continent and back in a featherdrake-drawn carriage. You really think we should be spending that kind of cash on this scammer, just because he's got the only ship leaving for the empire? Come on. Let's just walk there. Hell, if it'll convince you, I'll even carry you all the way there!"

He simply shakes his head. Ugh.

I take a deep, relaxing, and not at all sharp breath as I stand up to face the sailor once more. "Okay. Okay. You know what? Fine. Four viru? Great. Wonderful. I'll have it ready in two weeks' time. Does that satiate you, drake?"

He looks at me, and I can tell by the look in his eye that he knows I haven't got any better choice than this. The fact that I'm well over two heads taller than him doesn't matter in the least. A predatory smile tugs at his lips. "Sorry, but not quite, lad. Lots of people want to go with old Frilla. I'm afraid I'll need the payment by tomorrow at the latest, assuming you want to have a proper place on the boat and not get dragged by the rudder."

My claws twitch. Not thinking about much of anything, I slowly close my mouth and turn to look around. The harbor isn't exactly empty, but nobody's paying attention to us. This is far from the marketplace and the city center. I turn back to the sailor, and I can see the look on Simel's face, but it doesn't matter too much.

I take a step forward and grab the old sailor by the collar, lifting him into the air as I do, bringing his face closer to mine. His eyes widen a smidge and I glare right into them. "I'll get you your money," I growl, "but if you try to leave the city without us, I'll find you. I've got your scent. And by the time I've got you, you'll wish you took us there *for free*. Got that?"

His face doesn't even twitch. "Sure," he says, cool as a cucumber. "As long as you've got the money, there's no need to fret."

I continue glaring at him for a second or two before dropping him, though he unfortunately falls perfectly on his feet, not even a little scuffed.

Seething, I turn on my heel, Simel following along.

"Can you believe that? Four viru for a measly boat ride! Why, I should just . . ." I catch a glimpse of his eyes and pause. "Yeah. Yeah, I know. Still, I'm really . . ." I shake my head, trying to scatter the anger. "You're too soft, Simel. Those kinds of guys don't deserve that kind of mercy." He looks at me again and I shrug. "I know, sure, but we could find someone else to drive the boat. No, wait, *steer* the boat. That's the word. I mean, this is a *port city*, right? I'm sure they've got more captains than they do barmaids!" I frown for a moment. "No, wait, scratch that. Port city or no, it's still a city. Forget I said anything."

We continue walking. We have been living at an inn for the past couple of days, but if we'll need to stay here for two entire weeks, we may need something more . . .

I look at Simel. Simel looks at me.

"I wasn't going to!" I say, but he already knows. He always already knows. I don't know when he learned to read my thoughts, but it no longer scares me. "Still, I do think that . . ."

We step into the marketplace. It's bustling. More than usual. People are crowding by, chattering in hushed tones among each other. All I hear from the snippets of conversation is "Execution," and "Human," and "Child-eater," and that's all I need to hear. I share a look with Simel, and we allow ourselves to be pushed along by the stream. Being taller than the goblins, I have a good look at it all quite far ahead of time, giving me an excellent view of the platform before we actually reach it.

It's large and wooden, raised high enough for all to see, and atop it stands a goblin dressed all in WHITE, holding an axe. Next to said goblin is a man. Not a male goblin, nothing like that. A human man.

An actual human.

The fact that it's a human isn't completely self-evident, because at this time, said human is hunched over, head lowered onto a wooden pillory. He's completely naked, allowing his pink skin and long limbs and stubby ears to be on full display to the horrified populace. Now, don't get me wrong, I've never been too attached to the whole being-human deal, but hearing dozens—if not hundreds—of goblins around me whispering in jeering tones about how horribly disfigured this human man is isn't too good for my self-image. Not that it was any good to begin with.

As I stand watching the sight, the goblin clad in WHITE speaks. "This reprehensible Tallthing, this *human*, accused of the crime of stealing and eating the children of Ullum, has hereby been sentenced to death by beheading! And for those gathered who have never before seen a being such as this, do not be fooled by the REDness of its blood! These humans, as they call themselves, are not so much goblin as they are beast. A human burned the city of Acheron! A human brought war to this peaceful continent! And this human before us stole and ate *children*! For that, it shall now find penance in death!"

Huh. Stole and ate children?

I wipe the drool from my chin. Didn't know there was another man of taste in this city. Maybe I should have been more observant?

"P—please!" the guy shouts. The human guy, that is. "I don't—I don't know what's happening! Does anybody here speak English? Oh, God, please, I didn't do anything. I was just passing through. I have no idea what—"

"Listen to its incomprehensible language, crafted by no God! Hear the sounds of its sinful throat, bobbing and clucking like a layegg!" The goblin in WHITE raises the axe. "*Now we shall see if it still speaks without it!*"

With impressive strength, the goblin brings down the axe on the guy's neck. It got an inch in at most before getting stopped. The guy obviously screams because *duh*. Then the goblin actually had to lift the axe again to do a retry, and then another, and then yet another. By the point his head rolls, the goblin had been hacking at him for what felt like minutes.

I turn to Simel. "See, that's what you get when you try beheading a guy with inherent cheat skills and armor and stuff. All the humans who have reached this place naturally have really high levels, so honestly, executing them at all is kind of dumb. Like, they're here to fend off the god of kings's minions, so why get rid of them?" A little idea strikes me. "You know something? Back in the day, on Earth, sometimes instead of killing a guy, they'd just brand him for life. You know, so everybody could see that they were a criminal? Very effective. Just like with your lizard!"

Simel eyes me oddly.

I shrug. "Just an idea, of course. Nothing more to it."

Getting the money to pay for the boat was pretty easy. The problem was convincing Simel that I wasn't going to kill, rob, or loot anyone to get the money.

But I was able to cook up a pretty good half-truth. Basically, I told him that I'd been able to get one of the city's rich judges to pay to have me analyzed by one of his court mages. This was not a lie. I did, in fact, turn up at the house of one of the city's four high judges and tell him I was a human and that I was willing to give myself up for divine analysis. Furthermore, he did accept it. I really hadn't expected that one, but sometimes life does have its perks. What I didn't tell Simel was that I then pocketed a few of the judge's items and sold it to this one guy I found in a back alley at one point. If you're wondering why I didn't kill the judge, it's because—duh. It's a judge. I kill one of those and the whole city's guards will be after my ass like I'm a PlayStation on BLACK Friday.

Anyway, but then that guy refused to give me all the money I needed, so I killed him and took his organs to this other guy I met in a different back alley who made a living selling the things to reputable healers and temples, but then *he* wouldn't give me enough money either, so I got the names of some of his clients, BLACKmailed one of the richer ones, and just like that I had enough money to buy a boat seat. Yippee!

But explaining all of that to Simel felt like a bit much, so I kept it brief.

With the money in hand, I paid that damn sailor, but not before taking a deep whiff of his smell. And for the past close to two weeks, that smell is all I've focused on. I have been able to tell every single movement he's made. Where he lives. Where he works. The people he talks to. His family. His child.

I almost considered giving him a note saying if the ship didn't set out, I'd eat his family, but as it turned out, I didn't need to! The ship was all ready to set out when Simel and I arrived, meaning that I would not have reason to do good on the aforementioned threat. Darn it.

Still, we boarded the boat, finding it occupied by maybe a dozen other passengers, each odder than the last. A collection of oddballs, to say the least.

There was a farmer and his family; a judge and her handmaiden; a vagabond; a pair of siblings who must have each been ten years old at most; an apprentice sailor; and a lone mother with her baby. And then, there was me and Simel. I honestly don't know what we could be called, except for maybe a pair of travelers. Our duo could closest be compared to the vagabond, I guess.

Before we set out, the old sailor—the captain—gathered us all to explain how this was going to go.

First, the trip would take a month or two or however long the god of seas deemed it proper to take. Second, we were not passengers; we were cargo. If we did not like the treatment received, we would be tossed overboard like cargo. Third, we would receive three meals a day, at nine, one, and seven, respectively. If we did not show up at these times, we would not eat.

Tyrannical? Yes. Our only choice? No, but that's not what Simel thinks.

Regardless, all I care about is making it to the empire without Simel dying. A captain being high on his rulership doesn't really matter to me, no pun intended. The judge wasn't too happy about the rough treatment, but since this is the only option, she had no choice but to shut up. It was actually kind of satisfying to watch, but anyhow.

The captain ordered his few shipmates around, and after a few hours, the ship set out fully. Once the ship had left the pier, I took five steps to the railing and promptly puked my guts out into the ocean.

Hm.

Oh, Simel's next to me. Hey, Simel. What's with that expression? I can't tell if it's pity or if he's gloating. Or maybe it's some other emotion entirely. "I just . . ." I burp. Tastes like blood. Not mine, of course. "This is my first time on a boat."

He quirks an eyebrow.

"It's true!" I squawk. "Sure, I know, if I lived as close to the sea as I did, I should have been way more used to being on a boat than most normies. I just . . . I never really did anything like that. It just didn't happen, okay?" I feel my stomach clench and I lean over again, emptying out a bit of bile I didn't know I had left. "Eurghh . . ."

"Everything alright, sir?" someone asks. I glance over. Oh, hey, it's the sailor in training. "Are you seasick?"

"Yeah, don't worry, I just . . ." I feel something rise again but I swallow it down. As long as I don't think about the gentle bobbing of the boat, the lurching of the waves, and the rocking of the hull, I should be fine. I should be . . . "Urghh—!"

"Easy, there!" the young sailor says, patting me on the back. The touch makes me jolt a little, but I stop myself before I do anything bad. He smiles at me, all innocent. He's got dimples. His mane is carefully braided, much like most sailors. Everything about his face feels simple and easy. "Here, how about you sit down, sir? My father always told me that to sit in the shade and breathe a bit was best for seasickness. And if you permit me, sir, I could surely fetch you some tripseeds for you to chew on. It does wonders, that I can swear."

I furrow my brow at him. "Sure," I say. "Go ahead."

Simel looks like he has a lot on his mind, but the sailor boy appears completely oblivious to it, simply bringing me over to sit on an out-of-the-way bench on deck. Once I'm sat, he leaves, returning after a few minutes with a handful of little orange berries. "Here, sir," he says, nudging them into my hand. "Simply chew on one of these and you'll soon feel the nausea melt away."

I thumb the little berries in my hand. They're about as large as kernels of BLACK pepper, and as hard as one, too. Well, it can't hurt more than anything else I've experienced, can it? Shrugging, I pop one in my mouth and start chewing. It isn't especially sweet, and it has a slightly bitter aftertaste, but it does feel like my nausea is getting a little better. Interesting.

"You are aware that it is all hogwash, are you not?"

I look up to find the judge looking down her nose at myself and the sailor boy.

"I had my mage analyze them, and there is nothing in their properties to suggest any such abilities. It is merely superstitious nonsense," she says with a scoff, clearly taking her trip entertainment in watching the sailor boy squirm. "Didn't your father tell you that, boy?"

The sailor boy makes to speak but I'm a bit faster. "Okay listen yeah but you can't underestimate the power of the placebo effect, which you clearly haven't heard of or you would've let me keep chewing this thing 'cause I actually read a study about how at times the placebo effect could be just as strong as the real thing so even if it *is* just superstition or whatever it is still helpful in this moment also just so you know it's still effective even if you know that it's a placebo. Yeah."

She stares at me.

The sailor boy stares at me.

Simel sighs and looks away.

"Do—do you happen to be a learned man, sir?" the sailor boy asks. I don't have the heart to tell him that I'm probably younger than him.

The judge shakes her head. "If you would rather believe in superstition than fact, then you are clearly not a man of the gods." And with those devastating words, she leaves.

I keep chewing the seed, and then I swallow it.

The sailor boy slowly composes himself. "Well, there's all types of people, aren't there, sir?" As he watches her leave, his eyes suddenly widen, as though remembering something. "Oh! Forgive me, I almost forgot, but once you've finished chewing it, please spit it out, since the skin may cause the nausea to—" While he's speaking, I carefully stand up, move to the railing, and empty the last of my stomach's contents into the sea. ". . . worsen."

"I'm alright," I mumble. "I'm fine. I just need to . . ." I puke again. I think *this* is my blood. Not sure. "Okay, yeah, I think I feel better now."

The sailor boy seems beyond worried. "Well, erm . . ." He holds out his hand. "If it isn't too much of a bother, would you mind if I introduced myself?" I look down at his hand and up at his face.

I wipe the sick from my lips and the lips I'm wearing. "Lo," I say. "Lo Fennrick."

"Loe Feene . . . ?"

"That's my name—Fennrick."

He blinks at me. "Oh! Sorry, I just . . . I was worried for a second that you were about to vomit again. Erm . . ." He returns his hand to his side. "It is a pleasure, Sir Fennrick. I am Vann, son of Pettere."

I wave my hand. "No need for all the *sir* stuff. We're like the same age, dude."

"You are?" He looks me up and down. "Pardon me, si—erm . . . *Fennrick*, but you don't . . . I mean . . ."

Oh, wait, yeah, I'm wearing the skin of an adult. "Yeah, I've got this, uh, like . . . skin disease or whatever. People tell me I look like a fifty-year-old all the time, but I'm really only . . ." Squashing my eyebrows together, I count my fingers real quick. "Eighteen! I'm eighteen. Still eighteen."

He seems thoughtful for a moment, eyes falling to the deck below us. "You're younger than me?"

I purse my lips. "Um. Yup."

Going by the look in his eye, it would be fair to assume his world has just been shattered. Interesting to see.

After a minute or so, he finally composes himself enough to give a polite smile. "Well, Fennrick, it is still good to make your acquaintance, and I hope our ride will go well."

Surprisingly enough, just like Vann hoped, the rest of the boat ride actually went pretty well. I had sort of expected to have to fight sea monsters at some point, or at least a few pirates, but none of that happened. It was sort of, well . . . *quaint*. Which feels ridiculous when I say it like this, but that's what it was. The sky was usually blue, the wind was mostly on our back, and weirdly enough, I had company. I talked to Vann a lot, also making acquaintances with the other passengers. They were an interesting bunch, and once I got to know them properly, I found myself genuinely enjoying their company. Even stranger, they didn't seem all that opposed to speaking with me, either.

They would ask me about my and Simel's travels, and I would—simply enough—tell them. There was nothing inherently wrong with our travels. I could tell them the cities we'd visited without much fear.

After a little over a month, we arrived at the city of Yattisbay. I bid farewell to Vann and the others, and just like that, we were almost there. The empire was less than a month's travels away. For some reason, that thought gave me a strange sense of melancholy, knowing that once I brought Simel there and did the right thing, the floor would close, and I wouldn't get to meet him again until I reached Purgatory. Some little devil deep inside whispered that it didn't need to end, that we could keep traveling. I just had to mislead us a little.

But I couldn't. Simel trusted me to guide us right, and I couldn't betray that. Not my friend. Not like that.

So we continued. Of course, before we left fully, I made sure to sneak away in the night to get a bit of well-earned revenge on the captain. I had grown to miss the taste of goblin just a bit too much. Nevertheless, with that, my business with all of the ship and all that was concluded.

The empire was at hand.

It's Me, Your Prissy Princess

To recalibrate our current position, we are now camping out right on the border of the empire, in a little forest close enough to a village for me to steal from it but not close enough for Simel to realize that that's what I'm doing. Camping of this sort has been our modus operandi for months now, so there's nothing weird about it. No, the weird thing is that when I returned to our little campsite from wrestling a boar, I found Simel in a most peculiar state.

To be specific, he was standing behind an easel. Where did he even get that? Why does he have it? Also, where did he get a canvas to put on it? And what are all those tools and bottles he's got with him?

"Simel, what's all this?" I ask. He doesn't seem too surprised by my approaching, and once I'm close enough, he points over to a rock adjacent to his setup. I glance at it. "Are you going to paint that rock? I didn't know you could do still-life paintings!"

He makes a striking Gromit impression as he shakes his head and points at the rock again.

My jaw opens and closes. No way. Is he—?

My heart leaps in my chest and I jump over to the rock, taking a seat. "How do you want me to sit? Should I do a pose? How about this?" I do a few poses, flexing my spindly arms and making a bunch of silly faces. He just shakes his head. Oh, I see how it is. "Neutral, is that it? Fine, fine," I say, taking a more placid pose. Legs spread, hands on knees, facing straight ahead. Face set in a mask of complete apathy. I chuckle a little. "You know, this feels a little bit like a mugsho—"

He waves a little to the left. I scooch to the left. Then he nudges me back to the right. I follow along. He nods silently. I smile and let my body relax a little.

I can't see how he's painting, but going only by the ease with which he handles his materials, I'm going to assume that he's better at this than I'd previously expected. Okay, so now I just need to sit still. Perrrrfectly still. Not a single movement. None. At. All.

My eye twitches. It's probably just another hate message. I've been getting a bunch lately about staining the reputation of all humans or something. Making a mountain out of a molehill, as haters always do. Yup. So, since I already know what it is, there's no need to check it out. No reason for it to be from anyone I would actually want to get a message from. Not at all. Not. At. All.

I gulp.

I glance up at Simel. He's mixing colors. I look back at the empty air in front of my eyes. Under my breath, I mutter, "Messages."

<Status—Community—Top>
<Personal Messages>
<[NEW]SuperMoleman[F67]: Regarding the war in the middle continent>
<[NEW]HeyoMayo[F43]: I heard that u were to blame for goblins hating us plz turn urself in>
<[NEW]FarmerOfBlades[F57]: Hey again have u die yet?>
<[NEW]RatCarrier[F38]: My friend got hunged because of your dumb ****. Do you have emotion . . .>
<SuperMoleman[F67]: Checking in again, glad everything's going well!>
<[NEW]LoveBombDeluxe[F62]: If I ever find you in Purgatory I am actually killing you no matter what>
<. . .>

My hand shoots up to poke the new message, but it stalls midway up on account of the sheer power in Simel's glare. "Oh, I—I just . . ." I poke the air in front of me. "Insect. Saw a flyeater. Gone now. Heh . . ." He looks back at the canvas and I watch him for a second or so before letting my gaze fly down to the message I was able to bring up.

<SuperMoleman[F67]: Regarding the war in the middle continent Hey Kitty! I got your message, sorry about the late reply we were still visiting the Duchess of lat-inn and she had barred us from using status things, saying they're devices of the god of mischief, which isn't wrong technically speaking but still pretty weird. Anyhow, where are you now? Sorry again I've been too busy with all these diplomatic affairs to try to meet up. We'll

just have to wait until you get to purgatory properly, haha. I'm asking because I heard that the queen of ret-inn has been mobilizing her forces to advance on the empire of split horizons. If you and Simel are stuck in the middle of all that, I can't imagine it turning out very well. I don't think Simel will mind having to wait a bit with the whole deal. Again, and I know you don't like hearing this, but please try to refrain from doing anything rash, okay? Hope everything goes well!>

The war's really happening, huh? I'm not exactly surprised; it's more that I didn't trust the sources that much. However, if Moleman says it's true, that's a whole other situation. Not that it'll interfere with my plans any. No, as a matter of fact, it might just make it all that much more effective.

I glance up at Simel. He's focused. Great. Sliding down the status box, I began typing up a reply.

<PrissyKittyPrincess[F15]: U dnt need 2 worry bout da war im cool i gt a plan lolz gud luck w da kings n stff>

And then I quickly send it away, before Simel could so much as notice I was doing anything at all. Hehehe. Speaking of my plan, it might be a good idea to share it with Simel so he's in on it. Otherwise, it might come as quite a spook. I look up at him. He's focused on his painting, but none of this is going to come as any shock, so I'm sure he'll be alright.

"Okay, so, since our plan is to kill the emperor, I've been thinking about—"

He drops his paintbrush and a little rag and also a tiny sponge. For a long moment, he doesn't even move to pick it up. Once he does, and his face peeks beneath the canvas, he seems weirdly pale. He also gathers all of his things in a right rush, basically hurrying to hide back behind the canvas. Huh. I wonder what that was all about.

Well, might as well continue. "So, as I was saying, I've been thinking about how we might infiltrate the capital properly. Because it's a capital, right? You can't just sneak in and hope to get an audience with the emperor just because you're so pretty." I pause for dramatic effect like a slightly crooked defense lawyer. Simel isn't moving his paintbrush at all. Must be because he's so focused on what I'm saying. "And I'm sure you have a plan of some sort on how to do this, but . . . I think I've got a better idea." I wait. I kind of want him to peek out from behind the canvas again, but when he doesn't, I just continue without it.

"Remember how I've still got that princess's hide? Err—I mean, *skin?*"

He's sitting perfectly still now. Fully focused. Is he thinking the same thing as I am? No idea, but if he isn't, then I'm about to *blow his mind.*

"It's a simple plan, really. I've been thinking it over, and with all of the things in play, it should work. Your plan was to get us close on account of me being a human, right? We'd both get in trouble and then I'd beat him, et cetera, et cetera. And sure, that might work, but then the guy would be surrounded by guards. I mean, what kind of ruler would go before a convicted prisoner without a bunch of guards at his side? Exactly. However . . ."

I grin a little. *So simple! So easy! So quaint!*

"What if I approached in the skin of a regent thought to be dead?"

Now, Simel trembles. Excitement, no doubt. His plan may have been good, but now he sees how closed-minded he had really been.

"We'd be greeted with a parade. Orchestras. Jubilation. The emperor would have no choice but to meet us as a diplomatic envoy of peace. He doesn't want war, so this would be a godsend. And, sure, his dear prince would still be dead, but that's already been mourned aplenty. And, besides, we'll still be returning the crown, so it's fine, right? And then, when I defeat the emperor and clear the stage, nobody will be able to blame you. I mean, you're just a commander, right? Everybody will be looking at the queen and all of a sudden, she'll be in the wrong for sending her daughter to assassinate the emperor. Nobody will give you a second glance." I feel a laugh on my lips. "It's perfect, isn't it?"

He doesn't answer, but I know he's on my side. After all, I'm on his side, so that only makes sense.

It takes a moment for him to start painting again. By that point, I'm giddy with excitement for it all. I've never before felt quite so clever as I do with this plan. My only issue is how to fix it so that we'll actually be met with jubilations rather than suspicion. Sure, I'll be able to look exactly like her, and since my impersonate skill is at level nine it would be practically impossible for anyone to see through it, but what if they don't believe us?

Simel solved my problem before nightfall.

I only caught him doing it because I smelled an animal near the campsite, but when I found Simel handing a sealed envelope to a small bat-looking thing, I knew exactly what it was. He gave me a look like I'd caught him with a body and a shovel, but I just smiled at him. "You truly are a clever one, Simel."

To think he'd send the emperor a message saying that the princess had actually survived! Isn't that just devious? Technically speaking, this is just me assuming what the letter might contain, but I can't imagine what else it would say. Ah, I've always taken to underestimating his devilishness, haven't I?

Regardless, the message was sent, Simel seemed weirdly surprised by how positive I was toward the whole thing, and then the evening ended.

In the morning, we set out toward the capital to finally put an end to all of this.

"Do I look good? It feels kind of tight . . ." I tug at the frilly skirt a little. "And why does it have to be WHITE? I'd be more okay with a pink dress, honestly."

"A pink dress? Don't be silly, Your Highness. Such cheap, half-dyed articles could never properly fit your gracious form. This pristine WHITE, on the other hand, perfectly shows the gentle purity you are so known for."

My nose furls. Was that what she was known for? An image of a vomiting chimera flashes through my head. Yeah, no, I'll have to disagree.

Turning away from the seamstress, I look over at Simel instead where he stands in the doorway of my assigned room, looking markedly pale. I catch his gaze. "What do you think, Simel? Do I look like a pretty princess to you?"

He averts his gaze. The coward's way out? Possibly.

"I think 'pretty' would be an understatement, Your Highness," the seamstress comments with what I think is absolute honesty. Wonderful woman, really. Then she continues placing pins here and there to refit more parts of the dress. Just so we're all on the same page, this is the first time I have ever worn a dress and I am only wearing it to complete my princess disguise.

Of course, to be completely honest, the disguise had worked wonderfully even without an overly prissy gown.

It had almost been too easy to get in. For the sake of my disguise, we "borrowed" a drake to carry our things and myself. Combined with a dress I looted from a totally willing and breathing villager as well as the princess's very own crown—supplied by Simel—I made quite an impression when we rode up to the city gates.

"Isn't that . . . ?"

"But I heard she was—"

"It's her! It's Princess Swee-Swee!"

At the time, I wasn't exactly sure what the proper code of conduct was, so I just did a Queen Elizabeth wave by holding up my hand and rotating it one-eighty degrees back and forth. The guards greeted us by bowing, and we entered. Just like that! Those suckers didn't even check our ID, hah!

I kind of hadn't expected it, but we did successfully accrue a parade of sorts. There were guards riding behind us on big buff drakes, more guards at our front and sides, and the whole thing was eye-catching enough to form a crowd of a sort I hadn't seen since the third floor. We even got a little guide feller of some sort, walking at our side, telling us the way to the emperor's palace. Crazy stuff. By the time we got there, my wrist was kind of dead from all the waving. It'd probably have been better off if I'd gone to a jazz-hands competition.

Once we reached the palace, I had sort of expected that we'd get brought straight before the emperor, but not so. Someone—I can't remember who or where—had said something along the lines of *We can't possibly let the princess greet the exalted emperor in her travel clothes!* and then I'm pretty sure I heard someone whisper to Simel that *The exalted emperor is not quite ready for your visit. Please distract the princess while his grand self prepares the final aspects.*

Which is . . . kind of weird, but okay. I mean, don't get me wrong, just getting a procession of what feels like half the empire's army is great and all, but shouldn't he at least greet me now that we're here? Then again, this was on a mere day's notice, so . . . Yeah.

And that is why I am now in a little room off to the side, getting the final bits of a dress fitted. During this, the seamstress has commented on my height, my slim figure, the weird scars here and there on the princess's skin, and how cold I am. Luckily, she made no mention of the fact that I smell like rotting flesh, which might be because that's what I'm literally wearing. I've been wondering for a while how long a skin can sit in my inventory before it no longer works as a disguise, and going by what I'm currently wearing, it might actually take years. Insane.

A butler pops his head in through the doorway Simel's in, his eyes falling on me and then back at Simel. He steps inside, bows to the both of us, and says, "Your Highness, Your Majesty. His Excellency the Emperor of the Sun, Blind of the Seventh Heaven, is now ready to greet you."

I smile at him and lick both of my pairs of lips. "Oh, that's great!" As I step off the little fitting pedestal, the seamstress hurriedly removes the final few pins here and there, tying invisible knots of thread faster than I can see. I turn to Simel. "Shall we go, then?"

After a moment's hesitation, he nods back at me with an odd look of determination on his face.

We walk through the hallway, surrounded by what has to be at least a dozen guards, some in full armor. I'd be more flattered if the clinking and clanking of the metal weren't so annoying. But I can't kill them now. Hopefully, with my speed, I shouldn't need to face them at all.

Is it just me, or is this kind of awkward?

I'm not saying anything. Simel won't stop sweating. The guards all stink of fear. Maybe some witty banter would help the situation?

I look at Simel. His eyes are affixed to the front, back straight and brow furrowed. Yeah, no, if I said anything now, I'm pretty sure he'd leap out of his own skin. Is the emperor really *that* scary? Well, that's for me to decide, I suppose. In the meantime, if only to distract myself, I suppose I'll admire the architecture. It really is quite nice. Sure, every single doorway I step through forces me to hunch even more than I usually do, but the actual designs are very cool. Blocky. Almost brutalist in design. Yet at times, very human. Or goblic, as the goblins call it.

Looking out of the window, I see that the city itself is much the same in terms of design. Efficient. Structurally sound. Built in stone to last hundreds of years. Not very flammable.

We pass through the hallway and into a larger room containing a statue and a number of murals showing all types of war and divine-looking goblins and . . . and dragons? *They have dragons?!* No way. No *way*. How did I not know this before? It's *dragons!*

Damn, that's cool. Sadly, I don't have time to linger before we're brought into another room, filled with purple banisters showing a setting sun and some other stuff alongside a fair bit of gold and other precious metals. It's a cool place, but my eyes are fixed on the doors before us. Big. Intricate carvings. And if I take a deep breath, I can feel my skill activate, and my attention settles on a single presence in the room ahead of us.

The guards that had previously crowded around us suddenly step away, and a pair of servants take their places on each side of the door. They push the door open. Simel and I step inside.

There he is.

<Emperor of the Sun [BOSS]>

Seated atop a throne of gold and purple, wearing a cloak of deepest indigo and a collar of WHITE fur. The crown atop his head is adorned with various gemstones, somehow going down the back of his head to also become a pair of bejeweled rings around the base of his ears. His face has all the graveness of any king, with a malicious quirk to his lips that tells me his rule is all but benevolent.

Simel goes down on one knee before him and I follow suit.

His eyes slide across the room and onto me. I can practically taste the sweat on his forehead. Somehow, it feels as though his eyes see through everything I am, every layer of skin I wear, all the way down to my soul. He's got those kinds of penetrating, all-seeing eyes.

But apparently he doesn't have an ounce of manners, because he doesn't even so much as stand up to greet me—a princess.

Rather, he lets his deep-set eyes move from me, to Simel, and then back to me, before he finally says, "Princess Swee-Swee, my given daughter. How glad I am to see you alive."

I let my eyes move across the room. The only other people are a pair of servants behind us, by the doors. Witnesses, not enemies. I look back at the emperor. There's seriously only him here? Not even a single guard? Wow. I didn't think he was *that* arrogant, but you know . . . If he wants to get killed, who am I to refuse?

And only after almost a full minute of silence do I realize that he's waiting for a response from me.

"O—oh!" I say, totally not altering my voice to try to talk in a more lady-like fashion. "Of course, Father, I am certainly very happy to be not dead. Very cool, all things considered." He continues staring down at me. What? What does he . . . ? I glance over at Simel to find him holding a crown in both hands. Whoa, shiny! Oh, wait, uhh— "It is a great shame about your son, though. That is, my husband. To be. My former one. Yeah, sorry."

He gestures toward himself. Looking at Simel, I see him nudge the crown toward me. Ahh, I see how it is. Yes, hehe, thy will be done!

Taking the crown from Simel's hands, I stand up and move toward the emperor, holding it in both hands, walking carefully up the stairs to his throne, my body more relaxed than it really should be considering what I'm about to do. I'm next to him now, almost within arm's reach. My fingers clench around the crown in my hands.

He's right in front of me. Easy pickings. Neck exposed. Arms shown. Bowels easy to reach. Simpler than picking a flower. So many ways to do it. Bite. Scratch. Tear. Rupture. Slice, slice, slice, and it'll all be over. The right thing is at hand. I can smell his breathing. I can hear the beating of his heart. I can feel the warmth of his flesh. Almost quaint.

My fingers flex, my body tenses, my lips twist into a grin, my jaw opens, my eyes set themselves on the prize and I can practically taste his blood on my lips already—the sweet, sweet taste of doing what is *right*.

So easy.

So simple.

So—

"Wait!"

My hand, only slightly raised, freezes in place. Huh? Who was that?

I turn around. Not the servants. They're both gone. Not the emperor. Not the air. Not . . .

I look down and my eyes meet Simel's. "Simel?"

A pair of doors slam open and there's a rush of heavy footsteps, but I remain frozen even as a loop of barbed metal hooks around my throat and drags me down, spikes stabbing into the flesh of my throat as I crash to the floor, not even having time to realize what is happening before more such loops, each connected to a long metal pole, stab to grab all four of my limbs, pushing down my ankles, my wrists, my forearms, and my legs, all the while yet another slips around my thin waist.

Man catchers.

"Hold it down!"

"Don't let it get up!"

"More men on the legs!"

I'm pinned to the floor, but I can't fight back or think because all I can see is Simel where he stands across the room, atop a fine mat of purple, his chest rising and falling, looking at me as though I'm a wild beast that's finally been caught.

Well and proper.

XXIV

As Charged

I didn't fight back. They put chains on me, around every limb I have, and then they dragged me down to the dungeons, to the BLACK of the down there, and they chained me up.

Only when the gate to my cell was closed and locked did I finally snap out of it.

What is happening?

What happened to the plan?

Why would Simel . . . ?

I glance outside the cell. There are five guards in my immediate vision. Going by smell, there are several dozen more, leading all the way up and back to the throne room. I look at the bars themselves, and then at the chains I'm wearing. It wouldn't be impossible. Far from it. Almost easy. Simple. Q—

Wait!

I freeze up where I sit.

It *was* his voice. I know it was. I heard it loud and clear. He spoke. He can speak. Could he always speak? Why did he only do it just now? I don't understand. I don't understand anything anymore. I wish I could smell him so I'd know where he was, but the world is too cruel for that. Instead, all I can smell is the emperor, moving here and there with no real logic.

What should I do? Should I escape? Should I fight my way out? What else is there to do?

I shake my head.

I can't let myself fall to despair. The first mistake I could make right now would be to assume that the plan has ended. This is not the end of the road. It's just a little bump, that's all.

There has to be a reason why Simel stopped me.

But why? Why would he possibly want me to not take the chance? It would have been so easy. Could it be that . . . that *he had some other plan?*

A shock of realization zaps through me and the despair and uncertainty melt away in an instant.

That's it! Oh, man, do I feel stupid!

"Hahahahahahahahah!" I laugh, because it was so simple all this time!

The reason he seemed so apprehensive while he was painting me wasn't because he was stunned by how great a plan I was brewing, but rather because he knew how off the mark I was. And, even more so, that he couldn't tell me! Finally, it makes sense. He wanted to do his original plan for a reason, but he couldn't tell me why, so he had to forcefully push me into getting captured, somehow. Heck, he might even have mentioned that in the message he sent to the emperor, which would also explain why he was so startled by my discovery.

Oh, what a goofy situation this has become!

Still, knowing Simel, I'm sure this will all work out in the end. I'll be his blind and deaf sword, not knowing why or when to strike, but still doing it when the time is right. Of course, it would be nice to at least know a little about what the plan is. You know, just as a courtesy. I know that people usually don't talk to swords, but hearing what Simel is up to and what he's thinking would be nice, I think.

The rest of the day passes. No message from Simel.

The next day arrives and passes. No message from Simel.

The next day arrives and passes. No message from—

The cell is unlocked. I barely even have time to look up before a man catcher shoots out from the darkness, hooking around my neck. Now that I'm looking at it properly, the man catcher in question is actually held by four rather burly goblins, and while I'm mentally considering whether I can take them all on, one of them whisper-shouts to the others, "It may look like Her Highness, but that's an illusion—stay strong, brothers!"

Oh, yeah, now that I think about it, I'm still in my disguise. Not that it seems to have been effective in the way I wanted it to be, though.

While I'm thinking, the goblins holding the man catcher drag me to the feet by the loop while a number of other guards—each of them reeking of fear—rush inside the cell, undoing my chains and redoing new ones until I'm probably wearing more chains than I am clothes. Still, if I really tried, I think I could make it out of them. But that might hinder Simel's plans, so I present myself as passive while they grab the chains and pull me out, giving me no room to walk on my own.

Is it a bad thing that it feels slightly nostalgic to get yanked around like this?

Nevertheless, they drag me out, all in a big rabble around me. I can't tell exactly where we're going, but considering how we seem to be getting closer to the emperor, I think I might just be getting myself a second chance at doing the right thing.

That said, wherever it is we're going, there really are quite a lot of people, aren't there? It's choked with breathing and stuffy clothes and excitement and sweat.

Once we get there, I realize what this is at a moment's glance.

It's a courthouse. Inside the castle.

The whole thing is arranged almost like a church, with us entering through a large pair of doors to first bring us down a gallery of close to a hundred goblins, each dressed in fine robes of yellow and blue and orange. Are these the aristocracy? Wow, I don't think I've ever seen this many judges in one place. The way they stare at me like I'm a barely chained tiger almost makes this whole thing worth it. Still, a few of them view me—or rather, what they think I am—with confused pity.

The guards parade me through the gallery and to the main courtroom. There's a raised platform where two arch judges and a sentencer sit at their bench, alongside . . . the emperor? Why's he sitting with the arch judges? Don't tell me he's part of the verdite. Oh, and then there's also a woman on the other side of the judges, dressed no less extravagantly than the emperor and just as hard-faced. Going just by the way she looks, I doubt she's the empress.

As my eyes fall on her she suddenly notices me and visibly twitches, face softening immensely before turning away fully, unable to look at me. That's kind of weird if you ask me.

In the middle of the courtroom is a cage. The guards put me in the cage.

Hang on a second.

Why the heck am I in a cage?!

Hey, this is dehumanizing! I demand a fair trial! But I can't voice any of this before my eyes fall to one of the sides of the courtroom, where I see Simel sitting behind a desk, alongside a few other goblins I've never seen before. I almost want to smile and wave at him but that might ruin his plan, so I instead choose a more brutish expression of reluctant capture.

The cage clicks closed behind me and there's a moment of silence as the guards retreat, only two remaining close enough to act should I suddenly try to do dumb things with a vengeance.

And for just a moment, all is silent in the courtroom.

No, not quite. There's a quiet, muffled sobbing, coming from the judges' bench. Looking over, I see the woman in the crown cry just a little harder at seeing my face. Or, rather, the face I'm wearing.

One of the two arch judges glances at her before turning to one of the guards close to the cage. "Plaintiff, would you please remove . . ." He shakes his head. "Reveal the demon that hides in the flesh of Her Highness Swee-Swee."

The guard looks over at his colleague before reluctantly moving closer. He doesn't even seem like he knows where to start. Do I need to do everything? I bore my eyes into him. "My neck," I say. "There's a crease there."

He gulps and clenches the halberd closer. Nevertheless, he reaches out, arm trembling. His hand touches my neck, and I can see in his eyes how he can't align what he sees with what he feels. His fingers grope and eventually hook around a bit of open flesh, and I feel him twitch. He grabs the skin between his fingers and pulls up, peeling the skin off my head, removing the whole thing like the mask of a Scooby-Doo villain. The crown that previously sat atop my head falls to the floor with a melodic *clink* and for just a second nobody speaks.

A scream pierces across the gallery, instantly followed by exclamations of fear and disbelief. The only person in the room with no strong reaction is Simel, sitting off to the side, who simply stares at me. I give him a look in all the hubbub that strangely enough makes him wince, and then I turn back to the guard in front of me, still holding the princess's face. Ah, he's all frozen.

"What's wrong?" I tease. "I'm not *that* ugly without makeup, am I?"

And—*get this*—at that, he actually drops his halberd, falls on his ass, whimpers, and scrambles away! Wow. I guess a uniform doesn't make a man, after all.

I turn to the arch judges and smile. "So, is anyone going to get me out of the rest of this skin? It's kind of tight, and the dress is . . . Well, honestly, the dress is pretty comfortable, but not while wearing a literal skinsuit, heh." My joke did not land. Ouch, tough audience. Guess I'll just have to make do.

The same arch judge stands up and bangs his gavel, bringing silence over the gathered judges. "Silence!" His hawklike gaze slowly moves across the entire gallery before finally falling on yours truly. "Since the accused has now been revealed in its full, horrible glory," he spits, "we shall now begin this session properly."

His eyes burn into me, but I meet his gaze with even interest. Hey, it's not every day you get to be at a real court session!

"You stand before this court accused of the murder of the former king of Acheron, Parrus the Blessed of Two, alongside the killing of the capital of Acheron, the killing of Princess Swee-Swee of Ret-inn, and the killing of Prince Chepert of Split Horizon, alongside innumerable other offences to all hundred gods. How do you plead, human?"

I stare up at him. I glance at Simel. The urge is strong, but my friendship with Simel is stronger.

I open my mouth, and I speak.

"Guilty."

* * *

Mutters ripple through the courtroom again, silenced by the banging of a gavel. The arch judge's eyes train on me, alongside probably every other pair of eyes in the entire room. "You admit to your guilt, human?"

I shrug and point a finger at Simel. "You've got a good witness for it, right? I did it. I killed the king, and I killed everybody else in the city. He'd tell you the same story, so there's no use in fighting it, is there?"

He folds his fingers across the bench. "We have enough witnesses and evidence to more than satiate the Goddess of Law. Whether you did it or not is not in question." His eyes sharpen. "What we want to know is whether you have any regret whatsoever for the suffering your cruel actions caused."

I can feel my eyebrows furrow. "How's that relevant?"

And apparently that was a sufficient answer, because he turns to the other arch judge and the sentencer and shares a pretty long look. Then they turn to the emperor as a unit and the regent speaks, far louder than in the throne room, his voice echoing across the courtroom. "Why did you want me dead?"

My mouth opens and instantly snaps shut again. "Uh. Uhhh." I gulp, trying not to look at Simel. In the end, I find my eyes drawn to my feet, still wearing a pair of girly WHITE flats. "I, um . . ." I look up at him. "I'm just a crazy insane human who wants mayhem and death, I guess?"

Silence.

Simel didn't even blink. Which, hopefully, means that I didn't mess up his plan too egregiously.

The arch judges and the sentencer turn to the crowned woman on their other side. I can hear one of them say, too softly for the rest of the room to hear, "Would Your Majesty like to make any statement?"

She doesn't answer them. Too busy glaring at me, I suppose.

The arch judges share a few words before turning to me. "Are you aware of the kind of sentence your crime may bring?" I nod. "Do you confirm that your confession is the truth and nothing but the truth, as granted by the God of Truth?" I nod. "Were you coerced or otherwise forced to make said confession?" I shake my head. "Once more, do you accept responsibility for the demise of the capital city of Acheron demise, and for the death of its king, alongside the killings of the princess Swee-Swee and the prince Chepert?"

"That was me, yup."

"In that case," the arch judge continues, "combined with the statements regarding the crimes you have committed on your journey to reach this place, you will receive due judgment, penance, and punishment, so as spoken by the sentencer. Through the will of the Goddess of Law, you will now be judged."

The courtroom holds its breath as the sentencer speaks, his thin voice slicing through the thick atmosphere like a knife: "Us the high judgment finds the accused, the human Fennrick, guilty of massacre, of crown-killing, of murder, of home-taking, of robbery, of city-killing, of arson, of royal impersonating, of man-taking, of cannibalism, of tax evasion, and of mutilation. For this, you will receive no less than the death penalty. You will be beheaded by axe until your head is severed from your shoulders. Furthermore, on special request from His Majesty Simel the Blessed of Three, before your execution, your chest shall be branded by divine fire so that no being shall view your body as anything less than despised by the Gods and by all goblinkind."

I blink at him. I turn to Simel. He's staring at me. Branding? Like how . . .

Oh, that's clever. That's *real* clever. He's branding branding by getting me branded!

In that case, I assume his plan is not to have me escape right here and now, but rather to get branded first. I can just tear off the branded flesh later so it's not permanent or anything. In that case, this'll work out just great. I'll get branded, he'll save me, and then . . . Yeah. Sometimes, everything really does work out for the best, doesn't it?

And with that, the court is adjourned. What a quick and simple situation! They take me out of the cage and walk me back through the gallery, with all of the judges staring at me like I'm some exotic predator out for viewing. I chance a grin at one of them and watch with glee as its eyes roll up and it just passes out. No skill needed. Wow.

They bring me back down, into the dungeons, and chain me up once more. And just like that, I'm left to my own devices. The slightly funny part is that they didn't even tell me when they'd have me executed. It could be days, or it could be months or even years. Who knows?

Well, considering that they somehow got the entire queen of Ret-inn to come watch the court proceedings, I doubt they'd want to force her to stay months just to watch the one who killed her daughter get due justice. Hm. I wonder if this'll cause that war they were having to end? I mean, the queen of Ret-inn is literally at the capital of the empire. I assume that means they aren't on *that* bad terms anymore. Hmm.

Could it be . . . ?

Did Simel solve the war by getting me sentenced?

Whoa. Okay, *now* I understand his line of thinking. See, this is why open communication is key. If I'd known that he'd try to solve the war by using me as a throughline I'd be down for it in a heartbeat! Instead, now, we've got a bunch of miscommunication and dishonesty, which is the bane of all relationships.

He keeps proving me wrong about him. Even when I think of him as basically a demigod, he still ends up outshining everything I previously thought of him. Wow. I really couldn't ask for a better friend, huh?

Smiling, I lean back in my cell, only now remembering what I'm wearing. Oh, yeah. Skinsuit. Eugh, it reeks.

I may be almost fully tethered to my place, but that isn't stopping me. With all the agility of a cat, I begin gnawing off the princess hide, bit by bit, carefully avoiding tearing my dress because, well . . . Okay, listen, how often do you think I'm going to get my hands on a dress of such high quality? When I beat the floor, I bet it'll sell for thousands of points! Ah, I can't wait.

For some reason, a few of the guards outside my cell are staring, but none of them dare to say anything. Interesting.

In the end, I'm left sitting in my cell, wearing a dress and exactly nothing else. Even worse, in my own personal opinion, I don't look too bad in it. Just saying.

And then, not much of anything happens. Time passes. I spend it by meditating, doing some resistance training and meditating more. A few days pass. I was starting to fear it'd take weeks until the execution went underway, but apparently, I was just a bit luckier than I thought.

The guards that come to fetch me for the execution are dressed in much fancier armor than the normal ones, but it doesn't hide their faces. Meaning that I have a perfectly good look at the expression they make when they see the pretty dress I'm wearing. A glare was enough to keep them from saying anything about it.

They do the old man catcher routine, chain me up, and then off we go to my execution.

The whole palace stinks with fear, but as we move through it and to the outside, I get a whiff of fresh air, one that's practically thick with excitement.

There's a platform made of wood raised just outside the palace, next to a shining statue of some big goblin woman. Atop the platform stands a goblin clad in WHITE, carrying an axe, alongside a pillory, made with what seems to be marble. The fun thing here is that the platform is actually so big that it even holds three literal thrones, all with a front-row view of the action. All three are occupied. There's the emperor, with a few other crowned spawnlings standing at his side and back. There's the throne of the queen of Ret-inn, and then, next to her . . .

My eyes meet Simel's.

He looks so . . . *regal.* He's wearing an actual uniform of some sort, alongside a fur-collared coat, and on his head sits a crown. No, on closer inspection, it's not just any old crown, but rather the one I saw in his satchel, back in the desert. Not to mention that he seems to have a little royal sword of some sort, kind of like the poet king.

Would you look at that? Simel—*king!* Would it be wrong for me to be proud of him?

I can't know, because before I have time to think any more about Simel, one of the guards pushes me along, toward the pillory. But he stops me before we get there, shoving me to the floor by having the goblins holding the man catcher around my neck put their weight into it. I fall to my knees, and then no farther.

My chains are loosened for a moment but only to fasten me directly to the platform itself. And here we are.

I look out across the crowd gathered. Wow, there must be several tens of thousands of goblins gathered here. All to watch me do the right thing. Interesting. They're sure to have a memorable afternoon, that's for sure.

I glance at Simel where he sits. I chance a smile at him, but he doesn't react in the least. Ah, poker face, is it? I get it, I get it.

The emperor stands up. "My people! Before you kneels the dreaded killer of Acheron, who burned to cinders that which lived, killed its rulers, and felt no remorse! Not to mention its heartless slaughter of my given daughter and my own son. To those that have heard of or even met a human, the existence of this horrid demon is all the proof you need of the nature that governs all humans. However! You ought not to view these creatures' invasion as an unstoppable assault of demons. This creature was captured, and so will be all other humans who dare encroach on our divinely appointed land. They too shall face judgment!"

I watch in mild interest as a goblin carrying a branding iron steps up to Simel. Going by the way he's holding it, it's clearly not especially hot. Curious.

"Although this glorious empire places no faith in the hocus pocus of so-called magicians, we now employ the assistance of Simel of Acheron, its current king, to imbue this branding iron with divine properties. As sin has branded this human, so too will this iron brand it, purifying the flesh from the evils of its soul!"

The emperor continues speaking, thanking Simel for bringing me here and how the country should still mourn the prince and the princess or whatever, but I'm distracted by whatever kind of ritualistic magic Simel's doing. First up, he's using not a ring or something small like that, but rather an entire damn sphere, which looks much closer to a sovereign's orb than a crystal ball, despite it being crystalline. It's encased in strands of finely woven and engraved metal, designed to look like crawling vines, I think. As Simel holds it in hand, he puts his other hand on the branding iron and begins chanting. With every word he speaks, the branding iron clearly grows hotter, turning from its normal bronze color to a brighter yellow, until it eventually becomes a pure, horrible WHITE. Weirdly enough, it doesn't look hot. Simel is still touching it, and the goblin holding it doesn't seem perturbed in the least. Odd.

"Made of dragonheart, this branding iron will only brand the one culpable in the eyes of the Goddess of Law. Let us now see justice rendered unto this demon!"

The guy with the branding iron steps closer to me. Someone rips up the entire upper part of the gown I'm wearing, exposing my chest. Hey, that's my dress! It's not going to sell for anything if you rip it up, dumbo! Of course, my pleas go unheard and the man holding the branding iron steps closer. Now that it's this close, I can see what it portrays. It's about the size of a saucer, and the main image seems to be a crown, split in two by an arrow, the whole thing contained in a halo-like circle. I can tell that there's writing on the circle and crown, but since I'm looking at the thing mirrored, it's hard to tell what it's supposed to be saying.

He holds it closer. The air around it feels cold, like it's been flash-frozen. I squint at the lettering, trying to make out the words. Let's see: *The body upon which you find this brand has rendered unto death the city of Acheron and—*

The branding iron is pressed to my chest.

<THE GOD OF PAIN PITIES YOU.>

The iron is removed from my chest. Did I scream? My throat hurts. I don't know whether I screamed or not. The air echoes with stillness. WHITE. I look down to find the smoking brand on the right side of my chest, stuck there, clinging to my skin, onto the clear outline of my ribs. I can feel it in my bones. Burning WHITE. Freezing WHITE. There's a puddle of vomit in front of me. Did I make that? I don't know.

I take breaths but the pain in my chest keeps me from breathing properly. Pain. Pain. Pain. It hurts. I feel a sound mumble its way out of my throat, like that of groaning ice.

"And now," a voice says, from right behind me, from far behind me, somewhere, "we shall see that this creature is given the same fate as its victims, lacking only the mercy of the gods to accept it into the life beyond this!"

I'm brought to my legs. Chains are undone and redone and my head is placed atop the pillory. Pillowy. I want to sleep.

I look, and I see, just across the platform, my friend, my good friend, Simel, who watches me—*he's a king!*—he watches me, and I see him, and I wonder when the plan will take hold, when he will secretly send a spell my way, to grant me strength and life, to ease my pain, to relieve me of my worries, to let me spring from where I lie draped across the pillory, flying to my feet to finally do what's right, for the first time in my life, to make someone truly happy, to show that I can have friends, that I can be a good friend, even if I am only me.

"Let his head roll!"

There is a basket beneath me. To hold my head once it falls. But it won't fall. Simel will save me. He knows spells. He's a wizard, you see. And wizards are patient. They know when to strike, and when not to. And now he will soon strike to save me. I can see the executioner's shadow looming over me. He lifts his axe. Now it shall be done. Now I will be saved. Now he will grant me the strength and the will to do what is right. I know he will. I trust Simel. I trust him with all that I am. With my entire life, and with my entire death.

I trust him.

I trust him.

I trust him.

The axe is raised high, high, high, high. Above it all. Above me. Above everything that I am and ever will be. Its shadow hangs before my shadow. But I trust Simel. I trust him. I trust him.

I glance over at him. Time stops moving.

He's looking at me. I see that. I see him looking at me as I look at him. He doesn't look away. I don't look away. His eyes are determined and steadfast. They shine and they burn and I see in them something I have seen for almost half a year now, something that has been in his eyes for so long, something indiscernible and human and unsaid—something dark, always there. I see that nameless darkness, and I see what it is, I hear his eyes speak, a greeting, finally telling me, whispering the name of that darkness, of what it is that looks at me when Simel turns his eyes to mine.

I hate you.

I am glad to see you judged.

I see your death and I see justice.

I hate you, I hate you, I hate you. I hate—

The axe falls.

My head jerks back, to the side, letting the axe only strike through my mouth and jaw, severing it partially, leaving my lower face to dangle as I dislocate both of my wrists and pull them straight through the barbed shackles. The iron spikes within flay my flesh but compared to the pain still lingering in my chest—compared to what's in my heart—it is nothing. With my wrists freed and still on my knees I deftly sever the heels of my would-be executioner, slicing up his throat once he falls atop me. This all took place within a matter of mere seconds.

<Goblin (Lv.13) Defeated.>

Only now do the guards holding my man catcher collar react, jerking me back and away from the executioner, pulling me from the pillory. Acting fast, I dislocate both of my feet, letting their efforts unintentionally free me as I'm dragged to freedom. Now I grab the man catcher, starting a tug-of-war with the guards holding on to it. However, the second they begin bracing against me with their body weight, I let go, allowing myself to be brought along as they go tumbling. Using this short respite, I wrangle the handle out of their hands, and rather than spend time trying to fiddle with the locking mechanism, I simply pull it over my head, not caring as the spikes gouge long wounds along my face, neck, and skull.

Freed, I turn toward the emperor.

<Emperor of the Sun [BOSS]>

He blanches. "S—someone stop it!"

I can hear the shouting of the crowd and the barking of the guards, but it doesn't matter anymore.

I leap, twist, and shear my hand through the throat of the closest guard.

<Goblin (Lv.12) Defeated.>

Another is before me, and I pierce my hand through his chest.

<Goblin (Lv.16) Defeated.>

A bare neck presents itself and my claws slice across it with ease.

<Goblin (Lv.15) Defeated.>

I dance through them, reaping without thought or effort.

What little is left of my WHITE gown soon becomes RED and I don't think anymore. RED flies in crisp beads and I see the enemy before me and the enemy quivers in my sight, crawling back in his throne, his little crown sitting all topsy-turvy, but there aren't any more guards. There's just the RED, and the meat. And him.

He whimpers under my gaze.

I look down at my hand, covered in RED.

I return my gaze to him, and when I look down at my hand, I find his throat in it. I lift him up, grip tightening.

Do the right thing.
Do the right thing.
DO THE RIGHT THING

I do the right thing.

<Emperor of the Sun [BOSS] Defeated.>

I hear breathing. I smell flesh. Warm blood. I see, next to the throne, a little spawnling, with a crown on its head and eyes full of the darkness named hatred.

<You have cleared the fifteenth floor.>
<You have received 1,000 points for clearing the floor. You have received an additional 1,000 points for being the first to clear the floor.>

I move toward it, hand of RED emptied of what it once called father, mind buzzing with what needs to be done what has to be done what ought to be done what should be done *what will be done.*

<For clearing the stage completely, you will receive an additional reward.>
<To repay your debt, the additional reward has been traded for 5,000 points.>

I feel something.

<Chain.>

I blink. Now he's in front of me. Eyes of darkness, holding one of the spawn-lings, pointing at me with a sword held in his other hand.

<Responses have been ignored for the sake of the vote.>

I move to touch him.

<Chain broken.>

He doesn't move. He doesn't move. He doesn't move at all.
I hold out both hands. Spread my arms. Open my chest.

<To repay your debt, the floor clear reward has been traded for 1,000 points.>

Through a jaw not held in place,
choking on tears burning down my cheeks,
I say,
"Please."

<You will now be returned to the lobby.>

The last thing I see before I go away is his eyes,
burning with a darkness named hatred.

EPILOGUE

Just like last time, just like before, just like in his memories and just like in his nightmares, the creature disappeared, leaving only a pair of bloody footprints in its wake.

And still, although he knew that the creature was gone, that it had been taken back however briefly to the hell it called a *lobby*, Simel did not move. He continued holding Trygg, the fourth son of the emperor, as tightly as though he might at any time be swept away by a dragon, pointing a sword at the empty air.

"D—Dad!"

Only when Trygg gave such an exclamation did Simel finally allow the boy—only eight this summer—to cast himself from the older man's arms, running across the drenched execution platform to fall at the side of his father, where he lay tossed to the side. "Please, Dad, no . . . !"

Only now did the world begin to turn again, as the other princes, six in total, ran to the emperor's side as well. The oldest, Hark, simply knelt at his side, holding the others back by unspoken authority. He rolled him over. A deep, purplish bruise in the shape of the creature's hand stained the emperor's neck like a patch of mold. Hark looked over his shoulder, toward Simel.

"Your Grace," he said, voice heavy yet as clear as the chime of a church bell, "could you do his last rites?"

For the first time in several minutes, Simel felt himself breathe again, and he stood up, righting himself. He staggered across the platform, kneeling beside the prince to put one hand to the emperor's heart and one to his own. "*Oh Gods of one hundred beginnings, blessed be your multitude, take into your arms this mighty soul . . .*"

He spoke, and the world held its breath, and for a few minutes, the blood on the platform and the bodies that littered it weren't there anymore.

"*By the grace of the God of Endings, and the Goddess of Tomorrows, veri—vera—varum.*"

The first prince held his eyes closed for a moment, and then opened them again, shining with a determination beyond his years. "If it isn't against your beliefs, would you please do the same for the rest that have fallen?"

Simel gave a simple nod. For the past months, he had done nothing but last rites, blessing each soul taken by the monster he foolishly brought here.

As Simel moved toward the nearest guard, the crown prince turned to him fully. "Thank you," he said. Simel froze midstep. "Thank you, Your Grace."

Pressing down the bitter bile in his throat and the burning in his eyes, Simel nodded, and moved for the closest body.

Simel hoped, in his heart, that there would come a day when he would no longer have to do the last rites of those his foolish mercy rendered dead. And yet, somehow, he knew that he would never repent. The penance of death and the forgiveness it granted was not his to receive.

And he would not rest until that justice had been done.

ABOUT THE AUTHOR

Palt is a Sweden-based author of isekai, short horror stories, and some fanfiction. He is currently working toward a degree in criminology. In his spare time, Palt enjoys drawing and playing the trombone.

Podium

DISCOVER MORE

STORIES
UNBOUND

PodiumEntertainment.com